Dear Neighbor,
Drop Dead

Saralee Rosenberg

A

A V O N

An Imprint of HarperCollins*Publishers*

HarperCollins books may be purchased for educational, business, or sales promotional use. For information please write: Special Markets Department, HarperCollins Publishers, 10 East 53rd Street, New York, NY 10022.

FIRST EDITION

Designed by Diahann Sturge

Library of Congress Cataloging-in-Publication Data
Rosenberg, Saralee H.
    Dear neighbor, drop dead / Saralee Rosenberg.—1st ed.
        p. cm.
    ISBN 978-0-06-125377-5
    1. Suburbs—Fiction.   2. Domestic fiction.   I. Title.
    PS3618.O833D43 2008
    813'.6—dc22   2007045089

08 09 10 11 12   OV/RRD   10 9 8 7 6 5 4

Dear Neighbor,
Drop Dead

Also by Saralee Rosenberg

Fiction

FATE AND MS. FORTUNE
CLAIRE VOYANT
A LITTLE HELP FROM ABOVE

Dedication

To my parents, Doris and Harold Hymen, with love and gratitude from your funny girl.
(Now will you buy a copy?)

In celebration of the 70th anniversary of the Kindertransport, the British rescue operation that saved ten thousand Jewish children from Nazi persecution

Acknowledgments

Dear Readers,

In previous books, I have thanked family, friends, and colleagues for their love, encouragement, and support. But enough about them. It's time to acknowledge people that I may never meet but who mean the world to me—my readers. All ten of you. Oh fine, there are more, but according to my publisher, not as many as there need to be. More on that later.

Meanwhile, I want you to know how much your e-mails and postings inspire me. Most are kindhearted and full of praise, but even the ones suggesting I would be better suited to selling panty hose at Macy's are read and considered. With such busy lives, that anyone would take time to express their views on my books is a huge boost (disclaimer # 1: the really bitchy messages get printed and used to line the counter when I shuck corn).

But here's what I love best: when readers share details of their lives and tell me how touched they were because they could relate to my stories and characters. Some even accuse me of eavesdropping! Wish I could take them all to lunch to say thanks (disclaimer # 2: lunch is out until my ass is no longer the same shape as my chair).

Now about this new novel: it took a year to write and revise, and there's a good chance I went through so much paper we lost a tree in Oregon. But if it makes you laugh and cry and you end up loving it, let me know. Just as important, let your friends and family know. With fierce competition for attention from the three Is: the Internet, iPods and *Idol*, emerging writers like myself are getting lost in the shuffle. Your word-of-mouth praise can make all the difference.

Again, thank you for reading, writing, caring, and sharing. Otherwise I *would* be selling panty hose at Macy's, not that helping women look ten pounds thinner isn't a noble cause.

Best,
Saralee Rosenberg
Saralee@saraleerosenberg.com
www.saraleerosenberg.com
September, 2007

No one can make you feel inferior without your consent.
Eleanor Roosevelt

Confidence is that feeling you have, right before you understand the problem.
Harold Hymen

Prologue

August 2000

"Listen to her message." Mindy Sherman replayed the call for her husband. *"It's Beth from next door. I'm free today between four and six."* "What do you think she means? Is she saying, let's hang out for two hours, or is it more like an open house sort of thing?"

"Beats me." Artie pulled a desk lamp from a moving box. "Just show up at four and see how it goes . . . man, this is ugly. Where should I put it?"

"In the shed along with everything else your mother gave us."

"Wish I could." He made a sad face. "The Kramers took the shed, remember?"

"Oh, right . . . I still can't believe we didn't notice that at the walk-through. Anyway, don't worry. I'll buy you one for your birthday."

"That's a long time from now . . . maybe when you go next door, ask if we can share theirs. Did you see the size of it?"

"Yes." Mindy peered over at the Diamonds' backyard. "My

mother's condo isn't that big. . . . What do you think I should wear? I don't want to look like I'm trying too hard."

"You look fine the way you are. Please stop obsessing over this."

"I'm not obsessing. I just want to make a good first impression . . . did you notice her license plate? It says FSHN CRZY ."

"Fishin' crazy?" Artie stretched.

"Duh, this is Long Island. Try fashion crazy. Nadine is totally intimidated by her."

"Quick. Name three people who don't intimidate Nadine. And you can't go by your friends. Besides, we're here one day . . . you really think she expects you to be all decked out?"

"Yes . . . how does my hair look? I should have let Josie cut it one last time before we—"

"Mindy! Stop! You're a very nice person. She's gonna love you. I'm sure you two have lots in common."

"Like what? That we both drive silver cars and have ovaries?"

"Exactly." Artie hugged her. "You're the next Lucy and Ethel."

"You know in real life they hated each other."

"In real life they laughed all the way to the bank."

"Which bank?"

"Oh." Beth opened the kitchen door. "You brought the children."

A red-faced Mindy shifted three-year-old Jamie on her hip while five-year-old Stacie clung to her leg. "Sorry," she started to sweat. "Turns out they didn't have work today, ha-ha . . . No, see, my friend Nadine was in Mommy and Me with you. She said your daughters were around the same age, so I just thought—"

"They are the same age, but this is my Calgon hour."

"You're taking a bath now?"

"No, it's my time to relax. My au pair makes sure the girls are occupied. Do you have a live-in?"

"The cleaning lady slept over once when we had a wedding in the city."

"I meant do you have a nanny or an au pair?"

"No. Should we maybe come back another time?"

"Would you mind?"

Oh my God, that wasn't a serious question.

"Mommy, are we havin' a playdate now?" Stacie tugged at her shirt.

"Maybe another time, sweetie."

"I'm five." She waved one hand at Beth.

Jamie stopped sucking her thumb long enough to hold up three fingers. "I'm dis many."

"I guess you might as well come in," Beth sighed. "The kids are in the den with Bridget, but I don't like any running around before dinner and baths. I need them in bed by seven."

"Oh, wow! I'm lucky if I get these guys down by eight thirty. My husband doesn't usually get home until—"

"Whatever." Beth ushered them in. "Bridget! Upstairs!"

Mindy didn't want to appear like a gawking tourist, but the kitchen was nearly the size of her whole downstairs, and the gray granite was so rich looking against the black lacquer cabinets. Ah, but maybe Artie was right that they would find common ground. Oprah was on.

"Your kitchen is gorgeous," Mindy gushed.

"It would be nicer if the tiles weren't cracking . . . we're suing the contractor . . . Bridget, I need you now!"

"Hallow little cuties." A tiny blond appeared, no bigger than a child herself.

"Mindy? Bridget. Bridget? Mindy. What are your girls' names again?"

"This is Jamie." Mindy stroked the baby's hair. "And this is Stacie."

"Let them do a quiet activity." Beth handed Bridget a laundry basket." And take this down with you. And for God's sake, no Play-Doh. I'm still finding pieces in the carpet."

Bridget nodded and took the girls' hands.

"She seems sweet," Mindy said.

"Don't ask." Beth rolled her eyes. "I'm calling the agency before my ninety-day guarantee is up . . . Do you like tea?"

Uch, no! "Sure. Who doesn't?"

"Herbal or Lipton?"

There's a difference? "Whatever you're drinking is fine."

"Do you have a crazy neighbor from hell?" Oprah laughed. "Oh, this is gonna be a good show today. . . . I can hear those cell phones ringin' now!"

"I saw this one already." Beth started to change the channel.

"No wait," Mindy blurted. "I didn't."

"Listen to this next story," Oprah said. "It's from twenty-eight-year-old Marie Morgan from Cranberry, New Jersey. Her next-door neighbor was so mean that she invited the entire block for a holiday party, but left out the Morgans because she said their house was an embarrassment. . . . Then she had the nerve to borrow Marie's coffee maker and not return it."

"I swear they make half this stuff up," Beth turned to Mindy. "And whose business is it who you invite to a party? Don't you agree?"

"Absolutely," Mindy gulped.

"So do you do a lot of entertaining?"

"Not really. The holidays I guess, but it's mostly family."

"Good. I hate reciprocating strictly out of obligation. What does your husband do?"

"Oh, um, he's an optometrist. He works for his dad."

"An optometrist? That's not a real medical doctor though, right?"

"And Marie, how did you feel when this neighbor put you on the spot?" Oprah asked.

"I'm turning this off." Beth took out mugs. "I'm sure you'd rather hear about the crazy neighbors who live around here. Believe me, I could tell you stories. . . ."

Dear Oprah, please repeat this show right away. I am in very big trouble. Love, Mindy.

One

Eight Years Later

"Have you seen my Costco card?" Artie brushed and spit. "I could have sworn it was in my wallet."

"It was." Mindy dried her face. "Then I confiscated it."

"I knew it!" His baby browns were on high beam. "What the hell did you do that for?"

"Because normal people who go in for batteries and a roast chicken don't walk out with six cases of Gatorade and a kayak."

"Not just Gatorade. Fierce Grape! You know the kids go crazy for that flavor."

"Fine. But a kayak?"

"It called out to me."

"Hello? I'm your wife. I can prove you once got seasick in a hot tub."

"I was on medication."

"It's not funny, Artie. We are so broke right now."

"You still shouldn't have returned it without asking."

"Hey, you bought it without asking. Besides, I had to get it out of here before you gave it a name. Remember Fluffy Cat?"

"You were just as sad as me when she ran away."

"Whatever." Mindy shrugged. "Just tell me what's so important that you have to get."

"Can't. It's a surprise."

"You want to surprise me?" She swatted him with a towel. Say to me, 'Mindy, honey, I made a big deposit. We get to keep the house for another month."

"Why do you always have to be so negative?"

"Damn! That's right. I was supposed to pop the champagne when our checks bounced."

"I told you that wasn't my fault. It was a bank error. Now can I have my card back?"

"After you tell me what you're up to."

"Okay, but you're ruining my secret. They got in these really nice sheds for the backyard and I thought, wow, perfect birthday gift for Mindy."

"A shed from Costco," Mindy repeated, "for my birthday?"

"Well, technically for both of our birthdays. You promised me one when we moved here, remember? And you're the one who is always complaining about getting all the crap out of the garage. If we had a shed, we'd have a place for the crap."

"Or . . . we could throw out all the crap, skip the shed, and buy me a new dryer."

"Then you'd accuse me of being one of those jerks who buys his wife house gifts."

"A shed isn't a house gift?"

"No, it's for the outside, and I was going to let you pick the color. C'mon. Think about it. In the winter, you wouldn't have to stand out in the freezing cold cleaning off your car."

"I thought that's why we had kids."

"I'm serious. You'll thank me for this. Plus, where else would I put the kayak?"

"Doesn't matter. I returned it."

"That's true. Fortunately, Ira found the same one at his Costco, and you know my brother. Had to brag that he saved me money 'cause the tax is less in Jersey."

"Oh my God. What don't you get, Artie? I don't want a kayak, I don't want a shed. . . ."

"Then what do you want?"

"I want what every woman wants. A massage therapist named Ivan and a closet full of boots."

"Not me." He hugged her. "I just want a shed."

Mindy shoved her cell phone under her pillow, fearing that the constant vibrations would wake the kids. She had hinted to her best friend to please stop text messaging so early in the morning, but when Nadine was bored, everyone had to feel her pain.

did u open the letter? Nadine wrote.

Mindy laughed. She knew her so well.

no 2 scared . . . u do it

y do I hafta do everything

'cause lifesabitch n ur my friend

She lay back down, careful not to land on an arm or a leg. With her luck, she'd end up in *Newsday*: MERRICK MOM SQUISHES CHILD TO DEATH. FAILED MEDITERRANEAN DIET TO BLAME.

Now that the kids were getting older, she and Artie were

trying to crack down on this co-sleeping habit. "C'mon guys. Give us a break. Stay in your own beds!" Only to have their pleas ignored when the eldest translated for the younger two. "They're chill. They full out love us."

So no surprise when Mindy awoke to find body parts dangling in every direction, as if this was the set of a horror flick. But who was she kidding? She felt well rested, and as every parent knew, sleep was the new sex. Besides, nothing pleased her more than pajama scent and taking attendance. All three children were here and blessedly safe.

Eleven-year-old Jamie and her Orphan Annie curls were burrowed under a pillow. A gentle nudge found six-year-old little Ricky lying at the edge of the bed. And when she groped the floor, there was thirteen-year-old Stacie, a former delight now turned premenstrual shrew.

Still, Mindy was not naive. She fretted about the proper age to break up this party, much as she'd agonized over how old the kids should be when they stopped showering with her. Thankfully her mother-in-law, Rhoda, VP General Motives, was happy to second-guess her.

"In the old days families slept together 'cause they had no choice. But you've got a four-bedroom house and the kids are big now. . . . What are you waitin' for? To get knocked unconscious from a kick in the head?"

Artie had his doubts, too. Would their kids grow up thinking orgies were normal?

Mindy drifted off. Maybe the true story of the Sherman family bed could be the inspiration for a book, plus or minus some dramatic license. The saga would begin when a nosy neighbor reported their scandalous sleeping arrangements to the child welfare authorities. Then faster than you could say "bed-in-a-bag," the community would be in an uproar. There would be the requisite death threats, the innocent kids being pummeled at recess, and naturally, the fledgling civil liberties lawyer who took the case to the Supreme Court and won!

Enter TV's title-weight champs, Larry King AND Barbara Walters, duking it out over who would get the exclusive interview with the brave mom from Long Island who had come out of the linen closet to defy the child experts.

But the best would be the *People* magazine spread featuring Mindy and her new svelte body, which would drive her next-door neighbor Beth crazy. "That can not be Mindy Sherman. She's never looked that good. Bet they Photoshopped her."

Sadly, the alarm rang, the fantasy faded, and Mindy had to rejoin the show in progress, a duet of gushing water. Outside, the heavy March rains were testing their aging gutters while in the master bath, Artie sang in the shower.

During the week he was so fastidious about his morning routines, Mindy could tell the time without having to peek at a clock. God forbid he should miss the 6:40, as if he was traveling on the Long Island Railroad and the rates were lower if he showered off-peak.

At least his daily ritual offered her a little solitude before she had to make lunches, look for lost sneakers, and write excuse notes, most of which were filled with lies about homework. It was the main reason they'd gotten their dog, Costco (Dollar Tree was too long).

But maybe Nadine had a good idea. She should open the letter from Downtown Greetings to find out if she'd made it through the first round of their contest, not that she actually expected the popular card company to like her entry. This way when they informed her that she'd been eliminated, she wouldn't have to fake her disappointment, like actors who lied that it was an honor just to be nominated.

Still, the idea of participating in a talent search did seem as exciting now as when she'd read the article in the paper. The writer and artist who teamed up to develop the most original new greeting card line would split a hundred grand and receive a one-year contract.

She may have been too pitchy to perform on *American Idol*, she thought when she downloaded the entry form, but compete with other writers to create a hilarious line of cards? Hello, destiny! And if she God forbid won? She would use the prize money to pay off the loan from Stacie's bat mitzvah. Maybe even shop at Bloomingdales instead of use it as a shortcut to Sbarro pizza.

Plus, this could be her chance for career advancement, not that she was suggesting that anything could top working reception three days a week at her father-in-law's ophthalmology practice. "Mrs. Katz, you shouldn't drive yet. You just had your eyes dilated. No, a cab home is not included in the fee."

Mindy was especially encouraged after Nadine read her entry. "I'm dying, this is so funny! They'd never know you just were flying through the house on your PMS broom."

But while waiting to hear back from the judges, Mindy vacillated between euphoria and dread. In one fantasy, they were so enthralled they said, "To hell with the contest. We have a permanent position for you." Other times she could hear a Simon Cowell type skewering her. "You call this funny? I got more laughs reading the instructions for my Chia Pet."

Now as she dug through her end table drawer for the envelope, she felt the tension mounting. She so wanted to participate in this competition, if for no other reason than it gave her a good out to abandon the much ballyhooed project she'd begun on her fortieth birthday, a memoir entitled, *Where Have I Been All My Life?*

Sadly, in the year that passed, she, a former flower child, still had no clue what her purpose in life was, or how several decades had come and gone with her biggest achievement being that she had a brownie recipe everyone wanted.

Trouble was, whenever she fretted about her lack of inspiration, Artie would tell her to stick to what she knew—stain removal and getting through to Ticketmaster. Also, that she needed to have a better attitude. But this was so unfair. Most days of the month she was a very positive person. In fact, not only was she cautiously optimistic about this contest, she even had faith. Maybe if she held the envelope to the light, she could make out the word *congratulations*.

"Great. You're up." Artie peeked out from behind the bathroom door. "Gotta talk to you."

She jumped, stashing the letter under the comforter.

"You okay?" he asked.

"I guess . . . did you recently buy a kayak?"

"Me? The guy who's going to need a Dramamine drip on the cruise? Yeah, absolutely. I went over to Yacht World with Thurston Howell III and we picked out a nice one."

"Never mind. I must have dreamt it."

"I thought you spent every night with Dr. McDreamy."

"Used to. Now I think he's co-sleeping with your Dr. House."

"No! Not Dr. House!"

"Why are you guys talking so loud?" Stacie grumbled.

"You want it quiet?" Artie snapped. "Sleep in your own goddamn room for a change."

"*Shhh,*" Mindy scolded. "They don't have to be up yet." She scrambled to the bathroom.

He stared at the envelope in her hand. "Is that an eviction notice?"

"And you call *me* negative?" She closed the door. "No, it's the letter from Downtown Greetings. It came yesterday but I was too chicken to open it."

"You're kidding. You've been waiting weeks to hear from them. Although I still think it's stupid that they didn't just e-mail everyone."

"True. Why would a greeting card company have any use for the post office?"

"Good point." The five-nine teddy bear in brown curls laughed. "So let's open it."

"I'm afraid. It's like when I had to open all those letters from the college admissions offices. Big envelope, you're in. Little envelope, you're calling Antoine's School of Beauty. I just don't want to be disappointed by one more thing."

"Why do you always have to assume the worst? Why can't you ever think, hey, today could be the day everything goes my way?"

"That's exactly how I think. It just never happens."

"Fine. Then don't open it 'til Christmas."

"But what if they loved me? You think I'm hilarious! And besides, whenever I work on my memoir, I never get past the second page, and what are greeting cards? Two pages!"

The sound of a loud, hacking cough coming from their bedroom stopped them cold. "Little Ricky!" They eyed each other and ran.

"Mommmm!" Jamie screamed. "The little dweeb just coughed all over me."

"Did not." He coughed again.

"He's gonna puke," premed Stacie presented her case.

"No he's not!" Artie stared her down. "Come here, buddy." He carried his son to the bathroom in case Stacie got lucky with her diagnosis. "You okay?"

He said yes, but Mindy felt his forehead. He was warm and the coughs were coming closer and closer together like contractions.

Please God. Not when they were T-minus four days until lift-off . . . the start of their first vacation in years: a Caribbean cruise, courtesy of her in-laws, who wanted the family together to celebrate their fortieth anniversary. Even Mindy's widowed mom, Helene, had been invited.

Granted, the week would be a mixed bag. Mindy would have to celebrate her birthday with her in-laws, eye doc Stan and Rhoda, a woman with more opinions than a retired judge; Artie's brother, Ira, Mr. Hedge Fund, his wife, Dana, Queen of Tofu, their two children, Brandon and Abigail, aka Satanic Cretans. And adding to the merriment? A relative newcomer, literally.

Artie's seventeen-year-old son from his first marriage, Aaron, with whom he'd only recently been reunited, had unexpectedly said yes to the invitation to join them, forcing a fast, unrehearsed explanation to the kids as to how they had a half-brother in Oregon who had tattoos and a garage band called Pee-Nis.

"Sounds like an amazing time," Nadine said over lunch. "I can see the headline now: LONG ISLAND MOM JUMPS SHIP . . . MOTHER-IN-LAW DENIES INVOLVEMENT."

"I'll be okay." Mindy laughed. "If I have to, I'll barricade myself and conduct a scientific study on exhibiting patience in confined quarters."

"No. The only study you should do is calculating how long it takes you to punch out Rhoda for all her kvetching. 'My soup is cold. . . . I asked for well done. . . . What do you mean there are no more feather pillows?'"

Normally, Mindy loved Nadine's Rhoda impressions but now it only added to her angst, for no matter how much she dreaded being pent up with the whole, annoying Sherman family, she had waited an entire year for this vacation and would cry for the entire next one if she didn't get the chance to sunbathe, island hop, and drink like Cinderella on her night off.

At least now she finally had a convincing reason why her kids should be sleeping in their own beds: contagions that screwed up important plans. But what to do? This was her only day off before they left and she had a thousand errands to run.

"Ricky, honey. Throw up if you have to," she suggested. "You'll feel much better."

"No." He shook his head. "Don't like to. Do I have to go to school?"

"Yes," she replied to her husband's of course not.

Sure. Would Artie have to cancel his color appointment at the swanky Maximus salon and have to spend the whole cruise wearing a Mets cap? My, that would look lovely on formal night! Maybe she could leave Ricky home for an hour and run over there. Too crazy! This was a touch-up, not an emergency appendectomy. What if she picked up Stacie early from school and she babysat? No. She had play practice and Mrs. Morgan was threatening to kick out anyone who missed another rehearsal. And with all Jamie's *mishagas* about scary noises coming from the attic, how could she be left in charge? Not even her mother could bail her out. She was already in Florida, visiting her twin sister, Toby, whom she'd invited on the cruise, as it would have been her anniversary, too, if only Toby's husband hadn't dropped dead two years earlier.

But Artie was right. Why think the worst? Ricky was just congested. "Don't worry, sweetie." Mindy kissed him. "You'll feel better after you take some medicine."

"Okay," he said, then vomited on the rug.

Mindy tried reading the clock on the microwave but didn't have her contacts in yet and her glasses were upstairs. What good was it having family in the optical business if perfect vision wasn't part of the deal?

She tore through a junk drawer and found a red frame with rhinestone elephants that screamed, hello, I have no taste. And who cared what time it was anyway? Her son was sick, her day was shot, and if Rhoda got on the plane and felt a sniffle, she would diagnose it as pneumonia and never let Mindy forget that HER child had ruined THEIR special anniversary trip, for which they paid an ungodly sum AND generously invited her mother, Helene, who then had the NERVE to invite her sister.

As Mindy contemplated this disastrous turn of events, she searched for medicine, then caught a whiff of aftershave. No matter how she pleaded, Artie was so heavy-handed, his scent trumpeted his arrival.

"Hey, nice glasses." He opened the fridge. "Maybe I should carry those in the store."

"That's where I got 'em. Which probably explains last month's sales figures."

"Impressive! Shermy gets a three-pointer." He pretended to shoot hoops. "Anyway, I never got to tell you what I needed to tell you before."

"Oh yeah." Mindy gathered enough cold medication to knock out Ricky's entire first grade class. "What's up?"

"I got Mr. Waspy Banker to have another meeting with me."

"How is good ol' Waspy?" She grabbed the thermometer, too. "Maybe this time you'll believe me. The guy's a blue blood. You *have* to wear a navy suit."

"I will if you will." Artie took a large gulp of juice.

"No, no. Between the dandruff and his little breath mints, he creeps me out."

"Please?" He fell to his knees. "My only experience begging is in bed with you."

Mindy laughed, but saw the worry in her husband's forlorn face. "When is the meeting?"

Artie bounced up. "Today at nine."

"You sound like a commercial for Regis and Kelly," Mindy

sighed. If only her optometrist husband hadn't been so quick to buy into a new optical chain called Eye-Deals, he might have heard that the franchise fees were exorbitant and customers hated the selection and prices. The only clear vision she had now was of bankruptcy court.

"We'll take Ricky with us," Artie persisted. "By this afternoon he'll be bouncing off the walls like always."

"No, he won't. He's got a fever, a cough, and he threw up. What if it's strep?"

"See what I mean? You always have to think the worst! It's not strep. Let's just send him to school, and if he doesn't feel good he can go hang out with the nurse."

"I hate parents who do that and you know it. What is wrong with you?"

"I'm a desperate man, that's what. I've been reworking the numbers and I think I can prove we'll have a decent cash flow for the next fiscal year, but you're the better talker."

"You'll do fine. Besides, it's my day to drive."

"Let the kids take the bus for God's sake. Why do you have to carpool every day?"

"Stop! I've explained this a hundred times. It's just easier, okay?"

"How is it easier? You have to get up, get dressed, drive to the middle school, then come back and drive to Lakeside."

"It's easier because the buses come so early, and the kids always have so much stuff to schlep with their instruments and sports gear, and then they call me from school anyway to tell me they forgot their lunch or the envelope with the field trip money. . . . Trust me, it's a lot less stressful when we drive and make sure everyone has everything they need the first time."

"Fine. Whatever. I'm tired of arguing over this. Just call Beth and see if she'll switch."

"I can't. As soon as she sees it's me on the caller ID, she won't answer."

"Then go on line and IM her."

"Can't do that either. She blocked me."

"Why?"

"Because it's Tuesday and I have type-O blood! How the hell should I know?"

"What if you create a new screen name? Then you can at least see if she's online?"

"Oh screw it. This is getting stupider by the second. I'll just be brave and call her. "

"'Atta girl."

"I mean what's the worst she can do? Report me to the National Association of Minivan Moms? 'Mrs. Sherman, one more violation and we're taking away your five-year jacket.'"

When Artie laughed, his whole body erupted like a shaken can of Coke. It was one of the things she loved most. That and his capacity to eat anything she made without complaint, as long as it didn't up and bite him first.

"Oh. And out of curiosity," she asked, "what happens if the bank turns us down again?"

"No big deal," he hugged her. "We'll lose the store and probably the house."

"Fantastic!" she shrugged. "At least then you could stop feeling bad that we never got to buy a shed."

"Oh man," Artie sighed. "I always wanted a shed. I wonder if they come in three-bedroom, two-bath . . ."

Two

Beth Diamond was the next-door neighbor from hell. Stunning to the point of distraction but with a chip on her shoulder bag. If she wasn't complaining about your barking dog, she was accusing you of stealing her Saturday night sitter. And pray that this preachy, sancti-mommy didn't hear you discussing plans for your child's birthday party.

"Please don't feed the children cake and ice cream, then hand them goody bags filled with candy. Saying no makes it so difficult on caring mothers like myself."

But where this MILF[1] stood her ground was with her tall, toned body. While most of the other moms were waging daily battles against gravity and Pepperidge Farm, Beth would roll out of bed, throw on those low-lying Juicy Couture pants, pull her hair into a ponytail, and still turn heads at Starbucks. So unfair to the girls who slaved away at the gym and resorted to the latest diet craze just to fit back into their jeans after indulging in fast food and vodka shots.

---

[1] mother I'd love to f---

"I'm on the Master Cleanse Diet, Mindy. It's so easy."
"Oh, I heard. Pine-Sol for breakfast, Windex for lunch, and a
  small, sensible dinner."
"Ha, ha. No. It's a ten-day fast. You just drink lemon juice,
  maple syrup, and water."
"Great. No need for an autopsy then. The cause of death will
  be stupidity."

When Mindy first met Beth, she assumed the story went like this. Nice Jewish boy meets blond shiksa goddess, waits for his mother to remove her head from the oven, then marries the green-eyed beauty. Only to overhear Beth's mother call her by her Hebrew name, Batyah.

Turned out her cover-girl face had nothing to do with swimming in Christie Brinkley's gene pool. It was an inheritance from her regal-looking German-Jewish parents. Sadly, Mindy's Polish ancestry hadn't been quite as charitable, though Beth claimed that was a lousy excuse.

"No reason you can't get a decent haircut, drop twenty pounds, and let those nails grow!"

Sometimes Mindy would retaliate with away messages that friends would "get" were about Beth. But that kind of jousting took a lot of energy and she hated stooping to her level.

"How could someone so beautiful be such a misery?" Mindy would ask Artie during pillow talk. "Every day I have to listen to her go on and on about whose daughters aren't as bright and athletic as hers, and whose bar mitzvah was pitiful because the sushi was tough. And get this. When I asked her to sponsor me for the Walk for the Homeless, she said no. So I go, 'But, Beth, these people don't eat for days at a time.' So she goes, 'Really? I admire their willpower.'"

"No E-ZPass for life," Artie always said. "Sooner or later she'll have to pay the toll."

But after eight years of observing Beth's charmed, I'll-take-one-of-these-and-two-of-those existence, still no signs of ill fortune. No big weight gains or financial losses. No major crises or scandals. Not even an occasional run-in with a bad perm. To the contrary, Beth Diamond lived a sparkling five-carat life.

Mindy was about to pick up the phone to call her when a shiny balloon floated past. Little Ricky had brought it home from a party, and as with all the other junk in the house, it seemed to move from room to room until Artie threw it out or posted it on eBay.

She grabbed hold of the ribbon and glimpsed at her reflection. Was she really as unsightly as Beth claimed? She framed her roundabout face with her signature cocoa curls and sighed. In spite of a warm olive complexion and engrossing M&M eyes, she had yet to make peace with her portly, middle-aged train wreck of a body.

How could she? In this era of jaws-of-life jeans, it was every mother's dream to shop where her daughter shopped while prancing in front of the other moms who kept pulling their shirts over their asses. Oh to have the little salesgirl fetch you a size two that ran small.

And what would happen if Mindy did lose those twenty pounds? Would Beth finally show her a little respect? Yes! As little respect as possible! Therefore, no reason to pass up the leftover Munchkins on the counter. Mouth awash in yummy sugar, she pushed "T.B." ("the Bitch") on the automatic dial.

"What is it?" a breathlessly annoyed woman answered.

Damn caller ID.

I'm good, thanks. You? "Hi there," she swallowed. "I need a small favor."

"With you it's never small."

Did you really just make a crack about my weight? "Okay. Anyway, Artie just asked if I could go to this meeting at the bank with him this morning, so I was wondering if you—"

"Forget it. It's your day to drive. Plus, we're in the middle of a challenging art project."

Art projects on a school day? That would go over big at her house. "Come, children. It's seven a.m. Let's make popsicle forts." Lord knows where those sticks would end up.

"And why didn't you clear this with me sooner?"

"I swear he just mentioned it like two minutes ago, but it's very important that I go."

"Damn you," Beth whined. "If I drive, I'll have to cut the project short, and the girls will want to resume tonight, which is impossible because I have the PTA fashion show and I never picked up the outfits I'm modeling. God I hope they don't do to me what they did last year. Seriously, do I look like a size eight . . . no, Jessica, the gray gives the sky better definition. Emma, please stop dropping the pastels. They're very expensive. Honestly, Mindy. I agreed to this car pool to make my life easier, not harder. But this constant switching around business is a pain. Next year I'm starting a new one."

A new car pool with whom? The Mongolian housekeeper down the block? Nobody who spoke English wanted to deal with Beth. Or anyone over a size eight.

"What switching-around business? I asked you maybe once or twice the whole year!"

"Not according to my records." Beth jabbed at her BlackBerry. "This problem started on October fourteenth."

Ohmygod! She was keeping track? October fourteenth. What was October fourteenth? "Wait. That was Artie's grandmother's funeral."

"Whatever," Beth continued, "then in November I had to drive three days in a row."

"Yes, because I had to have my gallbladder out."

"A totally unnecessary surgery if you followed basic dietary guidelines. All I'm saying is I don't appreciate being taken for granted. I am not your private chauffeur, and from now on—"

"What?" A flustered Mindy pretended she was being called. "Okay, be there in a sec . . . Beth, sorry, I have to go. Artie is yelling for a plunger . . ." *Because I can't take your shit!*

"Did you call her?" Artie yelled from upstairs.

"Oh yes." Mindy raced to the foyer. "And not only did she accuse me of being a food whore who treats her like a chauffeur, she's threatening to take her car pool business elsewhere."

"She said that? Wow! Call Morgan Freeman. Tell him we've got an idea for a sequel called *Driving Miss Crazy.*"

"Exactly!" She laughed. "Now do I have your permission to kill her?"

"Not until the country-club jails get Tivo . . . but what did she say? Will she drive?"

"Nope. She requires a week's notice in writing. Of course that's never the case when she needs a favor. I swear she is the worst person ever, and don't you dare start defending her."

"I'm not. But remember how nice she was when my grandmother died? She made that amazing dinner so we could eat when we got home from the cemetery. And that time Ricky's igloo collapsed the night before it was due? She spent hours helping him rebuild it."

"Fine, so she occasionally acts nice. I still hate her and would appreciate it if you—" The phone rang. "Oh, joy. Twenty bucks says it's her calling with more accusations."

"Why don't you let me handle this?" Artie followed Mindy into the kitchen. "I know she intimidates you."

"She does not!" Mindy took a deep breath. "She just scares the crap out of me, but this time I'm going to speak my mind."

"Right." Artie rolled his eyes.

"I've decided that I will drive today because you're giving me no choice," Beth started in. "But there is a way you can make it up to me."

Raise your girls so you have more time to shop? "Sure. Anything."

"It so happens I will not be available to drive on April twelfth."

"No problem." *In most states, car pool changes aren't even misdemeanors.*

"Actually, I will be in Chicago on business and I'm not sure what day I'm getting back."

Beth had business in Chicago? Wasn't that generally limited to people who worked? "Are you going to one of Richard's conventions?"

"Frankly, I don't see what concern it is of yours why I'm going, but if you must pry, I've been invited to participate in a creative competition sponsored by a Fortune 500 company."

"Oh God." Mindy collapsed in a kitchen chair. "The one from Downtown Greetings?"

"Yes. How did you know?"

"Go get the letter!" Mindy ordered Artie. "Run!" She watched him scurry off. "Faster . . . The reason I know about it is . . . well, I entered it, too. The writing contest part."

"You can't be serious. I, at least, have an award-winning art portfolio from my days at Grey Advertising. What do you have?"

"What do I have? *What do I have?* I have years of experience buying cards. I'm a very big sender."

"Wow. Great résumé! At least when they see my design work, they'll know they're dealing with a pro."

"I guess. But the contest rules did say no experience necessary."

"So? Contest rules always say no purchase necessary, but do you believe that?"

Yes?

"Well what did your letter say?" Beth snapped. "Are you in? Are you going?"

"I'll let you know in a sec . . . Artie, where are you?"

"Sorry." His cheeks were flushed. "It fell behind the waste-basket."

"Probably an omen." Mindy took the letter, but her vision was blurred. "I can't read this." She handed it back to him.

"For God's sake," Beth snorted. "We're not talking about a four-year ride to Harvard."

"No, I mean I don't have my contacts in yet . . . what's it say?" She began to pray.

"Hold on. It's a little confusing . . . We liked your entry, yadda, yadda, yadda . . . thousands of qualified applicants . . ."

"I knew it! They rejected me."

"Well, of course." Beth yawned. "You're an amateur."

"And that's why we look forward to having you join us at the Oakbrook Hills Marriott on Thursday, April twelfth, at nine a.m.!"

"I'm in?" she squealed.

"Looks like it." He hugged her.

"I'm in! Oh my God, I'm so excited, I'm in!"

"You're kidding?" Beth moaned. "Look and see if it's addressed to you."

"Yes it's addressed to me." Mindy cried as if she'd won the contest. "I'm so happy. Artie was right. You have to stay positive."

"Well don't get all cocky yet," Beth said. "It's only the preliminary round. And let's be clear about something. I didn't enter this silly thing because I'm a bored little housewife who needs a hobby. I'm doing it strictly for the networking opportunities, so please don't expect us to hang out or anything."

"Sure." Mindy didn't dare retaliate now that Beth had agreed to drive.

"And one other thing," Beth went on. "I'm just reminding you to take in our mail while we're away next week. I stopped the papers, but Richard likes to see the bills right away."

"Beth, wait. I can't help you out. We won't be here either."

"Really? You guys never go away."

"Well, it's been a while, I know." She watched Artie head upstairs.

"What are you, like driving to Atlantic City?" Beth snickered.

No, the Queen of England invited us to Balmoral. "Actually, it's my birthday and my in-laws' anniversary. They're taking the whole family on a cruise to the western Caribbean."

"A cruise? Oh, gross! Those ships are like giant bacteria magnets. You board healthy and next thing you know, a thousand people are stuck in their cabins with Legionnaires' disease."

And Artie calls me *negative?* "We heard they're taking extra precautions now."

"Whatever. What are you doing with your mail?"

"Filling out one of those vacation stop cards at the post office."

"Well do that for me, too, then, because I have so much going on before we leave."

Not me. I have three kids and a job. I wish I could think of good ways to kill the day.

"Wait," Beth said. "Maybe Nadine could take in our mail."

"But she doesn't live in the neighborhood." *And she's my friend, not yours.*

"Well I'm not going to pay her if that's what you're suggesting."

"I wasn't suggesting anything." *Oh my God!*

"By the way, when is that new family moving in next door to you?"

"In a few weeks, I think. Why?"

"I could have asked them . . . What's their story anyway? Have you met them?"

"Yes and they were very sweet. I just can't believe Nancy and Paul moved to Atlanta."

"Well in my opinion, she was crazy to say yes."

"She didn't have a choice. Paul was transferred, got a big raise and a promotion—"

"Oh, please. Not in a million years would I ever allow Richard to uproot our family. This is what happens to wives who let their husbands make decisions. Anyway, what's their last name? I'm curious if it's the family I heard about."

"Don't remember. But she's a dentist and he's a something or other."

"That was helpful . . . Do they have kids?"

"Yes, a little boy around two or three and I think she looked pregnant."

"Better her than me, but if it's who I think, she has a sister who is building that humongous house on Halyard Drive."

"Oh gee. I would love to be on the open bay."

"Yeah, never gonna happen."

"Beth! Oh my God!"

"What?" she whined. "I'm just saying . . . Anyway, the sister is supposed to be this hotshot divorce lawyer. I heard she scares the crap out of husbands."

"Well I'm sure she's very nice when she's not in court."

"Who cares? It'll be like having a watch dog in the neighborhood. Might come in handy one day if—"

"Beth, sorry to cut you off . . . I gotta go. Thanks for driving today. I'll make it up to you."

"Damn right! And I'm picking a day when it's pouring out, like now."

No, you'll pick a day like Hurricane Katrina.

"What happened?" Artie returned, wondering why Mindy's hand was Krazy Glued to the phone.

Her eyes welled. "Where should I start? She's mad that we're going away, she said cruises suck, she's already got an attitude about the new neighbors, and get this . . . she entered the contest!"

"What can I tell you?" He checked the time. "At least you stole some of her thunder and got her to do us a favor. Sounds to me like things are looking up."

Mindy nodded and wiped her eyes.

"Mommy!" Ricky yelled from upstairs. "I throwed up again."

Beth laid on the horn. Finally the Shermans' garage opened. It was bad enough she had to do the runs to both the middle school and elementary school this morning without having to be made to wait on top of it. "Oh, good," she mumbled, "here comes Miss Chubby Cheeks."

"Mommy, stop it," twelve-year-old Jessica said. "You promised you wouldn't say mean things like that anymore. Stacie's my friend, and Mrs. Hanley says when you say bad things about people you're hurting yourself worse 'cause—"

"I don't know what you are talking about. I am very nice to her. I just don't understand why she has to be so loud like her mother and it's ridiculous that she's always got crumbs on her clothes. She's thirteen years old already. Look like a young lady!"

"Hey, Jess. Hi, Mrs. Diamond," Stacie sang. "My mom said to say thanks for driving."

"Any time," Beth muttered.

"Mommy?" Jessica asked. "Can me and Emma go over to their house after school?"

"Not today. We have to finish shopping for our trip."

"I don't think you could anyway," Stacie said. "Ricky was barfing this morning."

"Oh Christ!" Beth snapped. "It better not be the flu! Jessica, do you have your hand sanitizer in your backpack?"

"But Mom! Mrs. Hanley says that stuff is bad for you. It takes away the good germs."

"Enough with the Mrs. Hanley nonsense already. Is she leaving for Aruba in four days?"

* * *

By the time Beth finished both school runs, she had six minutes to make it to her nail appointment. Of all times to be driving behind the USS *Imbecile*. Didn't this guy know the accelerator was on the right? Finally he turned and Beth started to cruise down Sunrise Highway, fortunately behind a FedEx truck. They were always in a hurry, too!

She just wished her right eye didn't feel so saggy. Oy! What if the Botox had been injected too close to her eyebrow and she had the dreaded droopy eyelid? That's what happened to her friend Jill. Except that Jill had gone to one of those clinics that got sued for using illegal batches, whereas Beth had gone to a board certified plastic surgeon chosen by *New York* magazine as "the eye guy you want to see."

She dropped the vanity mirror to take a quick peek, just as the FedEx driver decided not to run the yellow. Didn't he have packages to deliver by ten thirty? She slammed on the brakes but was already on the truck's tail, and the rain-slicked pavement showed no mercy.

Within seconds she was eating an airbag. Fortunately it was lo-carb.

Three

It was after two when a bedraggled Mindy arrived home from the pediatrician, the bank, the hair salon, and Burger King. Just as Artie predicted, Ricky had a little nothing virus and was ready to rock and roll. She, however, was dying to crawl under the covers.

Waspy said he'd review Artie's figures but wasn't making any promises. So now the only guarantee was that she'd be up nights working at her full-time job: worrying about their future. Thankfully she could count on being kept company by the Artie Sherman Trio: snoring, farting, and teeth grinding.

En route to the powder room, Mindy noticed that the answering machine was blinking like crazy, which could mean only one thing. Everyone in her immediate circle was having a personal crisis that only she could avert.

In just the past week, she'd watched Karen Gold's kids after school so that her neighbor wouldn't have to rush home from the city. The next day, Mindy waited for the painter at Meryl Shechtman's house, thereby enabling Meryl to keep her appointment with her therapist. And in an uncharacteristic act of chutzpah, Mindy posed as a tough-talking lawyer in a phone conversation with the electrician who had botched a lighting installation in Nadine's kitchen. So convincing were her threats, the guy hightailed it back to work that afternoon.

As for who was calling today, however, every call was from Beth. Seems she had smashed her new Lexus *"all because you are so goddamned irresponsible" (beep) "and you forced me to be late" (beep) "and this never would have happened if you had driven like you were supposed to" (beep) "and my face is an absolute mess. I'll see you in court." (beep)*

"Hey! Did I tell her to drive like Danica Patrick?" Mindy asked the answering machine. It was no secret that Beth had been picked up for speeding so often, a cop gave her a season ticket.

Then the phone rang and she froze. Ever since Ricky decided his tree house wasn't complete without caller ID, they had to go back to answering the kitchen phone the old-fashioned way: guessing.

"Hello?" she answered. *Please be a chimney cleaner.* "Hi. No, I didn't listen to my messages yet ... Oh. Sorry. Yeah. I must have had my cell on vibrate ... Oh my God. Are you all right? That's unbelievable! First Domino's is slowing down, now FedEx. Who can you trust?"

But the news didn't end there. Seems that the Diamonds' auto insurance policy only had a small rental allowance, which forced Beth to choose between "some shitty little tin box from Detroit" and a Korean car with cloth seats "and NO NAVIGATION!"

"I should never have let Richard handle these matters," Beth fumed. "How the hell does he expect me to show up at the club with some little piece of crap car?"

"I'm really sorry, Beth," Mindy fought the giggles. "But at least you weren't badly hurt. That's the main thing."

"Oh bull! My eye droops, my cheek is bruised, and my whole face is red from powder burns from the airbag. I look like I went ten rounds in the ring. Wait until everyone hears what you did to me."

"Mom! Mommy! Mommmm!" little Ricky screamed from the staircase.

"Jeez!" Mindy said to Nadine. "If I was passed out on the kitchen floor, my kids would step over me to get to the fridge. But the second I pick up the phone . . . What is it?" she hollered.

Ricky rushed into her bedroom, cheeks flushed with news. "Emma fell. She's crying."

"Oh my God, Nadine, I gotta go . . . If I suddenly disappear, check Beth's trunk."

Mindy flew downstairs to find Stacie, Jamie, Jessica, and Ricky all huddled around Emma, who was crumpled in a ball at the bottom of the staircase. She was holding her ankle and sobbing. "It hurts. I want my mommy."

"What happened?" Mindy demanded.

The elder statesmen, Stacie and Jessica, started talking at the same time. "We were just playing hide-and-seek."

"Ricky was it and Emma couldn't find a good place to hide."

"She musta tripped on something running away."

"I can't feel my fooooot. . . ."

Mindy looked around. The staircase was beginning to re-semble a mini landfill right down to the falling debris. But clut-ter had never been an issue the Shermans spent much time debating. Beth's kids, on the other hand, lived in a hospital-clean house. The first time she and Artie got the grand tour, she whispered, "What? No velvet ropes?"

Now as Mindy looked down at a tear-faced Emma, she won-dered about the rumor that Beth used to glue coasters to her baby bottles. Unfortunately, she would have to ponder that when she wasn't dealing with a medical emergency.

"Mommy and Daddy just went to visit the car at the body shop, honey. They'll be back soon. Can I take a look?"

Mindy was no doctor, but it didn't take four years of med school to diagnose swelling. Although the injury appeared minor, this was no garden-variety kid. A Beth Diamond offspring was someone who was taught to call boo-boos abrasions. Lord knows what a simple sprain would be called. Probably a million-dollar lawsuit.

"Emma, I think what we have here is a twisted ankle. I know it hurts, but you're going to be fine." *I, on the other hand, will be leaving town momentarily.*

"Should I get some ice?" Stacie piped in.

"Excellent idea. And some Tylenol, too."

"But she vomits from Tylenol," Jessica cried.

"I know, sweetie. It's for me."

Finally, Emma's loud wails tapered off and she could talk. "I just want to go home!"

"Okay, but first I think we'll let Dr. Kornfeld have a look at you."

By the time they returned from Mindy's second trip to the pediatrician's office that day, Emma was enjoying the attention and the neon ice pack strapped to her ankle. She had, in fact, suffered a slight sprain. She'd be good as new as soon as the swelling subsided.

The kids wanted to make a human stretcher for her, but Mindy teased that they shouldn't get carried away. At ten years old, long-legged Emma was already so tall, she had no trouble putting her arm around Mindy's neck and hopping.

Pity that just as they reached the front door, the Diamonds

returned from the body shop. Richard hadn't even put his Range Rover in park when Beth ran to Emma.

"Oh my God!" She pushed Mindy aside. "What did you do to my little girl?"

With all the excitement, Mindy hadn't prepared a speech. The kids were better rehearsed as they'd already told the story in the doctor's waiting room. They all started explaining at once.

"Just stop!" Beth stammered. "Look at me, Mindy! I'm a wreck. My face is a wreck. My car is a wreck. . . . And what is the source of all my pain? You! But silly me. I leave two healthy children in your possession for maybe what? An hour? Sure enough, I come home to find that my daughter has been maimed!"

"She's fine. Honest. We just got back from Dr. Kornfeld's. She took a little spill on the steps and twisted her ankle. That's all."

"That's all?" Beth echoed. "You don't think it's a problem that Emma will have to hobble through airports now? And what did he say about the pool? Will she be allowed to swim? I swear it's not just annoying to live next door to you, it's dangerous! I'm going inside to call a realtor!"

"Seriously?" Mindy had to disguise her delight. "You would consider moving over this?"

"No, you will!" She scooped up her baby and headed home.

Whenever Mindy needed a good cry, she locked herself in the basement bathroom. Not only would her family be unable to hear her down there, she couldn't hear them either. *"Mommmm! Stacie took my iPod and won't give it back!" "Mommm! The little loser won't get off the computer!" "Mommmm! I think my retainer got thrown out!"*

Unfortunately, holing up in there forced her to try to make sense of not only her problems but also the former owner's attempts at decorating. Between the gothic light fixtures and haunted-house wallpaper, she felt like she was an extra on the set of *Friday the 13th*.

When they moved in, Artie swore he'd torch the bathroom before he'd ever take a crap in there, but a hundred other fires had to be put out first. Therefore, it remained in its original state, like an accident scene the police cordoned off until further notice.

"Hey." Artie knocked. "Let me in. C'mon. You'll feel better if we talk."

Mindy unlocked the door and wiped her nose. "Nothing is going to make me feel better. This has been the most awful day ever. I just want it to end."

"It wasn't that bad. Tomorrow things will look different."

"Yeah, they'll look worse. You think Waspy is going to write us a check tomorrow? You think Beth is going to wake up and decide not to sue me? Maybe I'll win the lottery so I have enough money to fly to Chicago. I don't know why I was so excited about entering that stupid contest. We can't afford for me to—."

"*Shhh* . . . We'll figure it out. Just . . . I don't know . . . keep it together for like five minutes. My mom is on the phone with the kids and wants to talk to you about the cruise."

"No! I can not deal with her right now. Tell her I've read all eleven of her e-mails and I will pick up number fifty sunscreen and get the passports from the vault."

"Yeah. *Uh*, that's not why she called. Seems there was a little mix-up with the cabins."

"Oh my God. We're not all together?"

"No, we're together. I mean really all together."

"What the hell?" Mindy screamed.

"Calm down. Just calm down. Something must have gotten screwed up with the reservation when we added Aaron and Aunt Toby. Instead of giving us an extra cabin, they canceled one, and since the cruise is sold out, we're just going to have to punt. My mom was thinking maybe you and Dana could bunk with two kids and—"

"No! I'll go crazy if I have to listen to Dana's stupid lectures about trans fats wrecking my small intestines, and about how Ira bought her another piece of jewelry she doesn't really like, or how when they redid their master suite, she wished that they'd made room for a Jacuzzi."

"Fine. I'll make you a deal. You talk to my mom, and I'll call Ira and tell him to have Dana cool it with the BS."

"But he's worse than her with all his stupid little gadgets and the pictures on his cell of his Porsche from every angle. I just don't get why everything has to turn into such a goddamn disaster!"

"Relax. Okay? You're not helping the situation by carrying on. God I hate PMS days!"

"Excuse me?" she poked his shoulder. "What does PMS have to do with this? You think I'm imagining these problems or that I want to be under all this stress. You think I like feeling powerless? I swear if you say one more thing, you'd better get a running start because I will kill you with my bare hands and I am running out of places to hide the bodies. Do you hear me?"

"Loud and clear. Kids, get your sneakers!" Artie yelled. "We're getting TCBY. Mom needs a Mississippi Mud Thriller Chiller!"

What to call the in-laws? That is the question newlyweds ponder, though not in Artie's case. After his third date with Mindy, he told Helene that he was going to marry her daughter and started calling her Mom. She was so thrilled that a doctor's son was falling in love with Mindy, she started calling him sonny boy and made him dinner every night.

Rhoda, on the other hand, made it clear to Mindy that she had no interest in being adopted. "My two wonderful sons are my children. I'll answer to anything but mother."

To his credit, Stan Sherman offered to let Mindy call him

Dad, though she never found out if this unusually gracious gesture was because he'd always wanted a daughter or that he genuinely liked her.

But how quickly that old familial feeling could dissipate. When Mindy mentioned she would like to start working reception part-time in his office, "Dad" suddenly changed his tune.

There would be terms, he told her. She had better not expect to earn a dime more than the others, and if she tried pulling rank, she'd be out the door. "I don't need the girls kvetching that you took an extra ten minutes for lunch."

Mindy assured him she understood, never expecting that it would be Stan who took advantage. He made her come in on her days off, yelled at her for mistakes made by others, and often sent her on personal errands he couldn't be bothered with.

T-minus two days before the cruise, he realized he'd forgotten to pick up his new tux and told Mindy to get it for him on her lunch hour. "But be back by one. We have a full afternoon."

"I don't believe him." Mindy called Artie on the way to her car. "Why should I have to schlep all the way to Garden City? I have my own errands to run!"

"Just do what he asks, okay?" he pleaded. "He's treating us for a whole week."

"I don't care. I'm so sick of this. I'm going back in and telling him what I think."

Artie had no such fear. He had heard his wife terrorize customer service reps in India, but confront Stan and his hard-boiled temper? Just the thought would make her break out in hives. And yet, what Artie didn't realize was that something inside his wife was churning.

She was tired and stressed as usual, but she'd also just returned from visiting her eighty-seven-year-old grandmother at the nursing home. A Holocaust survivor, and the only feisty member of Mindy's lineage, of late, Jenny Baumann was an equal opportunity destroyer who woke up combative and didn't close her eyes until someone had gotten a piece of her mind. "The only reason she's still alive is because God is afraid to meet her," Mindy would joke.

Yet every time she left there, she'd say to herself, Mindy, you need to be more like her. Open your mouth! Stand up for your rights! Demand that the peas not be undercooked!

Brimming with an eerie determination, Mindy returned to the office on a head of steam, shut Stan's door, and zoned in on his temples. If it was a bad day and he was ready to blow, his lobes would be purple and pulsing like Shakira in concert. Thankfully they were resting.

"I was thinking, Dad, "she cleared her throat, "since the tux place is right by Roosevelt Field, maybe afterward I would run over there and get some shopping done."

"Forget it. The girls would never let me hear the end of it."

"Oh. Really? Well okay then . . . I guess you'll have to get the tux yourself."

"Can't." Cue left lobe. "You know I'm booked solid the whole day."

"*Hmm*. Tough call." She stood with hands on her hips like she'd seen Rhoda do. "Lose an afternoon's billings or give Mindy a few hours off?"

"Have you lost your mind?" he looked up.

"Very possibly . . . Aren't you glad you're the first to know?"

"What the hell is going on with you? Do I look like I have time for games?"

"No." Her heart pounded as if she'd just missed her exit and hadn't a clue how to get back to the highway. "See, here's the thing . . . Dad . . . It's times like this that I feel very unappreciated. Remember back when I first started? It would take you days to return calls to patients because everything was so disorganized.

Now, thanks to me, lab reports get filed immediately and put in the right charts. And what about my great scheduling system? Patients love me because they know I'll get them in right away and they won't sit around the waiting room all day . . . And you do realize that because I handle so much of your phone work, you're not losing time talking to people who just need their prescriptions refilled . . . Oh, and what about the other day when I figured out that Mrs. O'Hagan had early signs of temporal arteritis, and I made her go right to the emergency room? If she'd waited for you to come back from your golf game, she could have gone blind. So I was thinking . . . aren't I entitled to a few hours off for all my hard work and dedication?"

"No! You're entitled to a paycheck!" Stan groused. "And you get a damn good one!"

"Forget it." Mindy headed out. "I hate when you're like this!" *Oh my God . . . Artie is going to kill me . . . not exactly the best way to start a family vacation he's paying for.*

"Come back here," he ordered.

The obedient one stopped.

"You have a helluva lot of nerve marching in here like this."

"I'm sorry. I just feel that—"

"Let me finish, for Christ's sake. I listened to you, now you listen to me. Go get my tux." He reached for his wallet. "And then, I don't know, go buy you and the kids some nice things to bring on the trip."

"Really?" Mindy stared at a wad of hundreds.

"But we keep this between us." He returned to his charts. "Understand?"

"Deal!" She trotted to the door.

"And Mindy? If you ever pull this shit again, don't bother coming back."

"I know . . . although, hey, you've got to admit I was right about everything."

"Not everything," he grumbled. "Mrs. O'Hagan had dish detergent in her eye."

An hour later, tux in the trunk, she was searching the Roosevelt Field lot for a spot and could barely contain herself. She had time, she had money . . . she was Beth!

But funny how the instant she thought of her neighbor, she spotted a small blue sedan with a rental sticker on the bumper that was just like the model Beth was driving. And the only reason Mindy knew that was because the second Beth had gotten home, she'd dragged Mindy outside to see the "piece of crap car" that was all her fault.

Mindy said a quick prayer that they didn't run into each other, only to head toward the mall entrance and spot a very familiar face sitting in a silver Mercedes coupe, next to an older man who was not her husband. Beth?

Couldn't be. Mindy's new contact lens prescription needed an adjustment. Then again, she'd just seen the rental car parked by the exit. And when the woman waved her Streisand-long nails, fluffed her blond hair, and laughed with dramatic flair, Mindy knew there was no mistake.

As if by telepathy, Beth sensed she was being watched and looked out. When their eyes locked, it was hard to tell whose face showed more fear.

Would this be a bad time to remind you it's your day to drive the kids home?

Mindy thought about taking a picture with her cell. If she'd learned anything from watching *CSI*, it was the importance of the eyewitnesses at a crime scene committing details to memory in the event they were ever needed to testify. Instead, she fled as if she were the guilty party, but not before getting a glimpse of the man's vanity plate.

BODYDOC? Was he the guy repairing her car? No, this was Beth. BODYDOC had to be a plastic surgeon. Maybe the one she saw in the city. Had he been headed to his house in the Hamptons and offered to look at the damage to her face from the accident?

Mindy was so wound up, she didn't realize she was standing in the middle of Nordstrom's cosmetics department.

"Care to try the latest fragrance from our signature collection?" The lady in red asked.

"What?"

"It's essence of patchouli," she whispered as if she were revealing the Colonel's secret recipe.

"Oh . . . um . . . no thanks."

"You should really sample it." She spritzed a card, waving it above her head.

Mindy gagged. *What happens when you mix Glade with Raid?*

"Why don't you stop by the counter to try a different—"

"Sorry . . . I can't do this right now. I just spotted my next-door neighbor in a sports car with a man who isn't her husband, and I am in shock."

"Not as much as his wife will be when she finds out," she smirked. "I should know."

"I just can't believe it—"

"Oh, honey, it's so common." She leaned in as if to share a trade secret. "The fragrance industry would be dead if it weren't for all the screwing around on the side."

"Really? I'm so naive. I never think these things happen except on TV."

"Well, don't jump to any conclusions. Unless you saw them doing it—"

"No. They were just talking."

"You know, you seem like a nice lady." She scanned the crowd for a real customer. "Maybe you should just forget the whole thing."

"Are you kidding?" Mindy laughed. "This could be the opportunity of a lifetime!"

"Why?"

"Because it just gave me an idea for a new book . . . Bed Beth & Beyond."

"Oh, you're a writer?"

"I am now."

Four

"Girls! Knock it off! I can't take all this screaming," Beth called from her bed. "You've got your own rooms, your own laptops, your own cell phones. What's left to fight about?"

"Look what your lovely daughter did!" Jessica ran in holding a Juicy jacket. "She wore it without asking and then got something totally disgusting on it!"

"Did not!" Emma bellowed from her room. "It's Kim Cho's fault. She dropped her lunch on me."

"Shut up you little slob . . . now it's all gross, Mommy. I am never going to wear it!"

"Like hell you won't! I paid almost two hundred dollars for that outfit. Just go downstairs, give it to Marina, and tell her you need it for school tomorrow. Meanwhile, it wouldn't hurt you to be nice to your sister. You know she has a serious ankle sprain."

"No she doesn't. She was just in the den playing DDR and she was on the second level!"

"DD what?"

"Dance Dance Revolution! The game where you follow the

arrows and dance on the mat? Daddy bought it for her after she helped him clean the garage."

"Emma!" Beth screamed. "Are you kidding me? Dancing on your bad ankle?"

"I hate you, Jessie! You are the worst sister evah!"

"It's not fair," Jessica whined. "The little dork always gets to wear my clothes, but if I touch one thing of hers it's like Jessica, give it back. Wear your own stuff!"

"Would you stop? I have a migraine and you're making it worse. Just go tell Marina to wash that by hand, and then you'd better get going on your homework. You know, Jessica, if you expect to be the speaker at the Founder's Day ceremony, you need those math grades up."

"No I don't! I keep telling you Mr. Ryan loves me, but I don't even care anymore because Whitney and Mallory are like sucking up to him and now they're probably going to get picked."

"That's ridiculous. Daddy helped his son get a job. I'll call him tomorrow."

"No! You ruin everything when you call. My teachers all hate you."

"Oh, please. I happen to be very highly regarded at your school, but fine. If you don't want my help, I won't call. Just don't come crying to me when you're not picked to be the speaker."

"I DON'T CARE ABOUT BEING THE SPEAKER, OKAY?" Jessica ran out of the room screaming, "You're the only one who cares so you can brag to all your little friends at the club. You're the worst mother evah!"

"Well excuse me if I happen to like being proud of you," Beth hollered back, then pulled the covers over her head.

So unbelievable! After devoting her life to these girls, the little ingrates were turning on her with their big mouths and bad attitudes. She did not deserve to be subjected to such snotty, obnoxious behavior. They were the worst daughters evah!

And what of her demanding parents? Even from their condo in Palm Springs, they made it clear that in exchange for their generosity over the years, they expected frequent calls, visits, and annual travel plans that included them.

On top of that, Richard was making life impossible. Blah, blah, blah, money was tight and they should let Marina go. But this business about letting the girls make their own decisions about their extracurricular activities was crazy. It was never too early to be thinking of college applications. If he didn't let her handle this, they would both end up at one of those no-name New York State schools. Not happening. Her car would have a Brown or U.Penn decal if it killed her!

But what was really getting to her was Richard's constant harping about updating her résumé and meeting with headhunters. She had zero interest in returning to the work world, which would feel like a prison sentence, not to mention, what would the neighbors think?

Fortunately, the opportunity with Downtown Greetings came along, and Beth was able to convince him she could submit the winning entry in her sleep. "I know what they're looking for," she'd said. "They're like every other client. They want new and improved only exactly the same."

Richard laughed, relieved that Beth hadn't lost her uncanny business intuition in spite of her long sabbatical from her days as an assistant art director. Sure enough, she received the letter informing her that she'd made it into the first round of the competition and handed it to Richard.

"Read this. I think you'll be quite impressed."

"Excellent." He examined his receding hairline in the mirror. "Split a hundred g's and get a one-year contract. Now all you have to do is win."

"Oh, I'll win, because I'm sure as hell not getting a job. Everyone would think we were in trouble."

"We are." He winced. Had his six-foot frame shrunk?

"Oh, please. My parents are loaded."

"That's right. They are." He stretched to prevent further erosion. "We're not."

"So? They just gave Brad fifty grand to open a business. Which if I know my brother, he dropped half of it in Vegas already. I'm sure if we're in a jam, they'll be happy to match that."

"We don't need handouts, okay? We live better than ninety-five percent of the people in the world."

"Forgive me. I forgot you're Jimmy Stewart, I'm Donna Reed and it's a wonderful life."

"That's right, it is! But we've got the girls' bat mitzvahs coming up, college to save for, you keep talking about buying a place down in Boca, and now if Allstate says your car is totaled, who has to come up with the down payment for a new one? You? No me. So all I'm saying is be reasonable. You've got very marketable skills. Help me out here."

I do help him out, she thought as she flipped on the TV. I'm raising our children! God! This was not what she had bargained for at this stage of life. They should be comfortable by now, not needing her to return to a career she hadn't pursued in fourteen years. Besides, what ad agency worth its billings would be interested in a forty-year-old mom whose greatest success of late was running the most profitable Scholastic Book Fair in the district?

And now with her and Warren picking up speed, she worried about careening out of control on Crash and Burn Road. What was she thinking when she let herself get dragged into drinks with Jill and her cavalcade of bored/lonely/revenge-seeking housewives who frequented Bryant and Cooper and the other swank north shore steakhouses on Fat Wallet Thursday?

Only on Long Island would there be a night designated for a gathering of those who were married but still shopping or divorced but still hoping. A night when even men with small change could score, as long as their wallets were well endowed.

"I'll take that to go," a bald, fat man salivated on Beth as if she were a juicy thirty-two-ounce porterhouse.

"We are so out of here," she said as she grabbed Jill's hand. "You said this would be fun."

"It is." She let go. "Relax. Have another drink."

"Everyone here is married!"

"Or was . . . Don't look now but there's a very hot guy eyeing you at the end of the bar."

That guy was Dr. Warren Ross, a top plastic surgeon with an office on Park Avenue, a home in Amagansett and an Upper East Side penthouse recently featured in *Vogue*. Twice divorced but currently unattached, he was checking out the Thursday night action on his way to the Hamptons in the hopes his takeout order would include a top sirloin and sex.

Subtle was not Beth's strong suit. She had to peek, but even in the dark-lit bar, the piercing Ralph Lauren eyes and tight gray curls stood out. She turned to Jill and fanned her face. He was hot! Taller than Richard and dashing in Armani in a way her husband would never be.

He bought her apple martinis and between the liquid courage and tingling touches, her hair fused to her skin. And though she turned down his offer to be wooed for the weekend, she did take his card. Should she ever succumb to the knife, what better than to be in the hands of a surgeon who was offering a full examination?

Two weeks later she went for an initial consult—at the Garden City Hotel.

After two glasses of wine and some R-rated groping, she confessed to finding him utterly adorable, but still could not allow herself to be his next piece of meat. To which he replied, "I know you're as hungry as me, and I'll wait."

Now several steamy encounters later, the last one in the parking lot of the Roosevelt Field mall, Beth was tormented by inde-cision. Join the ranks of married people who kept lovers on call, or bail before she surrendered body and soul to a surgeon who could scar her for life?

She hoped the vacation in Aruba would force her to come to her senses, as hooking up with a plastic surgeon was terribly cliché. Though admittedly her bigger fear was finding out how many patients BODYDOC had previously bedded, and if he dis-posed of them as quickly as he did his rubber gloves.

And yet, was it so wrong to fantasize about how different her life would be if they had an affair? If she didn't have to deal with Richard's nagging, her daughters' fighting, and Mindy, the next-door neighbor from hell, turning her already stressful life upside down?

Oh God. Mindy. Beth had momentarily forgotten about their sighting at the mall and shuddered at the thought of her fat-ass neighbor wanting to get even after all their years of sparring. One call to her idiot friend Nadine, and word would travel as if the talk was about former Merrick bad girl, Lindsay Lohan.

Maybe if she went online and chatted with Mindy, wished her a great trip, she would be so stunned by the friendly gesture, she would think twice before turning into gossip girl.

Beth ran into the adjoining study to turn on the computer. First task after logging on was to unblock Mindy, much as she hated the idea of seeing her screen name on her handpicked buddy list. But hallelujah! She was online. Finally something was going her way!

> diamondgirl (8:06 p.m.): hey just wanted to wish you guys a good trip

No response. Mindy must be downstairs and forgot to put up an away message.

diamondgirl (8:07 p.m.): richard mentioned something about wanting to book a cruise this summer . . . let us know how you like yours

Still nothing.

diamondgirl (8:07 p.m.): thanks for taking care of the post office. so hectic before a trip

Finally a reply.

mindymom3 (8:09 p.m.): yah

Beth took a deep breath.

diamondgirl (8:09 p.m.): wanted to talk to you about today . . . really no big deal
mindymom3 (8:09 p.m.): k
diamondgirl (8:10 p.m.): just ran into an old friend from Syracuse and ended up getting coffee
mindymom3 (8:10 p.m.): w/e

Beth paused. What the hell was "w/e." Oh yeah. "Whatever." Duh.

diamondgirl (8:10 p.m.): you looked like you were in shock . . . just wanted to tell you it was nothing
mindymom3 (8:10 p.m.): ???
diamondgirl (8:11 p.m.): old friends catching up . . . turns out he's single . . . would be a good catch. Know anyone who wants to be fixed up with a rich plastic surgeon?
mindymom3 (8:11 p.m.): no

Strange, Beth thought. Normally you couldn't shut Mindy up, so the curt replies had to mean one thing. For God knows what ridiculous reason, Mindy was pissed at her and maybe thinking it was payback time, in which case Beth had better set the record straight.

Fingers flying, she shared some wild tales of her and Warren's bawdy undergrad days at Syracuse, certain it would clear up any misunderstandings. "It would be pretty funny if you thought for even a minute that we were an item. God, no. Warren and I are just old friends."

But in her haste to cross the finish line, she blew right past the red flags, never stopping to think that someone other than Mindy might be at her computer; perhaps an easily distracted seventh grader who was supposed to be working on a report on the War of 1812.

In fact, Stacie was on her parents' computer, as the last laptop sighting was the backyard, and Jamie was on the one in the den and refused to budge until she checked out her gym teacher's profile on MySpace. So when Beth started jabbering away, Stacie, quite bored of the Battle of New Orleans, was happy to take a commercial break and join the show in progress . . . until she realized Beth's instant messages were getting a little too dicey for adolescent eyes.

She is so whacked, Stacie thought as she copied and pasted the entire conversation, forwarding it in an IM to Jessica next door.

MetsGoStacie (8:11 p.m.): btw . . . wat is up with yor mom????

And then because Stacie was thirteen and accustomed to transmitting her every thought instantaneously to as many people as she liked, she also forwarded the convo to her best friend, Danielle Cooper, and nine other friends and wrote, *omg . . . Jessies rents mite b gettin devorct*

And then because she was thirteen and texting was the next best thing to being there, she popped this little grounder to her softball team:

so not lookin good for jessies rents

And then because she was thirteen trying to act sixteen, she went on Facebook and wrote on Jessie's wall:

sorry bout ur rents. . . . here if ya wanna talk xoxoxoxo lyl

And then because today gossip traveled at laser speed with precision accuracy, within seconds of Beth's signing off the computer and pouring herself a glass of wine, Jessica was in her room sobbing over the awful rumors.

Beth heard the crying but assumed that her hormonal teen was still carrying on about her Juicy outfit being ruined. Jessica should only know what it was like to have real problems. Only to turn and find Jessica crying as if she'd just received devastating news. But as any parent of a middle school child knew, it just meant that she'd found out someone was having a party and, horror of horrors, she wasn't invited. Cue up lecture number sixty-two. Life is not fair.

"I hate you so much!" Jessica screamed, throwing a copy of her mother's conversation in her face. "Why do you always have to be so mean to Daddy? And don't think me and Emma are gonna live with you 'cause we're not. We don't wanna be like Corey Halpert. Oh, wow! He's real lucky! He gets to see his dad on a Webcam. . . . great life, Mom! Thanks! Just what we always wanted. Virtual visits!"

"What are you talking about?" Beth recognized the conversation and felt faint. "Oh my God . . . where did you get this?"

"From Stacie and like sixteen other people. Isn't that great? You're such a lovely mother I had to find out from like the whole world my parents are getting a divorce. God I hate you so much. You are the worst mother evah!"

"Would you stop saying that?" Beth shook. "Nobody's getting a divorce. Oh my God, I can't believe Mindy would do something so awful. Who does that, Jessica? Who gives a child a copy of a private conversation?"

"Mommy!" Emma yelled from her room. "Everyone is saying bad things about you and Daddy. Amanda's mom wants you to call her right away because her sister is the best lawyer. Why do you need a lawyer?"

"Oh my God, ohmygod, OH MY GOD!" Beth handed her wineglass to Jessica and demanded her shoes so she could run next door. "Both of you turn off your computers and your cell phones this instant! You speak to no one the rest of the night!"

What to call the boy? That was what Mindy had been pondering ever since seventeen-year-old Aaron replied to Artie's e-mail and said yeah, he guessed he would go with them on the cruise to celebrate his grandparents' anniversary, though he hadn't seen them since he was three, he'd never met his half-siblings or cousins, and didn't much care for big crowds or Calypso.

What had prompted Artie to invite him Mindy didn't know either, though her husband was prone to doing most things on impulse. Case in point, they were the owners of both a failing franchise and a Mini Cooper. ("At least we could say we drove a BMW.")

Not that Mindy blamed Artie for desperately wanting to repair the damage done by Davida, his bizarre ex-wife, who fourteen years earlier had taken their then toddler son to visit her childhood friend in Allentown, Pennsylvania, and decided, presumably on a whim, that it would be an awesome adventure if she and Aaron joined Ellie on a little jaunt to San Francisco by way of a used station wagon and enough dime bags of pot to make them rich by Cleveland.

Ten days later they stopped in Portland, Oregon, to visit Ellie's cousin, Walter, a biker/musician/name the stereotype, where a doped-up Davida fell in love over hash brownies and something called Starbucks, then called an already terrified Artie to say, "Queens sucks! We're staying."

Thus began a prolonged and expensive custody battle for Aaron, resulting in Artie getting nothing more from the judge's decree than holiday visitations and attorneys' fees.

Over the years he had begged Davida to let him have a real and meaningful relationship with the boy, only to hear a young Aaron say in a phone call that he didn't remember who Artie was, his dad was Walter, but it would be okay if Artie sent him birthday and Christmas gifts.

Christmas gifts? His son who had been blessed by two generations of rabbis at his bris wasn't being raised Jewish? His heartbreak was incalculable, yet to his credit, he remained hopeful that one day he and Aaron would reunite. That day took fourteen years to arrive, yet Artie was prepared for active duty when the call came. "My mom's in rehab again. Walter's dead . . . an overdose . . . Would you maybe wanna hang out one day?"

Artie flew out the next night, met his son at a Holiday Inn near the airport, and gave him his word that they would never lose contact again.

Now as they waited at LaGuardia, a nervous Mindy fretted over how the kids would respond to him, how Artie's family would treat him, how she would feel about him, and, mostly, what to call him. Technically she could refer to him as her stepson, but doubted that would roll off her tongue. Perhaps Artie's boy? His Royal Highness, the Prince of Portland?

Didn't matter, for it was a sullen young man who got off the plane and said all of four words ("My suitcase is green"). En route to Long Island, he mumbled that he was tired and slept the entire ride, as if he were still the sleepy toddler Artie used to strap into a car seat and take to the Bronx Zoo. Probably best, Mindy thought. For of all the things making her nervous about this night, the most perverse was that Aaron would judge them based on where and how they lived.

Though lot sizes in south Merrick were so nominal that home-owners would be woken by the sounds of garbage pails being hauled down their neighbor's driveway, and though the streets were so narrow, oncoming cars had to wait their turn to pass, the suburb was home to some of the most exclusive waterfront houses on Long Island's south shore, particularly the gated es-tates, once headquarters to mob bosses who needed to be close to the rum-running action off Hempstead Bay.

And though their block was not quite in that league, every home had undergone major renovations and was a shining ex-ample of what refinancing could buy. Save for one: 1359 Daffo-dil Drive, aka the Sherman house, the lone vestige of proof that these dwellings started as modest split-levels and high ranches. Number thirteen fifty-nine had no distinctive landscaping, no brick exterior or Belgian block walkways. Not even their cars were updated.

But funny how the things you worried about never happened, while the stuff you never saw coming could completely blindside you. When at last they pulled into their driveway, there was a welcome committee to greet them. Only it wasn't their kids who ran out of their house, it was Beth and Richard Diamond.

Five

"I can not believe your mean, irresponsible daughter!" Beth shouted the second Mindy got out of the car. "I hope to God you ground her for a good, long time!"

"She's just a kid, Beth." Richard trailed her. "Why are you blaming her for something you did?"

"Hey, guys?" Artie was so mortified his voice quivered. "What's going on here? Sounds like a little misunderstanding."

"Oh no." Beth went nose to nose. "There's been no misunderstanding. I don't know how you are raising your children, but mine would know better than to—"

"Do you hear yourself?" Richard pulled her aside. "You're such a hypocrite. You expect a thirteen-year-old to take responsibility for her actions, but you're an adult who can't do that."

"For the last time, nothing happened! Okay? But will that stop the whole neighborhood from talking behind my back now? I don't think so."

"Guys. Guys," Artie pleaded. "Can we just put it on pause for a second? I want you to meet my son, Aaron Findley."

Aaron gestured hello and headed to the front door singing.

"Every single day and every word you say. Every game you play, every night you stay, I'll be watchin' you . . ."

"Cool," Richard nodded. "Your boy likes Sting. . . . Look, I'm really sorry about this, Artie. We'll straighten everything out. I promise."

"Forget it," Artie gritted. "Aaron hold up."

"What is going on?" Mindy asked Beth and Richard, though she had some idea.

"I'll tell you what." Beth stood with hands on hips. "Your daughter pretended to be you on line when we had this whole conversation. Then she had the nerve to make a copy of that conversation and send it to Jessica and apparently a hundred other people, and then, are you ready? She started this rumor that Richard and I are getting a divorce!"

"Really?" Mindy had to fight the giggles. "Does this mean you unblocked me?"

"What?" Beth snapped.

"Oh, come on . . . you don't think I figured out that you blocked me?"

"You blocked her?" Richard said. "Why?"

"I don't know what you are talking about, Mindy, but clearly you are not hearing me. Stacie did a despicable thing to me and she owes me an apology. . . ."

"Would you stop?" Richard raised his normally calm voice. "Clearly you feel guilty about something or you wouldn't be—"

"Oh my God! Shut the hell up! Nothing happened. NOTH-ING!"

So this was the trick to fighting with Beth, Mindy thought. Get Richard to do the heavy lifting, though she did feel sorry that he was the unwitting victim here. And at least she was getting validation that she hadn't imagined the scene in the parking lot earlier in the day.

"Okay look," Mindy said. "This is awful timing, but I'll go in and talk to Stacie and try to get her side of the story."

"There is no other side to the story." Beth fought tears. "That little brat decided to be a big shot and ruin my good name and now everyone is making these awful assumptions and—"

"Hey!" She felt another power surge like the one that came over her when she took on Stan. "Whatever she did, you have no right to call my daughter a brat, okay?"

"Really? Then what do you call a child who doesn't know right from wrong?"

"I don't know. The same thing you'd call an adult who doesn't know right from wrong? I saw you at the mall today in that man's car and it sure looked like you guys were having fun. And where there's smoke, there's—"

"Don't you dare finish that sentence," Beth choked. "There is no smoke, no fire—"

"You were in his car?" Richard looked ready to cry, too.

"Where are you going?" Beth watched him leave. "Now look what you've done, Mindy!"

"Look what I've done? Wow. You are unbelievable. But you know what? If Stacie did do something wrong, then I'm glad she did it to you!" Mindy walked off.

Her only regret was that she couldn't turn to see the look on Beth's face after that knockout punch. But at least she could gloat. For the first time, she was the reigning champ. Pity the trophy ceremony would have to wait.

"Can you explain any of that?" An angry Artie was pacing in the kitchen.

"Possibly," she replied. "Where is he?"

"Bathroom."

"Did the kids come down to meet him?"

"Nope. Stacie is in her room balling her eyes out and Jamie and Ricky are hiding in the basement. Beth scared the crap out of them."

"Oh my God . . ."

"Yeah. Not exactly the John Boy returns to Walton Mountain party I expected."

"He's very cute though," Mindy whispered. "Just, you know, a little strange."

"And we look normal? He's probably on the phone trying to book the next flight home."

"We'll explain everything. I'm sure he'll understand. Let me just go talk to Stacie and try to calm her down."

But then Aaron returned looking so helpless and confused, his wavy brown hair still matted from the car ride, Mindy offered him a hug and a snack. He declined both as he drummed on the table and asked for a beer.

Her first instinct was to say hello, we don't serve minors and please stop tapping on the table. But Artie, a soft touch and a once aspiring drummer, didn't want to offend. He found an Amstel Light in the garage and showed Aaron to the TV in the den.

"Relax. It's not like he'll be driving," Artie whispered. "Plus I'm sure he's done a lot worse than this."

"Great . . . a wonderful role model for the kids."

"Oh stop. I drank when I was in high school and I turned out okay."

"I know . . . it's just, he looks so depressed. His clothes are ratty, his hair is scraggly, his teeth . . . They do have dentists in Oregon, right?"

"Why are you already judging him? So he's a little rough around the edges? He's been through hell, but he's basically a sweet kid."

"Sorry. You're right. He's great. Very cute. Can't wait to fatten him up."

* * *

Mindy had to maneuver through a minefield of dirty clothes, clean clothes, books, and several pairs of UGGs before she could reach an inconsolable Stacie, who was slumped in a corner of her room holding her stuffed animals. She stroked her daughter's hair and said she could win a hundred bucks if she could recall the color of her carpet. It didn't make her laugh.

Stacie cried that she felt very sorry about what she had done, but was mostly worried that if Beth and Richard got a divorce, Jessica would blame her, get their entire grade to hate her, then she wouldn't be invited to any more bar or bat mitzvahs.

"That's what you're so worried about?" Mindy chuckled.

"No, I'm scared Jessie will never talk to me again," she cried. "I really thought I was helping her."

"I know, but it was still dumb to pretend you were me.... Not to mention, you are so grounded for going on Facebook. That's only for high school and college kids."

"Mom! Everyone I know is on there and it's all they do.... Do you want me to be left out?"

"I guess not." Mindy sighed. This teen terrain was so scary, and what could be more terrifying than the thought of your child being a social outcast?

"Do you think they'll get a divorce now?" Stacie wiped her nose.

"I have no idea, sweetie. But if they do, it won't be because of anything you did."

"I would die if you and Daddy got a divorce."

"Never gonna happen. It would take us years to save up for the lawyers."

"Stace, you ready to come down and meet Aaron?" Artie stuck his head in. "He's very excited to meet you."

"Really?" Mindy asked.

"No, but he's in the den looking fairly miserable. I thought we could give him the old Shermaroo, let's get ready to rumble, high-five welcome."

"No!" Stacie snapped. "I'm not doing that. It's stupid."

"Oh, come on, sport. It's such a great family tradition. I bet he'll think it's fun."

"Not if he's normal. He'll think we're a bunch of dorks."

"I'll take my chances," he replied.

Sure enough, the Shermans, aka the starting five, lined up for their long standing tradition of welcoming guests while Artie did the play-by-play, as if they were in Madison Square Garden before a Knicks game. It was all hoops and hollers, except for the visiting rookie who barely slapped hands as he made his way down the line.

"Told you this was stupid." Stacie checked her cell. "Can I go to do my homework now?"

"How about we all have some ice cream?" Artie shot her a look.

"Great idea!" Mindy clapped. "We'll have a get-rid-of-it party before we leave."

"Ice cream! Ice cream! Ice cream," Ricky chanted.

"No thanks," Aaron said. "How far's New Jersey?"

"Depends on where," Artie replied.

"Not sure . . . Been talkin' to this kid online. . . . He said I could hang with him and his band."

"Tonight?"

"Whatever. Yeah. I guess."

"I don't think so. It's at least a good hour away. Maybe more."

"I drive you know." He air strummed a guitar. "Don't need you to take me."

"No I know. It's just that the highways around here are pretty confusing. And Jersey drivers . . . forget about it. Plus tomorrow's going to be all kinds of crazy. Last day before the big trip! Hey, do you need nice pants or shirts? A few of the nights you have to be dressed—"

"I brought stuff . . . not an idiot, Art . . . *'I didn't mean to take up all your sweet time, I'll give it right back to you, one of these days.'*"

Artie blinked. The kid was quoting Hendrix AND dissing him at the same time?

Mindy bit her tongue. She and Artie had wondered what Aaron would call him, but Art wasn't on the list. No one called him that. To his parents he was Arthur, to his brother, Ira, he was still Tank, a throwback to his former fat days when he was as big as a Sherman tank, and what she called him depended on how big a favor she needed.

"I'm not saying you couldn't handle it." Artie looked crushed. "It's just that we're all excited that you're here. We'd like to hang with you, too."

Stacie snickered, always amused when her dad tried to sound cool.

Little Ricky, a most intuitive child, came to the rescue. "I wished you could meet my dog, Costco."

"Costco?" Aaron drummed on his thigh. "Ya mean like the store?"

"Yeah, but he went on vacation and didn't come back yet."

"Your dog went on vacation? Cool."

"It's a New York thing." Artie winked while the girls rolled their eyes. Sadly, it remained a mystery how their beloved Shih Tzu had escaped the backyard.

"Mommy, what if Costco comes back when we're on the cruise?"

"Oh. *Um.* Maybe we could leave his bowl outside by the kitchen door."

"Yeah. He'd like that." A satisfied Ricky turned to Aaron. "Are you really my brother?"

"That's what they tell me."

"'Cause my dad said you are."

"Do you want me to be . . . '*Oh, brother, brother, brother, I know you've been layin' back a long time.*'"

Ricky ignored the song. "I dunno. Do you like the Mets?"

"Baseball's okay."

"I have Mike Piazza's rookie card. It's worth a million dollars."

"Cool."

"Does it hurt to get a tattoo?"

"Yeah. A little."

"Do you smoke, 'cause it's really bad for you and my teacher said you'll die if you do."

"You'll die anyway, man." Aaron shrugged. "But no, I quit . . . cigs were costin' me too much."

"Do you like to go on cruises?"

"Don't know," Aaron shrugged. "Never been."

"Me either. But you like Disney, right?"

"Not sure," he hesitated. "Never been."

"Mom! He's never been to Disney. . . . When we come back can we take him? Can we?"

"*Um*, well, not this year . . . but hey, we could definitely take him to the circus."

"Yeah, yeah! The greatest show on earth," he squealed. "Do you like the circus?"

"Not anymore." Aaron looked away.

"Could you teach me how to play the guitar?" Jamie said, blushing.

"How old are you?" He strummed an invisible instrument.

"Almost eleven."

"That's about how old I was when I learned. Who do you like?" Her eyes lit up. "Justin Timberlake!"

"Then no." He stopped. "Can't teach you. That's not real music."

"What Aaron means, honey," Artie said, "is that he's more into the classics, like Hendrix and Clapton and—"

"I think you look like Stacie," Jamie blurted.

"You know," Mindy nodded, "you do. I was thinking the same thing."

"Okay, we do not look alike." Stacie groaned, but studied him to see if they were right.

"No really," Mindy said. "You both have the same big brown eyes, the same coloring, and that cute dimple on your chin."

"Oh my God, shut up Mom." She buried her face in a pillow.

"Duh, Mommy," Ricky said. "Aaron's a boy. He can't look like Stacie. I think he looks like me. . . . Do you want to sleep in my room 'cause we all sleep with my mommy and daddy?"

"You are so freakin' gay!" Stacie threw the pillow at him and Mindy laughed. Artie, however, reacted differently.

"Uh-oh." Mindy saw his tears. "Here we go . . . Your dad gets a little emotional."

"Sorry." Artie waved an apology. "I don't know what came over me. It's just so great, seeing all my kids together, everyone talking and having fun. . . . I prayed for this day for so long and I was starting to think it would never happen . . . but see? You can't ever give up." He hugged his boy. "So good to have you here . . . so good."

"Whatever." Aaron stood soldier tall, though clearly not at ease.

Ice cream night at the Shermans' was a cardiologist's delight. Mindy was big into toppings, putting out a spread to rival Baskin-Robbins. But while everyone dove for their favorites, ignoring her pleas not to get the sprinkles on the floor, Aaron begged off, mumbling something about the long day and wanting to go online.

Artie brought him down to the guest room in the basement and apologized for the hideous bathroom while Mindy tried to enjoy her sundae without letting her mind wander too far from the hot fudge. And yet she worried.

Here was a seventeen-year-old who was never hungry and always tired. A boy who thought nothing of asking for an alcoholic beverage and whose parents had been in and out of rehab. A boy who dressed like a rocker, quoted lyrics from before his time, and had tattoos on his neck. Did anyone say drug habit? Or was she just being negative like Artie always accused?

For the rest of the week her eyes would be wide open for signs, but not nearly as wide open as they were about to get.

"I need a place to stay tonight." A red-eyed Beth was standing at the front door.

It took a moment for this to register. Five-star Diamond Beth wanted a room for the night? Would that be cash or credit? The same Beth who wouldn't drink Mindy's coffee unless she first rinsed the mug? The same Beth who had just verbally abused her entire family?

"Why?"

"What do you mean why? You saw the whole scene. . . . I just do."

Mindy stared, wishing Artie was there to watch Beth squirm.

"Trust me, I realize you're not happy with me at the moment, but I wouldn't be asking unless I was totally desperate."

"Thanks?"

"I can't look at Richard right now I am so angry with him. . . . He's treating me like a criminal and I'm not going to take it. Of course, it was okay when he fooled around."

Richard fooled around? Hello, Nadine? "Okay but see the thing is, Aaron is staying in the guest room, so I don't really have any place to put you. Could you maybe stay at Jill's?" *Or with one of your other snotty friends who look down on me because I don't wear my daughter's UGGs or drive a cute little convertible to Waldbaum's?*

"Mindy, c'mon. You know the whole goddamn story. . . . I can't go anywhere else. It'll just add fuel to the fire. Do you not get what I'm saying?"

"I do, but—"

"And look, I know your kids sleep in your room, so I'll just take one of theirs."

I'm sorry. Did someone report a missing Webcam? "How do you know that?"

"Oh, please. Everyone knows everyone's business around here. That's half the problem. So what's the deal? Can I stay?"

Mindy was confused. How could she be feeling sorry for the original "Mean Girl" of Merrick? A neighbor who made her so miserable, she'd started a file with a list of movers. Plus, it would totally stress her out if Beth went upstairs and saw all the suit-cases and laundry piled on the floor. And with the cleaning lady gone due to fiscal restraints, the kids' rooms were such pigpens, she wouldn't be surprised if they one day unearthed Carmen Sandiego. But that wasn't the worst of it. No matter how much she yelled, their bathroom was so gross even she hated going in there. The wet towels were multiplying, the toiletries were in-breeding, and there were no less than six brands of hair gel left on the vanity every morning.

"*Um*, things are kind of a mess up there right now with every-body packing and—"

"Fine. I'll sleep on your couch. I'll be up and out at the crack of dawn anyway."

"My couch?" *The one with the missing springs or the one with the rip in the arm?*

"Just give me a pillow and a blanket and I'm good to go." Beth walked through the center hall into the den. "Do you have down, because I prefer that?"

Okay this is my house, not a Ritz-Carlton, bitch. "Sorry. No, we're all allergic.

"Fine . . . Just give me whatever's clean. . . . And don't forget. Tomorrow is your day to drive."

Six

For most families, the day before a vacation feels like a pinball game. Once the ball is released from the shooter, the flippers move nonstop. There is so much to do (charge iPod, confirm limo), find (where are my green shorts?), pack (camera? check! phone charger? check! passports . . . shit), and worry about (what if the burglar alarm goes off and the police don't come?). It's a wonder anyone bothers to go away at all.

But for Mindy, the day began on full tilt. Not because she'd been woken at 6:00 a.m. to the sounds of Richard and Beth arguing about which of them would be taking the girls to Aruba. Not because Stacie had a temper tantrum about going to school ("Mom! All we do is watch stupid movies 'cause everybody's gone!"). Not because Oregon Boy was complaining that he couldn't find his favorite cartoons on any of the channels. Not even because her first call of the day was from Rhoda, who didn't bother asking if her grandson's visit was going well, she just wanted to know why Mindy hadn't thanked her for sending that e-mail providing important, last-minute packing tips.

No, the reason the day already blew was because Mindy couldn't find the five hundred dollars she'd put away for the trip, and retracing her steps had yet to help.

"You never used to be this bad." Artie paced in the kitchen. "Lately it seems like all you do is lose stuff."

"Me? What about you? When was the last time you left the house without having to run around looking for your cell and your keys. In fact, your definition of "I looked everywhere" means if it doesn't fall from the sky, you have no idea!"

"Whatever . . . Can you at least remember when you made the withdrawal?"

"Of course. It was the day we met with Waspy at the bank. You went into the conference room and Ricky and I went to the ATM."

"Good. That's a good start. Then what?"

"Then . . . I don't know. I put the money in an envelope and stuck it in my bag."

"Could you have dropped it?"

"No, because I remember seeing it when I had my color appointment. And after that we went to Burger King."

"Awesome. If you dropped it there, we can get it back with a Whopper and fries."

"I didn't drop it there! I never even opened my bag because I had a twenty in my pocket."

"Thank God. Okay, what else do you remember?"

"This is hard. It's been so crazy around here. . . . Let me think . . . Wasn't that the day that Beth had her car accident and left me all those nasty phone messages and e-mails. Oh my God! That's it! I think I stuck the money in the desk drawer by the computer."

"Thank you, Lord!" Artie did a dance in the end zone.

Only it didn't turn up there. Or in Mindy's pocketbook, her car, or the desk in the kitchen.

"I hate to ask," Mindy started, "but what if I didn't lose it? What if Aaron . . ."

"Don't even think it! In fact, if you want to accuse anyone of stealing, it should be Beth."

"Beth? Yeah right. Savings and loans come to her!"

"Maybe. But if she's leaving Richard, she might need some quick cash. Not to mention, last night she slept in the den, so she had time, she had motive, and she had opportunity!"

"Well thank you, Lenny Briscoe!" Mindy was near tears. "But think about it. Aaron was staying downstairs, too. Didn't he have the same time, motive, and opportunity?"

"He didn't have motive."

"You don't know that. There's a whole family history of drug addiction. What if he's one of those kids making crystal meth from Dimetapp? What if he's abusing OxyContin? Oh my God, he could have a stroke, or a seizure, or go into a coma, or—"

"Would you listen to yourself?" Artie snapped. "You've got him halfway to Betty Ford with nothing to base it on. Just admit it. You lost the money."

"That's the thing. I don't think I did . . . I'm pretty sure I had it when I got home."

"Fine. But leave Aaron out of this. He hasn't done a damn thing wrong."

"I'm sorry, I'm sorry, I'm sorry. . . . I'm just so upset right now. . . . I'm sorry."

Artie nodded. They were both stretched to their breaking points. "Problem is," he said, "whatever did happen, I don't think I can put together another five hundred to take with us."

"Why not? What happened to our overdraft protection?"

"We overdrafted it."

"That nice new bank card with the daisies?"

"Blew right past the credit limit to pay our medical insurance, plus I know how much you like heat in the winter. But hey! We've still got that two-hundred-dollar gift card for Home Depot."

"Oh jeez. We are so pathetic. How did we get here?"

"We're not pathetic. We're just in over our heads right now. But next month, we'll have that new nerd line that Johnny Depp wears. The kids will go crazy for it and sales could double!"

"Hey, Aaron." She swallowed. "Howz it goin'? Did you find the Cartoon Network?"

"Hey, son," Artie perked up. "Excited about the trip?"

"I guess," he shrugged. "Do you hafta call me son? It's weird."

"Oh. Really? Okay. Fine."

Yikes! "Would you like some breakfast?" Mindy asked. "We've got waffles, cereal—"

"Not hungry." He slouched in a chair.

"Oh come on. No extra charge. Comes with the room."

But Aaron wasn't much into humor. Seems in addition to his dark, tight curls, he'd also inherited his father's quick trigger for tears, like a malfunctioning sprinkler system. Apparently he did not have a song for every occasion.

"Hey. Come on," Artie nudged his shoulder. "Can't be that bad. Tell us what's going on. If you don't like your choices for breakfast, we can go take a run to the diner."

Aaron's face was streaked, his hair matted to his neck. "I can't do this, man. I can't go with you. You're all real nice, but I can't hack all the questions and everyone lookin' at me."

"Oh, you mean like last night when the kids bombarded you with questions?" Artie started to sweat. "They were just excited, but that's over now. Done and done!"

"I don't fit in. You're all so happy like."

"No c'mon. We're not happy at all. In fact at the moment we're pretty miserable. And I could be your wingman. Make sure everybody gives you space."

"Yeah," Mindy added. "And when we get on the ship, you can totally do your own thing. They've got tons of activities for teens."

Artie eyed her. Did Aaron look like the type who would be interested in activities for teens? He needed to hear the cool stuff. "What she means is they've got rock climbing and a basketball court on the ship. And I read that the lobby is nine stories high and—"

"I shouldn'ta come here. . . . My band needs me and my girl needs me, too. . . . They're all like when ya gettin' back, man?"

"Okay, look. . . ." Artie gripped an imaginary rod as if he were attempting to reel in a shark. "You'll be back before you know it, and I know yesterday didn't go great, but we really want you to give this a chance, give us a chance. . . . We all just need time to adjust. And a cruise is awesome. One big party! You got the sun, the pretty girls in bikinis . . . and it was going to be a surprise, but we're snorkeling in Cozumel and—"

"I wanna leave tomorrow. I gotta see my mom. She's in bad shape."

Leave tomorrow, miss the cruise, and maybe never come back? This couldn't be happening. Mindy took Artie's hand to show support, though to her surprise, he said that he wasn't going to argue. If Aaron wanted to leave, he could leave. "My dad always says, when a man makes his mind up, then that's it."

Wait. What? Since when did Artie quote the great philosopher, Stan Sherman? And what was the deal with him giving in so fast? He hadn't waited all this time to be dumped at the altar. A more likely reaction would have been if he locked Aaron in a closet until the limo arrived.

"Hold on," Mindy said, "let's just think on this before we do anything crazy."

Aaron rocked in his seat as if the music in his head was so much more compelling than listening to old people talk about activities for teens.

"The kids will be so disappointed, honey," Mindy tried. "It's all Ricky's been talking about . . . meeting his big brother. And the girls were just saying—"

"Let it go," Artie said. "I'll check online and see if we can change his ticket."

"But it's nonrefundable. We'd have to pay the change fee plus a higher fare because it's not seven days' notice, and Aaron, to be honest, money is a little tight right now."

"It's fine." Artie headed to the computer. "I don't want to force him to stay and then have him be miserable the whole week. We'll worry about the money later."

Mindy hoped Aaron might start to hedge, but no such luck, and now she was angry. So typical of kids today, she thought. Overindulged cowards. The least bit of conflict and they buckled. If everything wasn't microwave easy, it was *wah, wah, wah.* And now Artie was acting the same by giving up without a fight. As soon as he was out of earshot, she sat next to Aaron.

"We'll do whatever it takes to make you stay. You want to call your mom every day, so what if the ship-to-shore calls cost more than dinner? You want to have a few beers at the pool, so what if you're underage? You want to—"

"Why are you like buggin' me? Art said it was cool."

"No. Art said he wasn't willing to fight with you and I'm saying you're a quitter. You made the trip here, now see it through. If you run from this, you'll run from everything."

"*'And you run and you run to catch up with the sun but it's sinking. Racing around to come up behind you again.'*"

"Pink Floyd. Nice. But forget what they think. I want to know what you think. Did we offend you? Hurt your feelings? Are we scary?" She wiggled her fingers in his face.

"'I'd rather laugh with the sinners than cry with the saints. Sinners are much more fun.'"

"Billy Joel. Interesting musical tastes . . . *"'How many times can a man turn his head, and pretend that he just doesn't see?'"*

Aaron furled his eyebrow.

"Bob Dylan, my friend. 'Blowing in the Wind.' You didn't know that one?"

He shrugged.

"I think you've got some studying to do," Mindy teased. *"'I'm just a soul whose intentions are good, Oh Lord, please don't let me be misunderstood.'"*

"Cocker."

"Bingo. But you won't get this one. Perfect for a cruise. *I'm going, I'm going, where the water tastes like wine. We can jump in the water, stay drunk all the time.'"*

"'Going up the Country.' Canned Heat."

"Wow . . . we should switch iPods. I think you'll be impressed with my—"

"Don't have one."

"Really? But you live for music," she paused. "Well, no problem. We'll just share. Art has some pretty crazy stuff on his, although you'll probably hate what the kids listen to."

"You all have one?" His chin dropped.

"Yeah." And there it was. Her moment of Zen. So what if theirs was the smallest house on the block? Compared to how Aaron had grown up, he probably thought of the Shermans as rich folk from Long Island, what with their two cars, three computers, and five iPods. And then Ricky had acted so surprised that Aaron had never been to Disney.

While lost in thought, Mindy didn't notice the envelope lying on the table.

"Oh my God!" she gasped when she saw the familiar bank

logo. "Where did you . . . how . . . when . . . I knew it, I knew it, I knew it!" She banged the table.

"Sorry." Aaron drummed with two hands.

"That's all you can say? Sorry? You stole this from us!"

"Nope." He banged out a beat. "Ricky did."

"Right. A six-year-old was looking for an envelope full of cash. Is he planning to gamble on the cruise?"

"*'Because you're mine, I walk the line,'*" Aaron sang.

"Stop it. This isn't funny anymore. And what does the song have to do with . . . Oh," she laughed. "Johnny Cash . . . Clever boy, Aaron, but you better tell me what's going on or I'll—"

"Okay, all done." Artie returned. "It nearly killed me, but I did it. Aaron, you have a flight out from LaGuardia about an hour after we leave. A nonstop, too. Flight number ninety-four. You'll be home tomorrow by noon because you get the few hours back. Happy?"

Aaron said nothing.

"Yes, well before anyone goes anywhere, sonny boy has some questions to answer." Mindy waved the envelope in Artie's face.

"Oh my God. Is that the money? Where did you find it?"

"You'll never guess." She shot him an I-told-you-so look. "Aaron told me that Ricky took it. Ricky who picks pennies up off the street and asks people if they dropped them."

"Aaron?" Artie's voice went up by a half octave. "Spill it."

"I did, man. I'm tellin' the truth. Ricky came down last night and said he found all this money in a drawer and wanted to know if it was enough to go to Disney?"

"Okay, but why didn't you tell him to put it back?"

"He made me promise not to. Otherwise, no Disney."

"All right," Artie said to Mindy. "No harm done. He did the right thing and gave it back."

"Only 'cause you're lettin' me go home." Aaron drummed on the table.

* * *

The kids took the news of Aaron's change of plans better than Mindy expected, though it wasn't because they were the sympathetic sort. They were just very excited to finally be leaving for this much anticipated vacation. As with Aaron who had never been to Orlando, the Sherman kids were the only ones they knew who had never been on a cruise. Most of their friends not only had oft-stamped passports but a familiarity with the baggage restrictions for international travel. So while it would have been fun if Aaron had joined them, it was *woo-hoo,* Mexico here we come!

Artie, on the other hand, was trying to maintain his composure en route to the airport. While the kids were milking every minute of the cool limousine ride, a treat from their grandparents, he stared out the window, unaware that his older son was doing the same.

Mindy tried to bounce between her excited kids and the two somber men, only to realize that she was too drained to focus on either. In fact, she was already fantasizing about a beach chair and a cabana boy . . . located at a different hotel than her family. Now that would be a vacation!

But the second they arrived at the terminal, it was all chaos and keeping track of kids and suitcases and checking in and praying their bags didn't exceed the weight limit and calling Stan and Rhoda to find out where they were.

"Looks like we're all set." Artie counted baggage claim receipts. "Aaron, you'll stick with us until we board, and then you'll go ask which gate you need to go to."

"Cool."

"Ready everybody?"

But really. Can you ever be ready for the things you never saw coming?

* * *

The flight was late, the gate was packed, seats were scarce, and big traveling parties likes the Shermans' had to scatter to find any place to sit. So much for Artie's plan to use this time for a family huddle and to give Aaron a chance to bond and feel the love.

Naturally his hope was that he would enjoy all the good-natured kibitzing and wonder if he was about to miss the opportunity of a lifetime. Instead, Aaron got stuck between yoga-posing Aunt Dana and four-year-old cousin Abigail who cried, "Mommy, that boy smells bad."

Grandpa Stan came over and asked Aaron if he liked sports, and when he replied no, Stan returned to his seat.

Mindy was busy refereeing a fight between Stacie and Jamie over who got to use the Bose headsets. "It's my turn! Jamie got them in the limo."

Ricky and his cousin Brandon were racing up and down the aisles, annoying fellow passengers who had to shift their legs every time the boys flew past.

Meanwhile, Rhoda, whose seat backed up to Aaron's, talked to Ira about him as if he were in another terminal. "Such nonsense with the tattoos and the earrings," she snorted. "Wait until he's in the real world. The only jobs he'll qualify for are asking, do you want fries with that?" Good old Rhoda. Inappropriate for every occasion.

As for Artie? Mindy went to ask him a question and discovered he was gone. But wouldn't he have told her if he was going to the men's room or to buy a magazine? Unless maybe he'd decided to check on Aaron's flight. Come to think of it, why had no one said a word to her about Aaron's decision to go home?

Then when Artie didn't pick up his cell, she asked the family, but per usual, they were clueless. And oh how the mind can wander. Had creditors had him followed and taken him away for late payments? Had security discovered that he'd stashed a water bottle in his carry-on bag and were they questioning his motives? Or what if a resentful Aaron had tied him up and left him in a bathroom stall because his father had bought an iPod for everyone but him?

"Mom! They're calling you!" Stacie yelled. "They paged your name on the loudspeaker."

"They did?" She jumped up. "What did they say? Did anyone else hear it?"

Aaron, not wanting anything to interfere with his sulking, pointed to the gate agent.

Mindy tripped over her pocketbook as she raced to the counter. Sure enough, she had been paged. Mystery solved. Artie had felt chest pains and shortness of breath while waiting in line for coffee and had been taken by emergency medical technicians to the airport clinic.

"Go with her!" Rhoda pushed Stan.

"Me?" Stan waved her off. "I'm not a cardiologist. I can't help him."

"Dad!" Ira shouted. "Are you kiddin' me? You're a doctor. Go make sure they're not letting him die on the table!"

"My daddy is dying?" Ricky cried.

"Mommy!" Jamie punched Stacie. "She took my cell phone and won't give it back!"

"They all have cell phones, too?" Aaron looked faint.

Seven

When you learn that a loved one has possibly had a heart attack, there is no time to think or feel or even worry. As you rush to the scene, your only response is to pray from every pore that a competent doctor is on call and that by the time you arrive, the worst is over and the patient is being given a prescription for heartburn medicine.

You do not expect to find them hooked up to a heart monitor with their nose and mouth covered by breathing apparatus. You do not expect their skin to be as white as the paper on the examining room table. You mostly do not expect them to wink when the doctor isn't looking.

Mindy's eyes bugged out. Was Artie sharing this last moment of intimacy before he passed or letting her in on a joke? Because if this was a joke, she was going to wrap the blood pressure cuff around his neck and squeeze the pump until his temples bulged worse than Stan's.

Turns out the truth, like Artie, lay somewhere in between.

"I was hoping you'd bring Aaron," he said as Mindy wheeled him out of the clinic.

"Why? So you could beg him to come with us and say it was the wish of a dying man?"

"Sort of."

"You are such an asshole. Do you realize how terrified I was? I could have keeled over from a heart attack just thinking about you having a heart attack. And do you realize that they could have prevented you from getting on the plane right now? You're lucky that the doctor believed you when you said you were fine."

"Well, that and the EKG. Everything was normal. And I'm sorry about scaring you. I really was getting coffee when I started to feel chest pains, but I think it was probably from all the worry that my plan had failed and I was out of ideas."

"Wait. What? This was all part of a plan? Hold on. It's my cell . . . bet it's someone from your lovely family wanting to know if you're dead or alive, and where did I put the snack bag?"

"Yeah, where is everyone? How come nobody came with you?"

"I tried, believe me. But God forbid anyone should miss the boarding announcement and the first crack at the blankets. Hi. Yeah, no, he's fine. They don't think it was a heart attack, just palpitations from heartburn. We're on our way back. Oh no. The flight was delayed again?" She repeated for Artie's sake. "Bummer." *But good news! We won't have to squeeze in a funeral before we leave.* Wow. Your dad's concern for you overwhelms me. Now tell me about this stupid-ass plan of yours, and how come no one has said a word about Aaron not going with us?"

"Because I didn't tell anyone."

"Well that was really bright. Don't you think by day two they'd notice he wasn't there?"

"I didn't say anything because he's still going with us."

"He changed his mind?"

"No."

"You changed his flight again?"

"No, I never changed it in the first place."

"Artie, are you serious? You lied to him?"

"Hell, yes! They wanted four hundred bucks for a one-way ticket and the only available flight wasn't leaving until six o'clock tonight. What was I supposed to do? Let him wait around here all day by himself? Besides, I knew if he came with us, he'd end up having a great time."

"Oh my God! Then what were you doing yesterday when you went on the computer?"

"What do you think? Checking the weather in Mexico and watching Knicks highlights."

"So this whole thing was planned? You faked a heart attack and hoped he'd say he'd do anything if God saved you?"

"Well no. I wasn't planning on taking it that far. I thought I might pretend to be sick while we were at the gate and have him realize that he had feelings for me and that it might be nice if he got to spend time with us."

"Stupid, stupid plan. No teenager in their right mind would want to spend time with us. So now what, Dr. Phil?"

"I don't know. I guess I'm going to have to level with him. Tell him the truth."

"That you lied? That you never made him a new reservation? That he's going on the cruise and goddamn it, he's going to have the time of his life?"

"I like how you summed that up. Maybe you should tell him."

"Forget it. The only thing I'm going to tell him is that his father is an idiot."

No big surprise when they returned to the gate. The family was exactly where Mindy had left them, with one exception.

"Hello?" Mindy called out. "Anyone notice that Aaron is gone?"

"Daddy!" Ricky ran over. "You didn't die . . . can I ride on your wheelchair?"

"Sure. Where is your brother?"

"He's talking to a giiiirl." Ricky jumped on his father's lap. *"Ewwww."*

"What girl? Where?"

"Over there," he said, pointing to a corner by the window. "She's going on the cruise, too, and she has this big tattoo on her tushie."

"She showed it to you?" Mindy gulped.

"No, silly mommy! She showed it to Aaron. . . . Do you think they're gonna get married? Nana says you can get married on the ship."

"Nobody's getting married on the ship." Mindy glanced at Artie. "Divorced, maybe."

"Hey, look." Artie pointed to a happy-faced Aaron, who was strumming his air guitar. "One miracle requested? One miracle delivered."

"Not so fast. You have to go tell him the truth."

Artie nodded and headed to confession, though it was laughter that Mindy heard.

"He's a smart one all right." Artie came back. "He knew all along."

"No way."

"Yeah. He thought I went too easy on him after my big speech about never letting him out of my sight, so he went on line and found out flight ninety-four goes to London."

"And he was okay with that?"

"He is now." Artie high-fived her. "Melissa from Manchester over there sings lead in a girl band and looks like Miss July."

Even with its vast passenger list, tight living quarters, and assortment of strangers with whom you must mingle, once your bags have miraculously been delivered to your cabins and you are settled in, there is nothing quite like cruising for fun and relaxation.

Mindy got right into the flow by settling into a deck chair, as an indebted Artie had given her time off for good behavior before the ship set sail. While he and the kids were running around marveling at the floating playground, she was taking in the warm rays and reflecting on the most bizarre week of her life . . . save for the week she got married and Rhoda moved in with her and her mom to make sure the wedding details were being taken care of to her satisfaction.

How had she survived the craziness with Stacie and Beth, the endless e-mails from Rhoda, the encounters with Aaron, the run-in with Stan, the terror over losing all that money, and, finally, Artie's fake heart attack? She didn't know whether to laugh or cry, but the cool piña colada along with the warm, tropical breeze was helping to ease the pain.

She was so caught between neurosis and Nirvana, she didn't care what everyone decided about the sleeping arrangements, as long as she wasn't rooming with Dana. All she needed was to be woken at dawn for green tea and Tai Chi. "Don't knock it 'til you've tried it," would be Dana's mantra, which like a recorded message, would keep repeating on Mindy like a pepperoni pizza. Make that flaxseed and barley.

What did make Mindy happy was recalling the surprised look on Aaron's face when her mom presented him with welcome gifts. He didn't quite know what to say about the *NSYNC beach towel, which everyone but Helene knew was so yesterday. But the waterproof watch went right on his wrist, and when he smiled, it deepened the luster of his brown eyes, matching his dad's like a set of lost luggage that had finally been reunited with its owner.

Maybe Artie was right. This whole family vacation experiment was going to work out great. Everyone was in good spirits, the weather forecast was perfect, and now she finally had a minute's peace to speculate on her little victory with Downtown Greetings.

When was the last time she'd received any validation for having writing talent? Or any talent? Could she be so lucky as to have finally discovered her purpose in life? If only she hadn't mentioned her excitement to Artie over dinner that night, as it moved him a little too profoundly.

Maybe it was the emotion of looking around the table and seeing his entire family assembled for the first time ever. Maybe it was the relief that he was about to have a week's reprieve from his troubles. Maybe it was that when he looked at Mindy, he was overjoyed that she was still his best friend, still the woman who loved him and laughed with him. Or maybe it was just the bottle of wine he had polished off with Ira.

He stood up to make a toast to his wonderful family and beautiful wife, who was about to embark on an exciting career opportunity, which she so deserved.

"Sit down," Mindy whispered. "I didn't want to tell anyone yet."

"Why not? They'll all be so proud of you."

"May I remind you this is *your* family?"

"What kind of career opportunity?" Stan barked. Cue temples. "She's already got a job."

"No, no, I know Dad," Artie said. "This is something different. Something extra."

"Well, I'm not changing her schedule so she can go work somewhere else. It's bad enough I gotta rearrange things when it's Hebrew School and soccer. I'm running a doctor's office, not a day-care center." Right side vibrating.

"Dad. Relax. Mindy is still working for you. This is more like a contest she entered."

"A contest?" Ira butt in. "Mindy, what the hell? Now you're tryin' to win a job?"

"Here it comes." Mindy gulped the last of her wine.

"It's not what you think," Artie replied.

"Yeah. Who enters a contest for a job if they already have one?" Stan asked.

"Guys, listen." Artie tapped his glass with a spoon. "It's a writing contest for Downtown Greetings. Think of it as like *American Idol* for birthdays and holidays."

"I didn't know Mindy could sing," Rhoda said. "Stan, did you know she could sing?"

"Mom. It's not a singing contest, it's a writing contest. And she's going to Chicago because she made it through the first round of competition."

"I never buy Downtown Greetings," Dana sniffed. "They don't use recycled paper."

"You win, Mindy," Ira groaned. "You found something my wife doesn't like buying."

"When's she going to Chicago?" Stan's temples did the cha-cha. "If she takes extra vacation days, the girls in the office will never let me hear the end of it."

"Mindy, you didn't say anything about this." Her mom leaned over. "If you need me to watch the kids, you gotta let me know 'cause my mahjong weekend is coming up."

"Happy?" Mindy whispered to Artie. "I know I am."

"I think it's cool," Aaron muttered.

"What?" Artie cupped his ear.

"I'm just sayin'. She's funny, so her cards would be a hoot."

"Thank you, Aaron." Mindy patted his hand.

"Yeah. Don't listen to them." He stuffed pie in his mouth. "Anyone wanna go throw beer off the deck? Give the fish a good time?"

"I do! I do!" Ricky jumped up.

"See?" Artie was beaming. "My sons understand!"

"Oh, I understand, too," Stan grumbled. "I understand that once again I'm expected to be Mr. Nice Guy."

"You're a doctor, Papa." Ricky clapped. "Dr. Nice Guy."

"That's me all right!" He poured more wine. "Dr. Nice Guy!"

Mindy didn't want to be accused of being negative, but clearly the right destination with the wrong people never works, particularly if those people are staying in the same stateroom. Try as Rhoda did to accommodate everyone's wishes (hers!), the room assignments went like this: she and Stan would have the Royal Family suite ("Because it's our special anniversary and we're paying"). Ira and Brandon were bunking with Artie and Aaron. Helene and Aunt Toby got Stacie and Jamie, which left Mindy and Ricky in a cabin with Dana and Abigail, who, on the first morning, threw Mindy's new blush brush down the toilet and cried when mean Aunt Mindy yelled at her.

"Why don't you guys watch TV while we get changed?" Mindy tried to be sweeter.

"She doesn't watch at home," Dana sniffed. "Why would she want to watch here?"

"She doesn't watch television? Like ever?"

"There was that one time Plácido Domingo was on *Sesame Street* . . . Abby, honey, why don't you sing Aunt Mindy that song you learned about photosynthesis?"

But Aunt Mindy couldn't offer "Abby honey" her undivided attention, as she was distracted by Ricky, who had wrapped a plastic snake around his neck and was shadowboxing on their bed while making chimpanzee noises. Premonition was the term that came to mind.

Good thing she'd brought the walkie-talkies. She'd set the alarm early every morning, get coffee, find a quiet spot to detox from Dana, and have Artie locate her position. They'd just have to be a little more creative finding ways to meet for sex. To their surprise, Aaron became their ally. When Artie signaled, he'd round up the kids and promise to sneak them into the casinos.

Mindy's only hope was that he didn't expect them to return the favor so he could get it on with Melissa from Manchester. How did one have the "talk" with a seventeen-year-old who could probably give them a few good pointers?

Mindy sneaked into Artie's stateroom, turned on by the prospect of having a scandalous little midday birthday interlude, though it was with her own husband, so call off the paparazzi. She quickly changed into her favorite black negligee, saddened that it had fit much better before her long-term affair with Ben and Jerry. Although as her friend Rochelle liked to say, "Once a man's between your thighs, he's not askin' what the scale says."

But when Artie was a no-show, anticipation was replaced with anger. If he was hanging out at the Cigar Bar with Ira, no gift from a ship boutique would make up for it. This was followed by fear. What if the heart attack was real this time and he was lying on the bottom of the pool?

Naturally her first instinct was to call his cell, but one thing that hit you hard after the ship sailed was that you might as well toss it overboard, 'cause service was spotty to nonexistent and the kids had the walkie-talkies.

All she could do was pace inside the tiny cabin, watch CNN in Spanish, break into the minibar, and ponder if Dana and Ira were also finding ways to have sex, though she doubted from Dana's stiff I-don't-find-you-funny reactions to everything Ira said that she much cared. "Sorry, Ira. I have water Pilates at ten, my aromatherapy massage at eleven . . ."

By the time Artie turned the key, Mindy had changed back into a big T-shirt and shorts. "I don't know where you've been, but I turned down six good offers."

Artie, his face red and perspired from the heat, sat on the edge of the bed, staring out.

"Hello?" she waved her hand in front of his face. "Please don't tell me you got the cabin numbers mixed up and had sex with someone else, 'cause no offense, but you don't have that much to go around anymore."

"She died," he said.

"What? Who? Who died?"

"Davida." He waved a piece of paper in the air.

"Oh my God. She died? What does that mean?"

"What do you mean what does that mean? It means she crapped out. She's gone to meet her maker."

"No, I get that part. What does that mean for Aaron . . . for us?"

"What kind of question is that? I just found out like two minutes ago. I have no idea what it means. I'm in shock."

"Wait. Are you upset because your first wife died or your second wife is thinking we've got only ten minutes left for sex?"

"That's not even funny, Mindy. God! What is wrong with you? A forty-four-year-old woman who was bright and artistic and made beautiful patchwork quilts for half our neighborhood in Queens got sucked into a drug world and basically took her own life. . . . I think you would have liked her. . . ."

"Oh. Then I'm sorry for your loss. . . . I didn't know you had feelings for her anymore."

"I don't. . . . I'm just . . . I don't know what to do. Do I tell Aaron? Do I not tell him? Do I get him on a flight out tomorrow, when we get to Cozumel? Do I go with him?"

"I have no idea. Wait. How did you even find out?"

"I was down at the bursar's, buying tickets for the snorkel trip tomorrow, and the woman sees my name and says, sir, I think you just got a telegram. And I'm thinking, they still have those? Turns out it was from my ex-brother-in-law, Wayne, and it said,

"Urgent! Call me. Sad news." And then I'm like, damn, those ship-to-shore calls are so expensive. Should I wait until tomorrow and try to use one of those overseas phone cards?"

"But you had a feeling?"

"Well yeah, sure. I mean we knew she was in rehab, although people don't usually die there. . . . Anyway, I called and he told me she was supposed to be getting out in a few days . . . but they found her in her room this morning. They think it was a heart attack."

"Ohmygod!"

"Yeah. And get this. He also told me that Davida kicked Aaron out of the house a few months ago. Said she couldn't handle him anymore because he was too wild."

"Great."

"No, no. But that wasn't the real story. Wayne said she was the one who was too wild. She was totally strung out all the time and then she got arrested for auto theft or something. Anyway, Aaron ended up living with him and he said Davida wouldn't let him even come back to the house to visit. . . . Can you believe that? My kid was orphaned and homeless?"

"That poor thing!"

"Yeah, but Wayne said it wasn't his fault. He's a great kid."

"And what about Wayne? Is he a good guy?"

"When he's sober? A sweetheart. 'Course to him a balanced meal is a Bud in each hand."

"Lovely! What else did he tell you?"

"He said he was glad when Aaron moved in because he had been working for a roofing contractor and fell on the job and was still out on disability."

"Not a good combination. Alcohol and altitude."

"Right. Anyway, since Aaron had his driver's license, he could take care of the grocery shopping, the running around . . . he even worked as a part-time custodian so he could help with the expenses. Is this kid amazing or what?" Artie started to cry. "But he's been through so much."

"This is such a shock. When's the funeral?"

"Not going to be one. She's being cremated. Wayne said maybe they'd do a memorial thing when Aaron got back, but that most of her friends were either dead or too strung out on crystal meth to care."

"Jeez, we're sheltered."

"Yeah," he sniffed.

"Well, but at least if there's no wake, he can wait until we get back to go home."

"Okay, but when do I tell him?"

"Now. Today. You have to tell him today."

"Really?"

"Yes! If you lie about this like you did the flight home and your little heart attack, then strike three and you're out. He'll never trust you again."

"Fine, but do I have to tell him everything, 'cause there may be more?"

"More?" Mindy gulped. "His mother is dead. What else could go wrong?"

"Oh nothing much. Happy birthday. You might be a grand-mother!"

"A what? She raced out to the balcony. " Please tell me you're joking!"

"Don't you dare jump!" He followed her. "I am not joining AARP alone."

"What does that mean? Mindy hyperventilated over the railing.

"What do you think it means? It means sonny boy shtupped a girl and lucky us, there's gonna be a little baby in Oregon calling us grandma and grandpa."

"No, no. You maybe, not me. I may be getting old but I'm too young for this. I still get my legs waxed. Ohmygod!!! What did Wayne say exactly? Does he know for sure?"

"No. All he said was after Aaron left, he got a call from this girl in a band he'd been hanging out with, she was hysterical sobbing, said she was pregnant and needed to talk to him right away. What does that sound like to you?"

"Like an ABC after-school special." She paced. "So he has no idea?"

"None." Artie stared at the waves.

"Hold on . . . hold on. The day before we left, when he wanted go home, didn't Aaron say something about his girl needing him?"

"Yeah, he did. Shit!"

"This is crazy, Artie! What are we supposed to do?"

"Hell if I know. I'm still in shock that I get to have sex, let alone my son."

"It's unbelievable. One mother checks out, another checks in."

"That's good. Ambiguous is good. He won't have a clue what we're talking about. "

"Would you stop joking?" she yelled. "This is serious! You have to be straight with him. Get it all out there so he can start to deal."

"I can't do that. Then he'll always associate me with being the bearer of the worst news of his life and hate me even more. Maybe I'll get my dad to talk to him. When my grandfather died, he took me and Ira to a Mets game and told us during the seventh-inning stretch."

"Oh that's good. 'Son, there's been a death in the family. Have a hot dog.' And what if Aaron doesn't think his girlfriend being pregnant is bad news? What if he's thrilled and wants to run home and marry her?"

"You're crazy. No seventeen-year-old wants to be saddled with a wife and kid."

"Apparently you've never seen the ABC after-school specials. Some boys love the idea. It makes them feel manly and grown up."

"Whatever. Obviously I have no experience with any of this. Let's just agree to leave out this piece of the puzzle until we know for sure what we're dealing with. Maybe she's not pregnant, or maybe it's not even Aaron's."

"Agreed. But you're not gonna wimp out about telling him about Davida?"

"I'll tell him, I'll tell him . . . maybe at the next port I'll get lucky and find a baseball game and someone selling hot dogs."

Eight

It drove Mindy crazy whenever Artie insisted on asking his father's advice. Not that she didn't understand his desire to have someone older and wiser helping to solve his major life crises, it's just that Stan wasn't that guy. He may have been a solo practitioner in medicine, but at home he had a full-time partner, and she was hardly the silent type.

In fact, Mindy had laughed when she once took a message from a local playhouse inviting Stan for a callback. Though he had never mentioned a desire to act, she suspected he had tried out just to see what it was like to have a speaking role.

So when Artie decided that he would ask his father's input on handling this very delicate matter with Aaron, Mindy knew that it would be Rhoda and not Stan who dictated the terms, right down to the choice of words to break the bad news.

Mindy objected to her in-laws' involvement, though this was an old fight and the results were always the same. Artie, a forty-five-year-old husband and father would run to his dad for counsel, and Rhoda would call them a bunch of spineless sissies who should thank God she was there to advise them.

Sure enough, at the mention that Artie had an important matter to discuss, Stan and Rhoda beckoned their son to the royal suite, listened to the long, sad tale, and immediately took charge of damage control. Well Rhoda did, lest the displaced little pauper think he would have control over his kingdom.

"She wants to do what?" Mindy yelled when Artie returned from his little summit.

"Don't say it like that. I think it's a good idea."

"No. I'm sorry. You don't break the news into small bites like he's an infant."

"Why not? First we tell him we got word that his mom was pretty sick, give him a chance to get used to the idea, then tomorrow or the next day we tell him everything."

"Artie, haven't you realized he's a very smart boy? He'll call your bluff in a heartbeat."

"But he's only a kid. If we have a chance to ease him into this, I think we should."

"No, your mother thinks we should."

"That's not fair. I have my own opinion. It just so happens it's the same as hers."

"Really? And who would win if you disagreed?"

"Why are you getting so bent out of shape? I don't think it's wrong to want advice."

"I agree. I just think the person you should be asking is me because whatever gets decided, it's going to affect our family.

"Fine. Then what's your opinion? How should we tell him?"

"Well, first before we do anything, let's get more information."

"What else do you need to know? Davida is dead and next year Aaron and I could get the same Father's Day card."

"Very funny. But maybe let's call Wayne back and ask him the best way to tell Aaron, since he knows him better. In fact, maybe he should be the one to tell him, since it's a loss for him, too."

"Not a bad idea."

"Thank you."

"All right. I'll go back and talk to my folks. See what they think."

In the end, the match was a draw. Artie did call Wayne, only he was so wasted, Artie couldn't put much stock in his suggestion to break the news after letting the boy get drunk and laid.

And Rhoda, in her infinite wisdom, bought Aaron a five-hundred-dollar, TAG Heuer watch at one of the ship's boutiques, certain the gift would distract him from his pain. Though from experience, Mindy knew that the watch had less to do with pacifying him than trying to make the one Helene gave him look chintzy by comparison.

But alcohol, sex, and fine jewelry would hardly be antidotes for learning that your already vulnerable, disappointing life was taking yet another gut-wrenching turn. In fact, with Aaron's intuition already on high alert when summoned to the suite and given the watch and a generous slice of banana cream pie, his dessert of choice every night, he studied the choppy waters from the balcony as if he was considering his exit strategy.

The fixed stare freaked Artie. Suddenly he couldn't recall the words his mother had suggested. All that came to mind was Mindy's original question. What did all of this mean for them? Would Aaron come live with them or insist on staying in Portland? If he lived with them, would they have to add an extension? They were struggling to pay the mortgage and taxes as it was. What if he wanted his girlfriend and the baby to move in, too? And what about college? They had barely put away for Stacie, let alone handling even bigger financial obligations.

Mindy nudged him. Everyone was waiting. He looked at her and she knew.

"Aaron, honey," she went over and rubbed his back. "Very unexpectedly, we got a telegram from your uncle Wayne today . . . your mom . . . we have such sad news . . . she died this morning. . . . They think it was a heart attack. We are so sorry. But at least now her struggle is over. She's not in pain anymore."

Aaron blinked like a computer shutting down, then collapsed in a heap. The words had been slow to register but their meaning clear.

"*'Open your eyes, look up to the skies and see I'm just a poor boy, I need no sympathy because I'm easy come, easy go, little high, little low . . . Mama, don't want to die. Sometimes I wished I'd never been born at all. . . .'*"

"What's he doing?" Stan scratched his head.

"He sings when he's upset," Artie whispered. "He loves music."

"I love music, too, but I wouldn't be hummin' a few bars if my mother just died."

"Dad, it's famous," Mindy tried. "'Bohemian Rhapsody'? Queen?"

"A song about Queens? Which part? Flushing? Fresh Meadows?"

"No!" Even Artie was annoyed. "You never heard of Freddie Mercury?"

"*Uch.* You kids with all your crazy music. Now Sinatra and Bennett, that was singing."

"Shut up!" Aaron trembled. "Shut the fuck up!"

"Aaron," Artie started. "We're so sorry. We feel your pain. We'll do anything for you."

But sympathy was a useless commodity. He bolted for the door, screaming that he was glad his mother was dead because she was a terrible person.

They looked at one another until Artie asked if he should follow him.

"Go." Mindy pushed him. "You don't need anyone's permission to be a good father. Just ... you know, don't do all the talking. Try to get him to open up."

Artie looked at his dad for approval, who looked at Rhoda for approval.

"Oh my God! I can't take this anymore." Mindy raced to the door. "I'll go after him!"

"What's with her?" Rhoda asked.

"Believe me, you don't know how crazy she gets," Stan grunted. "With her, it's always that time of the month. Last week she practically held me up at gunpoint."

A twenty-five-hundred passenger ship that ran the length of three football fields was a terrible place to lose someone, especially someone who didn't want to be found. If only Mindy could ask her kids to join the search, as there was no one better at hide and seek. But best to leave them in the pool with their cousins and Ira so they wouldn't have to witness a young man's meltdown.

Question was, where to begin? The bars, in case he was able to convince a sympathizer to buy him drinks? A family that Dana knew from home suggested she try the fitness center. Maybe pumping iron would be a stress reliever, but no sign of him there. If it had been Mindy, she would have run to Johnny Rockets and the ice-cream parlor for their super deluxe anything, but as she well knew, Aaron wasn't an eater.

Fueled by fear that he might be so enraged as to try something reckless, she picked up steam and tore through the casino, the theater, the cafés ... up to the rock-climbing wall, the pool, the gift shops, and even over to the golf simulator. No luck. And by now, even with the cool breezes coming off the ocean, the sun and a wicked hot flash had turned her into a sweaty mess.

Not the best time to run into her mother and Aunt Toby, who were chatting with two gentlemen over coffee. From a distance, they resembled her father and Uncle Sidney, until she got closer and wondered if Artie had put the wrong prescription lenses in her glasses. Unlike her dad and uncle, these men had hair on their heads, fit bodies, and cruise wear from L.L.Bean.

Mindy also wondered if her mom and aunt were wearing glasses at all. Didn't they notice the men's wedding bands? Of course it would be great if they met someone on board, but this was no time to be laughing it up with other women's husbands.

Normally this thought would never have crossed her mind. But after the whole Beth fiasco, she was starting to think that maybe cheating was a hobby, like bridge or skydiving. And then there was that story Nadine told her about her across-the-street neighbors who took a cruise to celebrate their fortieth anniversary. The husband met a woman while waiting for a spa treatment, ended up leaving his wife, then married spa lady, figuring if she looked good in a bathrobe, she'd look good in anything.

Mindy ran to the table, introduced herself, apologized for springing bad news on them, and explained the tragic predicament about Davida. She also had the presence of mind to point out the obvious. "Mom, they're married," she whispered.

"I know, darling. We were with them and their wives last night. Don't worry."

"Not worried," she lied.

"They're here on a family reunion. They're traveling with cousins who are widowers. They're going to introduce us at dinner tonight."

Turns out Max and Mort Alter from the Detroit area were not only matchmakers, but experienced search-and-rescue workers. Max was a retired police detective who knew all about finding missing persons and Mort used to be a private investigator. First thing they asked was what was Aaron wearing, and had he met any girls on board?

Duh! Of course, Mindy thought. What seventeen-year-old

boy wouldn't want to seek consolation by nestling in the 34D breasts of Melissa from Manchester? But where to find her?

Normally, Max said he'd divide and conquer, but since there were no reliable methods of communication, they should survey the decks together, each being on the lookout for something different. Teenagers mingling, young people in the pool, a young man leaning over the railings.

Turned out Uncle Wayne had a leg up on the veteran cop as he knew Aaron best. The proof? His advice to get him drunk and laid came close. Aaron was discovered sitting in a dark corner of the Viking Crown lounge enjoying a blow job and a beer.

Mindy spotted him first and let out a cry, but not in time to prevent her mom, Aunt Toby, Max, and Mort from witnessing Melissa from Manchester performing oral sex.

"Go!" Mindy shooed them out before Aaron realized he had an audience.

"What are you going to do?" Helene whispered.

Take her refresher course? "What do you think I'm going to do? I'm going to talk to him. . . . Just go. . . . I promise I'll find you if I need help."

But first, Mindy needed a moment to regroup. She had no experience interrupting sexually active teens, and if this was a sneak preview of what Stacie and her little friends would be up to in a few years, they were moving to Amish country.

Focus, she thought. This was not about Stacie. It was about helping Aaron deal with his grief, though from the view from behind a plant, he hardly looked like a young man in mourning. And had he no shame? He was in a public place. And how could he cheat on the mother of his baby? Mindy had a few things to say about that, too. Focus, she thought. You have a job here!

"Aaron?" she took a few steps forward and waved. "Honey?"

He and Melissa looked over, more annoyed than ashamed. "Go away!" he ordered.

"I'm sorry. . . . I really think we should talk."

"Nothin' to talk about. Just leave me the hell alone."

"Aaron, you've just heard some tragic news. We want to help you."

But clearly he was already getting the help he wanted, for there was no further acknowledgment of her and she couldn't decide which was worse. That Aaron didn't care that he was exposing himself in public, or that he had already concluded that sex and booze were his preferred pain relievers?

Emotions stirred further as she realized how you could take the boy out of the gene pool, but never the gene pool out of the boy. From old family photos, she could now see the stark resemblances between Aaron and Stan as a young man, the tall, lanky build, the dark curls and deep-set eyes, even the strong chin, which she'd thought was Stacie's exclusive inheritance.

And though he was not from her bloodline, suddenly her maternal engine turned on.

"Aaron. Stop!" she tried again. "Melissa, honey . . . I'm sure your parents are wondering where you are. I heard they fixed the karaoke machine."

Alas, the beautiful young maiden got up, buttoned her shirt, looked for one of her flip-flops, and waved good-bye as if she'd just stopped over to watch TV.

"Let's sit over here." She motioned for Aaron to join her at a distant couch so as not to have to recall the crime scene, then chose her opening remarks. "So where did you get the beer?"

Aaron glared. If Melissa was forced to leave so that they could discuss underage drinking, this did not bode well for meaningful discussion.

"This is hard," she started over. "We're really not sure what to say or do for you. We feel awful, of course, and we want to do the right thing, whatever that is. We even wondered if we should wait to tell you until we got back, but we really respect you, Aaron.

You're so smart, and you've already been through so much. You deserve the truth."

"Thanks." He chugged his beer as if it was medicinal.

"Look. It's just a guess, but you probably think we're these spoiled, rich people who don't have any problems, let alone any idea what it's like to feel powerless all the time . . . and maybe it's true that we can't relate to what your life has been like, but that doesn't mean that we're uncaring. Both your father and I really want to help you through this. You just have to let us."

"There's nothin' you can do. And I don't need anyone's help. I've been doing everything on my own since I'm ten."

"I believe you, honey. You seem incredibly capable. But as much as you know, there is a lot you don't. Believe it or not, one of the first true signs that a boy has become a man is his ability to reach out when he's in trouble and say, hey, I need help."

"You don't get it. This isn't gonna matter 'cause my life's not gonna change now."

"Actually, this changes everything." *And you don't know the half of it.*

"Like hell it does! She didn't do nothin' for me anyway . . . my friends' moms were all nicer than her to me . . . I'll be okay."

"I understand where you're coming from. I'm just telling you that I know that emotions can change over time. Look, right now you're angry, so of course you're determined to keep doing everything for yourself. But what happens if one day you can't find a job, or you're confused about a relationship? It could make you feel lost and depressed. But if you have people like us around who truly care, we'll help you get back on your feet."

"Whatever." He chugged his beer.

"Not to mention, there are going to be lots of decisions like where you'll live."

"I'm not movin' in with you—you can't make me do that—I'm going home."

"Nobody is saying you have to move in with us, but you'll still need financial support, legal guardians. There's a lot of stuff that's going to come up." *Like say in nine months.*

"Oh thank God we found you." A breathless, windblown Rhoda barged in with Artie, whose strong aftershave did not mix well with the sweat on his tomato-red face. "We thought something bad happened. Aaron, you scared us to death."

Excellent choice of words as always, Rhoda.

"Aaron . . . how ya doing?" Artie leaned over to hug his boy. "We're so sorry. . . ."

"He knows," Mindy sighed. "We've just been talking about how to handle everything."

"Good! Now here's the plan," Rhoda announced. "I spoke to the captain, a lovely man from Nova Scotia, and he said that right after we take our family portraits tonight, Aaron can join him in the command center. Wouldn't that be fun, honey? Go home and tell your friends you got to steer a huge ship?"

Mindy looked at Artie. Was she serious?

"Mom," Artie said. "Let's do this later. It's a little too soon right now."

"What's too soon? There's nothing he can do to bring his mother back. He might as well have a good time. We're on a cruise, for God's sake! And I am NOT going back to the captain to tell him that this young man isn't interested in his very generous offer."

"Mom!" Mindy said. "Aaron isn't a child. You can't just make him forget his problems by taking him on a fun ride like it's Disney. He needs a chance to be alone and think."

"Think, schmink! All that will do is give him a chance to sit around sulking."

Um, he wasn't exactly sulking when I found him. "Aren't you being a little insensitive here?" Mindy eyed Artie as if to say jump in at any time. "What if someone tried taking you to Coney Island the day your mother died?"

"Why do you always have to twist my words?" Rhoda gasped.

"Mom," Artie pleaded. "Can we please not make this about you?"

"Of course I don't want this to be about me. And did I say Aaron shouldn't feel sad? I'm merely suggesting that he's here to have fun and fun he's going to have. Not that I would expect Miss let's everyone all sleep together and be treated like a baby for the rest of your life to understand . . ."

"Oh my God, Rhoda!" Mindy cried. "Why do you speak to me like that?"

"See what I have to put up with, Aaron?" Out came Rhoda's pointing finger. "Your grandfather and I were generous enough to take the whole family on this marvelous cruise, and believe me, we could have gone ourselves and been very happy not having to listen to the kids kvetching every few minutes about this one hit me and that one thinks the show is boring and why do we have to get dressed up for dinner again. Now I have to hear bellyachin' that I don't know nothin' from nothin' about what's best for a young man. She forgets I raised two wonderful sons who turned out better than good."

"Mom!" Artie yelled. "Mindy isn't saying that at all."

"No, it's okay." She raised her hands in surrender. "I know when I'm not appreciated."

"Here's an idea," Mindy whispered to Aaron. "How about I come live with you in Oregon?"

"Cool."

Nine

Mindy was trying hard not to be negative, yet she vowed to never look at a cruise brochure again and buy into the images of the happy people frolicking in the pool, enjoying gourmet meals, and laughing at the nightly entertainment. Truth be told, when you came with family, a cruise wasn't a vacation as much as a trip.

Proof was everywhere. Mothers trying to read in between dealing with whiny kids who were hungry, bored, or mad that somebody splashed them. Fathers getting drunk at the poolside bars so they didn't have to listen to their annoying kids and angry wives. Grandparents, especially the ones who had paid the freight, looking as if they couldn't wait to return home to their friends, people who were grateful for what they had, not complainers who felt the need to condemn every meal, excursion, and amenity as if they were judging a contest rather than the bounty of their lives.

With this being the final day on board, all Mindy wanted was for it to go by without drama, trauma, or anyone annoying the crap out of her. She wanted to feel rejuvenated so she could return to her getting-crazier-by-the-minute life with enough energy to cope. She wanted to hear a nice compliment instead of the usual assortment of hurtful remarks that made her dwell on the perfect comebacks. Mostly she wanted to feel love and pride for her daughters without thinking how unfair it was that by virtue of their short, round bodies, their net worth had already plummeted when compared to the premium placed on the skinny girls and their matching moms, who sauntered by in bikinis, stirring envy with each step.

Was this too much to ask?

"Now what?" she looked up to see a tense-looking Artie settle into his deck chair.

"What do you mean?" He lathered up in sunscreen, laid back, and shut his eyes. "Everything's peachy keen."

"Okay, who are you and what did you do to my husband?"

"Fine. We got several disturbing e-mails; Aaron is mad because I asked him not to fly right home after we get back; my mother is insisting you owe her an apology for accusing her of being insensitive; Ira won't stop hocking me about looking at vacation homes near theirs, which really pisses me off because he's only doing it to rub it in that he makes three times what I do; Stacie and Jamie are crying at the rock climbing thing because some boy said they were too fat to make it to the top; Ricky just punched Abby in the back and Dana is punishing him; oh, and I think I just saw my dad flirting with some blonde at the art auction on deck seven."

"Excellent. Care for a drink?" She toasted him with her Cosmo.

"At nine thirty?"

"I figured if I started now, it'll eventually get later."

"I'm not gonna lie. This cruise didn't turn out like I expected."

"Oh I know." She sipped the sweet drink. "Weren't the floor shows so lame?"

"And is it just me, or are we the only two people left in America without tattoos?"

"Sorry. It's down to you. For my birthday, I had your mother's name branded on my ass."

"Yeah. Sorry it was so awful. I promise I'll make it up to you when we get home. Meantime, can you patch things up with her so we don't have to get the silent treatment the whole way home?"

"No. I am so sick of the way she treats me. She says the most awful things and I'm supposed to take it because she's got this huge checkbook hanging over our heads. And I don't understand why you never defend me. Why don't you ever defend me?"

"I do. The problem is she's never going to change and you still keep sparring with her. Just ignore her like the rest of us do. Why do you think my dad was talking to that lady? It was weird. I've never seen him laugh like that; he really looked like he was having fun."

"Can you blame him? He wasn't being insulted for a change. Where is your mom anyway?"

"At the spa for the whole day. They're going to turn her into Cinderella."

"That good they're not."

Artie laughed.

"I just can't stand the way she always puts me down," Mindy sighed. "Not Dana. Never Dana. But here's an idea. Did you happen to notice if there's a hypnotist on board? Maybe I can be put into a trance: *Rhoda is a wonderful woman. Rhoda is so thoughtful. Rhoda—.*"

"Should come with a warning label, but forget that. We've got bigger fish to fry."

"Oh no. Please. Let's table that discussion, 'cause whatever new crisis just came up, I'm sure it will be as painful and horrible when we get home."

"Sorry. One of the items can't wait."

"Are you sure you don't want to order a drink first?"

"No. I need to be fully alert—oh my God—there's my dad with that lady again."

"Where?" Mindy scanned the crowd, but between the bright sun and every passenger dressed in tropical attire, it was hard to pick anyone out of the crowd.

"Don't look! I don't want him to see us."

"Too late. He's wearing a blue shirt and . . . okay, relax. He's not doing anything wrong."

"Oh. So it would be fine if I showed up at the pool with another woman?"

"No, but I'm sure it's totally innocent. Although remember that story Nadine told me about her neighbors who split up after their anniversary cruise? The husband met this woman at the spa and—"

"Mindy! I don't want to hear that. Oh my God. She's rubbing suntan lotion on him. Should I go over there and say something?"

"Like what? Excuse me, that's my father you're trying to arouse and if my mother finds out, she'll get last night's magician to make you disappear?"

"I can't believe what I'm seeing . . . my dad messing around in broad daylight."

"There seems to be a lot of that going around these days." Mindy thought of Beth. "But don't get crazy. They're not doing anything wrong . . . uh-oh . . . hold on. . . . She's rubbing his thigh. Whoa Betsy! Gettin' a little close to the family jewels there. But *aww* . . . Look. He's smiling. Oh, man. I hope he doesn't invite her to sit with us at dinner tonight."

"That's it." Artie sprung up. "I'm going over there. Today is his anniversary and this is no way to—"

"Artie, sit down. Let him enjoy the attention. After forty years with your mother, the man deserves a little happiness."

"What are you talking about? He is very happy. He's got his health, his wealth and a wife who has stood by him all these years."

"Fine. Then look at it this way. You weren't sure what to get him and now you know."

So much for world peace, an end to global warming, and being able to enjoy this last day of the cruise by milking it for every last moment of relaxation.

One of the e-mails Artie had read came from Inez, the book-keeper, who wrote to say that the store manager had been ar-rested last night for both DWI and striking an officer. His car was impounded, his head had to be stitched, and the only way he could make bail was to borrow the twenty-four-hundred-dollar deposit from the store. She wanted to know what to do.

Start a fire? Mindy thought, not that it would be good if life began imitating old Jewish jokes, like the one about two friends who owned factories in the garment district, and one says, "Sol, sorry to hear your place burned down and Sol says, '*Shhh,* not till Friday.'"

Unfortunately the e-mail about the store wasn't the only mood crapper. Wayne also got back in touch. Apparently, Aaron had missed a good part of the school year and would likely have to repeat eleventh grade, which was topic A at the truancy hear-ing he was a no-show for.

"Want me to go on?" Artie asked.

"No. I was just thinking. If I take the elastic band from my cover-up and tie one end around my neck and the other to the back of this chair, then you could pull really tight and—"

"Forget it." Artie took her drink. "You are not leaving me to deal with this by myself."

"Wait." She closed her eyes and took a deep breath. "This is the new me talking . . . *hummmmm* . . . none of this is life threatening and we still have our health, right?"

"Not sure. I think I might be feeling a real heart attack coming on."

"Oh, don't worry." She moved to his chair and rubbed his back. "I'll get in touch with the store and tell them what to do; I'll get the number for Aaron's school and speak to the principal; I'll locate his girlfriend; apologize to your mom; convince Aaron to stay an extra few days . . . oh, and I'm also going to win the contest from Downtown Greetings and earn lots of money."

"Wow! The new you is awesome. . . . Do you give blow jobs now?"

"About as often as you buy me diamonds and take me on nice vacations."

"Can you at least make sure my dad doesn't do anything he'll regret?"

They peered over their sunglasses to check the status. Blond lady with the shimmery gold caftan, aka Project Facelift, was now occupying the same chair as Stan, laughing at his jokes, which they knew could not possibly be that funny.

"Sorry." Mindy sighed. "This is beyond my scope of expertise."

"Maybe we can find out her cabin number and kill her in her sleep tonight."

"Love it! If we add murder one to our list of problems, we can kiss those monthly mortgage payments good-bye!"

Mindy and Artie were thrilled by how well their kids had gotten along on the cruise and wondered if by some miracle they had reached that enviable stage where they could travel as a family and enjoy the experience, rather than threaten to sell the kids off to the highest bidder. But alas, once they boarded the plane for the trip home, it was as if that magic spell had been broken.

Even before takeoff they were already fighting about whose turn it was to sit by the window and who was the moron/stupid/loser who threw chewed gum in the snack bag. But at least they were getting along better than Stan and Rhoda, who were not speaking at all, forcing the family to be U.N. interpreters. *Anyone on this flight speak bullshit?*

"Tell your father his slippers are in the blue carry-on, not that I give a damn if he's comfortable or not."

"Tell your grandmother if it's not too much trouble, she can lower her goddamn shade."

If only there hadn't been a mix-up at the spa with the time Rhoda was supposed to begin her day of beauty. That left her the hour to kill (almost literally) and a chance to search for Stan, who was by then cavorting with the "bimbo from Boca," a wealthy widow whom they'd met the night before at the Cole Porter Revue.

Rhoda sensed she had eyes for Stan, but never expected to find them sharing a deck chair and a drink. "Imagine my embarrassment. My humiliation. My husband of forty years carrying on with another woman like teenagers in the back of a Buick!" she cried.

Immediately she began dropping hints about which of their marital assets she expected to get in the divorce settlement, yet to the family's surprise, Stan tuned her out. There were no pleas for forgiveness on bended knee, no rushing to buy pearl earrings. In fact, his first reaction was to mention his plans for calling an old army buddy in Lake Worth to see about coming down for a weekend of golf.

"How far is that from Boca?" Artie asked Mindy at thirty thousand feet.

"Half hour tops."

"Great! No wonder I'm having chest pains again."

"Would you stop joking about that? That actually happened

in one of my favorite books. Remember *Claire Voyant*? This old man had a fatal heart attack right on the plane?"

"Really?" Artie sighed. "Were his parents splitting, too?"

Unlike an astronaut returning from a successful mission, Mindy did not have an easy reentry. Everywhere she looked around the house, there were piles of clothes and shoes that she hadn't had time to pick up before they left, prompting her to ask (bellow), did anyone other than her know how to bend at the waist?

Didn't think so! She might as well leave it for later and listen to their messages. Big surprise. Most were from Nadine.

"Was it great?. Did Rhoda behave? Are you dark? I'm so jealous. . . . Call me the second you land. . . ."

Though Mindy was grateful for their years of friendship, she had been happy to have the reprieve from Nadine's incessant chatter through voice mail, instant messages, and text messages. And what could she really say about the cruise? That it was memorable, but for all the wrong reasons? That they came home with more problems than when they left? Unfortunately, if she didn't return Nadine's call, how could she check her e-mail?

Once she signed on, everyone on her buddy list would know that she was back. But good news. According to Nadine's away message, she and Peter were out for the evening, which meant that Mindy could use the Internet in peace. Only to log on and find a snippy e-mail from Beth in Aruba.

Richard came. We're talking. Do you know a good real estate appraiser? Oh and thanks to my car accident my face is a mess and I can't sit in the sun. Best vacation ever. NOT!!!!

An appraiser? Were they planning to refinance or put the house on the market? Did that mean they were already think-ing divorce? Shouldn't they subject themselves to a torturous round of marriage counseling first? And, oh God. What if her in-laws planned this fast a split, too? Would it mean they'd sell the house in Great Neck and Mindy would get stuck having to make Passover every year? Out of necessity she'd agreed to make it this year because they were redoing their kitchen floors, but if this was a permanent change, she'd cry, because it was such a time-consuming, expensive holiday to host. And God forbid Dana would ever offer, not that the family had any interest in a hormone-free, macrobiotic Seder that compared the Jews' exodus from Egypt with rising sea levels due to greenhouse gas emissions.

They had only been home twenty-four hours when Mindy recounted all the things she'd lost on board the cruise. Her room key, her cruise card (twice), her sense of humor, and, by day six, her mind. What she did not lose was weight.

If only bathroom scales were programmed to forgive and forget the mounds of food and desserts consumed, or that ships from sovereign nations automatically disregarded the overindulging, releasing the extra cargo to the wind before disembarkment.

She tried to remember which of the thousands of calories she'd digested had been worth this guilt-ridden moment when she not only had to face the startling, near-pregnancy weight, but the painful discovery that even her fat jeans were snug.

"How bad is it?" Artie asked, though he dared not peek at the scale.

"Awful . . . Even my watch is tight. What about you?"

"Not terrible. A few pounds . . . I'll do extra time on the treadmill this week."

"I hate men. I diet for a month and lose thirty days. You spend an extra ten minutes working out and the scale moves. But face it. We're both too fat. By next Halloween we can go as Shrek and Fiona."

"I know. I just can't fight that battle on top of all the others right now."

"Fine, but let's at least agree to lay off the Chinese and Italian for a while."

"Why? What did they ever do to us?"

"You know what I'm saying."

"Okay, okay. But Aaron's whole world is about to unravel. How could we send him home on an empty stomach? Did you see how much he finally ate? I just wished I could have gone back with him."

"You'll go out to visit as soon as you can."

"I should have gone with him now. I'm his dad."

"There was no way you could have. Besides, Wayne will be there for him."

"I know. I'm just nervous about him going back to the house for the first time and then finding out about his girlfriend. He's going to need a mature, stable adult to guide him."

"Do we know any?" Mindy sighed. Nothing hurt Artie worse than thinking he might be letting one of his kids down. "How about being grateful that God made sure he was with family when he found out his mom died? Plus, now he knows how much we all care about him."

"That doesn't mean he won't go crazy and do something stupid."

"Artie, give him time to deal. He's very together for someone who's been through so much. I think he'll be okay."

"I hope you're right. It's just . . . I already miss him."

"Me, too. And I loved how he looked out for the kids right away like a real big brother."

"It was great . . . and did you know Jamie lent him her iPod for the flight home?"

"Sweet! I just hope he's a fan of Hilary Duff and *High School Musical*."

Artie laughed. These were the times he felt like Tevye the milkman on a bittersweet journey. First came the joy of getting to know his son, then the sorrow of having to see him go too soon. And was it necessary for God to make his financial burdens so heavy? If only he could have said, screw work. I'm going with my son.

"Mom!" Stacie yelled. "Jamie took my retainer and said it's hers, but I think she left hers on the cruise."

"Oh my God. Are you serious? I can't take this anymore."

"And the bee-ach just called. She's coming over."

Beth was coming over now? But it was so late.

"I left something here last week." Beth marched in without waiting for an invitation.

"Okay." Mindy followed her into the den, sorry she was wearing baggy sweats. Then again, Beth thought she was a sight for sore eyes no matter what she wore. "How did the vacation work out?" It felt strange trying to make chitchat.

"We got through it." She looked under the couch. "Did you guys have fun?"

"It was great, yeah. Really memorable. . . . What did you lose?"

"Nothing. Never mind. I must have misplaced it somewhere else. Oh, screw it! The truth is," she hesitated, "I didn't lose anything. I came over to talk to you. I was afraid to call from the house because my girls might hear, and I sure as hell am never e-mailing you again. I needed to let you know I can't drive this week."

"Excuse me?"

"I know what you're thinking, but just remember how many times I helped you out."

"I have no problem helping you; it's just that I'm working three days this week."

"What about Nadine or your mom?"

"Nadine's son has his big music audition at Indiana and they're flying out tomorrow, and my mom is still in Florida."

"Artie?"

"It's going to be so crazy at the store . . . where are you going anyway?"

"I'm taking a leave of absence."

"Isn't that for teachers who go out on maternity?"

"Look. You obviously know things are not great at my house. I just need time to think. Did you gain more weight on your trip?"

"Wow. You never give up. Yes, but I'll spin the wheel and pick a diet. I can lose it the Mediterranean way, the French-don't-get-fat way, the Jenny way . . ."

"What about just eating sensibly and taking a brisk walk every day . . . and take your girls with you."

"Beth, oh my God. You are so mean."

"No, I'm honest . . . and believe me, I know how they'll suffer if they have to spend their teen years hiding under baggy clothes. The world is a cruel place."

"It's a cruel place because people like you think they have the right to judge."

"I don't judge. I sympathize. I was fat all through high school. Bubba Beth they called me." She blew out her cheeks.

"No way."

"If I hadn't burned the pictures, I could have proved it to you."

"Well you'd never know it."

"Because I work at it constantly . . . and trust me, I could out eat even you. So before you go pay good money to one of those diet places, at least try my way."

"Your way. The Beth diet."

"Yes. Couldn't be more simple. Don't confuse a fork with a shovel, eat real food not chemistry experiments from a box, drink a gallon of water every day, eat only things you enjoy but in small portions, eat every meal on a salad plate, don't ever eat while walking, driving, or standing over a sink, and get out there and walk every single day. I promise you'll never be fat again."

"You make it sound so easy."

"It is. It's the rest of life that's a bitch!"

Mindy hesitated. This was the most personal they'd ever been. "What are you and Richard going to do now?"

"Not sure . . . I'm on my way to a friend's house in the Hamptons to think things out."

"With that man in the Mercedes?" she guessed.

Beth looked away, red as the peppers on her list of approved foods.

Ten

Taking the kids to see the Ringling Brothers Circus was a cherished family tradition, and though every year there was great anticipation to see the latest death-defying stunts, Mindy still thought the best act was watching the plate spinners jump from pole to pole. How carefully they choreographed their steps, knowing one slight miscalculation would cause the delicate balancing act to reel out of control. Just like life. One ill-timed move could bury you under the rubble of broken hearts. Oh, how she related!

She felt so bad for Artie, who returned to work determined to get a handle on his business problems, only to be met by a pile of bills, an angry customer who wasn't fitted properly, and two police detectives investigating his manager who had been arrested.

She felt awful for Aaron, who was at the threshold of a new chapter in his life, one fraught with adult problems, but without benefit of a sober adult to guide him. When Artie had called to make sure he'd arrived safely at Wayne's, Aaron told him that no, Artie couldn't speak to his uncle because he'd apparently been on a bender and was passed out on the kitchen floor, but could he borrow one hundred and forty-three dollars to pay the electric bill so that he could have the lights turned back on?

She felt pity for Beth's children, who had been left in the precarious position of having to defend their mother's good name without any understanding of what she was doing, or with whom.

Richard, too, had her sympathy. He had run over early this morning with heartfelt apologies for having gotten them sucked into this craziness, but if they could help him out with the car pool that would be awesome because his ad agency had been pitching a piece of Nike business, and the presentation was this week, and if they could also give him a hand with getting the girls to their after-school activities, dinner was on him.

Mindy felt bad for Stacie, who'd found out that her best friend, Danielle, had been invited to three more bar and bat mitzvahs, making her total twenty to Stacie's eight. So like any mother who felt her child's pain, Mindy promised to text Stacie if any invitations had come for her while they were away, but there were none. Correction. There was one, in a big blue box, but it was for Jessica and put in their mail by mistake.

Mindy even felt bad for Rhoda, who was bewildered by her husband's crazy antics. And though she had threatened to throw the bum out, all she really wanted was for this tail wind to blow over so they could return to the days when she was boss and Stan agreed.

Mostly Mindy felt sorry for herself. She had so wanted to participate in the Downtown Greetings' contest, but with their lives under siege, and their checkbook in need of a winning lottery ticket, how could she justify spending money on airfare and hotel when they were already swimming in debt and still owed money toward the kids' camps?

Time to resort to her trusty allies, Chips Ahoy and the deep, meditative state where she would visualize being at a secluded spot by the ocean, smelling the salt air, feeling the cool breeze, listening to the soothing waves, and holding Mr. Waspy's head underwater.

Too bad she didn't have the survival instincts of Bill Clinton, a man who could decompartmentalize his worries like dividers in a sock drawer. She, unfortunately, was more the Monica type, imbibing in food, drink, and folly to put herself out of her misery. But before she could raid the pantry, she got a text message from Nadine.

so mad gonna be away 4 ur pb party . . . wanted new coach bag w/ scarf . . . look 4 me

And there it was. The first plate to crash. This wasn't just a text message. It was a reminder that weeks ago Mindy had agreed to host a pocketbook party for her neighbor Karen, and it was scheduled for tomorrow evening.

Yes she would get to pick out a free bag in exchange for her hospitality, but it would only be a fake, and was she that anxious to carry a look-alike designer pocketbook that she was willing to turn over her den to twenty cake-eating neighbors on a school night?

Not to mention, Stacie had warned her mom not to try passing off the free bag to her as compensation for babysitting Jamie and Ricky, as the bitchy girls at school could spot a knock-off from down the hall and wouldn't hesitate to inspect it for authenticity. "*Ew.* The stitching is crooked, and duh, everyone knows Chanel only has one *n*."

Mindy didn't have the patience to chat by text and called Nadine back. Maybe she would have some advice on how to get out of this party obligation.

"What should I do?" Mindy asked. "Karen will kill me if I

back out last minute, especially since David keeps telling her she's a terrible businessperson, but we just got home, and I have so much to do and I hate Karen's friends. They all think they're such hot shit because they drive around in little sports cars and have husbands who are afraid of them."

"I don't get why can't she do this at her house? It's huge."

"That's the problem. Every time people see how big it is, they don't end up buying very much because they're sitting there wondering what the hell she's doing selling pocketbooks."

"Yeah. What the hell is she doing selling pocketbooks? She doesn't need the money."

"That's what I thought, but she told me that David keeps her on a very tight budget and she was just tired of having to answer to him every time she went shopping."

"They're on a tight budget? What does that mean exactly? That they put in regular gas when they fill up their BMWs and the boat?"

"I don't know . . . not my problem. But what do you think I should do?"

"Maybe tell her that Ricky got lice on the cruise. She'll cancel in a heartbeat. But forget about that. Fill me in. What's the story with Beth? I heard she hooked up with some rich plastic surgeon. Did she really leave Richard?"

For as many years as she and Nadine had gossiped about her annoying next-door neighbor, now that Mindy had been brought into her confidence, it felt wrong to betray her. Not that Beth didn't deserve the slap in the face after years of being a neighbor abuser.

But no time for chitchat as a second plate was crashing. Stacie was sending her a message from school, in spite of the rule banning cell phones. Didn't matter. She, like every other kid, thought nothing of text messaging all day long to complain about unfair teachers and which kids were being mean.

MOM y didnt u text me! I need 2 no if IM invited 2 Justin Weinbergs
... Danielle thought I was but then Tracy sed her mom sed that Justins
mom had 2 cut the list so shes not sure

Mindy didn't dare tell Stacie that no invitations had come in the mail. Not only would this break her daughter's heart, she'd probably go and bomb her math test next period, and if she didn't keep up her A average, Mr. Beller might not recommend her for the honors class next year, and then she'd cry that all her friends would think she was an idiot.

Mindy decided to lie and say she hadn't gotten to the post office yet and not everyone received things on the same day. Maybe it would be in tomorrow's mail. At least this would keep the plate spinning a little while longer. But wait. Was that the sound of another one falling?

"Oh, thank God you're home." Artie called from the store. "You are not going to believe the call I just got."

"Any chance it was Publishers Clearinghouse?"

"I need you to get me on a flight to Portland either tonight or first thing tomorrow. Aaron just called. Turns out Wayne wasn't drunk when he got home. He was dead!"

"Oh my God! He was dead? What does that mean?"

"What do you mean what does that mean?" Artie screamed. "Why do you have such a hard time with this concept? His mother's gone, Walter's gone, and now Wayne. He has no one left in the whole friggin' state of Oregon to care for him other than some pregnant chick who may expect him to drop out of school so he can support them. That's what it means!"

"Okay, okay. I'm sorry. I'm in shock, too. Start over. Tell me what happened."

"I don't have time. It's crazy here. Some lady from the child welfare agency took Aaron back to her office and is waiting for me to get back to her with my flight information."

"Does she know about the baby?"

"Mindy, I don't even know if *he* knows about the baby."

"Okay, but how is he? Was he singing?"

"I don't know. I only spoke to him for a minute before he handed the phone to the lady. . . . God, this is such a nightmare. Everyone who raised him is dead from an overdose. . . ."

"I know this might sound crazy, but maybe I should go instead of you. Who's going to manage the store if you're gone?"

"James."

"You didn't fire him? He was arrested and he stole a store deposit."

"He's getting me the money back. Just get me a flight."

"Artie . . . wait. Hear me out. You're not good with this stuff. You get so emotional."

"Would you stop? He's my responsibility. I'll be fine. Maybe call your mom to see when she's getting back from Florida. If she can watch the kids, you can at least open and close the store, make the deposits . . ."

" . . . do the laundry, the food shopping, all the car pooling, work at your dad's office, have a pocketbook party . . ."

"What pocketbook party?"

"Never mind. You just gave me the perfect out. . . . Rest in peace, Wayne."

Mindy wanted to call Beth but was hesitant, just as she was when she had to call the pediatrician in the middle of the night. She never wanted to be thought of as one of those panicky mothers who didn't know the difference between a routine question and a serious medical emergency. But then she thought screw it. Her crisis trumped Beth's hands down.

"I was actually going to call you," Beth said.

"You were?"

"Yeah. Did you get that e-mail from Downtown Greetings?"

"I have no idea. I haven't had two seconds to pee let alone check my mail. It's been such a wild morning. Do you mind my asking where you are?"

"I told you. In the Hamptons . . . at a friend's house. That's all I'm going to say!"

"Look, I'm not trying to be nosy. I'm asking because I have some really crazy stuff going on here and I can't do all the driving myself. I need your help."

"Oh, please! I can see right through your little ruse. Richard put you up to this."

"No he didn't. This has nothing to do with him. Artie has a six a.m. flight tomorrow to Portland because when Aaron got back he found out his uncle died, and that was after finding out a few days before that his mother died, and we don't think he knows that he may have gotten this girl pregnant, and then our store manager was arrested over the weekend for—"

"You're babbling, Mindy, and I have no idea what any of it has to do with me, but I am not coming back yet."

"But you don't understand. I can't handle your problems and my problems and—"

"Well, I'm sorry. Richard needs to get it through his thick skull that he can't keep blaming me for every goddamn thing that goes wrong. It's not my fault that he was passed over for a promotion. Maybe if he was spending less time drinking and more time focusing on his clients, he'd be getting bigger bonuses and could stop hocking me about going back to a job I'm no longer qualified for, or young enough for, or whatever the hell that asshole headhunter said that was so totally lame."

"*Um*, okay. That was a lot of information."

"Whatever," Beth puffed. "Now you know why I'm doing this."

"Are you smoking?"

"Yes."

"Oh. I never saw you with a cigarette before."

"Well don't get all preachy. I'm not a chain-smoker. It's just when I'm stressed."

"Whatever . . . Look, I'm really sorry you guys are having a hard time, but do you think maybe you could run away a different week? My mom is still in Florida and with Artie leaving tomorrow, how am I going to get everyone to school, then open the store, get to work, be back in time for the afternoon run, get everyone to—"

"Just tell Richard he's going to have to help out."

"But he's your husband!"

"Exactly, and I'm sick of him always leaving everything in my lap. Now the car pool is HIS problem."

"Okay, but they're *your* kids! Can't you ask Jill or some other friends to help out?"

"How many times do I have to explain this? It's bad enough that *you* know what's going on, I don't need the whole neighborhood discussing my business. I'm sure you'll figure something out. You're good like that. Shit, he's back and he told me not to smoke in here. I have to go."

Mindy was stunned. It was big news to discover that the Perfect Diamonds had marriage and money troubles, and that Artie was right, there was no such thing as an E-ZPass for life, eventually everyone had to pay the toll. And then for Beth to suddenly dump all those problems on Mindy was even stranger. Only a few days earlier she'd accused Mindy of maiming her children. Now she was leaving them in her care?

An hour later, she was still so riled, she had vacuumed the entire house, cleaned all the bathrooms, and did three loads of laundry. She just wished there was someone with whom she could vent. She couldn't burden Artie. He was frantically trying to pack last week's work and now this week's work into what would be his only day in the store.

Nadine, of course, would gladly listen, but she'd promise not to breathe a word, then spread the gossip fast as a blogger. And forget Karen. She hated Beth and didn't give a damn about her problems. Her only concern was that Mindy was trying to back out of her party commitment, and that was impossible. She had no way of telling people that it was off.

"I sent out like a hundred e-mails and who knows how many people forwarded it?"

"A hundred e-mails? I don't have room for that many people. You said it would be maybe twenty, twenty-five at most."

"Well maybe it will be. I never know who's going to show. They just come."

"Okay, but what if Ricky has lice?"

"Mindy, I don't care if he has all ten plagues! Just tell him to stay upstairs. I spent two days on a buying trip for this party and I got such cute stuff for summer, but I'm already out the money so you have to do this because David will kill me if I don't make it back, and I also don't want to start breaking out in hives, which is what happens when I get very tense. Remember last summer? I overdosed on Benadryl and almost had to go to the hospital? You have to do this for me! It's life and death."

"No, of course. Life and death. Can't wait . . . Who doesn't like a new pocketbook?"

Eleven

If deleting spam was an Olympic event, Mindy would be a gold medalist for speed. She was not interested in Hoodia at wholesale or hey dude, getting hard in ten minutes and satisfying her girlfriend, she just wanted to read the messages that came from people she knew. But in her haste to get rid of the waste, an e-mail from Downtown Greetings nearly got cut.

This must have been the one Beth asked her about, and good thing she read it, for she learned that for some odd reason, she'd been awarded a scholarship that covered her travel expenses. All she had to do was download the agreement form and return it signed within five days. Wait. What? She'd won something?

Incredible. Perchance a turning point? Then Dubious and his cousin Doubtful dropped by. At Artie's request, she had tried distancing herself from them, but they kept hanging around, like party guests who wouldn't leave.

Yet as much as Mindy wanted to believe the scholarship offer was valid, she didn't want to be naive. What if it was a come-on like those too-good-to-be-true credit card offers that helped consolidate your debts, only to discover you had just agreed to pay stiff penalties for late payments?

It reminded her of the time Nadine's son, Jonathan, got approached at the mall by a woman asking if he'd ever considered a career in modeling. He went home so excited that he could earn enough money to pay for college because he had "the look." All his parents had to do was sign a contract with the modeling agency, and fork over fifteen hundred bucks for a photo shoot that would guarantee he'd be assigned the most lucrative jobs.

Now Mindy was pissed. Being scammed was even worse than being spammed. And her anger coupled with stress, on top of eating anything that said chocolate is thy name, meant one thing. It was a PMS day. And the only good that could come from this confluence of hormones and hunger was channeling that energy into writing a nasty response to the company, accusing them of snaring innocent writers into their cruel hoax. She'd show them how crafty she was with words!

"Oh thank God you're home."

Not again! But it wasn't her husband hitting the replay button. It was Beth's.

"Richard?"

"Mindy, I am so sorry to do this to you, but I need your help. If she leaves now I'll go crazy. You have to stop her."

"Me stop her? But she already left."

"Are you sure? Damn her! After all these years!"

"Wait. You didn't know she left last night?"

"What are you talking about?" Richard smacked his desk. "I just spoke to her and she was at the house. She promised to wait till I got home tonight to talk."

"Really? I spoke to Beth this morning and she was . . . not there."

"Not Beth! Marina! Marina is the one I need you to stop from leaving."

"Marina?"

"Yeah. What a time for her to bail!"

"Because of Beth leaving?"

"Because I have to go out of town tomorrow."

"I'm so confused. When did she quit?"

"Just now. She called and said she'd been interviewing with other families, and one made her an offer this morning for a lot more money and today was her last day."

"Oh my God. That's awful." *Seriously? You're surprised?*

"Tell me about it. . . . I guess when she showed up this morning and found out that Beth left, she figured it was now or never. I mean she'd been asking for a raise, but I kept telling Beth we didn't need a live-in anymore. She's not working, the girls aren't babies. Plus, it's been so crazy with Beth and Marina constantly scream-ing at each other. Anyway, I couldn't tell if she was bullshitting or not, but if she really left, I am so screwed. That's why I thought if you talked to her, she'd listen. She always liked you."

"Okay, but to be honest, I know she's been thinking about doing this for a while."

"Damn! Then what the hell am I supposed to do now? Beth's car is done and I have to return the rental, not that I even know where it is because she took it, and remember when I said this morning that I had this major presentation for Nike this week?"

"Sort of."

"Well, seems there was some kind of screwup and Nike was expecting us to come to them, so now I've got to rush my kish-kes out first thing tomorrow. I'm getting too old for this Mindy. The ad game sucks. Anyway, how can I leave town if Marina's gone?"

"Well have you spoken to Beth?"

"I left three messages but she's not picking up. I don't know what the hell is wrong with her. Nothing I do is right, she's always mad at someone. My mom was saying it's probably a change of life thing. She went crazy, too, not that she ever left her family to go hide at the house of some guy she met at a bar."

"Wait. You know?"

"Of course! She had to throw it in my face that this rich surgeon thought she was amazing and was going to let her use his place out in East Hampton so she could think . . . the only reason I haven't gone out there to kill her is that he's out of town."

And the check is in the mail. "Can maybe your parents help out?"

"No, they're in Florida and my dad is still going through radiation. My mom won't leave him."

"Oh, right. Right. Of course. So like where do you have to go tomorrow?"

"Portland, Oregon. That's where Nike is based."

"Richard, no way! Artie is leaving for Portland in the morning, too. He has to go rescue Aaron. Are you on United's six a.m.?"

"No, American, but it leaves around the same time. Wow, that is crazy! Well, if he wants, he can share the limo with me. Agency's paying. No big deal."

"Actually, that would be great because otherwise I'd have to drive him."

"Good, good. At least now I can return the favor since I'm leaning on you like this."

"What do you want me to do exactly?"

"I guess try to talk Marina into staying for the week, 'cause if she won't, you'll have to take my kids until I can get back. God, I hate her."

"Who, Marina?"

"No. Beth!"

* * *

Forget plates crashing. This was Survivor, the home edition, only Mindy had no idea if she would get a commercial break. But no need to panic. She would call the people in her life and press one for immediate assistance. Or not.

Beth would not pick up her cell as she was too busy doing God only knows what with Mercedes Man.

Marina was sorry that Richard was in a bind, but after seven years of putting up with their nonsense, she had made up her mind to leave, especially now that this new family was paying her a hundred more a week, they just redid the maid's room, and there wasn't anyone in the family named Beth.

Mindy's mom was also very sorry, but now that she'd finally retired, wasn't she entitled to have some fun? Turns out that those nice fellows on the cruise, Max and Mort, were true to their word and hooked up Helene and Toby with their rich widower cousins, and the four of them were having a grand old time. "And they treat for everything. Won't even let us leave the tip!"

Rhoda, never one to lift a finger when you could pay someone else to do it, would not even hear of taking Mindy's place in the office for a few days, as she had barricaded herself in the house, unable to face their friends, let alone her husband's employees, after his childish behavior had sent her into a deep, he-doesn't-stand-a-chance depression.

Stan, meanwhile, wasn't buying any of his wife's high drama and told Artie it was about time she got a wake-up call, and that he was running back down to Florida for a few days of golf and that he expected Mindy to hold the fort down because if he left the other girls in charge, they'd put him out of business by the time he got back.

And Nadine, always good in a pinch, was in a pinch herself. She and Peter were en route to IU for Jonathan's music audition, and though their daughter, Rebecca, was being watched by Nadine's mom, she no longer owned a car and was afraid to drive one of those "monster truck" SUVs. Nadine needed Mindy to get Rebecca to and from the high school.

No big deal, Mindy thought. She'd feed and care for her children and Beth's children and get them to and from school and their activities, schlep Rebecca and her huge marching tuba, put in three days at the office, and then tomorrow night host a lovely party for Karen's customers, who really just wanted a night out and would schmooze for hours over cake and coffee while examining the pocketbooks, whispering that the copies weren't as good as they used to be and that Apryl Wynter was selling the same bags for so much less.

But really. She was so done with being negative.

Maybe if she called Artie at the store, he would say something inspiring. Wasn't that how it worked in the world of greeting cards? The right words could fix everything? Unfortunately, this was real life, and the only thing Artie said after only half listening to her was that he hoped she understood, but he wasn't coming home without Aaron.

"Can't leave him there. He's got no adult supervision, no support, and I don't care if he gives me a hard time."

"That's right. You say in your best Darth Vader voice, Luke, I am your father, and you have to do what I tell you."

"Exactly. He has to accept the facts. His new home is Long Island."

"Right. No, of course. He has to move in with us . . . maybe the girl and the baby, too."

She hung up and went online. Time to read all that spam and find out how much it cost to buy mega doses of Zoloft. Only to discover that Downtown Greetings had already sent her a reply asking her to call immediately because they had an important matter to discuss.

What to do now? Send a second e-mail apologizing for being a tad hasty? Explain that she had terrible PMS, and to please disregard everything she'd said because of course she would love to receive the scholarship? Better to call and plead ignorance . . . or maybe take a page from Stacie's playbook.

"Anna Jane Crandall's office," a young woman answered. "This is Olivia."

"Hi, Olivia . . . great name . . . loved you in *Grease.*" *Um,* this is one of the contest people? You sent me an e-mail this morning about your incredible scholarship opportunity. I was like wondering if you saw my reply?"

"Well I don't know yet. Who is this?"

"Oh. Right. Yeah. I'd tell you, but I'm afraid to on account of the fact that I just found out my kids did this really awful thing . . . they were on my computer reading my e-mails and then wrote back pretending to be me . . . And now I see the one they sent to you was so mean . . . I swear, they are grounded for life."

"Mindy, right? From Long Island."

Shit! "Yes . . . and look, I am so sorry because, oh my god, this is an incredible opportunity. I practically died when I read what they wrote."

"You have some crazy kids, that's for sure, but I know how they are with their computers. I have a bunch of nieces and nephews. This one time my nephew Anthony took his dad's credit card from his wallet, went online, and bought a monkey. A real live monkey, from like South America, or maybe it was South Africa . . . somewhere south."

"Are you serious?"

"Yeah. So then my brother-in-law gets this e-mail that the monkey is coming in to O'Hare on such and such a day and he'd better be there on time because otherwise there's this big penalty for cruelty to animals or something."

"That is hilarious!" Mindy was relieved to be talking to such a nice person.

"Yeah. Kids can do wild stuff," Olivia chucked. "So yours are off today?"

"No, they're at school."

"Oh. Then how did they read your e-mail? I just sent it a little while ago."

"Um . . ."

"And they must be geniuses because . . . wait . . . I have a copy right here. . . . I had to look up the word *egregious*. It's been a long time since the SATs."

"Okay." Mindy sighed. "I surrender. I wrote the e-mail. . . . I am so sorry."

"Thought so!"

"I am so bad at lying. That's why people love playing poker with me. But can I ask you something? If you knew I was making up a story, why didn't you stop me?"

"'Cause I understand why you wrote it . . . hold on, Anna Jane's on the other line."

When she returned, she said, "Mother of God, she's tough. 'Do this. Do that. Now, Olivia, now!' She is one loco lady."

"Hey, I hear ya. I work for my father-in-law at his medical office, and if it was legal, he'd beat me with a stick and tell me I had two bathroom breaks a day, use them wisely."

"You are funny," Olivia laughed. "That's why I picked you."

"*You* picked me?"

"Sure did. I picked all the scholarship winners. Matter of fact, the whole thing was my idea! But now Anna Jane is going around telling everyone she thought of it."

"That's so mean. By any chance do you know if she read my e-mail?"

"Lord, no! I deleted it. Otherwise you would have gotten one back that would have made yours look like a nursery rhyme."

"Oh, thank God . . . wow! You are a real lifesaver. Why are you being so nice?"

"Oh, girlfriend, I knew why you sent it as soon as I read it. It's PMS, right?"

"Yes! Exactly! Oh my God. I am going crazy today," Mindy laughed.

"Been there! I have the worst time—the bloating, the cravings . . ."

" . . . the mood swings!" Mindy chimed in. "Last Halloween my husband bought me a broom and said don't bother putting it away. You can use it all year."

"That's a good one!" Olivia laughed. "My fiancé tells everyone he marks my bad days of the month in big red circles so he knows when it's safe to talk to me."

"Hey, if my husband did that, every day would be circled in red. Don't bother her, feed her chocolate, carry a concealed weapon . . ."

Olivia laughed. "Mindy, I can't wait to meet you. And I sure hope you're on board now, 'cause your greeting cards would be a stitch!"

"Yes, definitely. And thank you for being so understanding. I owe you one . . . but um, could I ask you a question while we're on the subject?"

"Sure."

"Did you also pick Beth Diamond for a scholarship? We're next-door neighbors."

"Ohhh. Isn't that cute! Like Lucy and Ethel."

"Actually, more like Lucy and Evita. She thinks everyone should kiss her feet."

"Oh, I know someone just like her. My mom's next-door neighbor is a piece of work, too. Listen to this. The day my parents moved in, this lady comes over and doesn't even say hello, how are you, welcome to the block, here's some pie. She's screaming that their trees are hanging on her property and the fence needs to be moved because that's on her property, too, and she's got a tape measure and my mom is like, oh dear Lord, stop the movers!"

"That is crazy!"

"I know, so I get where you're coming from with her, but yeah, Beth got picked too because you should see her sketches. She's real, real talented."

"I know."

"But I can let you in on a little secret," Olivia whispered. "I bet it'll make you feel a whole lot better."

"I'm great with secrets."

"Okay then . . . it looks like I'm going to be one of the judges, on account of the fact that Anna Jane's boss knows I came up with the whole scholarship thing."

"Cool! But why would that make me feel better?"

"Because silly . . . I could make sure you won."

"Oh? Oh . . . Wait. What? That's not exactly kosher."

"Honey, not everyone keeps kosher. And if I work it so that you get the fifty grand for best writer, we could split it . . . It's just like you were sayin' before. You owe me one."

Twelve

When you marry a man with the same first name as your father, people jump to conclusions. They see a relationship rooted in desire to perpetuate a cherished bond, and in Mindy's case, they would be right. Her immediate attraction to Arthur Sherman was as much a tribute to his warmth and charm as to his beloved name. Saying it aloud drew her nearer to the times she felt safe in the arms of a loving man.

Her father was not one of those people who you heard was never sick a day in their life, then mysteriously dropped dead. To the contrary, Arthur Baumann spent years fending off disease like a fearless swordsman challenging each new chap to a duel. Twice he battled colon cancer and then an arthritic condition that would have leveled a less determined being. Yet true to his brave nature, he graciously accepted defeat, writing thank-you notes to his wife and children the day before he died.

Mindy's fondest memories of her dad were the times they spent debating great matters, such as which sports stadium sold the best hot dogs, and which cartoon character most deserved to be called superhero. But what she truly missed, especially during trying times like these, was his willingness to listen.

Though she held the degree in psychology, he was the one wise enough to understand a basic tenet of the human psyche. Someone in the throes of a conflict didn't need counsel as much as an outlet to hear their own voice. He would let Mindy go on and on about this person or that situation, never judging, only adding his classic "oy veys," then asking the quintessential question that would lead her down the right path.

Her greatest regret was that she never got the chance to tell him that he was her favorite superhero, and of course that not a day went by that she didn't think of him or wonder if he was okay. But the more years that passed, the harder it was to keep those lines of communication open.

Her old friend, Noah, a psychic medium, felt that her dad was still very much around her, and there were times, such as at Stacie's bat mitzvah, that she had felt his presence. But she also couldn't deny that most days the connection to him felt weak, like a dimmer switch that was gradually being turned down, leaving her to wonder if the idea of a loved one's spirit hovering was simply wishful thinking.

"I need a sign, Daddy," she whispered.

It was 4:30 a.m., and though Artie had told her it was ridiculous for her to get up to say good-bye, she said that since she'd been saved from having to drive him to the airport, the least she could do was be up to make sure he wasn't forgetting his phone or wallet. Good thing! She averted a disaster by thinking to ask if he'd remembered to leave her the store keys, which, of course, he hadn't. "That would have been awful." He kissed her good-bye. "I'll call when I land. Give the kids kisses. Tell them I'm bringing their brother home. . . . I hope."

Struggling to fall back asleep, especially since a restless

Ricky had already taken Artie's spot, she tried reaching out to her dad by closing her eyes and focusing on a picture she loved that was taken on that bright, promising January morning Stacie was born.

There was his moonbeam smile and laughing eyes as he held his first grandchild, his joy so palpable it leaped off the photo. Strangely, he was like this on most days, no matter the ills that befell him. She could walk into a hospital room where he would be barely visible behind the machinery and toylike tubes, and he'd wave and smile, as if they'd met at a diner and were about to dig into their favorite three-egg-and-pancake breakfast. If only she could see his smile again and hear his assurances that her future wasn't as bleak as it seemed.

If only he could explain a universe in which beat-the-system schemers like Olivia thought nothing of snaring honest people into a sting operation that betrayed fellow contestants. Or why so many married people like Stan and Beth seemed to be changing partners round and round, dancing right over their innocent families. What about the perilous addictions that ended young, hearty lives too soon, like those of Davida's and Wayne's? Was it all random or something more orderly and preordained, like a teacher's lesson plan?

"I need a sign, Daddy," she repeated. But none appeared.

By now she was so alert, all she could think about was the mommy minefield ahead.

Jamie had gym today, so she couldn't forget to stick clean sweats in her backpack. She still needed to help Ricky find his library books, and Stacie her brand-new tennis racquet. And what were the odds Richard remembered to leave lunch money for the girls? Not good, which meant that she would have to lay it out for them and wait to get paid back. Of course she could always make them lunch, but what was it that Emma was allergic to again?

And had she remembered to buy fresh bread after Ricky decided the birds in the backyard would enjoy challah and butter?

Only because she was overdue for a miracle did she end up getting her kids, and Beth's kids, and Nadine's daughter, Rebecca, and her sixteen-pound tuba, to school safely and on time, leaving her an hour before she had to open the store. Maybe the day wouldn't turn out so bad after all.

Then the phone rang.

"Can you pick me up?" A girl was sobbing.

Crap! She had just dropped everyone off at school.

"Rebecca?" Mindy asked. "What's wrong?"

"It's Beth," she choked. "I'm in trouble. You have to help me."

Beth? But with all the street noise behind her, Mindy could barely make out what she was saying. "Where are you?" she shouted.

"At a payphone at a goddamn train station. I don't know where the hell my car is, my cell died. You have to pick me up."

"Pick you up where? I have to go open the store because remember I told you our manager got arrested? And then I have to get to work and—"

"You don't understand. . . . I have no one else to call. I can't reach Richard, Marina's not picking up, I don't have any money on me, the ATM here is broken, the station is totally deserted, and I'm freezing!"

"Oh my God! Which station?"

"Babylon."

"Babylon? I have no idea where that is. What are you doing there?"

"This is where the asshole dropped me off, okay? He said it was where we left my car, but I've looked everywhere and it's not here and it was so late and I was drunk and he's not picking up his cell and I'm almost out of quarters and if you don't help me, it's going to be on your conscience when they find my body in a Dumpster and—"

"Okay. Calm down. Breathe." For a minute she forgot she wasn't talking to Stacie.

"I can't calm down. I'm in the middle of a disaster, okay. I'm begging you. Please come get me. I don't know what else to do."

"You can't call Jill?"

"I fucking hate Jill! If it wasn't for her and her stupid friends, I wouldn't be in this mess!"

Mindy was shocked. Her kids played the blame game all the time, but Beth was a grown-up. And how could she just drop everything? James, the store manager, had a court date this morning, so he couldn't open up, Stan would kill her if she was late. . . .

"Are you there?" Beth was shouting. "Why aren't you answering me?"

"I'm sorry! I don't know what to do. Stan will get crazy if I'm late and—"

"He's your freakin' father-in-law! Tell him you had an emergency and you'll explain later. Are you not getting that this really is an emergency?"

"You don't know my father-in-law. Okay, give me a second to think. Maybe I could go open the store first and then ask Christine to cover me at the office, and then since you'd be home, you could do the afternoon car pool—"

"Yes, yes, anything," she sobbed. "Just come. Please. Just come . . . and bring a jacket. I'm so cold."

Mindy couldn't fold a map let alone read one, her ancient minivan barely had a compass let alone a nice navigation lady who told you which way to turn, and she didn't have time to make a Google map. The only way to locate Beth's position was to rely on her trusty sense of direction, and gas stations every few miles.

She would not be like Moses, who got lost in the desert for forty years because he refused to ask directions.

At least as she sped down the zigzagging Southern State Parkway, one thing made her laugh. Only a few hours earlier she'd asked her dad for a sign, and now she was getting them every half mile. Bethpage State Park. Route 110 in Huntington. Wellwood Avenue.

Real funny, Dad, she thought as she grabbed donut chunks from the box on the passenger seat. And then it hit her that maybe this little rendezvous wasn't a mistake after all. Hadn't he always told her that getting lost was good for the soul? Yes! He liked to say that it could be good to get completely *farblunget* once in a while because it forced you down roads you would never otherwise have traveled, often discovering a much better route for your journey.

Now she got it! He hadn't been referring to driving; he had been talking about life. Being lost or unsure instilled fear, and fear was the conduit for change. The impetus for finding the better path. Without it, nobody would ever learn a damn thing.

That simple lesson brought Mindy to tears, making it difficult to make out the road signs. And yet she knew in her heart that she'd found the only one that mattered. The one that proved that her father was still very much with her, still guiding and directing her, especially when lost.

"Thank you Daddy." She blew a kiss to the heavens.

Mindy drove into the main entrance of the Babylon train station and, from a distance, spotted a haggard woman shivering on a bench beneath the train trestle. No way could that be her intimidating my-shit-doesn't-stink neighbor. But as she edged closer and saw the bare skin, matted hair, and large sunglasses, there was no mistake. Homeless people did not carry Louis Vuitton luggage.

It was like watching a 20-20 segment about a former rich person who was now living on the streets, knowing that millions of viewers were saying, there but for the grace of God go I.

Just before pulling up, Mindy remembered she'd wanted to toss the trash left in the car so she didn't have to watch Beth wipe crumbs off the seat and remove the soft drink cups as if they were viral science experiments. Not that a married woman who'd been dumped at a train station by her psycho lover should be in a position to judge.

When she finally approached, a stoic Beth grabbed her pocketbook and overnight bag, got in the car, put on Mindy's North Face jacket, turned on the heated seat, and buckled her seat belt.

"About time." She blew into a tissue.

Yep. It was Beth.

"Sorry. I had to stop at the store first and wait for one of the employees to show up, and then traffic on the Southern State was backed up and I wasn't really sure how to get here."

Beth finally muttered her thanks, but her voice was so low, only a dog could hear.

"Are you hungry?" Mindy asked. "Do you have to pee?"

She nodded yes, still shivering.

Mindy was in the mood for an Egg McMuffin with bacon, but given the company, she was too embarrassed to mention it. Where did health-conscious people eat anyway?

"How about that diner?" Mindy pointed. "I think we ate there once and it was pretty good."

"We have to find my car."

"Oh, right. Forgot about that. You really don't know where you left it?"

"We dropped it off Sunday night. I had a lot to drink. I thought I'd remember."

"But there's probably ten train stations in this area."

"Believe me, I'd rather be doing something other than schlepping up and down Sunrise Highway looking for a goddamn rental car that isn't even good enough to be stolen."

"Can you remember anything?"

"Yes. I think there was a Starbucks next to a tattoo parlor across the street."

"Well that certainly narrows it down." Mindy looked around.

"I'm sorry, okay? I feel horrible that this whole thing happened, and that you of all people had to be dragged into it."

Me of all people?

"That didn't come out right." Beth's eyes welled. "What I meant was that this situation is horrible enough without having to beg you for help. I know you hate me."

"I don't hate you." Mindy sighed. "I'm just not, you know, crazy about you."

"No, you hate me. A lot of people do. They don't say it to my face, but they do."

"Well, I'm not gonna lie. I do keep my Beth voodoo doll handy because you can be pretty mean . . . especially to my kids."

"That is not true."

"Really? What about that time you made that sleepover party for Jessie at that hotel in the city and didn't invite Stacie?"

"That was years ago. You're still bringing that up?"

"I have never brought that up," Mindy gasped. "I wanted to so many times, but after a while it was like what's the point?"

"Then why bring it up now?"

"Because. I don't know . . . I will never forget that weekend. Stacie cried nonstop. And this might sound dumb to you, but it affected all of us. We were all so depressed."

"Over a child's birthday party? It's not like the girls ever had the same friends."

"Beth, come on. They're in the same grade and they've played together for eight years. She was devastated."

"Well then I'm very sorry. . . . I'm sorry about more than you can imagine."

Mindy blinked. An apology from Beth was a first. She couldn't wait to tell Artie, who was always comparing their relationship to the United States and Cuba, neighboring countries with a history of hostilities.

"No, you know what?" Mindy said. "I'm sorry. You've obviously been through hell, and I'm going on about something that happened a long time ago. Let's just go in, get breakfast, and try to figure out a way to find your car."

"I don't know." Beth checked the vanity mirror. "I look like crap."

"So do I." Mindy grabbed her bag. "But it never stopped me from eating."

"Tempting," she quipped, "but I won't go there . . . and don't you have to get to work?"

"Actually, it turned out this lady Christine was happy to switch with me. She's got kids in college and likes the extra hours."

"And your father-in- law wasn't mad?"

"No, he was, but he's dealing with his own problems right now. He can't spend the whole day thinking about how much I disappoint him anymore."

The visit to the ladies room was a welcome relief. Difference being that when Mindy returned she looked the same as when she went in, unlike Beth who came back looking polished and beautiful, her hair pulled back in a smooth ponytail, light makeup perfectly applied. And, oh yes, there were her signature jewels, glistening like icicles from her neck, wrists, and fingers as if her marriage had actually been an ascent to the throne, her new title, Beth, Queen of Diamonds.

Mindy looked down at her imitation bling watch from the flea market and her modest engagement ring, which she remembered thinking was so spectacular when Artie proposed. Years later he promised her an upgrade, but three kids, a mortgage, several bad business decisions, and the need to pay for camp, braces, and bat mitzvahs later, her original diamond remained fused to her finger, testimony not to her wealth but her rich history with a man who loved her with all his heart.

How little she had in common with Beth, right down to their views on sating physical hunger.

Though Beth was starving, she was hardwired to count calories, ordering egg whites with a side of tomatoes, whereas Mindy couldn't imagine denying herself. Yet if she placed the order for her usual spread, Beth would surely carry on about fat people who made bad choices. Better to choose an egg-white omelet and pretend she was weight conscious, too. And thank God for the donuts she'd tucked away in her car.

"Oh my God, I hate this text messaging." Mindy picked up her cell. "Stacie doesn't leave me alone."

94 on my math test, mr beller loves me . . . justin says he might still invite me to his bar mitz. I HATE my lunch . . . no more gross 2matos . . .

"Does Jess do this to you, too?"

"No."

"Really? She doesn't bug you all day long?"

"She hates me. Why would she?"

"I doubt that." Mindy typed away.

"Doesn't matter." Beth yawned. "I hate text messaging. I hate all electronic gadgets. . . ."

"But I never see you without that BlackBerry thing. Isn't that how you kept up-to-the-minute track of our car pool?" *Oops. Strike that from the record.* "Miss, more coffee, please?"

Beth sipped her tea instead of breaking the cease-fire. "I don't know how I got here."

"I drove."

"I mean how I got to this point in my life."

"I ask myself that every day."

"Nothing makes sense . . . nothing makes me happy . . . everything I do turns out wrong, the people who supposedly love me are too self-absorbed to care what I want. You're probably thinking I deserve it."

"Maybe a little, but to be honest, sometimes I feel the same way. Artie and I are killing ourselves to give our kids this incredible life, but the harder we work, the less we seem to have. "

"At least you have a nice family." Beth fiddled with her fork. "I always see you guys outside doing things together . . . and you're lucky. Artie holds your hand and makes you laugh."

"Okay, never in a million years did I think you'd be jealous of me."

"Go figure." Beth shrugged. "I think when you're miserable, everyone's life looks better."

"I hear ya." Mindy nodded. Maybe they did have some common ground, though it was like finding eggshells in the mixture. Easy to spot, just too slippery to handle.

"I know this is none of my business," Mindy started, "but do you feel like talking about what happened?"

"No."

"Okay."

"Although I suppose that since I dragged you into this, I do owe you an explanation."

"It's fine. It's not like we're friends—"

"The truth is, at this point I don't even know what to tell myself. Warren turned out to be a total psycho. He could have really hurt me. The whole thing was insane."

"Well thank God you're okay. But it's funny. On the way here I was thinking about my dad . . . the things he would say to me when I was confused and angry . . . he was one of those big be-

lievers in everything happening for a reason . . . bad things being
good things in disguise. I bet he would have said that you got this
out of your system and now you and Richard can start over."

"Doubt it. We've been on a downhill slide for a while . . . He
won't even answer my calls."

Mindy looked at her watch. "He should have landed by now.
Maybe you could try again."

"Landed where?"

"Oh my God. That's right," Mindy replied. "You don't know.
He flew to Portland this morning for some big Nike thing. And
then remember I told you that Artie had to go to Portland for
Aaron?"

"Wait. Richard's not at work?"

"No. There was some kind of mix-up and Richard found out
he had to fly there. Anyway, they both got picked up around four
this morning. And strike me dead for repeating this, but he mentioned to Artie that he was going to talk to Nike about taking a
job out there."

"Richard did not say that! He knows I would never leave New
York."

"Well, I'm sure it was just venting."

"And I'm sure there was no mix-up. He just never pays attention to details. God, he's insane. Move to Portland, Oregon? I
dare him to even utter those words to me!"

"*Um*, then I don't suppose you want to hear the rest?"

"There's more? I'm gone for two freakin' days."

"Oh, it's been busy. Marina quit."

"Quit? Are you serious? Why?"

"Come on. You guys were hardly Alice and Mrs. Brady. She
said she found a family who was willing to pay her more; she left
a few hours ago."

"Oh my God," Beth gasped.

"Yeah." Mindy sighed. "And things don't look promising on

the contest front either. You know the scholarship thing? We were both picked, which was very cool, but I spoke to this lady Olivia who is one of the people running it, and it looks like she's on the take."

"I don't understand."

"Me either, but she actually told me she could make me the winner, as long as I split the prize money with her, so obviously the whole thing is a crock."

Just then the waitress brought their order and put Mindy's plate in front of Beth.

"Wait. That's mine," Mindy said as she watched Beth dig in. "Don't you want what you ordered?"

"Hell, no!" Beth inhaled the buttered toast. "Miss, can I have extra hash browns?"

Mindy stared at her. "The chocolate cream pie looked pretty good, too."

"Fine." Beth gobbled up the bacon. "Order it."

"A piece?"

"No. The pie."

Thirteen

If you live long enough, you see everything. So said the late Arthur Baumann. But one thing Mindy never thought she'd live to see was Beth eat anything other than nonfat, lo-carb tree bark. Thus it was quite a show watching her polish off every morsel on her plate, digging in to a chocolate cream pie, then grabbing the complimentary cookies on the way out.

"I remember seeing a Dunkin' Donuts down the block," Mindy teased.

"God no. I think I'm going to puke. I don't know why, but lately I'm so hungry."

"Join the club. New members always welcome."

"How about returning members? I was a blimp in high school. In fact this whole place reminds me of high school. It's like being in the cast of *Grease*. Can we please leave before someone starts teasing my hair?"

For an hour they drove down Sunrise Highway, stopping at stations in Amityville, Copiague, Lindenhurst, and two they couldn't identify. But alas there was no blue rental car. Mindy wondered if maybe the car had been stolen, to which Beth said, "You've obviously never driven it."

They were about to call the rental company to report it missing when Mindy remembered that Christine from her office, was married to an engineer for the Long Island Rail Road. Patrick might know which stations were located opposite a Starbucks.

"All of them," he said. "What else you got?"

Fortunately, he did think to mention that the Babylon stop had several huge lots adjacent to it, and people often forgot where they parked. He also suggested that they check the numbered stalls, as those were the ones designated for nonresidents.

Sure enough, Mindy drove around and there in a back lot in a numbered stall was the car.

"I don't believe it was here all along!" Beth punched the dashboard. "I am so mad!"

"You?" Mindy said. "I had a few other things to do today."

Beth fumbled for her car keys and started to laugh.

"You think this is funny, Miss Diamond?" Mindy used a stern teacher voice. "Do you want to share it with the class?"

"No. Sorry." Beth wiped a tear. "I swear I don't know what's wrong with me. I've just been through something so horrible and degrading and I was scared to death sitting on that bench in Jessica's little jean skirt thinking any minute I was going to be a rape victim and I must have been out of my mind when I packed because I had nothing better to put on. In fact this whole thing is insane: running away from home, ending up in some lunatic's house who weighed himself constantly and gave himself Brazilian waxes in places you don't want to know, then getting left at a train station without money, losing my car, having you show up in that ridiculous-looking sweatshirt—every time you wear it I cringe—"

"Wait, wait, wait." Mindy looked down at a family photo that had been screen printed on a bright pink sweatshirt. "What's wrong with it? My kids gave it to me last Mother's Day."

"Sorry. You're right." She made a face. "It's the thought that counts."

"That's right! God! This is what I can't stand about you. I took a day off from work to come rescue you and you're still insulting me. Why are you so mean?"

"I'm not trying to be. I just say what I think."

"Really? Okay. Let's see how you like it. I hate your long nails. They look like fangs."

"They do not," Beth said, admiring her French manicure. "And I'd rather have nails that were beautifully groomed than short stubs that have never been in range of a cuticle scissors."

"Excuse me, but I don't have the time and money to be so high maintenance, and furthermore, I cried when my kids gave me this sweatshirt. This picture was taken at Ricky's birthday party at Adventureland before he got lost. Can you imagine getting lost at your own birthday party? Anyway, the girls thought if this ever happened again, we could just point to the picture and say, hey, have you seen this kid?"

"Fine. It's lovely. I'm wrong."

"Yes you are. Plus, I love things with sentimental value. . . . I still have my macaroni necklaces they made in nursery school and the terrariums made out of Sprite bottles."

"As soon as they weren't looking, I threw all that stuff out. Who needs the clutter?"

"Oh, come on. You didn't love it when your kids did sweet things for you?"

"I wouldn't know," Beth sighed. "At least yours put some thought into your gifts. Last Mother's Day the girls had no idea what they were giving me because they couldn't even be bothered to wrap the box. They told Richard to let Bloomingdale's do it."

"Okay, so your life isn't as perfect as I thought. You're still very lucky. You're so pretty and you look like a teenager, you drive a beautiful car, you get to travel all the time, you don't have to work, you get to spend your days playing golf and having lunch at the club, and your house is to die for. . . . I love your stone fireplace with the burgundy couches— they remind me of a beautiful ski chalet."

"That's your big revelation? That I'm a spoiled brat?"

"No. I'm just saying it's so weird after all these years to find out that we've been jealous of each other. I'd kill to have half of what you have and you wished your family was more like mine."

"Maybe."

"And even though this whole situation is really sad, the way you ran off, the way you were treated by this jerk, I'm glad it happened."

"Oh, and I'm the bitch?"

"It's selfish, I know, but for the first time I'm seeing you from a different perspective. You're not this arrogant little snob. I mean you are, but there's another side to you. You can be sweet."

"It's a little known fact, so keep it to yourself."

"You like being thought of as a rich bitch?"

"Believe me, it has its advantages. Nobody dares to cross me."

"I can't imagine ever wanting to have that image."

"Mindy, if you had all the money in the world, you would still be you."

"You mean that in a good way, right?"

"Yes. You're a good person. It's possible I misjudged you."

"Possible?"

"Fine. I did . . . and now that I think of it, I'd like to repay you."

"You don't have to."

"No, I want to."

"Okay. You have this silver bangle bracelet I love that—"

"Not a chance. That was a birthday gift from my aunt. . . . I have a better idea. I'm taking you to see Nadia and having her clean up those eyebrows. Seriously, they're worse than my dad's. You've heard of waxing, right?"

It would have been great had Artie returned Mindy's calls while she was doing laundry, driving the car pool, picking up dinner, or straightening the house. Instead, while she was getting dressed, putting out refreshments for the pocketbook ladies, and helping Stacie study for a Spanish quiz—that's when he decided it was a great time to talk.

"I don't know where to start." Artie opened a beer. "Everything is such a mess."

"Where are you?"

"At some motel near Davida's house . . . Don't bother checking it out with Triple A. Just watch *Psycho*."

"Oh my God. Move the dresser against the door. Where's Aaron?"

"With the girl."

"Did you meet her? What's she like? Is she really pregnant? Is she keeping it? Do I have to learn how to knit?"

"Stop. Yes I met her."

"And?"

"And she's a lot older than him. Like maybe twenty-one or twenty-two."

"That's sick. He's just a baby. Can we have her arrested?"

"Give me a chance, okay? She seems nice for someone with a ring in her tongue, and there must have been a sale on tattoos 'cause she's got a lot of 'em. Also, not sure what color you'd call her hair. Rainbow, maybe? No wait, that's her name."

"Her name is Rainbow?" Mindy gasped. "Does that mean she's . . . multi-cultural?"

"Oh yes. A real combo plate. Part Native American, part black, even part Jewish."

"Really? Part Jewish?"

"That's what she said. Her mom's second husband owned a bagel shop."

"Ah-ha. Yes. That would make her a member of the tribe." Mindy laughed. "So what does she look like?"

"Actually, she's beautiful. Also big like bull.... She towers over Aaron, but then she's got this squeaky little voice that sounds like Stevie Nicks sucking the air out of a balloon. Go figure that she'd be the lead vocalist in a band; that's how they met. Aaron was jamming with them one night."

"Okay, but what's the deal? Is she pregnant? Is he the father? Is she keeping it?"

"Yes, she's pregnant and I have no idea about the rest. They went somewhere to talk."

"Well, how is handling it? Is he happy? Sad? Did he start singing?"

"I'll tell you this. He wasn't shocked, which means if it is his, and she does go through with it, he's going to fight me on coming back to New York."

"Any chance he's not the father?"

"Funny you should ask. She did mention this guy John twice, so who knows? Maybe she was trying to drop a hint."

"Okay, well let's pray, 'cause I'm still in shock that Aaron is now our responsibility. Could you imagine Rainbow and the baby, too? And what would they name it? Broken Rubber—would you stop it already?" Mindy yanked Jamie's arm to get her to stop chasing Ricky. "I'm not kidding. Leave him alone."

"He called me a doody ball." Jamie shook free.

"Richard Arthur Sherman! Do I have to tell Daddy you're using your garbage mouth?

"Oh and get this." Artie ignored the shenanigans. "Davida's dad is ninety-two years old and living in a nursing home in Florida, and when they told him that both Wayne and Davida were dead, he was like good, let 'em burn in hell, those no-good bums."

"He's probably senile."

"Actually, he sounded more with it than *my* dad. Anyway, they're both being cremated tomorrow and the old man told the funeral director to save money and put 'em in the same urn."

"Ew?"

"Yeah. But too late to worry about them. I'm more concerned with Aaron. He goes from being totally together to sounding like a three-year-old . . . do we know any good SAT tutors?"

"Not offhand. But everyone we know with kids in high school has one on speed dial. "

"Well start getting names because he never took them. He just thought he'd play in his band and get a big record deal, so who cared about college? Meanwhile, it looks like he may have to repeat his junior year because he was absent so much and missed a lot of work and tests."

"Oy-yoy-yoy. Okay, tomorrow I'll call the district and find out what we have to do . . . but to be honest, it still hasn't registered that he's coming to live with us. I just wish we had a bigger house."

"Trust me, compared to the way he's been living, our place will feel like Hugh Hefner's mansion, and Wayne's house wasn't any better. No food in the fridge, only three cases of beer, and these big bags of cat food in the garage. I was in this lady's office over at family services and started bawling. All I could think about was that my son was leading this god-awful existence and I didn't know. . . . I wasn't there for him—"

"Artie, you can't blame yourself. You tried for years to be a part of his life and they shut you out. At least now he's all yours."

"I know," he sniffed. "I know. Thank God."

"So have you talked to him about coming back with you?"

"Not really. I was waiting to see how the whole Rainbow thing went down, but I have to say. This is one beautiful city. You look out and see Mount Hood and the Columbia River and all these trendy restaurants and shops. This is a happening place!"

"We are not moving to Portland."

"I know. I'm just saying . . . We could have a real decent quality of life here. The air is clean, the schools are great, and everything is so much cheaper than on Long Island. I almost fell over when I saw Davida's electric bill. She was paying for two months what we pay for a day and you know how much I always liked the Trailblazers."

"We are not moving to Portland."

"Fine. I get it . . . but listen to this. Remember I used to talk about my friend Andy Levinger from optometry school?"

"No."

"Yes, you do. He was the guy who taught me how to ski, remember? I used to go with him on weekends to his parent's house in the Adirondacks. I could never figure out how he was like this fearless warrior on the slopes and such a pussycat with the rest of his life. Anyway, you're never going to believe this, but I saw his name on a billboard this morning. Looks like he moved out here, probably for the skiing, and now he's got a bunch of offices. I just called and left a message. Sounds like he's doing great. You never know if he needs help."

"Artie, have you lost your mind? We can not move to Portland. We have family here, friends, a business . . . Look I have to go now. The pocketbook ladies are at the door. I'll call you when it's over—wait . . . Find out if the women in Portland have these stupid parties. If they don't, maybe I'll think about it."

Next door, another conversation was taking place between spouses in Long Island and Portland, but it was of a much louder, angrier nature. Beth had returned home to find that just as Mindy had warned, she was minus both a husband and a housekeeper.

Her two daughters remained, of course, and though they were relieved to see their mother, they circled warily. She had hurt them terribly, leaving them fearful of their future.

Jessica was especially traumatized, since this possible split was coming at a most inconvenient time. Her bat mitzvah, the single most important event of her life, was scheduled for Thanksgiving weekend, a mere eight months away.

She had dreamed forever about her gala Saturday-night black-tie party, racking her brains to come up with ideas that would make it so much nicer than Melanie Lipsky's, who thought her reception was amazing because she had a band *and* a DJ, and the kids didn't have to eat chicken fingers. They had their choice of Chateaubriand and pecan-crusted sea bass, just like the adults.

Jessica would do better! She'd have the most awesome sushi bar and desserts from Serendipity. Plus, she already knew the dresses she would have designed (one for her service, one for her cocktail hour, one for her party); the invitations she wanted (no purple hearts and flowers); and the kids she'd invite versus the ones who had better pray to be on her guest list.

But now if her stupid parents were splitting, it would not only ruin her big day, but her whole life, just like her friends whose parents had gotten divorced. In fact, Amanda Kreiger's parents were fighting so bad, her mom supposedly took a piece of little Bella's dog doody and put it in her husband's chopped meat for dinner. "He gives me shit, I give it right back!"

But Jessica's parents weren't like that. They still loved each other, they just liked to yell. And even if they didn't still love each other, they loved *her* enough not to want to ruin her once in a lifetime bat mitzvah, right?

Unfortunately, from the muffled shouting coming from her mom's room, maybe Stacie had been right about them splitting.

"He told me he wasn't going to be there, okay?" Beth yelled. "He was just going to give me the keys and the directions."

"What am I? Stupid? 'Cause it's a real believable story. A guy you meet at a bar says, yeah sure, here's the keys to my house in the Hamptons. Have a nice day."

"What do you want me to say? That was the deal. I told him I was in a bad place right now and the last thing I needed was to complicate my life even further by getting involved."

"Really. A beautiful, married woman runs off and needs a place to stay, and he's like, that's cool. Help yourself to what's in the fridge."

"That's right."

"So then why did he dump you at a train station like you were garbage? Wasn't such a nice guy anymore, I guess."

"He got weird on me, okay? He turned out to be a big liar like you. I made him drive me back. We didn't have sex. You have to believe me."

"I don't have to do anything, Beth. Why even bother pretending we're trying to work things out? We've both been miserable for years and obviously you've already moved on or you wouldn't have done anything this stupid. The girls were scared to death. You have no idea what went on here after you ran off. Total hysteria."

"Richard, stop! I am very sorry. How many times do I have to say it? I know it was a horrible thing to do, but you screw up all the time and I'm supposed to look the other way."

"And here it comes . . . Let's get even time! Happy now?"

"No, of course not, and trust me, if I really wanted revenge, I've had plenty of opportunities before this. Ask your good friend Marty. He hits on me constantly. And why is it so hard for you to understand I just needed time to think? I don't know who I am or what I want anymore. . . . I'm always angry, I'm sick over the fact that the girls hate me so much . . . and believe me, you've made it very clear how you feel about me, too. All you ever do is complain that I'm this ungrateful bitch who spends money we don't have, but I'm not the one who wanted to join the club, and I'm not the one who sabotaged their career by pissing off management and—"

"Are you done, Beth? Because I can save us both a lot of time and trouble . . . I'm leaving."

"What do you mean 'leaving'? Where are you going?"

"Nowhere now. I'm staying in Portland."

"Why?"

"Because it's best this way. We'll be out of each other's hair."

"What the hell are you talking about?"

"And you accuse me of being an actor! You know exactly what I'm saying. . . . I want a trial separation."

"A separation? I don't believe this! Why do you get to leave? I should be the one who bails."

"That's for the lawyers to work out."

"The lawyers? Oh my God, Richard! Why are you being such an asshole? You have nothing on me other than one brief instance of questionable judgment, which compared to the shit you've pulled was a joke: the calls from Connecticut when you were really in Vegas, the money you took from my dad to invest in the market, then blew on that piece of shit Jaguar. Oh, and let's not forget your little indiscretion at the office. That was awesome taking money from our IRAs and paying those huge penalties so we could bribe your little friend before she filed a sexual harassment lawsuit. Well here's a news story for you! Guess who is building that huge waterfront house over on Halyard? A woman divorce attorney. Can't wait to invite her over for coffee."

"I don't get it. You've done nothing but bitch for years that you're miserable. Now I'm giving you an out and you're pissed?"

"I'm pissed that you're so out of touch with reality that you think you can run away and everything is going to magically get better. Get help, Richard! How long have I been begging you? Ten years? Eleven? Even your bosses back then were on your case, remember? David and Sam came to the house with the list of the top shrinks at Bellevue and told you to take a leave of absence with full pay? And what did you do? You threatened to sue their asses if they ever mentioned it again."

"They weren't trying to help me and you know it!" Richard shot back. "They were only trying to trap me into saying I needed counseling so they could legally fire me."

"I didn't believe that then, and I don't believe it now. But it's a prime example of how you rationalize everything, how you delude—"

"I'm not rationalizing anything. I admit I've screwed up, okay? But don't bullshit me either. You lost interest in us years ago. Why shouldn't I start over and take a job here?"

"Because it would be one hell of a commute. I thought you went out there to pitch a new piece of business."

"I did. But two of the top guys here have been talking to me for months about joining the team, and this morning we shook on a deal."

"Really, this has been going on for months and you never mentioned a word. I'm sorry. I don't believe you. I think it's just another one of your bullshit stories."

"Fine. Don't believe me, but I'm telling the truth. They offered me a senior VP position for a new digital media division and it's a great opportunity. The money isn't amazing, but in a year or two with all the stock options and profit sharing, I'll be rolling in it. Not to mention you know I always liked the people here, their business philosophy—"

"Oh my God. Would you listen to yourself? Their business philosophy? Wait until they find out that yours is taking three-hour liquid lunches, cheating on your expense reports, and blaming all your subordinates for screwing up."

"I knew you were too selfish to be happy for me."

"I'm sorry, did you say you want me to be happy for you? You fucking accepted a job all the way across the country without even discussing it with me!"

"What was there to discuss? You'll never leave New York and I want to start over. Besides, I've always loved it out West."

"That's not the point, asshole! You don't go and make a huge life-changing decision like this and spring it on me after it's a done deal. What do you plan to tell the girls? Sorry, love you guys, but I'd rather be close to great skiing?"

"No. I'll tell them that if they want to, they can come out here with me."

"Oh, this just keeps getting better and better! You're going to jump into a whole new career while taking complete responsibility for raising them? I'm not sure if you noticed, but they're a little old for day care! And wait until I'm not around to cover up for all your lies and nonsense and they realize their dad is a fuckup who can't even give you the time without distorting the truth. Oh, and there's one other small matter that apparently slipped your mind. . . . Jessica's bat mitzvah is in less than a year. I do hope you can still make it!"

"Of course I'll make it. I'm leaving you, not her!"

Fourteen

As pocketbook parties went, it was a decent turnout, particularly after Karen's cousin arrived with several friends from Dix Hills, the blinding-diamond capital of the world. They alone could make her night, yet as Mindy looked around, she saw more talking than shopping.

Not good. Karen needed to move the merchandise or face David's I-told-you-so speech. She'd been so sure that the ladies would go crazy over the selection, especially the red, quilted Chanel bag with the chain handle that, according to *New York* magazine was a favorite of those hungry-looking Olsen twins. But thus far, she had sold only two, and one was to Mildred Mayer, who kept asking about her return policy in the event her twelve-year-old granddaughter complained that the bag looked too fake to bring to school.

Frankly, Mindy could never understand why women who thought nothing of dropping big bucks for Marc Jacobs and Louis Vuitton would bother with the knockoffs. "They all say the same thing," Karen informed her. "I'm only buying this as a gift. Then I run into them at Bagel Boss and they're wearing it.

Who doesn't love a bargain?" Everyone does, of course, but not nearly as much as they love gabbing.

The ladies in skinny jeans sipped diet Coke while discussing breast implants, kitchen cabinets, the kids who got waitlisted at Brown, and the friend who lost twenty pounds on Weight Watchers thanks to the recipe for chocolate-cinnamon quesadillas.

All seemingly harmless chitchat, until topic A turned to local gossip, which at the moment centered around the rumored split between power couple Beth and Richard Diamond. Everyone had an opinion.

The marriage was a match made in hell. Richard had a good shot if he sued for joint custody, and in a unanimous vote, the women expressed disappointment that the once-sweet Jessica had morphed into her mother, right down to her unapologetic ambition and inherent sense of entitlement.

Given Mindy and Beth's history of conflicts, no one would ever expect to hear Mindy defend her, particularly since she had proven to be such a reliable source (yes, there's another Dumpster in front of the house, no, Richard did not buy that Harley, he's just test-driving it).

Now, as an insider, she saw things differently. The spread of gossip was viral, contaminating what would otherwise have been a sterile gathering. Yet rather than making people sick, it only masked the infectious belief that they were morally superior.

The irony was not lost on Mindy that at this very moment, Stacie was upstairs finishing a book report on the late Margaret Mead. She wondered what the famed anthropologist would have concluded had she immersed herself in the world of the upscale suburban mom, as she had done in a village of Samoan women back in the 1920s.

In their native habitats (a middle-class upbringing), these women appear to have normal behavior patterns that include conformity and good manners. But once they marry well and trade up to five-thousand-

square-foot houses, it can lead to major attitudinal changes insofar as self-importance and superiority, particularly if their husbands receive a Wall Street bonus.

This attitudinal change may last until the husband leaves the wife for a younger woman, or a younger man, or until the couple retires to Boca while still supporting their children. Though this is associated with stress and confusion resulting in a need for anti-anxiety pills, as long as the woman gets to keep the Mercedes and the co-op in New York, in time she will recover, particularly if her ex drops dead.

"Well, last summer we were out on Fire Island and bumped into Richard with this girl who he said was his assistant, but she sure wasn't using her hands to type."

Mindy moved closer. This little powwow she had to hear.

"Can you blame him? Beth is so mean to him. We used to go out with them all the time but we couldn't take her anymore. This one time we were having dinner at a great little place in SoHo and she started yelling at him because the poor guy wanted to order dessert. It was disgusting."

"Oh, I know, she's insane with the whole sugar thing. Emma once came over to play with Ali and I gave them leftover birth-day cake for a snack, and the next day Beth is yelling at me, 'Why would you feed them junk before dinner? What's wrong with fresh fruit?'"

"Well remember when she circulated that stupid petition trying to ban cupcakes from class parties? Oh, and no more bake sales either. Wasn't she ever a kid?"

"No wonder she likes Marsha Majors. I heard she makes her kids keep a food journal, then checks it every night to make sure they're not pigging out. Like they're really gonna tell the truth!"

"Wait. Speaking of petitions, wasn't she the one who wanted to remove books from the school library because they promoted sexual promiscuity? Then everyone found out she was having an affair with the principal?"

"No!" they all replied. "That was Marjorie Young!"

After Karen finally packed up and left, Mindy looked at the mess in the kitchen and said screw it until morning. After the day she'd had, she was entitled to take a hot shower, climb into bed with a big bowl of Lucky Charms, and watch last night's *American Idol* on Tivo.

But just as she armed the alarm, she spotted a tall figure with a fast gait approaching the back door. Please be a burglar, she thought.

"Sorry to bother you." Beth coughed. "You must be exhausted."

"Comatose is more like it." She yawned for effect, but stared at Beth as if she was catching a rare glimpse of a lunar eclipse. She looked so homely without hair and makeup, and dare Mindy say, old?

"I can't believe how much happened today," Beth fidgeted, looking over Mindy's shoulder to see if any of her kids were still up.

"Yup." *Please make this short. I'm so tired and I want my Lucky Charms.*

"Could we talk?"

Crap! What if the windows in the den were open and she'd heard everything? "Sure."

What little time Beth had spent in this kitchen, her routine was to wipe the crumbs off the chairs and check for food on the floor. Tonight, however, out of respect, she refrained from making faces. "So how was it? Did she have nice stuff?"

"I guess, but I'm probably not the best judge. I don't pay enough attention to the real bags to know if the fakes are any good."

"Looked like you had a lot of people though. Did she sell enough to shut David up?"

"It took a while, but most people ended up buying something. And then this one lady showed up with her daughter and bought like ten bags so that was good, but oh my god, was she obnoxious. I heard she got into Penn early decision, but obviously it wasn't based on a personal interview or using SAT words. All she said was, '*ew,* gross' and '*um,* noooo.'"

"Sounds about right. So what did you pick out for you?"

"This." Mindy fetched the Chanel bag. "Karen said it's the hottest thing."

"Wow!" Beth examined it with the eye of a jeweler. "It's a great fake. You can't even tell."

"I guess that's the whole idea, not that I understand why anyone would spend a ton of money on a designer bag that's as mass produced as the ones I get at Target. And don't hate me for saying this, but every time I see someone wearing Coach or Louis Vuitton, I think, wow, you just gave me permission to judge you. You're insecure, shallow, you can't think for yourself—"

"Really. So if one day I gave you one of my Michael Kors bags, you'd say no thanks?"

"Well no, I guess not. I mean I like nice things too, but—"

"Richard is leaving me!" Beth blurted. "He took a job at Nike just like you said."

"What? Mindy had to let that sink in. "Oh my God!"

"Mommmm!" Stacie yelled. "Tell the little bee-ach to get out of my room. I don't have her freakin' iPod!"

"Sorry, hold on." Mindy ran to the foyer. "Jamie! Get out of Stacie's room. You were supposed to be in bed an hour ago. You've got the Terra Nova tests in the morning."

"Are your kids usually up this late?" Beth sniffed.

"Unfortunately, yes. Just hold on. I'll go get my stun gun and be down in a second."

When Mindy returned, it was to a spotless kitchen. "Wow. Can you start tomorrow?"

"Don't laugh." Beth threw out a cup. "I may need a job . . . hopefully one that doesn't require hairnets or time cards."

"What's going on?"

"I don't even know where to start." Beth gazed outside. "Can I make some tea?"

"Sure . . . if you promise not to insult me by rinsing out the cup first."

"Stop. I'm not that bad." She looked in the kettle. "Oy. When's the last time you used this?"

"The Boston Tea Party." Mindy sat down.

"Sorry . . . I have this thing about being sanitary. I'd hate to start an outbreak of typhus."

"Knock yourself out . . . as long as you don't ask me to get up again."

"Sure." Beth sighed. "Can I get you something?"

"A case of beer and a straw."

"Too fattening. I'll make you some tea."

"I hate tea."

"You'll love mine. It's a special blend of . . . ," she began as she searched the cabinets. "Where are the tea bags?"

"You mean tea bag." Mindy rested her head on the table. "It's around here somewhere. Jamie and Ricky were playing catch with it this morning."

"You're joking, right?"

"Yes I'm joking . . . third cabinet on the right, bottom shelf . . . the only one I like is peppermint, and only after you add hot chocolate."

"You're very funny." Beth went into action. "I can't believe we were never close."

"You dare say that to me in a room full of sharp knives?"

"I'm trying to make amends. . . . I really need a friend."

"Why?" Mindy sat back up. "Don't you have a whole group from the country club and your tennis league? And what about all those girls you go to Canyon Ranch with every year?"

"They're around . . . I just don't . . . things are different now . . . they know me one way . . . I just can't . . . I don't want to be her anymore."

Suddenly Beth leaned over the counter and cried. It was a loud uncontrollable sob that would otherwise be heard at the news of a loved one's funeral and Mindy didn't know how to react. Had it been one of her children, or Artie or Nadine or her mom, she would have hugged them and stroked their hair. But this was Beth.

"I'm sorry." Beth blew into a tissue. "I don't know what it is about being with you. . . . I always feel like I can cry."

"I get that a lot. Here. You sit and I'll watch the tea. I promise you won't die from it."

"Thank you." She clutched a wad of tissues as if they could protect like Band-Aids. "Everything is such a disaster and I'm so miserable and I just want to blame someone, but the statute of limitations is up on my parents, and the girls have done nothing wrong, and Richard has done everything wrong, but I can't decide if he lies to me because I'm so unhappy with him or I'm so unhappy with him because he lies about everything."

"You *know*?" Mindy's eyes opened.

"*You* know?" Beth's eyes opened wider.

"I don't know what I know . . . I've heard gossip, but I really try not to listen because half the time it's not true . . . and the other half it is."

"I hate this town," Beth whimpered. "Why can't people mind their own damn business?"

"Oh, come on. You don't really think it's different anywhere else. We're all voyeurs today. Whether it's Paris Hilton or the family down the block, it's so much more fun to judge someone else's life. Then you don't have to bother looking at your own."

"I guess." She tried to collect herself. "So what's the word on us?"

"It doesn't matter."

"No, I want to know. I'm sure everyone here was talking tonight. What did they say?"

"Just stupid stuff. Someone thought they saw Richard with this girl on Fire Island."

Beth nodded, surprising Mindy. Where was the denial? The righteous indignation?

"Who knew? I could have saved money if I'd just had my neighbors do the spying," she mumbled. "I've spent thousands on private investigators and that stupid nanny cam."

"*Ew, ew, ew* . . . you think that Richard and Marina?"

"God no. She had much better sense than that. But don't you remember? Before Marina we had that Bridget, the au pair from Sweden who used to run around in halter tops and shorts and spritz on my ninety-dollar-an-ounce perfume right before Richard got home? I don't know what the hell I was thinking when I hired her."

"I do remember her. All of a sudden Artie started dieting. Did you ever catch them?"

"No, but I fired her anyway. You know how boring it is sitting through hours and hours of video day after day waiting for something to happen? The most I caught her doing was stealing my pistachio nuts. Anyway, my point is that I've always had to keep an eye on Richard. He drinks too much and he's a big flirt."

"So you've never actually caught him with another woman."

"Another woman, yes. A nanny, no, thank God. But trust me, he's never getting angel wings."

"I don't know what to say," Mindy sighed. "I'm in shock. To us, Richard's always been this stand-up guy who's so funny and helpful. A few weeks ago he came right over when Artie couldn't get the grill started, and he got Stephon Marbury's autograph for Jamie. Plus he's such a great dad. He's always taking the girls skiing and to Disney."

"That's the thing. When it comes to impressing people, he's the best. Then you pull back the curtain and his stories have more holes than a golf course. He'll be out of town on business and I'll say I heard on the news it's raining there and he'll say, no it's a gorgeous day. Then he'll come home and tell me he got soaked because he didn't have an umbrella."

"Well has he tried counseling? What about talking to the new rabbi? He seems pretty with it. You can't give up without a fight."

"All we do is fight."

"You know what I mean. You've been together all these years, and you have a beautiful home and a family. And what about Jess's bat mitzvah? You have to work this out."

"That's just it," she cried. "He called me from his hotel just now and said he wants out."

"I don't believe it. I've seen you together and family is his whole life. Remember the night we came home from the airport with Aaron? Richard looked like he'd been crying because he thought you were playing around."

"It's an act." She grabbed more tissues. "The whole thing is an act."

"No way!"

"That's how pathological liars are. I'm always telling him to forget Penn Station. He should get off at Broadway. And believe me, you're not the only one he's fooled. Why do you think his clients love him so much? He comes off as this boy genius who's funny and charming. Of course his bosses all know he's full of shit, but business is business."

"Then why put up with it? I can't even screw up the car pool without you getting crazy. He lies to you and that's okay?"

"No, of course it's not okay, but why do you think I get so upset over the car pool? It's because it's one of the few things in my control."

"Yeah, but still . . . How do you accept this kind of life?"

"My therapist says the reason I don't fight back is because then I'd have to acknowledge that I'm a hypocrite. When I started seeing Richard, he was engaged."

"You mean you found out later?" The kettle whistled and Mindy searched for clean mugs.

"No, I knew from the beginning," she sniffed. "She was always coming by the office. Richard was my boss at Grey Advertising. It's all so cliché. The whole story about long hours and tight quarters. He had an office with a couch and a door with a lock."

"So wait. That's the deal? Because you knew he was capable of dishonesty then, you think you have to put up with it now?"

"I realize it sounds stupid, but yes. The whole relationship started out on the basis of lies and deception, so how shocked can I be that he's doing it to me? And the other reason I tolerate all his crap is because, well, aside from my marriage, I have a very nice life."

"Wait. What? A bad marriage is a minor inconvenience? I could never live like that."

"You say that now, but it's not that simple. You look at what you've got versus what you'd lose, and don't jump all over me for saying this, but maybe the difference between us is that I have more to lose. I've got the house of my dreams, the freedom to spend my day as I please, we take great vacations, I've got medical insurance. You've heard of friends with benefits? This is marriage with benefits. It's just not love."

"That is so sad."

"I used to think so, too. Then I realized half my friends were in the same boat. They're actually happy they're out of love with their husbands. They shop all they want, have this great life, and don't have to deal with sex. It's like the cell phone ads. Nights and weekends are free."

"Well that doesn't sound very appealing to me. You deserve the real deal."

"No such thing." Beth sipped her tea. "Happily married is a myth. Women fake it like they do everything else."

"Not me . . . I mean yeah, I get so pissed sometimes I want to kill Artie, but I still love him." She toyed with the pocketbook. "Although I do agree that a lot of marriages are like this bag. You think no one can tell it's a fake, but that doesn't make it real."

"Huh?"

"Well, at first glance it looks authentic and there's no reason to think otherwise. But examine it closely and you'll see the stitching is crooked and the label is coming unglued. Maybe the reason the real bag is worth so much is because it will stand the test of time. Maybe the reason you're having such a hard time with Richard is because you accepted the knockoff."

"Lovely thought," she sighed. "I've got dozens of designer bags in my closet but my marriage is a fake . . . except for one major difference. My marriage has been no bargain. I've paid dearly for it."

"Fine, but now what? You can't just throw it out."

"It's too late."

"Not if you still love him. Do you?"

"I have no idea what that even means anymore. I know I used to. He was so smart and beautiful and he totally cracked me up. I couldn't wait to be alone with him."

"Well, look, I'm not saying take it back to the honeymoon stage, 'cause Lord knows the thermostat gets turned down for everyone. I'm just asking, is there enough heat to try?"

"Why bother? He's made it clear that he wants out."

"Yes, but what do you want? What if in spite of everything you still love him and he feels the same about you? I've seen the way he looks at you and as long as there's no Oscar statue in your living room, I don't believe it's all an act. I think he truly adores you."

"Who knows?" Beth threaded her tissues.

"Okay, let me ask you this." Mindy went on. "Whose name is the house in?"

"Both of ours . . . why?"

"Because I saw this doctor lady on Oprah who talked about an idea that might work."

"I'm listening. What's the idea?"

"Can't tell you unless I get my Lucky Charms."

"You have Lucky Charms?"

"The Costco size."

"I'll get the milk!" Beth raced to the fridge. "Do they still have those little green marshmallows? Dibs on those!"

Fifteen

The last thing Mindy needed after her all-night "cerealathon" with Beth was to get an early-morning wake-up call from Stacie. "MOM!!!! I got it!" she shrieked from the bathroom.

Ohmygod! "I'm coming!" Mindy hightailed it down the hall. "Mommy's coming."

"This is so gross!"

"Can I come in?" Mindy stood outside the door.

"No!" Stacie yelled. "You're going to slap me."

"I'm not going to slap you." Mindy laughed. "I don't even understand that silly tradition. Do you have the pads I bought you?"

"MOM! Oh my God, why don't you just yell so the whole block hears?"

"I'm not yelling. Tell me what you want me to do."

"I don't know. . . . My stomach is killing me and it went through my pajamas. I am not going to school."

"Let's take one step at a time. Just let me in so I can help you."

Stacie waddled over to the door and hid behind it. "I hate this! I'm gonna die if I get this every month."

"I remember saying the same thing." Mindy zeroed in on the

blood-stained rug and knew she'd better get it in the wash before Ricky saw it and started screaming there were monsters in the house.

"I wish I never had to have it!" she cried. "I'm not ready."

"I know, sweetie, but think of it as joining a new club. We meet monthly to eat chocolate."

"Jillian Wynter told me that once you get it you look pregnant and your jeans don't fit."

"Well, Jillian Wynter is wrong. Once you get it you automatically start to act like an adult who makes excellent decisions about not smoking, drinking, or hooking up with bad boys."

"You mean Britney Spears never got her period?"

"Good point! Let's get you some Advil and clean underwear and I'll show you how to wear the pads so you don't waddle. Welcome to womanhood." She gently slapped her face.

"Hey! You said that was stupid."

"I know, but I just realized why moms do it. They start to think about their daughters dating and they smack 'em around to remind 'em who's boss."

Mindy should have known that a morning that began with blood and screaming would be an ominous sign. If only she'd had time to consult with her online astrologer to find out what else was in store so that she could stock up on Oreos, the breakfast of cowards.

As of now, the day was scheduled to be a repeat of yesterday's chaos, hopefully minus the rescue mission in Babylon. She had agreed to do the morning car pool so that Beth could gather strength for her own brewing storm ("I must find a cleaning lady!"), but it still meant getting her three kids moving and Rebecca to the high school, then coming back for the other school runs, opening the store, and being at work by ten.

What she didn't need in the middle of helping Stacie and assuring her that yes, girls all over the world did attend school in spite of having their periods, was a phone call from Rhoda demanding the name and phone number of the accounting firm that handled Stan's medical practice. "I wouldn't have had to bother you on the phone if you'd answered my e-mails."

I'm surprised I still get your e-mails. I report them as spam! "Rhoda, I really wish you wouldn't ask me to get in the middle of this whole thing."

"Whose side are you on?"

"I'm not on anyone's side. I just want to go in and do my job . . . not to mention Stan signs my paycheck."

"Well I will certainly remember this the next time you need something from me! Where is Arthur?"

"You know where he is. He's in Portland with Aaron" . . . *and maybe moving there wouldn't be such a bad idea. . . .* "And aren't you getting a little ahead of yourself here? You don't need to see the books. I'm sure the two of you will work this out."

"This has nothin' to do with the books. I just like knowin' how things are run over there in case something ever happens to Stan and I have to take over . . . like a governor's wife. "

You mean in case you kill him? "Fine. Then call Edna. She's the office manager."

"We no longer speak. She's an incompetent oaf who can't keep her big trap shut."

"Rhoda, I can't deal with this right now. Stacie got her period, I'm trying to get the kids up, I have to drive Nadine's daughter to school—"

"Well, excuse me for interrupting your busy life, but I don't understand how one little favor is such a big megillah."

"Fine. The minute I get in I'll call you with the accountant's phone number."

"No. I won't be home. I have my 'mahj' game, a lunch date, and a root canal at three. Just e-mail me so I can get it later."

Mindy could have also done without the text messages from Nadine about Jonathan's audition and how he'd thrown up, and she was so nervous for him she couldn't stop crying, and Peter was yelling at her because she was making things worse, and not to forget that Rebecca had to be at school early for extra help.

Nor did she need the phone call from the unit coordinator at the nursing home saying that her grandmother's blood pressure was so high, they were taking her for tests and did Mindy want to meet the ambulance at the hospital or wait to hear from the doctor?

Mindy chose option B. She'd wait to hear from the doctor first. "Oh," the woman said. "And before I hang up, do you know anything about the pickle dish that was stolen from her?"

Damn! Not the pickle dish again. It was the dementia talking, of course. Right before she and her mom moved her grandmother into the home, they'd cleaned out her apartment and found a glass pickle dish with the Alexander's price tag still glued to the bottom. It was a nothing tchotchke, but Helene said she'd enjoy having it as it brought back memories of all the Sunday dinners she'd enjoyed at her then future husband's house. Only to have Grandma Jenny accuse her of stealing her most prized family heirloom.

Since then, Helene hadn't visited. Therefore it was unlikely that Mindy would repeat the story that she was still asking about the dish, let alone that she'd said that it had been taken by a ganef who had been stealing her blind for years.

Mindy collapsed in a kitchen chair, feeling ambushed by a morning that was less than an hour old. Hopefully all the bad news was now out of the way.

"Mom!!!" Jamie shouted from upstairs. "Alanna Decker's mom wants to know what we're doing for my bat mitzvah."

"I don't know what I'm doing for lunch today, let alone two years from now. Why is she asking?"

"I dunno. She just IM'd me."

"You aren't supposed to be on the computer before school, remember?" Mindy raced into the foyer. "Now sign off and get dressed. I have to go get Rebecca and you make sure Ricky is moving."

"I can't. I'm still printing my book report. Why does the bathroom smell like bird guts?"

"It doesn't smell like bird guts. Just print what you have to, then get ready. Wait. We didn't even get your bat mitzvah date yet. Why would Alanna's mother be asking about it?"

"Because their temple gave out their dates yesterday and her mom called ours to see who had the same date, and they told her it was me."

"Are you kidding me? The temple gave the date to a family who's not even a member before they informed us, the people who pay dues? That is so sick. By the way, when is it?"

"May 14, 2010."

"Nice! Maybe it's Mother's Day weekend, but why did Alanna's mom need to know?"

"Because they're having her party on a Saturday night like they did for her sister, and her mom said that since Alanna is one of the most popular girls in school, they would feel bad if someone with the same date also did a Saturday night and everyone went to Alanna's party."

"Are you freaking kidding me? That's what she said? Oh my God! What a piece of work! Well you know what? You go back and IM Alanna and tell her to tell her idiot mother that it is none of her goddamn business what our plans are, and I don't care if her guests are wearing black-tie pajamas to the Waldorf Astoria! We are doing whatever we damn well please, but not to worry because the way things are going, the only party we'll be able to afford is at a Wendy's that's open late."

"We're doing my bat mitzvah at Wendy's?" Jamie burst into

tears. "I hate you! That's not fair! Stacie got to have a real party. I hate you so much!" She ran to her room.

But mostly what Mindy did not need now was an e-mail from Artie saying he'd finally heard from Waspy and the bank was sorry, but not only were they denying the loan application, they were raising the rates on the current loan due to late payments, and Artie should let him know if he needed the names of some reputable liquidators.

Mindy grabbed a roll of toilet paper and cried into the balled-up mess. Without the bank's funding they were screwed, what with Jamie's bat mitzvah on the horizon, not to mention another child to support (possibly two), one of whom would be college-bound if it killed Artie, which it would likely have to, as the only way they could afford Aaron's tuition was if a life insurance policy paid the way.

"Why is everybody cryin'?" Ricky shook Mindy's shoulder. "You're cryin' and Jamie's cryin' and Stacie's cryin'. Did some-body die?"

"No, sweetie." She hugged him. "Nobody died. It's just girl stuff. Why don't you get your shoes and come with me when I get Rebecca? Then we'll stop at Bagel Boss. How's that?"

"Yeah. Yeah!" He clapped his hands. "Can we get egg sand-wiches, too?"

"Sure." Mindy grabbed her pocketbook. "If we're goin' down, it's not going to be on an empty stomach."

Though Mindy hadn't worked in nearly two weeks, she dreaded walking into the office. Despite her best efforts to conceal her red eyes, clearly she'd been crying and the girls would want an explanation. But unlike the imaginary conversation she'd had with Alanna Decker's mom on the drive over, 'none of your god-damn business' would not fly.

Most of these women had been together since Stan went into

private practice; they were family to each other, sharing all their simchas and sorrows and there was no such thing as a secret. You could beg all you wanted for a personal matter not to be discussed, but word would always get out, and even Stan would be in on it, though he swore he wasn't interested.

In today's little drama, however, he wasn't the observer but the subject. Apparently he'd come in this morning and told Edna he was leaving at noon and to refer their patients to the team of covering doctors until further notice, though he offered no explanation why.

So although the girls were polite and told Mindy they wanted to hear all about the cruise, in truth the only thing they wanted details on was what was up with Stan and Rhoda.

"What in God's name happened?" Edna barely let Mindy get her jacket off.

"What do you mean?" Mindy fumbled with her car keys.

"Oh, come on. We know something went wrong on the cruise. He's flying to Florida and she hasn't stopped calling."

"It's no big deal." Mindy coughed. "He's meeting an old army buddy to play golf."

"Right. And I'm leaving for Nantucket to sell my granddaughter's Girl Scout cookies. Come on! In ten years here, he's never taken this much time off."

"I wonder if Rhoda found out about Sydell?" Nurse Diana checked a patient file.

"I don't think so," Edna said. "That was years ago. I heard she died."

"Sydell?" Mindy looked up. "Who's Sydell?"

Edna and Diana looked at each other. "Nobody."

"No, come on. That's not fair."

"Well, give a little, get a little." Edna smiled.

"Fine. They had a little misunderstanding on the cruise but they're working it out."

"That had to be one helluva little misunderstanding if he's leaving town and she's asking all these questions about the book-keeping records."

"Mindy get in here." Stan motioned her inside.

Damn. Like I want to get dragged into yet another marital rift. But at least the lovely scenic view of the azalea bushes which could be seen from the guest chair would give her a focal point, like when she was in labor and needed a distraction from the pain.

"I'm putting you in charge this week." He scribbled notes on a pad. "As I'm sure you've already heard in great detail, I'm taking the rest of the week off."

"Putting me in charge of what? Edna is the office manager."

"I know who I employ, but you're family. I trust you will see to it that my patients are properly referred, and that under no circumstances are you or anyone to mention my personal affairs. Furthermore, you are to make sure that Rhoda does not set foot inside my office and if she tries to push you around then—"

"Wait, wait, wait . . . You can't honestly expect me to show Rhoda the door, Dad."

"Don't 'Dad' me . . . I'm counting on you to keep things from getting out of control here, and when I get back, there are going to be big changes. Rhoda and I are going our separate ways."

"Separate ways . . . You can't be serious. Wait, have you told Artie and Ira?"

"No. When you speak to Arthur later, you can mention it. And tell him to call Ira. I have to finish packing. What time is it?" He checked his watch. "Oy, the limo will be here soon."

"*Whoa.* Hold on! You expect me to be the one to tell your child, oh by the way, your father is leaving your mother?"

"He's not a child, he's a grown man with a family. He knows all about meshuggener wives."

"Hey! I resent that! If anything, I'm the sanest one in the bunch."

"Yeah, right," he snorted. "Every month I feel like you joined some crazy cult."

"Oh my God! You should hear yourself, acting all innocent."

"Did I ask for your opinion?" he said, glaring at her. "Now if you don't want to talk to Arthur about this, fine. I'll call him from the airport myself, but let me know now if you are prepared to carry out your duties this week."

"Yes, I am planning to do my job, I'm just not planning to do yours. If you have issues to work out with Rhoda, you are not putting me in the middle of them. Besides, where is your sense of responsibility here? Do you honestly believe the grass is greener over at Facelift Barbie's?"

"The nerve of you!" Stan's temples danced to the beat. "Take that back!"

"No! I can't stand it anymore. I'm just so tired of listening to men blaming their wives for their unhappiness without owning up to their own failings!"

"Other men are not my problem. And since when do you come to Rhoda's defense? You can't stand the crazy bitch!"

"I'm not defending her. It's that I can't stand watching people who think it's okay to turn their backs on the family they're supposed to love and protect. Look at Aaron and what it's done to him, having a mother and a stepfather and an uncle who cared more about their stupid drug habits than taking care of him. And then there's my next-door neighbor. He's been lying to his wife for years and thinks it's no big deal."

"I have never lied or cheated on Rhoda, so don't throw me into THAT pot!"

"Oh, really? You've never cheated? What about Sydell?"

"SYDELL? Where are you getting your information? From those blabbermouths?" He pointed. "If you're listening to them, you're crazier than I thought."

"Fine. Then who is she?"

"Sydell Baumgarten was an eighty-seven-year-old Alzheimer's patient who used to call me six times a day, and that's when she wasn't driving over here to tell me how much I reminded her of her son Alan, who died, only he wasn't dead, he was a bankruptcy lawyer in Westchester!"

"Oh."

"I don't even know how she got here half the time, but whenever she showed up, she was wearing underwear over her pants."

"Sorry." Mindy looked down. *I am going to kill you, Edna.*

"So be careful before you start making accusations! You know what my life with Rhoda has been like—a living hell! And if I've decided I've had enough, I don't need your or anyone else's permission to call it quits."

"Okay, okay . . . do whatever you want. Just . . . you know, try to consider your grandchildren's feelings when you break the news to them. They're going to be so crushed."

"I will handle this with the great care and sensitivity that I handle everything else."

"That's what I was afraid of."

Sixteen

When had marriage become as disposable as a lighter? Good for a few thousand flicks, then discard it for the promise of a bright new spark? After seeing the ease with which Richard and Stan could walk away from their wives with zero interest in rekindling the flame, Mindy felt guilty for not reminding Artie she was grateful he was such a devoted husband and father (even if their future was going up in smoke).

As soon as Stan's limo pulled away, she ran to her car to call him, thereby preventing Edna and the others from listening in as they always did. Unfortunately, Artie's phone went right to voice mail:

Hey it's me. Just wanted to say I love you, you're the best, and we'll get through this together. Also, it's not exactly cheeseburgers in paradise here either. Your dad is on his way to Florida and your mom is freaking. Oh, and Stacie became a woman this morning, but trust me, it wasn't as much fun as watching her take her first steps. Call me. Love you. Bye.

Mindy looked at the time to try to figure out where he might be this early in the morning. Aaron's school perhaps? Planned Parenthood? She'd wait another few minutes in case he got back to her and meanwhile, maybe she'd call Dana to fill her in. Not that she was easily reachable. On weekdays she was either at the gym, tending to her herb garden, or crusading for wind energy.

Even if they did speak, Dana would likely claim to have no interest in her in-laws' marital problems, unless, of course, it resulted in them deciding to sell their Great Neck estate and disposing of their valuable antiques, which the family knew she'd had her eye on for years.

In fact, just the thought of hearing Dana's whiny voice made Mindy reach for the Coffee Nips she kept hidden in a seat pocket. Nothing better than passing the time with her good friend Mr. Sugar.

She closed her eyes, letting her mind go into a random free fall, and what came to mind were conversations she'd had with her father about historic figures who weren't all that honorable. How he loved to snitch on famous people who were known for their great achievements, but whose private lives were tainted with scandal.

One story she never forgot was about Albert Einstein, a habitual philanderer who had an affair with his cousin Elsa, then married her and began an adulterous affair with his best friend's niece. Was this the real basis of his theory of relativity? Was Mindy thinking about this because of the events of the past few days? *Duh*, as her kids would say.

She was about to head back inside when she spotted a familiar car pull into the parking lot. Not that there weren't a lot of people who drove silver Infinitys. But only one would have the vanity plate, RHODAROUND.

Rhoda was not expecting to see Mindy jump out of her car and clutched her bag to her bosom. "Oh, for God's sake! I thought you were a mugger!"

"Sorry. I was just about to go back in . . . Don't you have a lunch date and a root canal?"

"I canceled them. What were you doing outside?"

"Trying to reach Artie. I didn't want everyone listening in. Why are you here?"

"What? Now I need an engraved invitation to come by my husband's office?"

"Rhoda, Stan already left."

"Good. I don't want to see the son of a bitch. I'm here to get all the family photos. I'll be damned if his patients are going to think, how nice, he's such a wonderful family man!"

"Thank God. I thought maybe you were planning to take the books to show a lawyer."

"What if I was? According to her, it's still marital property."

"You already spoke to an attorney?"

"The best of the best!" She waved her finger. "My cousin Doris's neighbor Adelle used this crazy broad in the city and got the whole kit and caboodle right down to the dog!"

"Hold on. Hold on. Dad had one little silly encounter. Aren't you overreacting?"

"Who's overreacting? Am I the one running down to Florida like a little Romeo?"

"I'm not defending him, but the two of you really need to talk. Maybe just listen to what he wants."

"Me listen to him? Oh no. No, no. He's gonna listen to what I want! How about a little respect, a little understanding— AND—the biggest goddamn apology of his life?"

"Did you ever think that maybe that's what he wants, too?"

"What do I have to apologize for? I didn't do anything wrong.... And you have some nerve butting in like this. How about if I want your opinion, I'll ask for it!"

Mindy gulped. After years of seesawing between ignoring Rhoda and killing herself to receive the tiniest praise, she had never interfered with her mother-in-law's handling of her affairs, as she'd made it clear that the only ones permitted to speak this candidly were her sons, and only if they chose their words carefully.

But now as she studied Rhoda's once regal frame, a countess embodied by rings the size of golf balls, she wasn't feeling intimidated. This wasn't the tough-talking it's-my-way-or-the-highway matriarch, but a vanquished wife whose dark roots revealed grays of sadness under the bright morning sun; an aging wife whose small, sunken eyes were shadows of confusion.

And how odd. It was the second time this week she felt sympathy for a woman for whom she'd previously felt nothing but contempt. But in spite of the reprimand, Mindy would be nice.

"Look, I'm sorry if I'm overstepping my bounds, but I am still family to you and—oh, hold on." She looked at her cell. "Oh, thank God, it's Artie. You go in and tell the girls that everything is fine and I'll tell him what's going on to see what he thinks."

To Mindy's surprise, Rhoda nodded her approval. To her son she would listen.

"Where are you?" Mindy didn't even say hello. "What did you find out? I was up all last night worrying about this baby, and then I must have fallen asleep and had this dream that you bought a house in Portland without asking, you didn't do that, did you? And then you wouldn't believe what's going on with Beth and Richard and your parents. I told your mom I'd ask your advice about—"

"Stop. One thing at a time. No wonder your computer always freezes. Let's take it from the top. Rainbow is six weeks pregnant, but she told Aaron he's not the father."

"Oh, thank God."

"Yeah, it's like I thought. It's that guy John's, but then it's like you said, too. Aaron *wanted* it to be his. He actually accused Rainbow of lying because he's only seventeen, but no matter what, he plans to help support her."

"Support her how? With rebate offers?"

"I don't know . . . he's a mess. He was sobbing in my arms last night because he wanted to be the father and I'm standing there thinking, what is wrong with him? He has no education, no home, no means of earning a living. I wouldn't have wanted to be dealing with this at his age."

"Yes, but think about it. You didn't just lose your mother. Maybe all this emotion about the baby has nothing to do with the baby. Maybe it's a delayed reaction to losing the only family he knew. How he could he not be a mess inside? His parents are dead, his uncle is dead. . . . Other than you, he has no one to call family. No wonder he wants one of his own."

"Wow, that psych degree comes in handy every once in a while."

"Not that it ever solves anything . . . When are you coming back?"

"That's why I called. We caught a flight this morning and are on a layover now. We land at LaGaurdia at two."

"Wait. You got Aaron to come back with you?"

"You'd be very proud of me. I told him that if he was going to be a father, the first thing he had to learn was how to be loving but firm."

"Impressive . . . You ought to try that at home. Anyway, don't hang up yet. I have to fill you in on your parents."

"No, please. I've got enough on my plate, and you're better at this stuff than me anyway. Whatever you do is fine."

"Really? It's okay to tell your mom to hire that divorce attorney she saw?"

"Oh, jeez. She met with a divorce attorney? No, of course, don't let her do that. Do you want her walking off with half of our inheritance, also called your retirement fund?"

"No."

"Then you must stop her or smite her."

"Smite her?" Mindy giggled. "Should I run over to Target to see what's new in the sword department?"

* * *

Real time was one of those modern day terms that had taken on multiple meanings, the most important of which was that it reminded us to live in the moment. Forget harboring old resentments or dreaming of tomorrow's redemption. Nothing was better than seizing the day.

In that spirit of here and now, Mindy ended her call with Artie and told Rhoda to come back outside. "I just had an idea and I want you to hear me out before you say no. Artie and Aaron are on their way back from Portland. I'm going to have to pick them up at two, so what if we drive back to your house first, I'll book you a flight, you pack a bag, and then come with me to the airport so you can fly to Florida, too."

"Me go to Florida? I can't do that. My hair needs a wash and blow."

Clean or dirty, your beehive always looks the same. "You look fine."

Rhoda stared. This was crazy talk. She was a sixty-seven-year-old grandmother who did not jump on planes, let alone to go plead with a husband who was acting like an ass. "Nothing doing! Rhoda Sherman does not chase men!"

"Look. I know you're a very proud person," Mindy said, "but so is Stan. Maybe that's why he paid attention to that other woman. It was just nice to hear someone say, 'you're a sweet, interesting man. I like you.'"

Rhoda's lip curled. She was livid but listening.

"That's why you need to be there. Not to show him who's boss, to show him you care."

"Go down to Florida. Today?"

"Yes."

"But I don't have a reservation. And have you seen the fares lately? Ridiculous!"

"Who cares? You've probably got more money in the bottom of that big pocketbook than I have in my checkbook. And did

Dad give a damn about the fares when he booked his flight?"

"I don't know . . ." She looked like she wanted to smoke. "What am I? A crazy teenager?"

"No, but it could be fun acting like one."

"You call fun going on a wild goose chase? And where would I stay? How would I get from the airport . . . it's too much for me! I like to plan everything nice and neat."

"Fine. Then sit home and wonder what he's doing, where he is, who he's with . . ."

Rhoda shifted.

"What if I call my mom? I'm sure she and Aunt Toby would pick you up and you could even stay at her place."

"But what if . . . ," Rhoda practically whispered, "what if he doesn't want to see me?"

"Are you kidding? He'll be thrilled to see you. He forgot his blood pressure pills. Oh, hold on, it's Stacie. That can't be good!"

It hadn't started out as a day like any other, so it was only fitting that it get more screwy by the hour. Though Mindy hadn't worked in two weeks, her job would have to wait. She went back into the office for her things and told the girls to hold down the fort and pray.

First stop was picking up a miserable Stacie at school so that she could roll up in a ball and die in the comfort of her own home, only there was no time to drop her off, she was going to have to make the jaunt to Nana's house and then the airport, where Mindy would drop off her miserable mother-in-law and retrieve her miserable husband and his miserable son.

By the time Mindy and Stacie were hauling Rhoda's bags from the parking lot to the terminal, she had the woman's undivided attention.

"You'll call his cell when you get down there and tell him you made a dinner reservation for the two of you."

"But I don't know the restaurants he likes. He takes care of those things."

"Fine. Then call and ask where he'd like to go."

"That's ridiculous. He's my husband, not a date."

"Rhoda! Yes he is your date!"

"I don't like that idea. I'm gonna give him Toby's address and tell him he'd better get his big, fat *tuckus* over there right now."

"Nana! Oh my God! That's so dumb." Stacie had forgotten about her cramps now that she was on an adventure. "That's not how you get a boy to like you. You gotta be nice and let him do all the talking and pretend like he's interesting."

"Glad to hear nothing's changed since junior high," Mindy said as she was about to walk inside the terminal.

"Mindy!" A man yelled. "Mindy Sherman!"

"Mommy . . . over there." Stacie pointed to the cab stand. "It's Jess's dad."

"Richard?" Mindy stopped so short, Rhoda nearly rear-ended her.

"Oh, thank God!" He hugged her. "It's like a miracle that you're here. Please tell me you're just dropping off, not heading out."

"Actually we're here for lots of reasons. Wait, were you on the same flight as Artie?"

"Artie? No . . . He's coming back today, too?"

"Yes. Rhoda, this is our next-door neighbor Richard, *an even worse husband than yours*. Richard, meet Artie's mother, Rhoda . . . we're dropping her off and then waiting because . . ." she looked at her watch, "Artie and Aaron are landing in a few minutes."

"Oh, fantastic. I swear I didn't know what I was going to do. I must have left my wallet in one of the bins at security and didn't realize it until I got on the plane. I have no money on me, no credit cards, Beth didn't pick up her phone, big surprise there. I was going to have to see if I could negotiate with one of the cabbies to take me to the city and borrow some cash from someone at my office, but this is perfect. I'll go home with you now. You have room, right?"

"Oh. Sure. Yeah. Of course. That's what minivans are for. We just have to go check Rhoda in and then head back down to baggage claim to meet Artie and Aaron."

"Great. This is great!" He hugged her again. "You keep saving the day, Mindy. I don't know how I am ever going to repay you."

Stop being such an asshole? "We'll talk. I have a few ideas."

Rhoda was not happy to have rushed her kishkes out only to discover her flight was running late. "It's a sign I shouldn't go," she quipped.

"No, it's a sign there's a storm down south." Mindy studied the big board. "Actually, this works out great because now at least you can see the guys before you go."

"What for? We just spent a week together and maybe I don't want to see anyone 'cause this is embarrassing for me. Me chasing my husband like we're Blondie and Dagwood."

"You have no reason to be embarrassed." Mindy checked the board again. "Hey wait. According to this, their flight is coming in a few minutes early. Let's everyone go down to baggage claim."

"No," the group said. Stacie needed to use the ladies' room, Rhoda wanted to buy a book, and Richard wanted to head over to customer service to report his wallet missing. Maybe he'd luck out and they'd tell him they'd found it and it was coming in on the next flight.

At last they were assembled, just in time to greet Artie and Aaron, who couldn't have looked more confused. Artie had no clue why he was being met by his wife, his daughter, his mother, and his next-door neighbor. And Aaron, who was bewildered enough, kept his eye on the baggage carousel, as if he might hop on and head back to the hangar.

Mindy hugged them both, promising that the situation was

easily explainable and that if Aaron had been worried that he was going to miss a crazy family life, he had nothing to fear.

Minutes later, they all wished Rhoda good luck, waving as she rode the escalator to the gate, stoic like Nurse Nightingale, en route to mend a once healthy marriage that had deteriorated from neglect.

"Did she take her cell phone?" Artie asked as they waited for the bags to come out.

"Nope." Mindy watched Stacie and Aaron ignoring one another. "It's still charging."

"She's had it for two months already."

"Yep. Still charging."

"Are you sure this was such a good idea?"

"Getting her a cell phone or sending her to Florida?"

Next leg of the journey was heading to the car. Until *bashert*, the hand of God, joined the party, twisting circumstances like pretzels. "Papa!" Stacie ran off, just as they were crossing from the terminal into the walkway.

"What the hell?" Mindy tried to follow her daughter's youthful sprint, but it was as if the Red Sea stopped parting. There were so many travelers and bags in the way, she lost sight of her.

"Did she just see my dad?" Artie asked. "I thought you said he left already."

"I thought he did," Mindy started to sweat. "He should be in the air by now."

"Unless the poor kid's hallucinating from all the blood loss."

Mindy didn't even know how to respond. "Richard, you're a lot taller. Can you see her?"

"Think so." He stood on his toes. "She's wearing a yellow sweatshirt and jeans?"

"Yes!" Mindy said.

"Yeah. I see her. She's with an older man."

"Oh my God." Mindy felt faint. "I don't understand . . . What should we do? Rhoda's probably at the gate already."

"We?" Artie started to sweat. "I think we have to have her paged, 'cause if she gets on that plane and then finds out he never left—"

"I know, I know . . . don't even say it. Okay, you guys wait here and I'll run in."

"Well hold on," Richard said. "Looks like Stacie's heading over here."

"You guys are absofuckingfreakin' crazy," Aaron said, then yawned.

"What the hell is everyone doing here?" Stan stared at Mindy. "Why aren't you at work?"

"Dad, we'll explain later. She was just trying to help out." Artie backed away. "Jeez. How much did you drink?"

"Nothing. One or two beers." He started to sway.

"Oh, man." Aaron laughed. "The old guy's toast."

"Young man, I'm fine. . . . Has anyone told me what the hell you're all doing here?"

"You go first." Mindy's heart pounded. "What happened to your flight?"

"Didn't get on it." He shrugged. "It was delayed coming in from Atlanta, so I stopped at the bar . . . had a few beers . . . guess I forgot to go back to the gate."

"You forgot or you changed your mind?" Artie asked. "'Cause guess who's upstairs waiting to get on a flight right now to meet you in Florida?"

"No." He blinked and swayed. "Rhoda? What'd she do that for?"

"Because Mindy told her it was a good idea."

"Okay!" Mindy yelled. "I get the point. This is all my fault. . . . Let me go get her."

"Then give me the keys and the parking stub," Artie said.

"We'll get the car, maybe get Diamond Jim Brady over here some coffee. Just call us when you have her."

"Good idea. Here." She was fumbling for her keys when her cell rang.

"Hey, girlfriend! You are never going to believe who we just ran into."

"Nadine, hold on. I have to call you back. I'm in the middle of a crisis here. I'm at LaGuardia and have to go find Rhoda before she gets on a plane to Florida, or my ass is grass."

"Oh my God, that's so funny. That's who we just bumped into."

"Wait? What? Where are you?"

"LaGuardia. We just landed. We went standby from Indianapolis early and—"

"Nadine! Stop! Do you know where Rhoda is?"

"Yeah, she's at the gate. That's what I'm trying to tell you. We were walking off the plane and I heard this woman screaming at the counter lady about her seat and I said to Peter, 'wow, that sounds just like Artie's mom . . . you know that loud, annoying bark . . . and I turn around and there she is. So we go over to say hi, but she didn't seem interested in talking to us . . . not that she ever does."

"Oh my God . . . I don't believe this. Are you still in the terminal?"

"Yeah. Why."

"Because you are about to be knighted. Go back to the gate and get her. She can't get on that plane."

"What's going on?" Artie asked.

"I'll tell you in a sec– do you read me, Nadine? Run. Go get Rhoda. Tell her that Stan is downstairs with us . . . he never left."

"What if she already boarded?"

"Nadine! Just go get her. Pretend it's an episode of *24*! The clock is ticking . . ."

"Okay, okay. Peter . . . wait up . . . we have to go back and get Rhoda.. there was some kind of mix-up . . ."

"Wait, wait," Mindy said. "Is your car here?"

"Yeah."

"Perfect, because I've got me, Artie, Aaron, Stacie, Stan, Richard, and hopefully Rhoda, plus all their luggage. It's gonna be tight."

"Oh, that's so cute," Nadine laughed. "We'll have our own little car pool. Beth will be so jealous."

"Oh my God. Beth . . . the car pool . . . I told her I would get the kids from school today. If I switch with her one more time, I won't get my merit badge!"

Seventeen

It was fine with Mindy that Rhoda refused to speak to her when she got in the car, though Mindy did have one regret. Just when she thought they were bonding, she had to hear little quips from the backseat about meshuggeners who liked spending other people's money on outrageous airfares with no refund policies. Stan, too, gave her the silent treatment as he was unhappy she'd abandoned her post at the office, though in his buzzed condition, and having played with the notion of playing around, who was he to grumble about being irresponsible?

But the real source of their mutual anger stemmed from having to be questioned by the Port Authority Police and their not-so-friendly dogs after they tried retrieving their luggage. Seems their travel plans had raised suspicion, as they had both made last-minute reservations on Delta, both checked two bags, then checked in for their flights an hour apart but never boarded.

"Come on. Do we look like terrorists?" Stan began his appeal. "I'm a Jewish doctor and my wife is a grandmother of five." But when that didn't fly, he appealed to their personal experience with marital spats. "We had a little argument. I was running down to Florida to shoot some golf. Then my idiot daughter-in-law suggested to my wife that she go down, too, so we could try to patch things up."

It was a believable story, but not convincing enough to get them off the post–9/11 hook. They were both banned from flying for thirty days until their backgrounds and alibis could be verified, which meant they would have to drive or take the train to Florida to make their good friend Alan Gordon's surprise birthday at the end of the month. But good news, at least Stan and Rhoda were talking again. First order of business? Removing Mindy from their wills.

"C'mon." Artie unpacked his suitcase, sniffing his T-shirts to see if any could pass the smell test. "You've got to admit this was one of your stupider ideas."

"It was not stupid—here, just give me those; I'm doing a load of whites next— if he'd have gotten on the plane like he was supposed to, everything would have been fine."

"No, because if he'd gotten on that plane and my mother found him with that woman, it would have been a great day to be a defense lawyer!"

"Fine. You want me to say it was a stupid plan? It was a stupid plan." Mindy took more clothes out of the hamper. "But at least they're speaking again. That's an improvement."

"Not usually. I'm just grateful that Stacie was with you and spotted my dad. Otherwise he might still be stumbling around the airport while my mother was searching the bars in Boca."

"True . . . But you know what I do feel bad about?"

"That you didn't get a picture of my mom's face when she saw my dad in the car?"

"Actually that was funny. She was trying so hard not to laugh.

No, what I'm sorry about was all the craziness when Aaron arrived. . . . I wanted things to go smoothly. Poor kid has been through so much."

"Tell me about it. When I got to the house, he was so freaked out about me taking him back here I was almost ready to let him stay and fend for himself."

"Why?"

"Because it's been a shitty life for him, but it's still the only one he knows. I just had visions of him sitting in his room here, counting the days until he turned eighteen and could declare free agency."

"Yeah, but what kind of life would he have without any parents around? He deserves stability and home-cooked meals."

"Me, too. Where do I sign? But then I realized, what the hell difference does it make where he lives? He'll be miserable no matter what. And Davida's house was so disgusting, I couldn't decide between putting it up for sale or setting it on fire, and that was before going over to Wayne's place, which was filthy and had this cat smell that I swear will haunt me forever. Not to mention that they shut the power off."

"Oh my God." Mindy sat on their bed. "So wait . . . we can sell Davida's house?"

"You know the saying, when our ship comes in, with our luck we'll be at the airport?"

"We can't sell it."

"Well, because Aaron is still a minor, once we became his legal guardians we could. But I found out it could go into foreclosure soon. Apparently she owed back taxes, and she had all these legal bills from when she got arrested."

"Davida Findley?" Mindy sighed. "Never heard of her."

"Exactly, 'cause believe me, I also thought if the house was worth something, that's how we'd pay for his college. I swear I don't know what they were living on. She had no job, no insurance . . . looked like her only source of income was selling quilts, drugs, and brownies."

"Or drugs *with* brownies . . . makes you appreciate how lucky we are."

"No kidding." Artie handed her more dirty clothes. "We feel sorry for ourselves because we can't take a vacation every year. Aaron can't remember the last new pair of sneakers he got."

"It's amazing he's even semi-normal."

"No, it's amazing he's not a drug addict like every adult around him. We're going to have to get him tons of therapy."

"You think he'll go?" Mindy asked.

"We're not going to give him a choice. He told me he's been drinking and getting high since he was ten."

"Okay, now you're scaring me. What if he tries bringing drugs into the house?"

"That's the crazy thing. I think if he found out that Stacie was experimenting, he'd kick her ass."

"I can see that. And I would have to agree with you about him seeming responsible. On the cruise he was so protective of the kids . . . and I know they like him. When I told Jamie and Ricky he was back, they flew downstairs to say hi. They were so happy."

"You just made my day," Artie smiled. "Anyway, the other reason I wanted him here was, last night at the motel we were up all night talking about my business problems."

"Oh? He's a consultant?"

"No, but he has zero interest in sports and it beats talking about his future. Turns out when I told him how bad the store was doing because of the brands we have to carry, next thing I know we're online looking at the Eye-Deals Web site and he's making these awful faces like who the hell would wear that stuff and I'm like, that's the problem. So he says to me, well can you sell other things, and I go no, there are strict licensing agreements, so then he says, what if I created a Web site for you and you could sell whatever cool glasses you wanted?"

"That would be incredible . . . can you do that?"

"Why not? We'd be doing business under a different name. In fact, he even came up with one already . . . he said we should call it Outasight! Is that great or what?"

"Oh my God, I love it!" Mindy clapped. "It's so clever."

"Yeah. This kid is so smart, Mindy." Artie's eyes welled. "You had to hear him going on and on about the ways things are sold on the Internet today and how you use key words and this thing called search engine optimization to build traffic to your site, and I'm sitting there pretending I know what the hell he's talking about. That's when I said to him we're going to do this business together. Father and son. And he was like, yeah, great."

"You really think it could make money?"

"Are you kidding? The way things are going at the store we'd make more from a Web site. There's no overhead, no payroll—"

"If you build it, they will come?"

"Yep."

"Mommm!!!" Stacie yelled from the basement. "The bee-ach just IM'd me and wants to know when you're going online. She's gotta talk to you."

"Why does she keep calling Beth that?" Artie sighed.

"Okay! Tell her in a few minutes," Mindy hollered back. "Because she's still pissed at her for that night she came over here and screamed at her. Frankly, I'm not sure I've forgiven her either."

Mindy went to check on the kids, who were camped out with Aaron in the guest room. Never intended for large gatherings, let alone a teenager who'd hooked up his father's guitars and amps, the room was so small they had to crowd on the floor to listen to him play.

But rather than be in the moment, all she could do was survey the dismal decor. The cheap, we'll-get-rid-of-it-in-a-year bedroom set, a relic from their newlywed days; the shag carpet, a temporary fix after a flood; and bookshelves lined with Beanie Babies that a naive Mindy had been so sure would be worth thousands, as she had six of the original nine, including the coveted Brownie the Bear and Flash the Dolphin. "When they retire, we retire," she would tell Artie, eventually concluding that the only one getting rich off them was their creator.

"Don't worry," Artie came from behind and whispered, "we'll figure something out to make the room look nice."

"Doubt it. Not even *Extreme Makeover* could help."

"C'mon. Don't have a bad attitude."

"You're right. I'll think positive like in that book *The Secret*. I'll close my eyes and visualize a master bedroom suite and a check for fifty grand for those extra added touches."

"Is it too late to recall your old attitude?"

"Oh, come on. Visualization worked great on *Oprah*."

"Everything works great on *Oprah*."

Well, not everything.

When Mindy finally got to read Beth's e-mail, she learned that the advice she'd dispensed after watching Oprah's show on lying-cheating spouses was apparently not the right prescription for everyone. In fact, at the Diamond house, the message was swallowed like a bitter pill, resulting in side effects that did not vary.

Mindy felt terrible. The pretty doctor with the pretty new book had been so convincing when she said that her combination tough love—tough luck strategy was a proven way to "keep wild horses in the stable." The key was forcing the untrustworthy spouse to sign over their rights to the house and other marital assets if they ever disappointed again.

But when Beth threatened Richard via e-mail with this as-seen-on-TV plan, it didn't work as advertised. He name-dropped his father's divorce attorney, who was famous for keeping wealthy husbands happy.

The instant Mindy went online, Beth IM'd her.

> diamondgirl (9:07 p.m.): got any other brilliant ideas???
>
> mindymom3 (9:08 p.m.): sorry . . . it sounded like a sure thing . . . money talks
>
> diamondgirl (9:08 p.m.) : well money may talk but we're not . . . maybe you should stop playing therapist without a license
>
> mindymom3 (9:09 p.m.): im sorry . . . does it seem totally hopeless??
>
> diamondgirl (9:10 p.m.): pretty much . . . he said he rented an apartment near Nike's headquarters and he's happier than he's ever been . . . what would Oprah say about that???
>
> mindymom3 (9:10 p.m.) call dr. phil?

You try to be nice, Mindy thought when she signed off. All she did was make some well-meaning suggestions, just like she did with Rhoda, although that was a bust, too. So maybe Beth was right. She should get out of the advice business and stick to what she knew. How to remove blood stains from clothes (contact lens solution), take the itch out of bug bites (toothpaste or Preparation H), and treat kitchen burns (soak in egg whites).

* * *

Mindy didn't know where she was finding her nerve, but when Stan called the house early the next morning to say that he and Rhoda had decided to spend a few days at their country home in the Berkshires, she told him that she would be taking the week off, too.

"What has one thing got to do with other?" He coughed in her ear.

"Oh, come on. Be reasonable. If you're not seeing patients, why do you need a receptionist to open and close that little sliding window all day?"

To her surprise he didn't argue. Either he was learning he couldn't win or he secretly agreed that with Aaron's arrival, it was more important that she be home.

"But I'm real glad to hear you and Mom are talking again," Mindy said.

"Yeah, about what a busybody you are. Tell Arthur to give me a call tonight. I have to speak to him about an important matter."

"Okay. Wanna give me a heads-up?"

"If I wanted to give you a heads-up, wouldn't I say, oh good, it's Mindy, I have something to discuss with you."

"Do you really not like me that much?"

"Who said anything about not liking you?"

"So you speak this way to your friends?"

"Who said I had friends?"

Before their first baby is born, prospective parents can choose from an array of books, DVDs, and classes to help prepare for the blessed event and the challenging years to follow.

Before their first baby is born, eager parents are showered with gifts. Lots and lots of gifts, so that their precious newborn can ease through every stage in comfort.

Before their first baby is born, anxious parents can look to experienced family and friends for guidance and support so that they never feel alone in their quest to make the best decisions.

But when your first born is seventeen and literally falls into your life by a stork named Shitty Circumstances, there are no educational materials to show you the ropes, no baby showers to help offset the endless expenses, and certainly not many people to whom you can turn for advice, because really, how many parents could say they'd had a similar experience?

As Mindy lingered at the kitchen table, she worried how they would adjust. It was one thing when Aaron was a visitor, quite another to now have to think about the high cost of supporting him. He might well be the only teen on Long Island who didn't own the bare essentials: a cell phone, mp3, or laptop, let alone the quintessential must-have for the just-passed-my-road-test crowd, his own car.

Mindy was familiar with the lore of the student parking lot at their high school, a stokin', smokin' assemblage of Hummers, Beamers, and Benzs, while the teachers' lot was home to the usual assortment of age-ripened Camrys and spiritless minivans.

So it would take Aaron what? The first two periods of school to realize that his value had fully depreciated without these peer-worshiped possessions? It meant she had no choice. Right after registering him at the district office, they would head to the mall and run up the secret credit card she'd kept for emergencies. She just couldn't bear the thought of him walking the halls feeling like the Pauper from Portland.

And what were the rules of the house? Mindy considered herself fairly open-minded, but that's only because her children were still at the stages where they did nothing that wasn't doctor recommended or parent approved. The only cardinal sins were lying and text messaging at dinner. But Aaron was different—

more like a feral Mustang who was free to roam and difficult to domesticate. How could she restrict him now when all he knew was fight or flight?

By the time he awoke, Mindy had written a contract stating his duties at home and standards for acceptable behavior. He looked at it and laughed.

"This is a joke to you?"

"Best one of the day." He pounded the table.

"It's only nine thirty."

"Sorry." He tried wiping the smirk off. "Hold on . . . I gotta show you something."

Aaron returned with a motel notepad and waited for Mindy's reaction when she realized that Artie had written something almost identical and made Aaron initial each rule, starting with "Thou shalt not take money from desk drawers" to "you break curfew you break my heart."

"Oh my God!" Mindy laughed. "We are such nerds."

"Totally."

A knock at the back door startled them, and in walked Beth, loaded down with shopping bags. "Hi, I'm Beth." She shook Aaron's hand. "Remember me? The bitch next door?"

"Hey," he said, unsure whether to stare at the bags or Beth. Both were alluring in different ways and his interest in either made him blush.

"So we're talking again?" Mindy quipped.

"What choice do I have? I have no friends and you always have the good cookies from Trader Joes. Aaron, I thought you might like some of these things. My husband's ad agency works for Nike and they keep sending him all this stuff. Any chance you're a size eleven sneaker?"

"Maybe," he eyed the bags as if they held gold. "Not sure."

"Oh my God." Mindy peeked at the loads of merchandise. "It's his baby shower."

Aaron glared. Was she making a joke about Rainbow?

"Relax," she said. "I was just thinking how you were going to need so many things, and it would be great if my friends threw you a little welcome party. This is even better!"

"Knock yourself out." Beth handed him the bags. "Take it all for all I care."

"Thanks." He looked as if he might cry as he pulled out sneakers, T-shirts, and jackets.

"Best part is, it's a little taste of home." Beth smiled. "Although you probably had a ton of Nike stuff already."

"Not really." He unlaced a pair of sneakers that cost more than his entire wardrobe.

"This was so sweet of you." Mindy hugged her. "I can't thank you enough."

"No big deal . . . It was just stuff that was sitting around the basement."

But Mindy didn't buy the nonchalant response. From the way Beth was beaming, she knew she'd made Aaron's day.

"How do I look?" He wore a different sneaker on each foot, shorts over sweats, and a baseball cap with Tiger Woods's name on it.

"Like an athlete who just got a big endorsement deal," Mindy teased.

"Oy," he tried to check out his reflection in the window. "I was goin' for the pretty boy from Long Island look."

"Sorry." Beth shrugged. "For that you need to wear Polo and drive an X5."

"What's that?" he posed like a model.

"Oh, man," Beth looked at Mindy. "He's going to get one hell of an education here."

Maybe there was something to be said for the power of positive thinking, for just as they were admiring Cinderfella's new wardrobe, Artie called from the store. "Get down here right away," he said. "And bring Aaron."

"Why?" Mindy asked. "Is everything okay?"

"I'll tell you when you get here."

"Well, can you give me a hint? Is it good news?"

"Don't know yet."

"I hate when you do this. What's going on?"

"All I'll say is that I just got a fax and you have to read it to believe it."

Eighteen

Unlike need-for-speed Beth, Mindy was a cautious, courteous driver who never took out her aggression on other motorists, unless, of course, they started it first. Most often it was men in trucks cutting her off who caused her to curse, but not before telling the kids to cover their ears.

They never did, however, because what was funnier than listening to your mother power down her window and shout, "YoustupidmotherfuckersonofabitchpieceofshitIhopeyoudie"? But en route to the store in nearby Seaford, it was Mindy who could have been pulled over.

Nadine would have laughed had she heard that good-citizen Mindy had just blown past Lakeside Elementary, since Mindy was the one who had worked so hard to get the county to put up one of those electronic "your speed is" signs along Babylon Turnpike. This, in spite of the fact she secretly feared a malfunction. What if one day it inadvertently posted her weight instead?

"Do not ever drive like this," Mindy said to Aaron, who gripped the armrest. "I am merely demonstrating what you are not permitted to do."

"Cool."

"And take the tags off your clothes so people don't think you just robbed Sports Authority. When we get home I'll give you a card so you can send a thank-you to Beth and Richard. When is the last time you went to the doctor or a dentist. Remind me to make you appointments when we get home. Any interest in a haircut?"

"What is up with you, woman?" He ripped a tag off his cap. "You've gone psycho."

"Sorry. Artie's phone call got me crazy. I think it's good news, but he's hard to read."

"Well if it's bad news, why are ya drivin' so fast?"

"Good point." She laughed, though it didn't slow her down. In fact, by the time they got to the store, they were both so pumped they raced inside only to find Artie fitting a customer.

"Hey. How are you?" He waved. Was this the same person who had just insisted they rush over?

"I have no idea what's going on," Mindy whispered to Aaron, "but it better be good because I didn't get to shower yet and we have a lot to do today." She tried signaling Artie to ask what the deal was.

"Be right with you," he said as if she were a customer.

"Hey, Mrs. Sherman." James, the manager breezed past. "Sorry, can't chat. Busy today."

"Apparently," she replied. "See the problem?" she said to Aaron. "Nobody here under the age of sixty. In fact, there's usually nobody here period."

Aaron nodded like a young management consultant who was there to observe. Finally, Artie finished, then ushered them into his office, where he closed his door and exhaled.

Mindy should have warned Aaron that Artie's office would be a tight squeeze not only because of the limited square footage but because he was both a slob and a saver. Boxes of contact lens solution ran into piles of sales brochures which spilled over onto eyeglass displays.

It killed her when he misplaced something, then claimed he never had it to begin with, or that he left it in a certain spot and somebody moved it, or it wasn't lost, just temporarily concealed, only to be discovered weeks later under back issues of *Contemporary Optometry*.

"Look on my desk," he told Mindy.

"Oh, yay! I love a good scavenger hunt."

"Stop . . . it's right on top . . . that's it. The fax. Your hand is on it."

Mindy immediately recognized Stan's scribbling, proof that illegible handwriting was the first test one had to pass in order to enter medical school. But having worked for him all these years she could make out the message and read it aloud:

> *Arthur, Gone to the country house with Mom. She thinks we might have taken out a life insurance policy on Davida. . . . All our old files are in the attic there. We'll let you know if we find anything. Dad*

"Oh my God!" Mindy's hand shook. "What does this mean?"

"Well for starters it means that they're talking again, which my dad may be sorry about 'cause it's a long ride to the Berkshires when my mom is in one of her crazy moods."

"True . . . but what about the fax? This is incredible news, right? Now we just have to hope that they find the policy and that it didn't lapse because they forgot to pay the premiums."

"Unless it was one of those policies that got paid automatically from an investment account and eventually the dividends paid the premium . . . then it could still be in force."

"Oh my God," Mindy squealed, "it's like winning the lottery!"

"Yo! People!" Aaron was air strumming a guitar. "What are you guys talkin' about?"

"Well, my friend," Artie slapped Aaron's shoulder, "we just found out there's a good chance we'll be coming into some money soon. Your grandparents are on the way up to their country house to see if they can find a life insurance policy they think they might have taken out for me on your mom. And if they did, and it's still active, wow! That would so save our asses!"

Aaron blinked. "You'd get money 'cause my mom died?"

"Life insurance is a great concept, right?" Artie beamed. "It leaves survivors tax-free cash so they're not hurt financially when they lose a family member. I'm telling you, Mindy, if this actually happens, I'm becoming a true believer in that thing you heard on Oprah."

"You mean visualization?"

"Yeah, visualization. Remember yesterday when you said you were imagining getting a check for fifty grand? It could be on its way!"

"Oh my God!" Mindy and Artie hugged. "We're saved!" She hugged Aaron.

"I was trying to think of a fun way to break the news to you." Artie grabbed jelly beans from the jar on his desk. "I even thought about running out to pick up those Hundred Thousand Dollar candy bars, but then we got busy here, and how often does that happen?"

"A hundred thousand dollars?" Mindy gulped. "You think it could be that much?"

"Who knows? My mom doesn't do anything small. The policy could even be for a half a million or a million."

"A million?" Mindy felt faint.

"Then again," Artie grabbed more jelly beans, "they could get all the way up there and not find the policy, or like you said, find it and then realize it lapsed. It's hard for my mother to remember what she did last week let alone seventeen years ago."

"It would be my money though, right?" Aaron's breathing got heavy. "'Cause she was my mom?"

"Oh. *Um.* Well, no. Not exactly." Artie straightened his back. "We'd have to wait and see how the policy was written if they find it at all. But most likely, my parents made me the beneficiary."

"What's that?"

"A beneficiary is the person who's listed on the policy to receive the benefits when a death claim is made. Most times it's in the spouse's name because they're the ones with all the financial responsibilities."

"But you weren't married no more and I'm still her son."

Artie and Mindy exchanged glances. The look on Aaron's face had gone from sunny to ice cold with a wind-chill factor of ten below zero.

"You know what?" Artie coughed. "We're really getting ahead of ourselves here. We don't know anything yet. There may not even be a policy. I guess it was dumb to say anything until we knew for sure. . . ."

"Your father is right," Mindy continued, "but it reminds me of when the lottery first started in New York, and we bought a bunch of tickets and talked all night about what we'd do if we won, then had this huge fight because we couldn't agree, remember?"

"Yeah. You wanted to buy your parents a place in Florida and I wanted to get a boat."

"Needless to say we learned our lesson about counting our chickens," Mindy laughed, "so let's stay cool. Even if in the best-case scenario there is a policy and we get the money, it doesn't mean we have to go out and spend it. We'd want to come up with a plan."

"Exactly," Artie said. "Remember Nadine and Peter told us about Lee Rosenberg, that financial planner in Jericho? They swear by him."

"Oh, yeah. Great idea," Mindy said, "We'd meet with him, tell him our goals, and listen to his advice. He could save us a lot of money on our taxes."

"Maybe we'd even have enough to get you a car. Wouldn't that be awesome?"

"I hate you!" Aaron clenched his fist. "I hate you both!"

"Why?" Artie stopped chewing. "What did we do?"

"You're acting all happy 'cause my mom died. You people are sick!"

"No. You're misunderstanding. We're not happy that she died, we're happy that maybe now we'd have a way to take care of you."

"But it's MY money!" Aaron grabbed Artie's car keys on his desk and ran out the back door. "It's MY money!"

They chased him, but Aaron was younger, thinner, and had the benefit of brand-new Nikes on his feet. What he didn't have was the knowledge of where his father's car was parked so that he had to dart through a crowded parking lot, narrowly missing an oncoming UPS truck.

"Aaron! Hold up!" Artie shouted. "I can't run as fast as you. Do you want me to have a heart attack trying?"

Welcome to Jewish guilt. Aaron stopped, allowing Artie and Mindy to catch up. But for Mindy it wasn't the shock of having sprinted in moccasins that startled her. It was the realization she was seeing double. Both father and son looked bewildered by the other's disrespect.

"We're sorry," she panted. "That was really inconsiderate of us. We weren't thinking." She glared at Artie as if to say, nice job, dumb ass.

"Look," Artie said, reading her loud and clear. "Of course you're confused. We really screwed that up."

"I'm not confused, man!" Aaron yelled. "I know when some-one's gettin' fucked, okay? My mom died and that money should be for me and Rainbow and the baby, and so I don't have to live with your crap decisions. You don't know what I need, so don't pretend you do. I run my own life!"

"Aaron, listen." Artie panicked. "I said the same things to my father, but you have to understand. If there is a policy, it's a legal document."

"So what? You think I'm too stupid to figure out what it says?"

"I'm not even sure I could figure out what it says. . . . No, I'm saying that if my name is listed as the beneficiary then that's that, but it doesn't mean that I win and you lose."

"*'I am not what you see, I don't answer to you, please understand what I mean, while it gives me a thrill, it's all I can do, you realize I do it all for you . . .'*"

"Stop singing, damn it!" Artie snapped. "I hate when you tune me out like that."

"It's called "Cheat Me" by Dogwood," Aaron spit out.

"I'm sure it's one of the finest songs ever written, but give me a break. I'm trying to make you understand."

"Then you're doin' a great job, 'cause I totally get what your deal is."

Artie exchanged glances with Mindy. The look said stop me from strangling the kid.

"Hey!" She whistled to get his attention. "You're in shock right now . . . so are we. But we're trying to tell you that if this thing happens, it's good for the whole family."

"You're sayin' that now, okay?" Aaron stammered. "But I know how this goes down. . . . It's like when my mom promised me a new TV. As soon as the welfare checks came, her and my dad would go to Wal-Mart and buy all this shit and tell me they'd get me my stuff the next time, but there never was a next time."

"Wait, hold on." Artie tried putting his arm around his boy.

"No fair comparing us . . . Mindy and I said from the start that we would do whatever it took to make sure you had all the same opportunities as our other kids. We'd get you into counseling, hire tutors, start looking at colleges—"

"Aaron, look at me," Mindy said. "Do you honestly believe that if we handed you a big check and said hey kid, good-bye and good luck, you'd be set for life?"

"Hell, yes! You give me my money and that's all the help I need."

"You say that now," Mindy shouted, "but you're seventeen and clueless, which is why God invented parents. And believe me, we get that you've been cheated out of a lot of things and that you're just trying to protect yourself, but that's not what's happening here. Your father wanted you to be the first to know about this possible windfall because he loves you and only wants the best for you. If he was really looking to cheat you, you would never have known any of this."

Aaron studied his new sneakers and kicked pebbles.

"You know what I was thinking?" Artie kicked pebbles, too. "I knew your mom pretty well and I'm sure she felt terrible that she could never give you the kind of life you deserved. But now look. Whether we get the money or not, for the first time you're going to have a chance for a real family life, a future with great opportunities. That was always her wish for you, Aaron. It was always our wish for you."

"I guess." Aaron's lip curved, more retreat than smile.

Artie grabbed his boy and gave him a hug. Maybe John Boy had returned to Walton Mountain after all.

If the police could give tickets for driving while distracted, Mindy would have been pulled over, for as she and Aaron headed to Target, she couldn't concentrate on the road. Not when she was thinking about receiving a lump sum of insurance money at the same time she was trying to read her text messages. "Don't ever drive while doing other things," Mindy said. "It's very dangerous."

"Hell, that's nothing," Aaron laughed. "You should try rollin' a joint while changin' a CD and gettin' a blow job!"

"Aaron!" she clutched the wheel. "A little respect, please."

But truth was, she was happier talking to him than reading Stacie's text messages complaining about her moron social studies teacher who wouldn't let her out of class so she missed being in the cast picture that was going to run in the paper.

Or listening to Nadine's freak-outs about how it would be another few weeks before Jonathan heard from Indiana, and he was still undecided about his safe school, but meanwhile for good luck, he was refusing to wear anything other than IU's school colors, red and white.

Finally, a call with good news. The unit coordinator at the nursing home informed Mindy that her grandmother's blood pressure had dropped enough for her to be released from the hospital, and now she was back at the home, where she had resumed her normal activities, including mistreating the orderlies and accusing other residents of stealing her magazines.

But it was the call she got while shopping that made her pull over, though it was only a cart, not a car.

"It's Beth? Where are you?"

"Target with Aaron . . . are you okay? You sound terrible."

"I am terrible . . . sick as a dog. Can you pick up something for me like Pepto?"

"Sure. Of course. What are your symptoms? Do you have a fever? Diarrhea?"

"No, nothing like that. I'm a little light-headed and I can't stop vomiting."

"Poor thing. It's all the stress from Richard, or maybe your stomach forgot how to digest junk food. Aaron, over here." She waved, studying the contents of his cart. "Did you leave any-thing for the other customers?"

"Cool store," he blushed.

"Oh, I know. Visa loves it, too. What is all this stuff?"

"Nothin' . . . some things for my room."

"A snowboard, a basketball . . . Damn! You inherited Artie dis-ease. Were they out of kayaks?"

"They have those? What aisle?"

"Never mind. . . . Just go put everything back that is not ab-solutely essential to your health and well-being and meet me at the check-out in ten minutes . . . sorry, Beth. Aaron is having a Target moment. . . . Where were we?"

"I was saying I must have the flu."

"Well for that you need rest, fluids—"

"And my boobs are killing me, too."

"Your boobs?" Mindy dropped a bag of Tootsie Rolls. "Are you sure it's the flu?"

"The flu, a virus, whatever. Just find something to put me out of my misery."

"A home pregnancy test?" Mindy could barely get the words out.

"Oh my God, bite your tongue, Mindy. I am NOT pregnant. How could you even say something so stupid? There is no way!"

"Sorry. It's just that other than the vomiting, it doesn't sound like the flu."

"Well, whatever. I'm not pregnant. . . . My mother does this to me, too. Always has to think the worst. Diarrhea means Crohn's disease. Depression is Lyme disease . . ."

"Fine. Besides, you'd know if your period was late."

"I'm hanging up if you don't get off this subject."

"Plus, I'm sure you guys use protection."

"Yes, it's called anger and resentment. And I'm also on the pill . . . when I remember."

"When you remember?" Mindy shrieked, forgetting she was in public. "This isn't like cleaning the fish tank. You have to keep up with it."

"Would you stop?" Beth yelled back. "You are getting me very nervous and upset now . . . I'm sure I had my period last month . . . pretty sure. But, whatever . . . I couldn't be pregnant now because my husband left me, I'm forty fucking years old, and I'm sure all my eggs have hatched."

"*Um,* apparently you let your subscription to *People* lapse. . . . Do you know how many celeb moms are over forty? That actress from *Desperate Housewives,* Marcia Cross? She was like forty-four when she had her baby. And what about Brooke Shields and Courtney Cox and that one from the show about the woman president, you know who I mean. . . ."

"Geena Davis?"

"Yeah, her. I love her . . . anyway, I think she was closer to fifty, so all I'm saying is, the eggs don't always know what time it is."

"You're insane. . . . I'm sure it's just a twenty-four-hour thing."

Or a twenty-four-year thing. "You sure you don't want me to pick up a home pregnancy test? Remember the other day when you said you were so hungry lately?"

Silence.

"Beth?"

"No. There's no need. I am NOT pregnant. . . ."

"Are you sure?"

"No."

Nineteen

Aaron had gone from being enraged in the morning to exultant an hour later, and Mindy knew to attribute this sudden change in cabin pressure to flying high at Target. Never before had he experienced the flow of oxygen to the brain from shopping, but there was no denying his joy when he picked out hair gel, body wash, and three funny T-shirts.

In fact, he was in such a good mood on the way to the district office, he was calm enough to start asking thoughtful, curious questions about school, and if he could maybe work for Artie at the store. It gave Mindy hope that this harrowing climb up Blended Family Mountain would not have to end in a free fall.

But not so fast. While filling out the school registration forms, Mindy discovered how quickly Target Man could turn into Brat Boy. It wasn't that he refused to answer questions about his GPA, his extracurricular activities, and if he was ever tested for scoliosis. It was that he chose to misbehave, like a puppy who peed on the rug in the hopes of discouraging a family from bringing him home.

At first when he tried juggling the clown figurines on Mrs. Cassidy's credenza, she winked at Mindy as if to say, it's fine, I understand he's nervous. But when he laughed at her family photos and did a handstand while singing Frank Zappa's "Weasels Ripped My Flesh," not even quick-on-her-feet Mindy could explain his errant antics.

Plus, with his transcript and medical records still in transit, Mrs. Cassidy said she had no choice but to sum up her observations with the trifecta of labels: OCD, ADD, and immature social skills. This left Mindy with no recourse when Mrs. Cassidy told her that Aaron would be starting school in a remedial program. "And make sure he's medicated before he arrives in the building."

"Weasels ripped my flesh?" Mindy wanted to fling him against the car but feared that someone in the office would catch her and add "abuse victim" to his file.

"She was a dirtbag." He waited for her to unlock the passenger side.

"A dirtbag? All she did was ask you about your previous high school. What did you think we were there to talk about? The death of acid rock? I can not believe you behaved like that!"

"I'm seventeen. Law says I don't have to be in school no more."

"No, no. The only law that pertains to you is the Sherman Law, and that states very clearly that you will not only finish high school and bust your ass to get good grades, you will sit for the Regents exams, you will take the SAT's, and you will go to college and lead a productive life. Do you want to end up selling Cutco knives the rest of your life and force us to hit up our friends every year so you can win free travel?"

"You don't even know me. Why are you buggin' out on me?"

"Buggin' out? That's what you think I'm doing? Oh, right. Because with three other kids, a job I hate, and a failing business,

I was short of things that pissed me off. You want to know why I'm so angry? It's because you blew the chance to show off how smart and capable you are. Now Mrs. Cassidy is thinking psych wards and Ritalin."

"*'We don't need no education . . . we don't need no thought control . . .'*"

"Don't you dare sing "Another Brick in the Wall"! This isn't funny, Aaron!"

"It's just school . . . Any chimp can get through it."

"Oh, really? Well let me tell you something about chimps, 'cause Jamie just finished a big project on primates and I happen to remember a thing or two."

"You talk too much, woman. Let's just go."

"Fine, but we're still going to talk about this." She unlocked the door but refused to turn on the ignition.

"This is madness!" Aaron air strummed his guitar.

"Tough! I'm just warming up. And for your information, chimpanzees have this amazing capacity for exhibiting social behaviors. They're sensitive to feelings, they help groom one another, and they'll even risk their lives to save a fellow chimp."

"Stop trying to be my mom, okay? 'Cause you're not . . . and don't mess with my life 'cause I already know what I'm gonna do with it."

"Oh. So that's the grand plan? Help Rainbow with the baby, then sit around and write music and wait for some big producer to call and say 'Hey, Aaron, you're the bomb. Have your people call my people'?"

"The bomb?" Aaron groaned. "You are too cool for me, but yeah, at least I'd be doin' somethin' that made me happy."

"And you think this the life your mom envisioned for you? To drop out of high school, write a few chords, and call it a day?"

"Don't talk shit about my mom!"

"I'm not. We're having a discussion. I'm just trying to get you to understand that you could have an amazing future doing all the things you love, but it has to start with a decent education."

"Whatever . . . Art told me you guys don't have enough money for college."

"We don't have enough money for most things, but it hasn't stopped us yet. . . . And who knows? We could end up with that life insurance money. If not, we'll take out student loans. But trust me, if you think college is expensive, wait until you see what it costs you not to go."

"School's bullshit."

"Some of it is, I agree. I've always said they should make the kids take classes on handling money and crises. And it kills me that they don't teach leadership skills or how to make the most out of your creativity. But that's the thing. It's not what you learn in the classroom that makes school so important, it's what you learn about yourself: the things you're good at, how to get along with different kinds of people. And if along the way you do study something you enjoy, or you read books that move you, you'll have things to write about forever. But if your music is only an expression of your very limited experiences, then your songs will reflect that and nobody will buy them."

"Nobody's gonna buy them anyway . . . music sucks now . . . people are buying crap."

"Sorry. I was voted most negative in my family. You do not get to take my place."

"I'm not negative. . . . I know the truth."

"Oh my God, you do sound like me. People always tell me I'm so negative, and I say no, I just tell it like it is. But you know what? Maybe I do have a bad attitude."

"Nothin' wrong with that. I need pizza."

"Really?" Mindy lit up. "You like it now?"

"I dream about it. . . . Back home the box tastes better than the pizza."

"Then you know what? You just gave me a great idea. I have to drop something off at Beth's, we'll go get lunch and then have a little adventure."

Some adventure! Any time Mindy sat in traffic on the Long Island Expressway, she either fantasized about shooting out everyone's tires or having a car that could fly. Anything not to have to focus on all the drivers who should be ticketed for EBD (everything but driving). Was it too much to ask fellow motorists, especially the ones on her tail, not to shave, send text messages, or read the paper?

Clearly this spur-of-the-moment jaunt to Queens was a bad idea, and that didn't even speak to what the return trip would be like in the middle of rush hour. Fortunately, her kids all had after-school activities, so she didn't have to play beat the clock. But no question, her time would have been better spent had they gone home so she could have caught up on the bills and thrown in some laundry.

What stopped her from ripping the steering wheel out of the dashboard was the hope that her father was watching from heaven, as they were en route to visit his mother at the Beth Hillel nursing home, and bringing her favorite food, Sicilian slices from La Piazza.

Although this trip was intended to alleviate Mindy's guilt over not having visited in weeks, she also thought it would be good for Aaron to meet a Holocaust survivor. Grandma Jenny was proof that although life could be brutal and unjust, one need not ever lose faith in God.

A great plan until she hit traffic. Not that Aaron noticed. Like a battle-fatigued toddler who could turn any car ride into siesta time, Mindy had to smile. Aaron's baby-smooth cheek was pressed to the window, gold streaks sunning his hair. He appeared so young and unencumbered, a boy for whom the light would still shine if he chose an illumined path.

Oh to have a navigation system that could lead you through life, she thought. To be able to hear the soothing voice of a nice lady telling you to take a left at the intersection of Not Sure and Totally Confused. Or to make a quick U-turn before crossing a line in the sand. Or mostly to watch for road signs that pointed to danger ahead.

How ironic that at this point in the journey, she spotted a familiar sign for Little Neck, home to the Denny's children's clothing store where she'd first met Artie. It was also Aaron's place of birth.

What did her father used to say when she'd try to tell him a story? "Mindeleh, I can't understand if you don't start from the start."

Two weeks after she returned to the University of Buffalo to begin her senior year, her father was diagnosed with colon cancer, and she could not fathom leaving her mother to bear the responsibility of caring for him. In less time than it took her to decide what to wear to a frat party, she made up her mind to move home and finish school at Queens College.

It was a tough transition, juggling classes and hospital visits while filling in for her mother at Denny's, the children's clothing store in Little Neck, where Helene had worked for years. With her husband sick, rather than leave her boss in the lurch, she asked Mindy to fill in.

Trouble was, Mindy hated the job, as it required waiting on whiny, manicured mothers who'd wheel German-engineered strollers that cost more than her car and who weren't fazed by dropping hundreds of dollars to outfit their kids while the little darlings tore through the store, delivering ear-shattering cries if Mommy dared to try to stop their fun.

But the dad shoppers were even worse, screaming at their kids to hurry up and pick out what they needed so that they could get back in time to watch the game. And God forbid they had to wait in line to pay. They would groan about the long wait, fully expecting that if a woman was ahead of them, it was understood that they step aside, as their time wasn't nearly as valuable.

So it was an unexpected surprise when one Sunday afternoon, Mindy was shadowed by a young father who cared very much about picking out the right winter jacket and pajamas for his two-year-old son, Aaron.

His name was Artie, and though he was obviously married with a child, Mindy thought a lot about his gracious smile, quick wit, and undeniable love for his boy. She hoped one day she would meet a man as special as he was.

A month later, with her father having recovered enough to return to his job at a midtown accounting firm, and her mother having thankfully returned to her job at the store, Mindy was free to focus on graduating. She knew that her bachelor's degree in psychology would mean nothing careerwise until she went for her master's, but she was too stressed to think about graduate school and decided instead to take a year off and take any job that paid well.

The first "any job" she applied for brought her to Forest Hills Ophthalmology and the office of a Dr. Stanley Sherman, who was trying to hire a new office manager. Though Mindy had had no previous experience, it did not matter to Dr. Sherman. He admitted to being desperate, as his wife, Rhoda, had just given him her two weeks' notice. "It's fine if I have to work another twenty years, but she should get to retire?"

Mindy had a bad feeling after speaking with the grouchy doctor by phone, but she decided to at least interview and find out his deal. On her way in, she recognized a young man leaving Dr. Sherman's office. It was the sweet dad with the little boy she'd helped at Denny's.

When he held the door and smiled, she shivered. But it wasn't from the cold, it was from the heat. She found him cute in a teddy bear way, yet stopped herself from saying hello. Not only was he a family man, she was back to dating Noah, her former high school sweetheart. And yet, only that morning she told her friend Nadine that he didn't do it for her anymore, since he'd become a kosher-vegetarian-psychic trying to make millions selling his homemade hummus.

"How's your little boy?" Mindy blurted.

"What?" he jumped, unprepared for a stranger to ask.

"Mindy Baumann." She shook his hand. "I used to work over at Denny's.... Didn't I help you pick out a winter jacket for your son? He was so cute."

"Oh ... yeah, right. Thank you. I thought you looked familiar. Are you a patient here? He's my dad. I'm finishing optometry school. Artie Sherman. Sometimes I work part-time in the office. My life is such a mess. My wife took away my son. They're living in Oregon. Do you want to maybe get some coffee?"

"Oh my God. I mean sure, but I'm here for a job interview. How would it look if I went on break before I was hired?"

"Don't take the job!" Artie uttered so fast he surprised himself. "You'll hate working for my dad. He's crazy, and my mom's not really quitting. She just wanted a raise."

All true. And coffee it was. Then an official date. Then a second, at which point Mindy already knew that she wanted her parents and her Grandma Jenny to meet him, though she had the good sense not to mention he was married with a child.

As soon as Artie excused himself to use the bathroom, her grandmother rendered her opinion. He seemed like a nice boy-chik, it was just too bad that he hadn't gone to work on Wall Street like his brother, or better yet, planned on becoming an ophthalmologist like his father, who had an office in Queens, one on Long Island, and a vacation house in the Berkshires. "It's such a *shanda* when a bright young man like that wastes his potential."

"Well, he did mention he might still be thinking of applying to med school."

"Oy. That's crazy. You'll end up supporting him and then he'll leave you for a nurse."

When they married a year and a half later, Artie's single great-est regret was that three-year-old Aaron was not at the wedding to serve as ring bearer. His single greatest joy? That his bride had taken a pregnancy test hours before the wedding and whispered under the chuppah that their new life together would truly be blessed with new life.

Mindy parked in front of a row of modest two-family houses, shocked that she had found the block. Remarkably, the dwellings looked unchanged, with their postage stamp frontage and the fa-miliar Fedders air conditioners hanging from bedroom windows.

"Aaron, wake up." Mindy nudged him. "You'll never guess where we are."

"Your grandmother's nursing home." He didn't bother open-ing his eyes.

"No . . . c'mon. Wake up. We're at the house where you were born!"

"What?" he looked out. "Why?"

"Because the traffic was getting to me, so I pulled off and then realized this was where your mom and Art first lived. Does it look familiar?"

"No."

"Well, you were only two when you left, but isn't it cool to see where your life began?"

"It's okay," he shrugged. "When are we goin' back?"

"Don't you want to get out? Maybe ring the bell?"

"Hell, no! Am I getting a cell phone today?"

"Oh, come on . . . I know the experts say not to do this, but I thought we could see if someone was home and ask if they'd let us look around."

"Let's just break in. Now that'd be awesome!"

"We're not breaking in. We'll say hello, sorry to disturb you, but this young man was born in this house and we were wondering if we could maybe see his old room."

"The place means nothing to me. Can we just go?"

"Really? I thought you'd be so excited. Who doesn't want to see where their story began? Can I at least take a picture of you in front of it? It's that one over there." She pointed to a tan brick duplex with two front entrances and an American flag flapping between the doors.

"You're such a tool!" He grumbled, but opened the door.

"No, just sentimental. And if you don't cooperate, next I'll take you to where I was born."

"The old lady don't open the door for no one." So said the ghost of Lucy, a spindly, redheaded woman with a career-smoker rasp who had come outside for a cigarette and pointed to the next-door neighbor's. "Been here six years and don't speak a word of English."

"Excuse me?" Mindy noted the high-rise hairdo, the orange nylon jogging suit that swished with every step, and the white leather Keds, all remnants of the eighties. Had this woman escaped her time capsule?

"You thinkin' of buyin' the place?" She coughed. "'Cause they took down the For Sale sign last month."

"Oh. No," Mindy motioned Aaron to move to the right. "We thought it would be nice to take a quick picture. This young man was born here . . . just moved back from Portland, Oregon."

"Maybe tell her your garage code, too." Aaron squirmed.

"Aaron?" The woman squinted in the bright sun. "Are you little Aaron?"

He stopped in mid yawn.

"You remember him?" Mindy almost dropped her phone.

"A grandma never forgets a face . . . I used to babysit you when you was this big." She placed her hands together, her cigarette flopping. "I gotta get my boy out here. You remember Jimmy? He was maybe six or seven when you was born. He'd try playin' with ya, but you'd just be layin' there on your little blankie and he'd say, 'Ma, you said a new boy was livin' next door, when's he gonna be able to play catch with me?'"

Aaron said nothing. Was he being his usual, off-putting self or trying to dredge up any recollection of a boy named Jimmy?

"You're not the mother." The lady eyed Mindy. "She was an itty-bitty thing."

Thank you? "No . . . I'm wife number two . . . Mindy Sherman." She shook her hand.

"Yeah, yeah. Sherman . . . that was the name. Oh, good lord, I'll never forget the day she up and left with the baby. Never saw them two again. And my Jimmy, he cried and cried."

"They were close?"

"No . . . it was on account of the fact that Aaron used to play with Jimmy's big-boy toys and he liked this certain fire truck, see . . . my husband, John, God rest his soul, spent twenty-three years with Engine Company forty-five in the Bronx. Every week he'd be bringin' home another fire truck for Jimmy and Mikey, and I'd say, John, they got enough of them stupid things, I'm trip-pin' on 'em all day. Anyway, this one truck lit up, made all kinds a noise and Aaron here, that was his favorite. But that day he and his mom run off, they took it with 'em and Jimmy kept sayin', 'Ma, I want my truck back. . . . Make 'em bring my truck back.' I just never forgot that day."

"Aaron, any of that ring a bell?"

"So you knew my mom?" he ignored Mindy's question.

"Oh, sure! Ya can see how close you lived. Hard not to get to know the people, except of course for these folks. So many goddamn people livin' there now we can't keep track no more. You got the parents, the grandparents, the kids, the uncle from Sri Lanka, and not one of them stinkers knows how to come out and say good morning." She stared at the long lost boy. "So how's she doin', your mother? She still makin' those nice quilts? She made me a beauty for my birthday once . . . bet I still got it somewhere."

"She passed," Mindy whispered as if Aaron couldn't hear. "Just recently."

"Oh . . . well, very sorry to hear that. Gotta be rough on a young man to lose his mother."

"What's your name?" Aaron blurted.

"Darlene. Darlene Fitzgerald. Maybe you guys wanna come in and say hello to Jimmy? He's home almost a month now. Just got back from Iraq . . . second tour . . . sons of bitches in Washington sending these kids on a mission to hell, and for what? So they can come back all shot up. Thank you, Lord Jesus, for bringing him home alive," she looked around to make sure Jimmy couldn't hear, "but he ain't ever gonna be the same. His right foot got blown to bits in a Humvee, and his mind ain't the same neither. I thought fine, the government's gonna take care of him, pay for all his rehabilitation, pay for college, but good luck tryin' to get the sons of bitches to answer the damn phones, let alone send the money they owe him. You listen to me, young man. You stay in school and get yourself a good education so you don't gotta go join no stinkin' army and spend the rest of your life feelin' sorry for yourself. Yeah, come on inside." She finished her smoke. "Say hello to Jimmy. He's just sittin' around watchin' the TV. Meantime I'm gonna look for that quilt for you, Aaron, and I might just come across some pictures, too. Used to be real good about gettin' them in albums, but lately the arthritis's actin' up pretty bad."

Mindy looked at Aaron's puzzled face and knew he was trying to decide between racing to the car and holding the woman's hand.

"We'll just stay a few minutes," she whispered. "I swear to God I did not plan this."

"Then who did?" He looked around. "My mom?"

"Wouldn't be surprised." She rubbed his back. "You remember that fire truck?"

"Yeah," he swallowed. "Still got it."

Aaron sobbed the whole ride home, clutching the mildew-stained quilt his mother had sewn, each handwoven square a patchwork of her troubled past. Still, it was comforting to hold something she'd created from love, something that held the remnants of her life.

And on his lap? Several Polaroids, including one of him and Jimmy under the Fitzgeralds' Christmas tree, fighting over a fire truck. Who could have known that when their paths finally crossed again, they would both be soldiers fighting a war against abandonment?

Mindy prayed that this unexpected detour wouldn't prolong his agony, though from the way he clung to the quilt and the photos, it was just as Mindy's father had said. Getting lost was good for the soul, as it could take you down roads you were destined to explore.

Twenty

"Does that really help?" Mindy watched Artie pace as she dozed in bed.

"I don't want to fall asleep yet." He flicked on the news. "My parents still might call."

"They never call past eleven."

"Oh believe me, if they find that policy, they'll call."

Artie had spent the day trying to keep his mind off the fact that his parents were still searching for any record of taking life insurance on Davida. As of six o'clock, they had nothing to report, though their investigation did turn up a box of invitations left over from his bar mitzvah. "We thought the kids would like to have them," Rhoda sounded so pleased.

"Mom, throw 'em out," Artie begged. "Nobody cares about that stuff; just get back to looking."

"Believe me, we've been schlepping boxes down from the attic since we got here."

"I don't understand why you can't just call Henry's office. He handled your insurance stuff for how many years?"

"Number one, he's retired now, and number two, we didn't buy this policy from him."

"Why not?"

"Because at the time I was fighting with him. I didn't care for how he handled my mother's claims when she broke her hip."

"So who the hell did you buy it from?" Artie yelled. "My agent said if you know the company name, you call, give them your social security number, and they'll trace the policy."

"Stop yelling at me, Arthur. What do you want from me? It was a long time ago."

"I'm not yelling," he yelled. "I'm just upset. That money would be a huge help to us right now, okay?"

"If things are so terrible, talk to Ira. Who knows more about making money than a big success like him?"

"Mom! Stop! I don't need to talk to Ira. Just tell me what else you remember."

"Well, I was saying to your father that I remember how reasonable the premiums were because you were so young and in good health."

"I still don't understand how you could have bought it from some no-name company."

"It didn't sound no name at the time. They were advertising on Joan Hamburg's program on the radio. You know how much we trust her."

"All right, well just keep looking."

"Aren't you going to ask how your father and I are getting along?"

"Fine. How are you two getting along?"

"Oy. Don't ask!"

"I can't stay up another minute," Mindy said, and yawned. "I'm exhausted."

"You were busy today, that's for sure," Artie sniped.

You have no idea. I wonder why Beth never called. She must have peed on the stick by now. "Can you open the window?" She kicked off the covers. "I'm so hot."

"No problem," he mumbled. "It'll be in the forties tonight, but it's fine if I freeze."

"I'm sorry. Are you mad at me for something, because I didn't get the memo?"

"I'm just depressed. . . . I wish my parents hadn't said anything until they knew it was for sure."

"I know. It's driving me crazy, too. Can you lower the TV? I don't want to wake the kids. . . . Have you noticed they're sleeping in their beds since Aaron got here?"

Artie channel surfed as Mindy released her stress by talking.

"I felt bad when I had to call Grandma Jenny and tell her I couldn't make it again . . . although I think she was looking forward to seeing the pizza more than me. But then Aaron—"

"Don't you think I should have been the one to take him?" he cut her off.

"What?"

"I'm saying, did it ever occur to you that maybe I would have liked to have been the one to take Aaron back to the house? It was my house."

"Oh my God! You never said one word about taking him there, and it's not like I planned it. I told you. I saw the sign for Little Neck, then I saw the Denny's and remembered the house wasn't far from there. And how did I know there was going to be a Mrs. Fitzgerald who still lived next door, and would just so happen to come outside for a smoke?"

"I know you didn't plan it, but you always do that."

"Always do what?" She sat up.

"You always do things on impulse. You don't think!"

"Oh, really? Have I ever brought home a kayak from Costco?"

"I never did that. You dreamed that."

"Well, whatever . . . You've come home with a lot of other stupid things like those pool floats that light up. Ricky practically burned his hand off trying to figure out how they work. And look, I'm sorry if I stole your thunder, but that was not my intention, and you can't tell me that it was a bad thing that Aaron got to meet that Jimmy because he was one hell of a walking advertisement for staying in school. You had to see this big, strong guy just lying there like a lump with a missing foot. I thought Aaron might throw up. But at least now he's got that beautiful quilt to keep."

"Whatever," Artie paced again. "I'm just saying . . . This isn't working out like I hoped. Ever since we got home, he's not connecting with me like he is with you. You make him laugh, you're the one he's with when important things happen, like when he got all those clothes from Beth, and everything I do with him is wrong, like telling him about the life insurance money and having to watch him go bat shit because he thought I was stealing from him."

"That's why you're mad at me? Because you're jealous? Oh my God! I thought you'd be happy that I'm trying so hard to make him feel okay about being here."

"I am happy. Don't get me wrong. You've been amazing with him. . . . I'm sorry. I'm just so nervous and pissed off about more things than I can keep track of. . . ."

"Come here." She motioned him over. "I still have faith that things will work out okay. . . . Meanwhile, let's enjoy the peace and quiet. When's the last time we had real privacy?"

The phone rang and they looked at each other. Was this it? The moment of truth?

"We found it." Stan said. "Naturally it was in the last box we looked in."

"Oh my God, they found it!" Artie repeated for Mindy's sake.

"Thank you, God!" she clapped.

"Well, don't get excited yet. There's a problem."

"What kind of problem?" Artie watched Mindy cover her face with the blanket.

"We called the phone number listed on the policy and it's been disconnected."

"What's the name of the company?"

"Convertible Life and Mutual."

"Never heard of it. . . . Sounds more like an auto dealer, but I'll go online and see if there's a Web site. Maybe they moved and it's been so many years, they stopped forwarding the calls."

"We tried that already."

"Okay, then tomorrow I'll call my insurance guy. Maybe he's heard of them. Maybe they got bought out by another company and are doing business under a new name."

"Or not at all," Stan groused. "I don't know why I ever let your mother handle this."

"How much was the policy for?" Artie held his breath.

"Fifty thou."

"Fifty thou would be amazing, Dad. . . . I am not going to give up so easily."

"Good, because let's not forget the twenty grand you owe me from investing in the store."

"Right . . . How could I forget . . . ? Night, Dad . . . Thanks for your help." He hung up and turned to Mindy. "First thing to-morrow I want you to call Noah."

"Really? But you hate psychics . . . especially ones who are my old boyfriends. Didn't you once ask me never to speak to him again?"

"That was before I was in the middle of a meltdown. I can't take it anymore. Do we get the money? Do we not get the money? Does my business make it? Is Aaron going to be okay? Are we going to be okay?"

Mindy had a few questions for Noah, too, but ironically they weren't about her own life, they were about Beth's. And how strange was that? Up until now she'd been praying daily for the Bad Luck Fairy to pay her bitchy neighbor a visit. Now it was delete, delete, delete. She would be heartbroken if Beth was single, pregnant, and forty. If only you could pay Noah extra for the good-news package.

Mindy sat next to Noah Blum in homeroom their first day at Forest Hills High. Five minutes before the bell rang, this short, geeky stranger guessed what their teacher would look like. "He's a tall, thin gay guy carrying a Channel 13 tote bag." Not that this didn't describe much of the faculty, but she was amazed when a tall, thin man walked in carrying a Channel 13 shopping bag, as their schedule had listed the teacher's name as "Unassigned."

Later, Mindy hunted the boy down in the lunchroom and asked if he could guess what she'd be when she grew up. He said, "Older," and it was the start of their friendship. They spent hours discussing his psychic premonitions and their mutually lousy karma—coming into this lifetime with bad acne and the nobody-picks-you-for-gym gene.

Then, a starlit night and a bottle of Blue Nun wine brought Mindy and Noah to a new place in their relationship—first base. Which was immediately followed by second base (her new bra was killing her). Third base was the absolute most fun she'd ever had with another person, and, by then, was so aroused, she whispered in his ear that if he didn't finish the job, they would never speak again.

"I didn't see this coming, I swear." Noah begged forgiveness the next day.

"And you call yourself a psychic?" Mindy teased. "Forget it." She kissed his cheek. "I'm just glad my first time was with you."

They spent most of high school together, mutually agreeing

the party was over before she left for Buffalo and he Amherst College. They briefly reunited in their senior year, but when Mindy met Artie shortly after, it was no, no, no more Noah.

They tried staying in touch, planning at least one get together a year, but over time Noah became very in demand, as he was on call to the NYPD, the FBI, and legions of celebrity clients in the city who didn't poop unless he said it was a good time to sit.

And, too, Artie grumbled every time she mentioned his name, for Mr. "I've got a secret" hated the idea of someone from Mindy's past being privy to their future. Only once did he ask if Noah had predicted anything about their life together, and even then was reluctant to hear the answer.

Unfortunately, Mindy knew that Artie was still skeptical of magicians, let alone someone who claimed to have the ability to foresee the future. She doubted that desperation alone was incentive enough for him to change his attitude. So no point pestering Noah for answers that would likely be disregarded. Besides, every time she'd gotten in touch, her now twice-divorced ex made things uneasy by propositioning her.

Then again, they were so stressed out, it would be reassuring to hear that things were going to work out in the end.

"I wouldn't go if he makes you feel uncomfortable." Nadine poured more coffee. "I would just call. You've done phone readings with him before."

"Either way sounds scary to me," said their friend, Lori Wasserman. "Just knowing I was going to hear predictions about my future would give me nightmares."

"Are you kidding?" Mindy laughed. "Name three things that don't scare you." *Same for you, Nadine.*

They were sitting at Mindy's kitchen table, just back from their annual mammogram, a tradition they'd started after their dear friend, Marla, died of breast cancer. First they'd carpool to the radiologist's office in the afternoon, then open a bottle of wine, hopefully to celebrate another year of getting to "keep the boys." And if God forbid one of them received a questionable report, at least they'd have immediate love and support.

This year, however, the only way they could arrange their work schedules and be seen back to back was to start at ten in the morning, so the bottle of wine would have to chill. Meanwhile the conversation was plenty good-natured, like the ones they'd have back in the days when their kids were little.

Mindy liked Lori because she was good-hearted and not a gossip. Her one design flaw was that she was neurotic. Everything gave you cancer or heart disease or both. And dare you utter the words *trans fats, deodorant,* or *underwire* bras, be prepared for the dire warnings.

As a joke one Halloween, Mindy and Nadine went in on a government issued hazmat suit, only to have her cry from joy. "Thank you," she sniffed. "You have no idea how long I've wanted one of these. It's like my Victoria's Secret."

"The problem with talking to Noah," Mindy went on, "is that he's usually right on the money. I'd die if he told me things were going to get even worse."

"Don't be negative," Nadine said. "Maybe he'll see great things ahead."

"Based on what? The extraordinary luck we've had so far?"

"Based on the fact that it's your turn for a little good news."

"Knock-knock." Beth scared them with her rap at the back door.

"Crap," Nadine grumbled. She hated Beth and liked it better when Mindy did, too.

"Hi." Mindy unlocked the door and made eye contact. "How are you? Anything new?"

"Is your little coffee klatch almost over?" She peered in. "I have to talk to you."

OHMYGOD! "*Um*, well, see, we're celebrating our clean mam-

mograms and then going for lunch. Do you want to come in?"
She felt daggers in her back.

"No, thanks." Beth made a face. She detested Nadine as much
as the other way around, having to do with some stupid incident
that neither could remember, but the grudge held.

"When are you getting back?"

"I guess in a few hours." She tried to read Beth as if the answer
would flash in neon. Pregnant? Not pregnant? Pregnant? Not pregnant? Better yet, maybe Mindy would offer her a glass of wine. If
she refused, that would be a sign of the big, prenatal no-no.

"Okay, call me when you get back," Cool Hand Beth gave
nothing away other than more things for Aaron. "These are
Richard's, but who cares," she said, handing Mindy a bag. "Let
Aaron go through it after school."

"Actually he's at the store with Artie. We figured he's missed
so much, what's another few days off? And then Nadine invited a
bunch of Jonathan's friends over tonight so he can meet them and
at least see a few familiar faces on Monday. You sure you don't
want to come in? We were just talking about whether I should go
see this psychic I know. Do you ever have big, important questions you want answers to?"

"You know a psychic?" Beth clapped. "Who is it? Which one?"

"Noah Blum?"

"No way." She placed her hand on her heart. "You've been to
him?"

"If you want to know the truth, I've been on him," she chuckled. "We were a thing in high school, and then for a little while
before I met Artie."

"Is that good for a discount?"

"I wish." Mindy stepped outside. "What happened?" She kept
her voice down. "Did you do the test yet? You look calm. It was
negative, right?"

"Would you get off my case?" Beth whisper-yelled. "You don't need to be obsessing over this. It's not your problem."

"You say that now."

"Trust me, at my age and with Richard gone, there is no way I'm having a baby."

Mindy peeked in to make sure Nadine and Lori weren't eavesdropping. "But what about your period? Did you remember the last time you had it?"

"No, but it's only because of that damn perimenopause. Now you see it, now you don't."

"Oh my God, would you listen to yourself?" Mindy grabbed Beth's hand and moved her farther from the door. "You had sex, you can't remember if you took the pill, you can't remember the last time you had your period, you're vomiting, and your boobs hurt—you don't think, 'Houston we have a problem'?"

"I can't fucking be pregnant, okay?" Beth eye's welled. "I just can't!"

"Oh believe me, I understand. I had a little scare myself last year and Artie was practically talking me off the ledge. But you have to deal with the facts, so just march your ass back home and take that damn test!"

"I'm afraid," Beth sniffed. "What if I fail like I have at everything else? My kids hate me, my marriage is a disaster, I'm not qualified to get a job anymore, my only friend is you . . . "

"Well thanks for throwing me into that pot, but listen. You can't sit on this like you would a decision to buy a new bedroom set."

"I would never sit on that decision," Beth wiped her eye.

"Exactly. And this is almost as important. Now go do it and don't you dare come back here until you bring me that little stick!"

"You are such a bitch!" Beth headed home.

"I learned from the best!"

Twenty-one

There were times Mindy felt sure that Long Island was the sister city of Hollywood, with its confluence of wealth, power, and growing number of stunning, ageless women who by virtue of their rich, uninterested husbands had the time and money in which to find trouble.

At least it guaranteed continuous good gossip, like the time Beth's former friend, Jill, propositioned two men at a party and ended up nude in the hot tub with them, too stoned to notice one of them was her ex-husband's partner and the other a woman.

Mindy and Nadine loved feasting on these outrageous lapses in judgment, especially knowing the words *don't repeat this* were code for *it's open season on this idiot. Tell whoever you want.* But of late, Mindy was keeping mum on Beth and it was hard, especially with a miffed Nadine breathing down her neck. "You must know something. You two spend like every waking minute together."

"We do not. It's just that we finally called a truce. I thought you'd be happy for me. You of all people know how miserable she's made me."

"Which is why I don't get how all of a sudden you could be so buddy-buddy with her. She is such a bitch."

"Well she's being nice now. What should I do? Tell her to cut it out? And what's with the jealous wife bit? That's not like you."

"I don't know. . . . I guess I'm feeling left out. We don't hang out anymore, we hardly talk, and when we do, you're not doing any of the sharing. Even Lori noticed you've changed. That day we were hanging out at your house and Beth showed up, it was like you forgot we were there. And then when we went out to lunch, all you did was check your cell to see if she called."

"I'm sorry Nadine. I really am. It's just that she's got all these problems right now."

"What kind of problems?"

"Oh no. No no no. I'm not going there. I am not going to betray her trust."

"Betray her trust? Oh my God. We're talking about Beth, the neighbor who made you dig her car out after a snowstorm because she didn't want to ruin her new boots. The neighbor who called the town to accuse you of running your sprinklers on odd days instead of even."

"People change."

"Yes they do, but Beth never will. She's just using you like she uses everyone else."

"Excuse me, but she can be a very sweet, thoughtful person."

"She put an anonymous note in your mailbox that said, 'Dear neighbor, drop dead.'"

"Actually, that was my note. I put it in hers first."

"What is this? *Brokeback Mountain*? You guys are starting to sound gay. But whatever your deal is, don't tell me I didn't warn you when she dumps you and goes back to her old habit of making you feel like shit."

"Fine. You warned me. Now get off my case."

"Oh come on. Just one little hint . . . I heard she got drunk at a bar and—"

"Would you stop? How would you like it if I spread it around that Peter couldn't get it up if Regis and Radu personally came over to lift it?"

"I'd kill you. The difference is, we've been friends since college. How long have you been friends with Beth? Twenty minutes?"

"Nadine, drop it! I'm not saying another word."

"That's pretty sad considering she's been going around telling everyone that you're a mess and your house is a mess and it's a shame that Stacie and Jamie are going to end up fat like you because you know shit about proper diet and nutrition."

"She did not say that!" Mindy gulped.

"According to Elise Kruger she did. I bumped into her at the dry cleaners and she heard it from Stephanie what's her name with the orange skin who uses the same trainer as Beth."

"No way. After all I've done for her!"

"That's what I'm saying. She's a bitch. So is it true? Is she having an affair?"

"No, but Richard's leaving her and doesn't know she might be pregnant."

"Oh my God!" Nadine gasped.

"Shit!" Mindy felt faint. "I can't believe I just did that. You can not repeat this, Nadine. Do you understand? You can not open your mouth to a single soul because it might not even be true. I mean I'm the one who thought she was pregnant because she had all the symptoms and she hasn't been careful with the pill and couldn't remember when she had her period, but she told me she did the test and it was negative, and who knows if Richard is actually going to leave? He's just threatening because they're fighting all the time, but in my opinion, I think he really loves her, he's just got this huge problem with lying, so when he told

her the other night that he'd decided to live in Portland and work
for Nike, she couldn't tell if he was bullshitting or not."

"Oh, jeez," Nadine said. "That's a lot of information!"

"I know, but I wasn't kidding before. You repeat one word of
this and I will tell Peter that you did not go to the movies with
me last week, that you went to the craft fair at the Nassau Coli-
seum. No, wait. I'll tell Lori that you still smoke. Oh, man. That
will get you into major trouble!"

"Okay, okay . . . relax. You don't have to get all crazy. I'm not
going to tell anyone."

"Yeah, right. You're probably halfway through a group text
message."

"That is not fair, Mindy. Have I ever betrayed your trust?"

"Probably . . . but it better not be this time."

Stupid, stupid, stupid. Wasn't Mindy forever reminding her
daughters that trust was the most important thing in a relationship? And how could she be pissed at Nadine for blabbing Beth's
news when she had done the same? So which was worse? Ad-
mitting you were this huge hypocrite or living in fear of con-
frontation?

Not that Mindy would blame Beth for never speaking to her
again. In spite of all the mean, hurtful crap Beth had pulled over
the years, and the fact that payback was hardly out of line, Mindy
had done the unthinkable. She'd added yet another layer of pain
to Beth's suffering.

By evening she was having palpitations about the ugly, un-
avoidable showdown and the realization that she had jeopar-
dized the start of a new, promising friendship. Even the usually
oblivious Artie noticed she wasn't herself. When did Mindy not
devour sushi from Akari?

So when Beth left her an instant message that she needed to
come over right away to talk, Mindy's first thought was to grab her

keys and a bag of chips and head to her mother's house. Not that this was any great refuge. She'd end up confessing, then having to listen to the same tape she'd played for the girls about trust being the most important thing in a relationship. Plus, thanks to the Internet and cell phones, your business and whereabouts were easily traceable. Ditto for leaving your car in the driveway.

"Why didn't you get back to me?" Beth was standing at the door. "I know you're home."

"Oh, *um*," Mindy stammered. "I was just busy with the kids. Everything okay?"

"No, of course not. Can I come in?"

"Sure." She opened the door. *Please don't yell at me here. I don't want my family hearing what a terrible person I am.* "Did you hear from Richard again?"

"No . . . what is wrong with you? You're shaking. Did you see a ghost?"

Wait. You're not mad at me? Nadine actually kept her mouth shut? "I'm just a little stressed . . . been a long day."

"No shit! You must have told your lovely friend Nadine my entire life's story because I've spent the last few hours reading about myself on everyone's away messages."

FUCK! "Beth, I'm so, so sorry. It just blurted out and I—"

"Whatever. I don't give a damn anymore about who knows what. People are such goddamn hypocrites. We've got more important fish to fry."

"We do?"

"Yeah. Apparently that lady, Anna Jane Crandall, at Downtown Greetings was mighty impressed with us. She sent us an e-mail inviting us to Chicago to talk about doing some sort of creative project for them. Didn't you read it?"

"No, I haven't been online today. So, wait. There's no more contest?"

"Guess so. That crazy lady, Olivia, you spoke to made the

whole thing null and void. Anyway, here's the deal." Beth made herself a cup of tea. "She needs us to fly out Thursday and meet with her first thing Friday."

"This Thursday? That's only two days from now. I can't do that."

"Why not?"

"Because, I don't know. Who would drive the kids?"

"Screw it. It's time they learned to take the bus."

"Hello, Fox News? I'd like to report an alien abduction."

"Or," Beth ignored her, "maybe Aaron could drive them. He's not starting school until Monday."

"Seriously? You'd let a teenager who doesn't know his way around drive your children?"

"I'll take my chances. I have no choice."

"Wait. How can you leave town? Unless Richard is coming back."

"That's the other thing I had to tell you," Beth wrapped the tea bag around her spoon.

"Are we thinking those are his balls because you just castrated that poor thing?"

She looked at her still tight grip and laughed. "I hope he's feeling this. . . . The prick just e-mailed me that he's signing a one-year lease for this townhouse near Nike."

"Oh, man! Now I'm sorry I gave him a ride from the airport the other day. . . . I just felt so sorry that he lost his wallet."

"He didn't lose it."

"Yes, he did. He said he left it in one of those bins at security."

"I know that's what he told you, but the man is a pathological liar. He didn't lose his wallet, he was out of money because he blew through his cash advance."

"How do you know?"

"Because he told me. And you had to see how proud he was that he got you to believe his story."

"But he seemed so distraught."

"Mindy, the man could sell beer to the Mormons. The truth is, he never carries his own money or credit cards when he travels for business because he hates waiting to be reimbursed. The hotel and car are direct-billed to the agency and he just takes a big enough cash advance to cover his meals and incidentals. I guess this time he must have had some pretty interesting incidentals because he didn't have a dime when he got to LaGuardia."

"No!"

"Yes! Didn't I tell you he could have been an actor? He had me fooled for a long time, too. I actually thought he loved me."

"Beth, I'm sure he loves you and the girls, he just needs help."

"Then you tell him because I'm tired of begging." She sipped her tea. "Anyway, I just called my mother and told her the whole story, which was not easy because we're hardly the Gilmore girls. Anyway, she said she would be willing to fly in tomorrow to stay with the girls and then my dad would come in next week for Passover."

"So she wasn't freaked out when you told her? 'Cause my mother would have given me the you-made-your-bed-now-lie-in-it lecture. I think there's a Hallmark card that says that."

"A few years ago she would have done that to me, but she's finally mellowing. That, and her hearing is getting worse. It's possible she missed half of what I said."

"Great. So much to look forward to. Deafness, incontinence, nobody wanting to spend time with you unless you brought your checkbook . . ."

They were contemplating the joys of aging when Artie walked in. "I meant to ask if you called Noah? We really need to talk to him."

"Have you met Mr. Didja?" Mindy asked Beth. "Didja call the exterminator, didja pick up the dry cleaning . . . ? Yes, I called him, but he didn't get back to me yet."

"Is that a bad sign? You think he had an awful vision and now he's avoiding you?"

"No, I think it means he's busy helping the government locate missing tax evaders. It always takes him a few days to return my calls. Why are you so jumpy?"

"Mom!" Stacie yelled. "Is the bee-ach still here? I need help with math."

"Awk-ward!" Artie sang.

"Me?" Beth pointed to herself. "I'm the bee-ach?"

"It's our little code name for you on speed dial," Mindy chuckled. "Yes, she's still here." Mindy hollered back. "Daddy will help you . . . and please get Ricky into the shower."

"Well, if it's true-confession time," Beth whispered, "you're FS on our speed dial."

"Full of shit?" Mindy guessed.

"Fat slob."

"Oh my God! That's so mean!"

"Now we're even. . . . Can we please finish discussing the Chicago thing? I have to get home to talk to the girls."

"Sure . . . Brace yourself for some actual good news," Mindy told Artie. "Downtown Greetings wants to meet us on Friday, and they're paying for us to fly there."

"You're kidding." He stopped drinking. "Why you?"

"Because our entries were amazing," Beth said. "And apparently they've got some big board meeting coming up and want to announce a partnership deal with this fabulous new company called House of Cards."

"Who are they?" Artie asked.

"Us. We're House of Cards."

"We're a company?" Mindy spit out her coffee.

"We are now. We just have to print up business cards and bring them with us."

"Cool!" Mindy laughed. "What do we do?"

"What do you think we do? We develop clever greeting cards."

"Are we good?"

"Are you kidding? We've got me as the art director. We're unbelievable!"

"Do you have clients?" Artie asked.

"One . . . Downtown Greetings."

"Wait . . . who gets to be the president?" Mindy poked Beth's shoulder.

"That would be me also," she said.

"No, no. I am much more qualified. I have real presidential experience."

"Since when?"

"I was president of my Hadassah chapter for two years and I was awesome. But seriously, what's the real story here?"

"I just told you. Anna Jane thinks we're great, she needs a quick something or other to impress the board after they find out the contest was canceled, and it's Chicago here we come. And don't even think of not going because I need the job!"

"No one gets through E-ZPass without payin' the toll." Artie caught Mindy's eye.

"And you would know," she glared. Beth was suffering enough without him poking fun. If only there was a cure for Dumb Husband disease. "Would you please go up and help Stacie with her homework? Then go get Aaron."

"Homework, yes, Aaron, not yet. I just spoke to Nadine and she said the kids are having a great time and not to come until eleven. Apparently it turned into a victory party."

"Jonathan just found out he got into Indiana's music school," Mindy told Beth, "and he's out of his mind excited."

"That's great. I wish my luck would start to change."

"Me, too." Artie squeezed the soda can in his bare hand. "The bad news continues. . . ."

"Now what?" Mindy swallowed.

"Remember before when you said Noah catches tax evaders? Well that could be us."

"Oh, no! Lenny finally woke up and realized we hadn't filed since Clinton was president?"

"Leave him alone. You think it's easy doing people's taxes with an abacus? No, he just did our quarterly estimates and we don't have the money to pay them. Oh, and then we just got a call from some detective in Portland investigating a vandalism case at one of the schools."

"Oh my God." Mindy held her breath.

"Yeah. There's a warrant out for Aaron's arrest."

But what did you get when you mixed Jewish geography with six degrees of separation? The name of an attorney in Portland who happened to be related to a cousin of Nadine's uncle's second wife. And that wasn't even the coincidence. The attorney, Steven Hoffman, knew and remembered Davida Findley, as she had once donated a dozen of her handmade quilts for an auction for his pet charity.

After hearing Aaron's tale, including the latest twist that he was being charged with vandalizing school property, Steven offered to take the case on a pro bono basis in return for his late mother's generosity. Only trouble was, he was going to need Aaron back in Portland within forty-eight hours to post bail and to await a hearing with a family court judge.

"No problem," Artie told him. "I was hoping to get away for a few days."

"Plus, we love spending money we don't have." Mindy poured a glass of wine.

When confronted with the accusation, Aaron swore he had not vandalized any schools in years and that the Portland Police had picked him up in error for questioning once before. But while

Mindy and Artie desperately wanted to believe him, with a prior arrest record and now a new warrant, he had no choice. He had to answer the charges.

But funny how bad did sometimes turn to good, for being back in Portland allowed Aaron to collect more of his possessions and to see Rainbow. Meanwhile, Artie was finally able to get his hands on Aaron's official school transcript as well as Davida's death certificate, the biggest saving grace of all.

On a hunch, Stan had called the New York State Insurance Department and discovered that the company Rhoda bought the policy from had changed hands several times, but was still paying out claims. Furthermore, Artie was correct in guessing that the policy could still be in force if the premiums had been paid from an investment account and then by its dividends. With proof of the insured's death, he as beneficiary could file a claim and receive the settlement.

Still, he was careful not to do the happy dance when he heard the news, lest Aaron go crazy again for thinking his father was rejoicing that his mother died. But proof of her death would not be the only evidence they would supply that would change their luck.

The crime committed against Lewis Elementary occurred on a night that Aaron was cruising the Atlantic Ocean, and dated photos downloaded by Stan was the evidence they needed to prove he was not the defendant picked up on the surveillance cameras.

"Aaron's not going to jail?" Ricky tugged at Mindy when Artie shared the news. "No sweetie pie. He was telling the truth . . . he's a really good boy. Just like you."

"Now can we take him to Disney?"

"Not yet, but definitely the circus. It's coming up real soon."

"Aaron doesn't like the circus."

"He doesn't? How come?"

"'Cause the clowns are scary and they do bad things to kids. They made him pull down his pants."

"Oh my God! He said that? He said the clowns made him pull down his pants?"

"Yeah . . . but it's okay to go to the circus here 'cause that was only the clowns where he lived."

"Do you swear you're telling the truth, Ricky, because that's a very bad lie to tell?"

"I'm not lying Mommy. Aaron hates the circus 'cause-a the bad clowns. I don't wanna go no more either."

Twenty-two

Why was it that when you were in the middle of a storm that was blowing the roof off your house, and you were down on your knees praying for survival, the phone rang and it was someone trying to sell you vinyl siding?

There Mindy was, trying to book a return flight for her mother in Florida that would land in time for her and Beth to then catch a flight to Chicago, when the phone rang and Mindy heard Dana's whiny, aren't-I-special voice. "Hello, Mindy. How are the children?"

Not that Dana cared. The reason she'd called was to say that she and Ira had been discussing it and they were uncomfortable with the idea of Mindy and Artie making Passover because, well, their house was so small, and it would be such a tight squeeze to fit everyone into the dining room and besides, everyone knew Rhoda was a much better cook, not to mention she'd just spoken to Rhoda and things were more or less back to normal with Stan, at least they weren't threatening to split up anymore, and also, the contractor doing their kitchen floors was running behind and wouldn't be getting started until after the holiday so they could still make the first night as long as Mindy and Artie were okay with it.

Mindy took one of those deep-cleansing breaths Dana was always raving about and said, "You know what I think? I think that you should take your organic horseradish and your gluten-free matzoh and shove it up your ass because we are making Passover here just like we planned. My family has been looking forward to starting some new traditions, and so what if our dining room would be a tight squeeze? If you guys don't come, we'll have plenty of room and we won't have to worry that we only have service for twelve or that your bratty kids will destroy the place like they did last time they were here."

"Oh my God. It was just a suggestion!" Dana sniffed. "I wish you'd try gingerroot and passionflower. They really take the edge off."

"So does a bottle of red!"

"Whatever . . . I didn't know it meant so much to you to make Passover."

"Actually it doesn't. Way too much work, not to mention a huge expense. It's just that I don't understand why you always have to act like you're royalty and we're here to serve you. I mean you basically just told me we don't deserve to make a holiday because we don't live in a McMansion, but you know what? Forget it. I don't have time to deal with this right now. I'll tell Rhoda we love the tradition of having it at their house and that's the end of it. I have to go now."

"Wait, Mindy," she blurted. "I'm sorry. That came out wrong. I wasn't thinking. . . . The truth is it's not even why I called."

"It's not?"

"No. I was wondering, did Artie mention anything about talking to Ira?"

"Ira? Not really. Why?"

"Just curious. I thought maybe he happened to mentioned something to him about us."

"No, nothing. What's going on? Are you crying?"

"I'm fine," she sniffed. "Forget I said anything. I'm sure once Ira comes back to his senses he'll realize I'm right."

"About what?"

"You wouldn't understand. You and Artie are so good together. I'm sure he doesn't constantly belittle you or take off for days at a time. Ira can be being very difficult. I don't know how much more of this I can take."

Whoa! Not you guys, too. Did someone spike the Kool-Aid? "I'm really sorry, Dana. I had no idea, and if Ira did say something to Artie, he didn't tell me. What are you going to do?"

"I don't know. I was thinking maybe you could talk to him. Tell him that he'd better get his act together because you found out I was very unhappy and that is not a good thing."

"Me tell him? No, no. I'm out of that business. He's your husband—"

"Well that's what Stan suggested. He said you were able to talk sense into Rhoda, so maybe you could do the same with Ira."

"Oh my God, you've discussed this with Stan?"

"I discuss everything with him. He's an excellent listener . . . very understanding."

"Stan, our father-in-law Stan?"

"Yes. I don't know where I'd be if I didn't have him to lean on."

"Oh me too. He's so supportive." *Holy crap, Batman! I'm the last sane person on earth. Time to board the mother ship.*

Mindy was in a bind. She and Beth were en route to the airport, but it was not the victory lap she'd envisioned. If she closed her eyes, she either thought of Dana pouring her heart out to Stan, or Aaron's painful secret about circus clowns. If she opened them, she was sitting shotgun in a car driven by a woman who had confused the Southern State Parkway with the Autobahn.

Either way she felt nauseous, but with this being a factory-clean car, and with them already running late because Mindy forgot their box of business cards, she would never hear the end of it if she chose this time and place to puke.

But as Beth took hairpin turns, Mindy chose *A* for "Aaron." Oh, the injustice that his early life had been so tainted and that his childhood fears were still chasing him like hooligan waves. Weren't they supposed to weaken over time, not follow him to shore with an undertow of dread?

And of all things in which to be afraid. A clown's entire reason for being was to bring people joy and laughter, not embed fear like a microchip planted under the skin. But if it was true that Aaron had been molested by some sicko in a clown costume, it would explain why he had behaved so badly at that Mrs. Cassidy's office the day they registered him for school.

The clown motif in her office wasn't a decor choice, but an obsession, with every inch of space designated for a photo, figurine, or collectible. Clearly her intent was good. Who wouldn't enjoy being surrounded by smiling faces, other than perhaps a young man haunted by images of unspeakable acts, and for whom life was no longer a laughing matter?

It was so sad. Just when they thought they knew all there was to know about the boy's jigsaw life, they were still uncovering more pieces of the puzzle.

"Why are you still crying?" Beth asked Mindy as they waited at the gate area. "My driving wasn't that bad."

"Really? Remind me to grab some of the airsick bags from the plane and stick them in your glove compartment." She blew into a tissue. "You are aware that the posted speed limits are not just suggestions?"

"I wouldn't have had to rush if we didn't have to go back for the business cards."

"We wouldn't have had to go back if you'd have let me concentrate on my packing, but no, you had to call six times, should I bring the Donna Karan sweater or the Ann Taylor blazer, the Joan and David pumps or the Coach sandals? What do I know about fashion?"

"Good point. Half your wardrobe says the Mets. That would make me cry, too . . . and please tell me you brought something nice to wear to our meeting."

"Sadly, my choices were limited," she sniffed. "It was either my red checked skirt that doubles as a tablecloth or my black funeral suit, which is so tight, the only way I can zip the skirt is if I wear the pantyhose that makes your voice go up an octave."

"Great. So which was it? I hope not the tablecloth."

"No, I went back into the archives and found an old skirt that was kind of long and flowing and lets me breathe normally in case the supply of oxygen is cut off."

"Then why are you crying? You're getting insurance money you weren't expecting, Artie got his son back, and now you have this once in a lifetime opportunity to work with me."

"I know, but it seems like every time we get some good news, there's more bad news right behind it."

"Hey. I'm the one who should be crying. My husband left me, my daughters hate me, and my parents want to move in with me because they don't think I can handle everything by myself. . . ."

"I'm sorry," Mindy sighed. "I'm in shock. We've been through so much recently and the insanity just doesn't end. Things keep happening that boggle the mind."

"Yeah, but let's face it. We bring most of this on ourselves."

"Maybe . . . It's just that it's times like this I miss my dad so much. He always knew what to say to make things better. And it's crazy because he's gone almost five years now, but still . . . Every time the phone rings, I think it's him calling to check on the kids or tell me who he likes for the Mets this season. I'm so mad he's gone."

"Maybe he's not gone. Maybe he's the reason you're getting all this good news."

"I would love to think that." She blew her nose. "I really would . . . Do you remember the morning I had to rescue you at the train station?"

"It rings a bell."

"Well, he was definitely around me that day for sure."

"How do you know?"

"Because that was the morning that Richard and Artie left for the airport and I was so stressed out I couldn't fall back asleep. I kept asking my dad to send me a sign that he was with me but got nothing. Then a few hours later you call, and I had to totally rearrange my schedule to get you, and I had no idea where I was going, and I was so mad that I was having to do you this favor because I mean, what had you ever done for me? And then like out of nowhere, I start getting these messages . . . like about not judging the bad things that happened because they could turn out to be good things in disguise."

"You keep saying that." Beth checked her cell phone.

"You don't agree?"

"Not really."

"Well, I do. Look at Aaron. Everyone taking care of him died of drug overdoses within a few months of each other, which is horrible. But it turned out it was the only reason Artie got him back. And now for the first time, this kid has a chance for a decent future.

"And take the two of us. All these years we've done nothing but piss each other off and hurt each other's feelings, then something bad happens to you, I get forced into helping, and now look. We're becoming friends and working on a business deal together."

"Only because I'm such a magnanimous, forgiving person."

"Huh?"

"I still can't believe you told Nadine everything."

"I swear it just happened."

"You sound like Richard."

"I'm sorry but it's true. She was egging me on and on, telling me how you were telling everyone what a mess I was, and that Stacie and Jamie were going to be fat forever because of me, and I just lost it."

"That's ridiculous. I haven't said anything like that in weeks."

"But you admit to doing that before?"

"All the time. That's why I couldn't be too pissed off at you . . . more surprised than anything."

"Damn!" Mindy winced. "I wish I'd known before I threw out half my dinner from Akari."

"It's a start." Beth offered Mindy gum. "Anyway, when you first brought up that whole good thing–bad thing, I thought it was bullshit. My mother's entire family was wiped out in the Holocaust, and all I ever heard growing up was good was good and bad was evil."

"I know," Mindy said. "My grandmother's family, the same thing—not that she ever told us much. Just bits and pieces."

"Where was your grandmother from?"

"Poland. But when the Nazis started coming into power, her family moved to Vienna, thinking they would never invade Austria, but they were wrong. I know that her father was arrested for practicing medicine and sent to a death camp, and her mother went into hiding with her and her younger brother. And the only reason this family took them in was because my grandmother could sew. She made these exquisite lace tablecloths that sold for a lot of money. Of course the family took all of it, then kicked them out because they said it was getting too dangerous to let them stay. Anyway, long story short, my grandmother was one of the only ones in her family to survive. And the amazing thing is, until her dementia kicked in, she was one of the happiest people I knew. She made the most out of every day, always looked for the silver lining, never complained.

"That's why I get so mad at myself. . . . I have more money and freedom than she could have ever have dreamed of, but does that stop me from bitching about how hard my life is? It's awful how much we've come to expect, and the kids are even worse. They really think the world owes them something."

"Tell me about it," Beth said. "Mine are so overindulged it's nauseating."

"Get this," Mindy nodded. "The other night I'm watching *Grey's Anatomy*, which my kids know I have to watch in peace. Anyway, Stacie barges in and says I have to see the new Tiffany catalog because there's a necklace she wants for her birthday, which mind you is eight months away, and I said, are you out of your mind? I wouldn't spend seven hundred dollars on a necklace for me let alone for you and she actually cried and said, 'But Mom, I really want that. Don't you want to get me things I really want?'"

"Glad it's not just at my house."

"That's what I'm saying. It's not just the kids. I'm no better. You'd think that having a grandmother whose life was spared because she made it out on that Kindertransport, I would understand what's important and what's bullshit."

"The Kindertransport?" Beth stopped fidgeting.

"Ever heard of it? I'm always surprised how few people know about it."

"Yes, I've heard of it. That's how my mother got out of Vienna."

"Vienna? Really? I thought she was German."

"My dad is, my mother was from Austria. But yes, I know the whole story about the children who got out of Europe after Britain agreed to let them enter the country unaccompanied. That's how she escaped, and she was a baby practically. The story is unbelievable. Do you know what year your grandmother left?"

"I have no idea," Mindy said. "But I could probably figure it out. At my Sweet Sixteen I remember her telling me how she spent her sixteenth birthday leaving the Kindertransport and getting put on a ship to England. And now she's eighty-six. Do you have paper and a pen?"

"You can't do simple arithmetic in your head?"

"Not anymore. It's too clogged with nonsense like the inspiring, real-life stories of the *American Idol* finalists."

"Whatever." Beth handed her a Gucci pen and a Coach memo holder. Mindy stared as if she were looking at the queen's gold.

"What?"

"This is the difference between us. If you asked me for a pen and paper, I'd be handing you an ATM receipt and one of those little pencils from the miniature golf course."

"What can I say?" Beth laughed. "I travel first class. Just figure it out and then figure out my mother's, too. If I remember she had just turned four, and her birthday is in December. And this year she'll be seventy-four."

"She was four years old and she was all alone?" Mindy clutched her heart. "Oh my God. We don't let our kids get three steps ahead of us at the mall."

"She never told me much, and my father was totally Silent Sam. I just know it's an absolute miracle that either of them survived."

"Unbelievable." Mindy did the math. "Okay, my grandmother's birthday is also in December, so if she was sixteen, then that would have made it . . . December 1938."

"Interesting," Beth said. "I remember my mom saying how cold she was when she first arrived, so it could have been December. She was brought to some refugee camp in a coastal area that was nice in the summer but the winters were freezing."

"I wonder if their paths ever crossed." Mindy laid her hand on her heart. "Think about it . . . Both of them might have left from Vienna in December 1938."

"Not likely. There were hundreds of children who left then, and there was too big an age difference."

It is a fact of modern life that a phone call can rock your world. Your ex-wife has passed. Your estranged son wants to meet you. Your estranged next-door neighbor needs your help. The bank has turned down your loan application, an old life insurance policy remained in force, you've been chosen by a company to handle a creative project, your sister-in-law is an idiot, and your son has been accused of a crime.

But no phone call could compare to the one Beth made to her mother while she and Mindy sat on the runway waiting for their flight to take off.

"Mother, do you know the name Gittle Sole . . . Wait, hold on. I have to ask Mindy again. . . . What was her last name?"

"Soloweichyk."

"Mother, did you hear? Her name was Gittle Soloweichyk?"

"What's she saying?" Mindy could barely breathe.

"Nothing yet . . . Hold on, I'll put her on speaker phone." She hit the button. "Mom? You still there? I put you on speaker phone so Mindy can hear, too."

"Ver did you hear that name, Batya?" she asked. "Ver in God's name . . . ?"

Mindy and Beth locked eyes. Wait. She recognized it?

"Mom, we've gotta do this fast because we're about to take off, but Mindy was saying something about her grandmother being on the Kindertransport, so, of course, I told her about you. Not that I was actually thinking you would know the name."

"I know it!" she cried out. "I know it!"

"Oh my God! Are you sure?" Beth and Mindy held hands.

"Sure I'm sure. Even efter seventy years, you think I could forget? Gittle vas like a mother to me. I was a baby, Batya. Just four years old. You've heard the story. My mother put me on the train ven I vas asleep. Then I vake up and all around me are strangers . . . end I'm crying I vant my mother, end this girl hends me bread and says to me in Yiddish, 'Come to me little beauty. I em your mother now.'"

"Oh my God. And that was Gittle?"

"That vas Gittle. She vas no bigger than a child herself, Batya. But she took care of me on the train from Vienna, and then the ship all the vay to England. End another baby, too. A little boy, Oskar, but he died from fever. . . ."

"Mrs. Goldberg, it's Mindy. And you're sure this Gittle's last name was Soloweichyk?"

"Yes, yes . . . she made up little songs so ve could remember all the names."

"And what happened after you got to England?" Beth asked. "Did you stay together?"

"No, no . . . Vee ver taken all over. The older children vent to the hostels if they didn't have femily, and the younger ones like me vent to these holiday camps and vaited for foster femilies to take us. Vee got separated right avay. I vould ask people, do you know ver is Gittle Soloweichyk? One man told me she vent to Palestine, but I didn't know if thet vas true."

"Mom, they want us to turn off our phones now because we're taking off, but maybe you should buckle your seatbelt, too. . . . I know where your Gittle is. . . ."

"She's alife?"

"Yes! She lives in a nursing home in Queens."

"Oh my God in heaven. Mindy, darlink, vat is her name now?"

"Well, when she came to America, she changed her name to Jenny Solomon." Mindy wiped her eyes. "Then she married Abraham Baumann."

"Jenny Baumann . . . Oh, I em so happy right now! Thank you, darlinks, thank you."

"Bye, Mom, love you, talk to you when we land." Beth ended the call.

"This is so unbelievable." Mindy was shaking. "She had this whole story."

"I know, but do you honestly think it could be the same person? There must have been lots of little Gittles. Wait—how old is your grandmother?"

"Eighty-six."

"And my mom is seventy-four."

"So that would mean," Mindy looked at her math, "your mom would have been four, and my grandmother would have been sixteen . . . and bingo! That's what they told us."

"Then maybe it is true." Beth blew into a tissue. "But it's so crazy."

"Also known as *bashert*. Fate. God's will. Ultimate Jewish ge-ography: two girls, twelve years apart, one born in Poland, the other in Austria, both end up being taken to England with the older one caring for the younger one like she's the mother, then they get there, get separated, and never see each other again."

"Until seventy years later," Beth continued, "next-door neigh-bors on Long Island who barely speak find out that they would never have been born if not for the fact that God spared the lives of Gittle and Ruchel," Beth wept. "There are no words . . ."

"I couldn't help but overhear your conversation." The woman

seated next to Mindy leaned over. "That was quite an amazing story."

"I know." Beth wiped her nose. "We're in shock."

"You know what I can't get over?" Mindy sighed. "That it took seventy years to discover something so important to our families."

"Seventy years?" The woman smiled. "What a coincidence. That's how long it takes for a carob tree to bear fruit."

Twenty-three

Mindy and Beth did not know how they were supposed to go from making a sudden, shocking discovery about their family's histories to handling the hassles of modern travel: long waits at the baggage carousel, longer waits in the ladies' rooms, and a line out the door at the car rental counter.

It was as if they'd just spent hours watching a disturbing film about the Holocaust, then walked out into the bright sunshine and remembered it was no longer 1942. They were free to go about their business.

Still, Beth was so lost in thought, she forgot to have a hissy fit when the car rental agent informed her they were out of premium cars. Mindy was in such a daze she realized she left her carry-on bag with the business cards hanging on the hook in the bathroom stall, though she told Beth that her weak bladder was the reason for the return trip to the ladies' room. That, and she had to call Artie.

He had only left for Portland with Aaron yesterday, but what a heavy news day he was missing. Ricky's little bombshell that

Aaron might have been molested by a clown. The shocking call from Dana that she was on the outs with Ira and that Stan was her new best friend. But mostly the startling revelation that she and Beth had a shared history that was of epic proportions.

But did he pick up his cell? Of course not. He'd either forgotten to turn it on, charge it, find it, or take it off vibrate. Her best shot was to leave a voice mail and hope he could recall the two easy steps for message retrieval.

By the time they were en route to the hotel, they were both just relieved to have found the airport exit, let alone Interstate 88, though Beth did cross over four lanes of traffic and cut off a tractor trailer.

"And for my next trick," Mindy peered into her side view mirror to see if a cop had witnessed the maneuver.

"Hey . . . it's a new city. I'm trying to learn the shortcuts."

"And I'm trying to arrive with dry underpants."

"You're hilarious. You should think about writing greeting cards. Are you looking for the sign for Cermak Road?"

"Believe me, no one wants to find that exit more than me. You do realize you're tailgating an ambulance."

"Just keeping up with traffic, Officer. Just keeping up with traffic."

Nothing like a beautiful hotel suite to help you settle in. Especially one that didn't cost a dime and that had a fruit basket and a bottle of wine waiting. Even Beth, who was accustomed to fluffy robes and scenic views, was impressed by the size and the well-appointed bathrooms. "Downtown Greetings must want us pretty bad." She went right for the wine.

"Yeah." Mindy kicked off her shoes and collapsed on the couch "The question is why."

"I don't care why." Beth poured two glasses. "All that matters is they canceled the contest so we have zero competition, they paid our way here, and all we have to do tomorrow is charm them with a little tap dance."

"Yes, well before we shuffle off to Buffalo, can we please think through our strategy?"

"No need. You're forgetting I came from the razzle-dazzle end of the ad game. The key is to listen to what the client wants, lather, and repeat. They'll think we're brilliant."

"And you're forgetting that I've never even sat in on a business meeting before. I'd just feel more comfortable if we went in with a plan."

"Trust me. I've been in a billion meetings and they're all alike. Every client says, 'show us new concepts, real cutting edge,' then you do that, they hate it, and invariably they end up going with the same old, same old. They hate leaving their comfort zone. Besides, we're all they've got. We'd get the job if we walked in backward wearing togas and shower shoes."

"If you say so . . . I guess I'll go call home and then try to reach Artie again. Did you call Richard yet?"

Stupid question. From the speed at which Beth's smile faded, clearly she was happier in her own suite world, where she could escape all thoughts of the battle she'd left behind. Where she could think about the joy it would bring her mother to reunite with an angel from her past. Where she could reminisce about her glory days wooing clients and fantasize how she would impress the folks from Downtown Greetings so much, they would give her a chance to maybe set up her own company.

"No, I didn't call him." Beth plunked herself down in a comfy chair. "Nor do I plan to."

"I'm sorry," Mindy said. "I'm just so used to thinking of you as Beth and Richard, Richard and Beth . . . the kind of couple that would be married for a lifetime."

"Believe me, twelve years has felt like a lifetime."

"That's all you guys have been together? But Jessica is only twelve."

"Exactly." Beth chugged her wine. "Anyone who can do simple math without a calculator has already figured it out. . . . I was pregnant when we got married."

"Oh."

"And let me guess. You want to know if I would have married him anyway and the answer is yes. I was so in love it was ridiculous. I couldn't wait to see him, talk to him . . . I was obsessed as the kids say. But talk about being young and stupid."

"Don't say it like that. Don't regret a life that gave you a beautiful family."

"I guess . . . It's just that after making this incredible connection today between your grandmother and my mother, I finally realized something. Up until now, no matter how angry and disgusted I was with Richard, I was still thinking that I needed to find a way to make the marriage work because a divorce would be so unfair to the girls."

"And now?" Mindy asked.

"And now I realize the person I should be the most angry and disgusted with is myself."

"Why? You weren't the problem."

"It has nothing to do with that. It's that even though I grew up knowing my life was so much more privileged than my mother's, I took everything for granted, and now it turns out the only thing I was a victim of is my own shitty decisions. I've wasted all these years complaining about how much I hated my life but didn't do a damn thing about it because I couldn't stomach the idea of not having all the trappings, which is what they are. Things that kept me trapped in a life that made me angry and miserable . . . I even think that's why I couldn't be friends with you."

"Yeah, please explain that to me. Why did you hate me so much?"

"I didn't hate you. I just didn't want to be around anyone who was happy."

"Who said I was happy? Get me names."

"You're not happy?"

"Not really. No. Most days I feel like the old boxer whose manager makes him stay in the ring so nobody calls him a quitter. He's getting pounded, he's disoriented, he's in pain. . . . He just wants the fight to be over, but the bell rings and he's gotta get back out there for another round."

"Too bad I didn't know. Misery loves company, which I'm sure is why I hung out with Jill so much. No one is more bored, lonely, or pathetic. I used to walk away thinking at least my life wasn't as pitiful as hers."

"How pitiful could it be when you're driving around in a little white Mercedes convertible to go food shopping? Even her daughter drives a nicer car than me. . . . It kills me. I pull up in a minivan with a crack in the bumper and Kayla's tooling around in a brand-new Range Rover with her initials painted on the door. And everywhere I look, all these young girls are walking around with real Louis Vuitton and Chanel."

"I agree it's sick. And they're too young to understand that this is a life sentence. Once you go down that road where you have to have the latest, the hottest, the most expensive . . . there's no going back. You become like an addict. If you don't have it, you'll die. You'll even put up with a lousy marriage just to be able to walk into Saks and spend twelve hundred dollars on a Marc Jacobs pocketbook."

"You spent twelve hundred dollars on a pocketbook?" Mindy threw a couch pillow at Beth. "You could buy a new washing machine for that."

"You could buy a lot of things for that. And the deal with Jill's daughter? She may be driving a nicer car than you, but Jill and Mitch had to get an order of protection for her because she was in an abusive relationship and too strung out from alcohol and OxyContin to notice."

"Oh my God . . . what are we doing to our kids?"

"That's what I'm saying . . . I think this is my wake-up call. I have to get a grip on my life and my daughters' lives before we completely lose touch with reality. I owe it to my family who never had the chance to fulfill their dreams."

"That's pretty profound."

"I know . . . empowering yet simple. And the irony is, it really is what I tell the girls all the time. You want something out of life? Don't wait to have it handed to you. Go get it!"

"But what does all that mean for you and Richard?"

"That it's shit-or-get-off-the-pot time. I either have to throw myself into this relationship, force him to get help, and then do whatever else it takes to get us on track, or file for divorce. I can't be in limbo like this anymore. I'm going to make a decision and then commit to it."

"Wow. That's amazing that you thought all that through in such a short time," Mindy said, sighing. "The only thing that occurred to me is I think I forgot to bring a top for my skirt."

As far as Mindy was concerned, she was already a winner. She'd gotten a free trip to Chicago, a night in a beautiful suite, and a nice dinner at the Mexican restaurant in the hotel. Too bad that lucky feeling started to fizzle like her fajita.

"Have you been listening to them?" Beth nodded at the two men at the next table.

"Yeah. The tall one just said something about Wal-Mart and private-label greeting cards."

"And I could swear the other guy used the words *presentation* and *Anna Jane* in the same sentence. Excuse me," Beth cleared her throat and continued, "we couldn't help but overhear . . . Are you meeting with Anna Jane Crandall at Downtown Greetings tomorrow?"

"Yeah." The tall guy grunted, irritated by the interruption until he checked out Beth and corrected his posture. No man could be rude to a beautiful blonde. "Are you in on this, too?"

"What do you mean, too? We thought we were the only ones."

"No, there's a bunch of us. Half the people in here are presenting tomorrow. And then we found out there's another group coming in on Monday."

"What do you mean presenting?" Mindy gulped.

"We put together a bunch of concepts and storyboards." The man ranked her a zero and turned to Beth. "Chris Corbin." He shook Beth's hand. "This is my partner, Nick DeMarco."

"I'm Beth, and this is my partner, Mindy."

"Howdy, Partner." Mindy waved. She refused to be ignored.

They grunted hello but turned back to Beth.

"We're confused," Beth said. "All we were told to do was make up business cards."

"Yeah, us, too," Nick replied. "We're Card Sharks. What about you?"

"House of Cards." Mindy leaned in: "So, wait. You were told to put together a thing?"

"Yeah," Chris said, and kept eating. "We basically just did what they asked in the e-mail—a ten-minute dog-and-Sony show. We're on the retail side already. We know the drill."

"We never got an e-mail." Beth put her fork down.

"What are we going to do?" Mindy asked. "We've got squat."

"Sucks to be you, man." Chris chugged his beer.

"Well hold on." Beth smiled. "Maybe you could give us a copy of the e-mail."

"Maybe I could, sweet cakes." He winked. "But what's in it for me?"

"What's in it for you," she winked back, "is the satisfaction of knowing you did a very nice thing for your colleagues. Plus, I'm a former art director. . . . I might be able to give you some pointers if you wanted me to critique your presentation."

"Hell, no. We don't need another opinion, we need the work." He laughed in her face. "May the best man win." He toasted with his beer.

"I told you we needed a strategy." Mindy checked her cell for messages as Beth unlocked their door. "Are you sure you never got an e-mail about this?"

"I'm positive, but I brought my laptop so if you want, so I'll go online and check."

"I guess it doesn't matter." She threw off her shoes. "Either way, we're screwed."

"Well, not necessarily . . . Richard installed that Power Point program and I used it a few times for PTA stuff. If we come up with some ideas, I could turn them into an okay presentation."

"But what good will that do? We don't even know what they're looking for."

"True, but I just thought of an idea."

"For a line of cards?" Mindy asked.

"No. That's your department."

"My department? Aren't we a team?"

"Absolutely. You're concepts and I'm execution."

"No, no. You said you were Miss Razzle-Dazzle. Miss Lather and Repeat. The one with all the experience."

"Relax. I didn't say I wouldn't brainstorm with you, but listen. Remember when that Chris guy mentioned that half the people in the restaurant were here for Downtown Greetings?"

"Yeah."

"Well, let's go back downstairs and see if we can find someone else to help us out. Not everyone can be as much of an asshole as him."

"No, wait," Mindy said. "Better yet, let's find one of the e-mails from Anna Jane. Didn't she give us her cell number?"

"We're not calling her now. It's too late."

"I don't care. We came all this way and it's not like she's ten and has a bedtime. This whole thing has been wacko from day one and I want to know why!"

It took a game of telephone tag, but Mindy did eventually reach Anna Jane. Not that it cleared up the confusion.

"No need to kill yourselves for the presentation," she said. "Save the good stuff for me."

"Excuse me?"

"This is for your ears only," she lowered her voice, "but I am resigning from this loony bin very soon to set up my own little endeavor, and I would love to work with you girls."

"Wait. What?" Mindy eyed Beth as if to say wait until you hear this. "Are you saying this thing tomorrow is all for nothing?"

"Well, no. Not for nothing. You could still be considered for the freelance project. I am just saying if we work together on my thing, it is a sure thing."

The team from House of Cards gave it their all, for maybe an hour. Creating clever greeting cards was harder than it looked, like watching bad commercials all night and bragging you could do better, only to discover that filling thirty seconds of airtime was a mean feat.

But it wasn't a wealth of ideas that was lacking, it was motivation. Hard to get fired up about a competition, especially when with each passing glass of wine, the only thing on which they could agree was that, like Mindy's pocketbook, it was a fake and not even a good one at that.

"So in conclusion," a teetering Mindy picked up her shoes, "we would like to thank Downtown Greetings for the nice night in Chicago, but House of Cards is folding."

Normally when Mindy drank, it was lights-out the minute her head hit the pillow. But now, not even the luxurious down comforter brought sweet dreams, for she was too busy fantasizing about stuffing it in her suitcase, courtesy of Downtown Greetings.

Was she a pharaoh in another lifetime that she deserved such crappy karma in this one? Why did it have to be that every time she came close to getting what she wanted, God laughed and said, "Ha-ha, Mindy, not so fast, I'm not done with you."

The cruise she'd waited a whole year for had sucked. The insurance money that was an unexpected windfall was going to have to be split with Stan. The contest she entered was totally bogus. Which all meant one thing: her father wasn't totally right. Maybe bad things could be good things in disguise, but it could just as easily work the other way around.

"Send me a sign, Daddy," she whispered as she so often did in moments of despair. "I need to know if this is all going to work out."

Twenty-four

It's never the stuff you worry about that happens, it's the stuff you don't see coming that incapacitates you like a Taser. And nothing like five-thousand volts of electricity to get your undivided attention.

"What time is it?" A startled Mindy opened one eye to find Beth shaking her shoulder.

"I don't know. Two-thirty maybe?"

"What's wrong? Why are you up?" *It better be good.*

Beth threw herself onto the unmade part of the queen bed and sobbed into a pillow.

"Did you have a bad dream?" Mindy fumbled for the lamp.

"Yes, a horrible dream," she cried harder. "Then I woke up and it was all true. You were right! I am pregnant!"

"Pregnant?" Mindy bolted up. "How is that possible? You said the test was negative!"

"I lied. I never even opened the box until a few minutes ago. Now look." She waved a plastic stick. "Pink is the new black. . . . I swear I'm going to die!"

"Don't say that!" Mindy's heart raced. "Start from the beginning. Tell me everything."

"There's nothing to tell," she gagged. "I was too freaked out to take the test the day you brought it over. I just thought I hadn't gotten my period because of some hormonal screwup, but obviously that wasn't it because I feel like shit, I've put on all this weight, and it looks like my body's been taken over by this alien being."

Mindy held the stick up to the light. The pink YES was unmistakable and she didn't know what threw her more, that Beth was pregnant or that she'd been right all along. "This is scary."

"Ya think?" She wiped her eyes. "And don't start in on that whole bad news can be good news crap. This is a disaster. I wanted to LEAVE Richard, not have another child with him!"

"Well then you do what's best for your own survival. Nobody has to know."

"I can't have another abortion, okay?" Beth choked. "I had one in college and almost died from the hemorrhaging, which was so bad I needed a second D and C, and then a blood transfusion, plus I had this thing called sepsis . . . a high fever and then the chills. Why do you think I married Richard when I found out I was pregnant with Jessica?"

As Beth and Mindy sat in the darkened living room sipping tea, one thing was certain. Whatever was scheduled to have taken place this morning was a scratch. There would be no meetings, no opportunities for advancement in the greeting card industry—just two moms glued to hotel couches, grappling with the implications of a pink stick.

As best as Beth could figure, she was in her second trimester, and though she had yet to feel signs of life, this stage was eerily familiar—the heavy breasts, the stretched abdomen, and the endless urge to pee. Was this God's way of punishing her for having undergone that risky late-term abortion in college, which nearly took her life?

At the time she pledged she would never succumb to another, but like a broken spell, that promise had returned to haunt her amidst circumstances that were far graver than when she was nineteen and clueless. She would be bringing an unwanted baby into a broken-down marriage with little hope for a meaningful family life.

"How could you even think that this baby wouldn't be loved?" Mindy asked. "Maybe you just need time to let it sink in."

"No, I don't. Time isn't going to change anything. I don't want more children or responsibility, and I certainly don't want to be even more tied down to Richard. Plus, I would rather die than get as big as a house. Can't you just see the looks on everyone's faces when I show up wearing maternity clothes? My kids will be mortified, especially Jessica. When Jordy Schreiber's mother got pregnant last year, she was like 'Ohmygod mom, that is sooo gross'!"

"This is good," Mindy said. "Express your deepest fears . . . maybe you'll hear yourself say something that gives you hope."

"Would you stop with the Oprah babble? I have no hope!" She rocked in a fetal position. "Everyone thinks I lead this charmed life but I'm a fraud! I have a shitty marriage, our finances are a mess, and my daughters think I'm this selfish bitch. It wasn't supposed to be like this. . . ."

Who knew, Mindy thought? All these years she'd watched Beth's lavish lifestyle from afar, teetering between envy and disgust: the beautiful family, the showcase house, the great cars and vacations . . . It suddenly gave new meaning to House of Cards. "Maybe try to look at the big picture," she started. "You're beautiful and talented, you've done a great job raising your daughters, your parents are supportive of you—"

"I don't want a baby!" Beth screamed.

"Okay, but think about this. Only yesterday we were talking about how precious life was, and about how the only reason we were even born was because God spared your mom and my grandmother. Maybe this is a sign."

"Yes, that I should have made birth control a higher priority! If I have an abortion, it's a huge risk medically. If I have a baby, it's a huge risk emotionally and financially. I swear to God I should just throw myself down the stairs. . . ."

"Would you stop? I understand you're in shock, but this is not a death sentence. Lots of women have late-in-life babies and it works out great."

"Well, good for them, but I'm not one of those mushy, maternal types who goes all gaga over little kids. The greatest day in my life was when I didn't have to do those boring mommy-and-me classes anymore. I can't go back to that life. I've done my time!"

"I know, but look how fast those years went."

"Whose side are you on?"

"Yours, but I'm trying to get you to see this from a different perspective. You're only focused on the negatives right now."

"That's right. There are no positives."

"There are too! How about the fact there is no greater joy or anything that gives you greater hope than holding a life you created? And oh my God, the baby clothes are so cute now!"

"Whatever . . . I just don't understand how with everything you know you could tell me to go against my better judgment here. Do you honestly think Richard will somehow magically transform into this wonderful husband, and Jessica and Emma will be thrilled at the prospect of having a baby in the house, and my friends will shower me with support, and I'll look back and say 'Thank you, Mindy, thank you for showing me the light? This baby was the greatest thing that ever happened to me'?"

Mindy blinked. Had Beth accused her of having a positive attitude? "You're right. I don't know what I'm saying. You woke me out of a dead sleep, hit me over the head with this . . . It's like what happened when we found out Aaron's mother died . . . I just started blabbing."

"If only I'd left him when the real estate market was at its peak. We could have sold the house for over a million and both started ove. . . ."

" . . . Artie's cousin went through this, too. She already had three kids and went nuts when she found out she was pregnant again. Now that kid is the love of her life. . . ."

" . . . Jessica would be starting college when this kid was starting kindergarten. . . ."

" . . . I was really nervous about having a third child, but there's something so special about the baby in the family . . . like Olympic gold. . . ."

" . . . I don't even know how to tell Richard . . . he's just crazy enough to think this is good news. . . ."

"I thought of something else my dad used to say. He'd tell me that the worst thing about anger and fear was that it made you overreact. Like when the stock market plunges and everyone rushes off to sell, he'd say to me, if you panic, you lose. . . ."

"Did you hear a word I said?" Beth looked up.

"No, did you hear anything I said?"

"Not really."

"Well I was making a lot of sense."

"Nothing makes sense right now." Beth cried out. "Oh my God!"

"What? What is it?"

"I think it just kicked—the alien's alive!"

"It's not an alien," Mindy laughed, "it's your baby."

"I know." Beth hugged the pillow. "I know."

Nothing wrong with cell phones. It was the addiction to using them that stirred anger and anxiety if someone with whom you

were in constant contact suddenly stopped answering or returning calls. Mindy had been trying to reach Artie since early yesterday to no avail, and the mystery deepened when her mom told
her she hadn't heard from him either. Of all times for him to be
missing in action . . . Mindy fumed as she packed her suitcase.

"Any luck reaching Artie?" Beth yelled from the other bedroom.

"No, and I'm so pissed! He always does this to me. He leaves
me a message, then shuts his phone off. Or I leave him all these
messages, then he walks in the house and asks what's new?"

"Maybe something is wrong." She walked in. "Didn't he almost
have a heart attack recently?"

"Thanks for the reminder, but if he's lying in a hospital bed
somewhere, don't you think I would have heard from Aaron
by now?"

"Unless maybe they were both in an accident."

"Why do you always have to be so positive and ruin everything?" she mimicked her. But it did remind her to try Artie
again, and miracle of miracles, he finally answered.

"Where the hell have you been? Why didn't you call me back?
I've been worried sick!"

"Sorry," Artie answered in a fog. "I lost my phone and just got
it back a few hours ago. . . . I didn't want to wake you. What time
is it?"

"Around seven your time I think. You wouldn't believe what's
been going on."

"Hold on. . . . I'm grabbing my jacket and going outside. Aaron's
asleep. We just got to bed like two hours ago. Where are you?"

"Chicago. The contest thing was a disaster. It's not even worth
it to stay. We're heading back to the airport to see if we can
change our flights."

"That's too bad, but you know what, then? Why don't you
come here instead?"

"Come where? To Portland? Why would I do that?"

"I have my reasons and your mom is with the kids. What's the difference where you are?"

"Arthur Sherman, you better promise me you didn't buy a house."

"No," he said, and laughed, "but I could. We could afford it."

"Thank you, Bill Gates. Now put my husband back on."

"I'm not joking. I have some amazing news to tell you."

"Oh my God! We got the insurance money?"

"Yep, but that's not all!"

It's never the things that you plan on that go right, it's the things you don't see coming that can turn your life around. While Beth finished packing, Mindy sat on the bed and listened to the tale.

Seems that after Aaron resolved his police matter, he insisted on going back to his house to search for the toy fire truck that once belonged to little Jimmy Fitzgerald. But after tearing apart his room and the garage, he lost hope of finding it. Then he remembered the boxes in the basement.

The last thing Artie wanted to do was spend time in a dungeon that reeked of mildew, beer, and cat urine, but Aaron was on a mission. "I got something back of my Mom's, now I wanna give Jimmy something back that reminds him of his dad."

It was too noble a cause not to help, so Artie helped dig through shopping bags and old cartons, only to find a box shoved in a back corner underneath a garden hose and back issues of *Guns and Ammo*. Unlike the others, it wasn't labeled, "Keep out Sucka" or "Nunna Ur Beeswax."

At first it looked like nothing more than piles of bank statements, until Artie realized he was holding the deed to the house, which was attached to a closing statement proving that Walter had bought it for cash over twenty years ago.

"What does that mean?" Mindy's heart raced.

"It means that after probate, we can try to sell the house, pay off the back taxes and legal bills, then set up a nice little college nest egg for Aaron. A broker told me that this neighborhood was getting hot again and the place could be worth as much as two hundred thou. Maybe more. How amazing is that?"

"I am so happy for him, Artie. And you must be so relieved."

"You have no idea . . . but wait. There's more."

"Let me guess . . . Walter also owned stock in Microsoft."

"You're close," he laughed. "Davida bought stock in Starbucks."

"Holy shit! We may have to call him Prince Aaron."

"How about Prince Artie?"

"What?"

"Yeah. The stock certificates were in our names: Arthur and Davida Sherman."

"What does THAT mean?"

"It means that I'm going to stop bitching about spending four bucks on a cup of coffee because it looks like my insane bride bought the stock from our joint brokerage account."

"You had that much money?"

"Hardly, but I was thinking back. Ira had just started working at Merrill Lynch and was under a lot of pressure to meet his quota, so my dad had me open an account, and every few months he'd throw in a few thousand to give to Ira to invest. And no surprise here, Davida played the market like she played the horses. But she must have had one hell of a strong hunch about Starbucks, because I found stock certificates for fifty thousand shares dating back to 1994, the year she left me."

"Did you say fifty thousand shares?"

"I did."

"*Whoa!* I wish I could multiply in my head."

"Trust me, after you carry the one, it's worth . . . I don't even know how much, but a lot, and the funny thing is, I'm more in shock that we almost tossed the box. We were hauling so much crap from the basement, we weren't even bothering to look at what we were throwing out."

"So what made you open it?"

"I don't know. It looked more official for some reason. But isn't that crazy? All these valuable documents were just rotting in a basement."

"Shows you how out of it they were." Mindy sighed. "But wait. What about the fire truck?"

"I saved the best for last. . . . We found it in a box of old baby clothes and it looked brand-new. Aaron is so psyched to bring it over to the Fitzgeralds'. I swear I feel like I won a contest."

"Funny you should say that," Mindy laughed. "That was supposed to be me."

Mindy and Beth were so unglued, it was a toss-up who had the better head to drive. They settled on Mindy, as she feared Beth would intentionally drive into a guardrail. But en route to O'Hare, Mindy had a brainstorm that stole her concentration, causing her to change lanes without looking. "Sorry, sorry." She clutched the wheel. "I must have blanked out for a second."

"Fine by me." Beth stared out the window.

"I was thinking," she started, "and just hear me out before you say no. . . . Why don't we both go to Portland?"

"Are you nuts? The last person I want to see is Richard."

"I know, but think about it. It would give you the chance to have a heart-to-heart conversation without the girls interrupting, and sometimes a change of scenery works wonders."

"You don't know what you're saying. When I tell him I'm pregnant, he'll get all spiritual, do the happy dance, and then tell me it's great news."

"But that's good. You want him to be excited."

"No I don't. It'll all be for show. The second it's old news, he'll go right back to his old tricks. I'll never know where he is, how much money we have, if he's telling me the truth about work . . ."

"But think about this. He's out there now because he wants desperately to start over."

"Yes. Without me!"

"Or maybe because of you . . . Maybe he's trying to get it together so he can come back to you and say look, I'm doing it. I'm handling my new job, I'm getting counseling—"

"Mindy, we're not some Lifetime movie starring Valerie Bertinelli! Richard is hopeless."

"No, he's not. He sounds as lost and scared as you."

Beth fidgeted with her engagement ring.

"And you have to admit, he'd be so shocked to see you, it would really make him think about your relationship. I mean who flies across the country unless they mean business? Plus, you have to admit this whole thing with both of our husbands ending up in Portland is bizarre. It has to mean something important is happening in the cosmos, right?"

"Maybe," she sniffed. "But I wouldn't even know what I'd say to him, where I'd start."

"It's like I told Rhoda; it doesn't matter what you say. The fact that you're there is the only thing that's important."

Beth didn't answer.

"Oh, please say yes? I have such a good feeling about this."

"Are you always such an optimist?"

"No, never, I swear. It's my first time."

"Then what's up with you? Why do you care if I have this kid?"

"Are you kidding? It would be a dream come true. You'd finally be fatter than me!"

Twenty-five

It was déjà vu all over again: Artie, Aaron, and Richard standing around an airport due to unexpected circumstances, each lost in thought. Artie wondered if Richard knew Beth was pregnant. Richard wondered if Aaron knew he was wearing his old clothes. Aaron wondered if Artie believed him when he said he wanted to marry Rainbow. Then a woman's cry diverted their attention.

Richard was the first to spot the somber-faced airline personnel dotting the crowd, but it was Artie who heard mention of United's flight 671 from Chicago and the chilling words, *please identify yourself to the agents.*

It's hard to remember the details of your day only hours later, but there is no forgetting where you were the minute you learned that the plane on which your loved one was a passenger was doing figure eights over the airport to burn fuel before bracing for an emergency landing.

"This is the same thing that happened on that Jet Blue flight a few years ago." A woman raced past them on the way to the airline's Red Carpet Club for a briefing.

"What did you hear?" a breathless Artie followed.

"Did you get through to someone on board?" Richard book-ended her on the other side.

"My sister's at home watching CNN." She beat their stride. "They're reporting the landing gear is messed up. They'll have to do one of those foam flops. Hope the runway is long enough . . ."

"It may not be mechanical," a heavyset man tried keeping up. "My wife's boss knows a guy at the NTSB. They're thinking hijacker."

Artie felt chest pains. Plane crash? Terrorist plot? This couldn't be happening. But when a terrified group assembled in a packed conference room, reality hit. A drama was unfolding without benefit of a script and the reaction was immediate. Grab your cell phone and laptop and get the facts.

Unfortunately, phone contact with passengers would be im-possible, as the signals had been scrambled to prevent radio in-terference with the tower. Or as one distraught husband said, "The SOBs are probably already doing spin control."

In youthful defiance, Aaron leaped over a chair and headed for the door. "I can find out what's goin' down," he said. "I gotta friend whose dad works here."

"And I know the guys who left Fallon to set up the ad agency that won the United account." Richard's heart was pounding. "They might know something."

Artie nodded, unable to mask the terror in his eyes, or the guilt. Had he not talked Mindy into switching her flight, both of their wives would be back in New York and out of harm's way. How he prayed not to be one of those unfortunate souls quoted in the paper whose story reeked of irony. *I thought it would be nice if she came to Portland.* "How do you think they're doing?" he asked.

"Are you kidding?" Richard checked his cell for the tenth time. "Beth goes nowhere without Xanax. She probably took the whole bottle by now. Damn! No service in here. I'll be right back."

"Richard, wait!" Artie grabbed him. "There's something I need to tell you ... about Beth."

"I know what you're going to say, but I know my wife. She wasn't going to leave me."

"No, no. That's not it. . . . She may not have taken the Xanax . . . she's pregnant."

"Pregnant?" His voice ricocheted over the crowd noise. "What the . . . are you sure?"

"Positive. Mindy told me she did the test last night. That's what she was coming to tell you."

"Oh my God." He clutched Artie's shoulder. "Oh my God . . ."

Artie was pacing at the back of the room, wondering how anyone could remain seated let alone focused on the hastily done Power Point presentation that was supposed to reassure them. Instead it was creating more angst, giving people things to fear that they hadn't yet considered.

"The A320 airbus is one of the most reliable, technologically advanced commercial jets out there," a veteran pilot droned on. "Similar incident in Los Angeles a few years back . . . nosewheel jammed ninety degrees in the wrong direction . . . passengers and baggage were moved toward the rear of the craft . . . no fatalities."

Artie couldn't listen. All he could ponder was what he'd say when he called home. He was awful at this job. Mindy was the rock, the one who knew the right words to put everyone at ease. How would he ever survive without her?

"We're doing everything humanly possible to minimize the risks: burning forty-six thousand pounds of aviation fuel, putting less stress on the plane reduces chances of an explosion. Fire trucks and emergency rescue workers standing by on the tarmac . . ."

He checked his watch. They'd been circling for an hour. One

more to go. Thank God they wouldn't have a view of the touch-down, but would they hear the sirens?

"The pilots will keep the nose gear off the ground as long as possible. Runway 28L is eleven thousand feet. FAA doesn't rec-ommend a pre-foam, depletes supply in case of fire, can't com-promise the brakes . . . may be able to evacuate using air stairs instead of slides . . ."

Artie was in such shock, he didn't notice Aaron crouched in a corner until he heard a familiar voice: *"I'm afraid of aeroplanes, even though I like the way it feels to be a person in the sky . . . one day we'll come crashing down, what will I do, never had a chance to say goodbye . . . close my eyes . . .'"*

Now his stomach was in knots. This wasn't just any song. It was "A320," the Foo Fighter hit from the *Godzilla* soundtrack. He liked it, too, he just never imagined it would one day be his theme song. "Believe me, I'm freaked out," he said, "but these guys are so well trained."

"Not good." Richard found them. "It's a full flight . . . hundred-thirty six passengers and crew . . . they've never had a major crash here before. Let's hope they know what the hell they're doing!"

"Oh my God, would you cool it?" Artie gritted.

"Right. No, of course," Richard backpedaled. "My buddy at the agency said the pilot just has to pop a wheelie so he lands on the back tires. Sure beats losing an engine!"

Artie didn't know which was worse: thinking that every passing minute was bringing the plane closer to its life-or-death land-ing or being surrounded by a room full of strangers who were crying, praying, and chatting, their random words of fear and faith wafting in the air.

"Hey, c'mon." Artie had to lift Aaron off the floor. "You heard the guy. The second the plane lands, they start the evacuation and everyone gets out."

"You believe what you wanna believe. I know the truth!"

"What do you mean?" Artie's heart raced.

Aaron waved his arms in a big circle and made a loud popping sound.

"What the hell are you talking about?"

"My friend's dad is off today but I got to talking to some guys on the ground crew." He looked up in tears. "They said the wind's not comin' from the west, so it's gonna be real hard to control the plane now. . . . They're gettin' ready for a crash and burn!"

"Oh my God!" Artie shuddered.

"Why do you have to keep saying *God*?" He rocked like a baby. "There's no such thing."

"You don't believe in God?"

"Wouldn't matter if I did. He doesn't believe in me!"

"That's crazy. Of course there's a God. I mean it's fine to question your beliefs. Even Mother Teresa had doubts. But this is no time to abandon ship. If ever you needed to believe in a higher being and—"

"Stop tryin' to sell me, okay? I used to go to church and pray and it did shit for me. You think I wanted to grow up in that house? You think it's fair I've been losin' people left and right, or that a plane full of good people might blow up 'cause my mom wants to get even with me. I know I shouldn't have called the cops on her, but I thought we were all gonna get killed . . . all these guys livin' in our house, stealin' our things. 'Cause of me she had to serve time; wouldn't talk to me when she got out. . . ."

Artie was riveted, momentarily forgetting that his wife's life was in jeopardy. All he could focus on was his son's painful confession and his sad, convoluted belief that there was some karmic connection between his dead mother and the innocent people in peril.

"Hey, look. It's your call if you want to talk to God, or Allah, or the Good Humor man. But please tell me you believe in something, 'cause I can't think of anything worse than not having faith. And how you could think you had anything to do with this situation? You're an innocent bystander."

"You're only sayin' that 'cause you're my dad, but you gotta see the truth. Somebody up there hates me.... I go on a vacation and my mom dies, I come home and my uncle is dead, I go back to New York and find out I'm under arrest in Portland. I get back here and now a plane full of people is getting fucked! It's me, man. Don't you see? Anything to do with me is doomed!"

Artie tried to process the sad revelation that his son felt like a marked man, yet he couldn't contain his glee. "You think of me as your dad."

"Duh."

"No, I mean when we first got together, you kept calling me Art."

"Just a name," Aaron said. "I'm not retarded. You're all I got now."

"Mindy thinks you're great, too." He wiped his eyes. "She'd do anything for you."

"I know.... Somethin' happens to her, we are so screwed!"

"Nothing's going to happen.... God knows we need her more than he does. "

Artie had lost track of how many diet Cokes he'd downed, how many steps he'd paced, how many tears he'd shed, how many times he'd called home, how many times he'd wished he'd never asked Mindy to change her plans. But the bottom line was the same. If not for finding the Starbucks stock, he never would have suggested that Mindy book a last-minute flight. So the money wasn't even in his pocket yet, but it had already altered his life, and not for the better.

And who was he to tell Aaron not to question God's existence? He had a few concerns himself. How could a compassionate God shower him with wealth, then take away the woman who was his wife and best friend? Was it written in the script that he wasn't entitled to happiness and success at the same time?

An energized Richard ran over. "Good news! I asked one of the guys up there if a pregnant woman would be one of the first off and he said yes. That means Mindy would be right behind Beth."

"Good, good!" Artie had to force himself to focus. "What else did he say? How much longer are they going to be up there?"

"Another twenty minutes maybe. Half hour tops . . . I can't be-lieve they're not shutting down the airport for this. The terminals haven't been evacuated. It's like business as usual out there."

"That's strange because I heard someone say the tarmac looks like an army invaded— rescue workers, fire trucks, ambulances. Have you been drinking?"

"Yeah, but not enough." Richard blew into a tissue. "I swear to God I've never been so scared in my entire life. The thought of all these people strapped in their seats not knowing what's going to happen to them is blowing my mind. I don't know what I'll do if she doesn't make it off that plane. I've screwed up so royally. . . ."

"Want to know my one regret?" Artie whispered. "That I never bought Mindy a nicer engagement ring. I know how much she wanted something a little bigger. I could kick myself now. I blew money on such stupid stuff when I could have used it to show her how much I loved her . . ."

"I just want to make things right, especially with a baby coming," Richard sniffed. "I hope to God they're okay. . . ."

"What the fuck!" A bewildered Aaron looked up from his crouch position. "We need to start prayin' or somethin'."

Some choice! Wait around for word of the landing or follow one of the staff into a room where a small closed-circuit televi-sion had been set up. Artie was astounded by how many people jumped at the chance to watch, as if this was a Hollywood movie, not a potential real-life tragedy.

Richard opted to watch so he didn't have to spend another minute in a crowded conference center listening to people's annoying cell conversations or well-meaning clergy.

Artie was still undecided because of Aaron. How could he let this young, troubled kid possibly witness a plane blowing apart? He'd carry this image to his grave, although sitting around staring at tables of food and drinks thinking Mindy had left this earth would be more surreal.

Only to look around and realize that while he had been contemplating his terrible options, Aaron was once again making his own decisions. He was gone.

"Call his cell," Richard said. "We've only got another few minutes."

"We didn't get him one yet." He wiped a sweaty brow. "Where the hell could he have gone?"

Everyone with whom they'd spent the past few harrowing hours had a suggestion. Try the men's room, the vending machines down the hall, the newsstand, even the roof. Maybe he was trying to catch sight of the landing from there, no matter that he could be arrested for trespassing.

Artie was so torn between shock and anger that at the very moment he was supposed to be bracing for a possible disaster, he was cursing out his kid for his senseless acts.

"We gotta go." Richard nudged Artie. "He'll show up eventually. Poor kid's probably hiding under a couch."

"You don't know my son. When he runs away, he looks for blow jobs."

"God, I love this kid!"

Artie looked around the room full of brave people who had said that no matter how terrified, they wanted to watch the land-

ing. Of course in this day of dazzling, fifty-inch televisions with
state-of-the-art high-definition images, none of them expected
to have to gather around a small black-and-white set from the
days of *The Ed Sullivan Show.*

And rather than looking out for fellow survivors, people were
elbowing for a better spot. But it was in the midst of being shoved
aside that Richard saw an image on the screen that made him
wonder if maybe he'd drunk too much after all, for now he was
seeing things. "Is that Aaron?"

"Where?" Artie wedged himself closer to get a glimpse.

"Over there." Richard pointed to the top right of the screen.
"Yeah, that *is* him. . . . Those are my Nikes. . . . Look, do you see
him? He's wearing a helmet and a yellow raincoat!"

"Son of a bitch." Artie stared. "How the hell did he get out
there? I'm going to fucking kill him! He could die!"

"Where are you going?" Richard grabbed him.

"What do you mean? I have to have someone go get him. He
can't be out there."

"Sir, there isn't time," some woman from the family assistance
team said. "I don't even think we can notify one of the squad
captains now; it's too late. The plane is about to touch down."

"Oh my God!" Artie crouched down. "Oh my God . . . how
could he do this to me?"

"Wait. Look," Richard waved him over. "One of the guys just
gave him a hose and stuck him on a truck."

"Oh man! I bet it was one of the guys he talked to when he
went downstairs to find his friend's dad. . . . I can't watch now."

"Yes you can. You're the one who said we had to stay positive."

"Yeah, but that was before my idiot son decided to play fire-
man! The kid always loved fire trucks. . . . Just yesterday we were
cleaning out his old house and found this one from when he was
a baby. I bet he went out there for Jimmy Fitzgerald. . . ."

"Or for Mindy," Richard patted Artie. "No way does he want to lose another mom."

As people held hands bracing for the landing, they gasped. Just before touching down, the plane suddenly thrust upward, banking steeply to the right before soaring back into the air. Nobody had mentioned the possibility that the attempt would be aborted at the last second.

"I have no idea," the head supervisor said, knowing that everyone would demand an explanation. "Obviously there was a problem. Maybe the angle was bad or the wind speed . . ."

"Practice makes perfect," a young woman crossed herself.

"They're coming back . . . they're trying again." Richard sounded like one of the play-by-play announcers on *Monday Night Football.* "Holy shit, is that smoke?"

Artie wished there was a split screen so that he could monitor the landing while trying to keep an eye out for Aaron, and oh God, Richard was right. The nose of the plane was on fire, raw flames and plumes of gray smoke were ripping across the belly. "Oh my God!" Artie cried.

"Land!" Richard screamed. "Fucking land the plane already!"

"Why aren't they foaming down the runway?" someone yelled.

"I'm gonna be sick." A man ran out.

Then in an instant, the plane came crashing downward on its belly like a cannonball, but instead of decelerating, it was picking up velocity on the wet pavement, sliding from side to side like a mad skater. Suddenly the screen went white, obliterated by huge sprays of foam shooting from every direction. With zero visibility, the only things to focus on were the piercing sounds. Sirens, alarms, water dousing from hoses, the crackle of flames, people screaming?

In the corner of the tiny screen, they could spot signs of life:

passengers sliding down a chute, then running, slipping, tripping, grabbing hands covered in foam. . . .

"I think I see my son!" a woman cried. "I think that's him! That's his jacket!"

A panicked Richard and Artie were glued to the screen. Weren't Beth and Mindy supposed to be among the first ones off?

"Ain't that your kid?" a man nudged Artie. "Looks like he's carrying somebody . . . oh Christ . . . he fell!"

"Get up, Aaron!" Artie shouted as if he was watching the Jets in overtime. "Get up! Run!"

"Can you see who he's with?" Richard squinted.

"No, they're too far away . . . wait, hold on, is that Beth? I see some light-colored hair . . ."

"Oh my God! That *is* her! he found her!" Richard hugged him. "He found her!"

"Yeah, but where's Mindy?" Artie gulped. With dozens of people fleeing, it was near impossible to make out faces. "C'mon Mindy! Show up!"

A moment later, Richard high-fived him. "I see her. . . . it's definitely her!"

"Where?"

"Right over there," he pointed. "Looks like she's carrying someone, too . . . an older man maybe. It's hard to tell."

"Oh my God, you're right. It *is* her!"

"She's unbelievable, Artie!"

"I love you honey," Artie said as tears streamed down his face.

"They made it!" Richard hugged him. "They goddamn made it!"

"Thank you, God!" Artie fell to his knees. "Thank you, thank you, thank you!"

"We're driving home," were Mindy's first words when she tore through the terminal doors and collapsed in Artie's arms.

"Whatever you say." He kissed her. "Although they mentioned something about giving us free flights back."

"Free?" She laughed, afraid to let go, as this was the moment she'd prayed for. "Okay, maybe."

Then Aaron walked in, received a hero's welcome, and hugged Mindy so tight she well understood his meaning. They were family to each other from this day forward.

"You're grounded." Artie slapped him on the back.

"For what?" Aaron removed his fire helmet and shook out dust and debris.

"What do you mean for what? For scaring the crap out of me."

"Fine. What's my punishment?"

"I don't know. Haven't thought about it yet."

"Doesn't matter. I'm just gonna appeal. I have an in with Judge Mindy."

"That's right," she said, wiping her eyes. "Aaron can do no wrong. You wouldn't believe how many people he carried out, and the smoke was getting so awful."

"Fine!" I'll make it a light sentence." Artie laughed. "No allowance for a month."

"Fuck that, man. I'm as rich as you now!"

"True. Then okay, just give me your word you're done with the dangerous stunts for now. I swear I thought I was going to lose both of you, and I don't know what I would have done."

Aaron couldn't respond because he was whisked away by a reporter from one of the news channels.

Meanwhile, Beth and Richard were huddled in a corner, both at a loss for words. They had forgotten that beneath the hardened surface of hostilities lay a foundation of love and companionship.

Mindy looked over and smiled, sensing that Richard had just asked Beth if she was pregnant, and she looked in his eyes and nodded yes. Together they cried, knowing how difficult it would be to cast aside the years of hurt and pain, yet understanding that the only way to reconcile this near-death experience was to get their priorities straight.

"I swore if you walked off that plane, I was going to do anything you asked," Richard said.

"Funny, I swore the same thing. If I walked off that plane, you were doing anything I asked."

"Let's call home and then get the hell out of here so we can go celebrate our amazing luck."

But there would be a long delay, as most of the passengers couldn't bear to leave the airport cocoon, their experience so traumatic they wanted to maintain the bond that had united them. For the next few hours it was all about hugging, retelling the tales, taking pictures, drinking champagne, exchanging contact information, answering reporters' questions, praising the airline crew, and celebrating life and love.

And making resolutions, for not one among them felt they could squander this second chance to get it right. Yet the one with the greatest resolve was not a passenger but a hometown boy who in a moment of terror had heard a calling to rescue innocent people, not in the name of obligation, in the name of courage.

Mindy had been the first adult who had ever cared enough about him to hold him accountable for his decisions and to urge him to be brave in his pursuits. It was in her honor that he tore out onto the tarmac.

The next day his picture was in the *Oregonian,* but it was the caption he loved best: AARON FINDLEY, LOCAL HERO, FUTURE FIREFIGHTER. He bought extra copies in the event he was ever arrested again.

Twenty-six

It took five days for Mindy to be able to wake up and not have as her first thought the life-altering event that had changed her outlook. She was over the shock that finally they would have money in the bank. Gone was the need to break into hives when the credit card bills arrived.

Recovery from the plane crash would take much, much longer.

But because she hated long car rides and wanted to hurry home to see her kids, say nothing of the offer of free flights and the extreme odds against lightning striking twice, Mindy agreed to fly back. Also, Beth refilled her Xanax prescription and offered to hand over the bottle if there were any terror-filled moments on board.

The first two days home flew by in a frenzy of phone calls, e-mails, and spontaneous celebratory gatherings with family and friends, offering endless chances to recount the unforgettable story and the heroics of Artie's son. Even News 12 and *Newsday* came out to interview them, citing the miracle landing that spared two Merrick families from a terrible tragedy.

But it wasn't all joie de vivre. Little Ricky and Nadine were directing unprovoked anger toward Mindy, and it took a show-down to discover their motives. A sister-kicking, toy-throwing Ricky was struggling to cope with the idea that his mommy almost died and that now she liked his new big brother better than him. "He came here to be with Daddy, not you."

Nadine, supposedly older and wise, was sour grapes over the fact that the *Newsday* piece had referred to Mindy and Beth as best friends. "And what am I? Chopped liver?"

Probably not a good time to mention to either of them that she and Artie had seriously discussed relocating to Portland. But after spending two days there, and getting an impressive grand tour led by Aaron, Mindy could no longer dismiss the idea as "absofuckinfreakincrazy."

The turning point came while having dinner with Artie's old friend Andy Levinger and his wife, Tracey. Such nice people and their stunning mountain-view home with tennis courts and a pool caught them by surprise. Did Mindy and Artie dare to dream?

Turns out Artie had guessed right after seeing the billboards advertising Andy's optometry centers. He'd moved west for the skiing, met a nice girl, and created new roots, ending up with a beautiful family and a comfortable lifestyle that they thanked God for every day. Even better, Andy was excited about the idea of spreading the wealth.

His own small franchise was thriving, but he desperately wanted a business partner to help him expand. Even more amazing, Andy happened to know two buddies from optometry school who were also unhappy Eye Deals franchisees and who had spent the last few months gathering evidence for a class-action suit, as there was mounting proof of financial wrongdoing against the owners. "They've been cooking the books from day one."

News from next door was equally surprising. Richard and Beth had also spent their first few days together reflecting on their future. Beth was adamant that if she had this baby, it would have no bearing on her decision to stay in the marriage. The only thing that would convince her to work this through was if Richard agreed to get counseling, be open about his daily life, and promise never again to deceive her.

Richard gave her his word, assuring her he understood that he had just gotten the wake-up call of his life, he was sorry from the bottom of his heart for his behavior, and he desperately wanted to keep their family intact. Under one condition: that Beth consider selling the house and moving to Portland. "You've got to admit, this opportunity with Nike is incredible, and we'll have the best chance of starting over if no one knows our whole story."

"Not on your life," she'd said at first. Not with Jessie's bat mitzvah coming up and her parents getting older, making travel more difficult. And then there was their house in which they'd invested so heavily. How could he even think about asking her to walk away from her brand-new Aster Cucine kitchen and Jenn-Air appliances? Maybe other people could pick up and move to another part of the country, but she was a New Yorker. She did not live in cities not within driving distance of Bloomingdale's or Neiman Marcus.

But when Mindy confided that she and Artie had been talking about making this move, Beth hedged. She had been impressed by Portland, the cost of living was affordable, the schools were great, the skiing was amazing, and their new custom-built home could be on a large piece of property, rather than a postage-stamp-sized lot that allowed your neighbors to watch your comings and goings.

"I'll think about it," Beth returned from Mindy's and said to Richard, though she could barely breathe when the words came out.

"Yes! What made you change your mind?"

"Looks like Mindy and Artie are serious about it, and I don't think I could live here anymore if she wasn't next door."

"So it has nothing to do with wanting to stay married to me?"

"Not really, no," she said, giving him a half smile.

With life beginning anew for the Shermans and the Diamonds, it was only fitting that they be preparing for Passover, the festival ushering in spring and the season of renewal. Each year, Mindy offered to arrive early at her in-laws house to help set the holiday table, though it meant having to listen to Stan complain that the matzoh balls were too soft, while Rhoda yelled at him to stay out of the kitchen. But this year, there was a sweetness to their voices, a sign that like two horses who'd spent a lifetime pulling the family cart, they were back in step, still leading the way.

As Mindy carefully laid out each utensil and glass, she took great pleasure from seeing the gleaming silver, the bone china, and the embroidered silk linens handed down over three generations, for it brought her back to when she would help her mother in much the same way.

How she had loved setting the table with the "good" dishes, then proudly placing her Bubbe's candlestick holders next to her father's silver *kiddish* cup, all while savoring the sweet smells coming from the kitchen.

But no question; nobody prepared a holiday meal like Rhoda. Each year she would bring out one delectable dish after another. The carrot tzimmes, the assortment of kugels, the homemade gefilte fish with white horseradish. Even Dana, the hard-core health nut who insisted on bringing vegetable chopped liver, would be caught nibbling pieces of the soft, mouthwatering brisket.

And how auspicious that it was tradition that the youngest child at the Seder table ask the question, why is this night different from all other nights? For on this night, they would be joined by Aaron, the little boy whose presence had once brought so much joy to Artie's family and who, like the Israelites, had been snatched from his home, praying that he might one day be returned.

Mindy couldn't wait to see Aaron's reaction when he toured his grandparent's waterfront home or when he read the passages from the Haggadah. Would he take an interest in the holiday rituals, other than the one that ordered drinking four glasses of wine?

And in keeping with the spirit of the holiday, welcoming strangers in a strange land, Stan and Rhoda graciously invited Beth's entire family so that they could celebrate together the miracle as great as the Red Sea parting . . . their families reaching this day with everyone alive and in good health.

But the miracles did not end there. For the first time in seventy years, Beth's mother, Ruth, could be seated next to another important guest, Mindy's Grandma Jenny. Though infirm and of sound mind only on occasion, what better way to commemorate freedom from bondage than to reunite the former refugee, Gittle Soloweichyk with her onetime charge, Ruchel Freund, of Vienna?

Mindy had gone over to the nursing home the day before to try to explain the story to her grandmother, who said she understood. But that was no guarantee that she would remember that tonight was Passover, let alone that she was reuniting with little Ruchel.

Dayenu. It would have been enough to have just one of these blessings. But to have them all? She felt so blessed.

The minute the tall, still regal-looking Ruth arrived, she went right over to Gittle, hugged her beloved guardian, and began speaking to her in Yiddish. But the elderly woman showed no signs of recognition. "Keep going," Mindy said. "Half the time she doesn't recognize me at first either." So Ruth shared stories and songs, even showed a picture of her in her mother's arms that was taken months before the Kindertransport departed. Still nothing.

"Leave her be for now," Helene suggested. "She's like an old car on a winter morning . . . she needs a little time to warm up before she's good to go."

"Maybe show her the pickle dish." Mindy laughed.

"Oh yeah. Good idea." Helene brought it over to her. "Ma!" she raised her voice so she could hear. "Remember this? The pickle dish you wanted back?"

"No," she said, and waved it away. "Ver is Abe?"

"Abe is gone, Ma. . . . Arthur, too. But Mindy and I are here."

"Ver? Ver is Mindeleh?"

"It's me, Grandma. I'm right here."

"Ver's your mother? Is she coming?"

"She's here." Mindy kissed her and turned to Ruth. "This may take a while."

"It took seventy years," she hugged her. "Vat's another few hours?"

By the time Stan began the Seder service, Mindy was holding back tears. As she looked around the table, she saw not friends and family, but people who had journeyed here with rich stories of love and loss, escape and redemption, and mostly of survival. And though they may have been strangers, they were united in their unbroken faith and their belief in God.

How great to see Beth and Richard seated between her parents and their children, all so prosperous looking. Yet their suffering had never been allayed by their wealth, as it was true that there was no such thing as an E-ZPass for life. Mindy hoped that like the Israelites who were given a second chance, they, too, could rebuild and go from strength to strength.

As for Ira and Dana, it was yet unclear where their marital journey was headed. A normally boisterous Ira arrived barely uttering hello, except to Mindy, whom he said he was happy to see. "We would have missed you around here, kid. Nobody else keeps Dad in line like you." But his attempt at humor was thinly veiled, as Dana had no problem showing her hand. "Well, what do you know? At least he appreciates someone!"

Mindy took Artie's hand and smiled. How lucky she was to have had a loving partner and trusted friend all these years, and a father for her children who, like her father, believed that protecting them was both his duty and his privilege.

And what of their children? They were living in a world that placed so much value on material possessions and that rewarded entitlement without effort. Her hope was that in spite of their newfound prosperity, they had instilled in them a desire to enrich not their pockets but their souls. To live life with a generous spirit and a devotion to family, for that would be the best legacy they could possibly inherit.

Then there was Aaron, so handsome looking with his cropped haircut and clothes from the mall. Interesting how he blended in with his siblings and cousins like the missing patch in a quilt, yet without sacrificing his own unique style. Not many boys would dare to cut the sleeves off an expensive Abercrombie polo or attach their iPod to a pocket-watch chain.

And though he might not have understood the prayers his grandfather was chanting in Hebrew, he did recognize the language of love. Proof came at the end of the meal when it was time for the children to find the afikomen, the hidden matzoh. Little did Aaron know, his cousins weren't looking very hard, as they were warned to make sure Aaron had beginner's luck. There was a gift waiting from the leader, Papa Stan, and it had Aaron's name on it.

Not one to show great emotion, Stan could not hold back his saltwater tears, for it gave him such joy to present Aaron with a photo of a beautiful baby boy sitting on his grandfather's lap, celebrating his first Seder.

"Is that me?" he asked.

"It sure is," Artie sniffed. "I don't know where they found it, but it's you at this very table."

"Welcome home, son," Stan kissed his cheek. "Welcome home."

"Ruchel!" Grandma Jenny suddenly called out. *"Hab keine Sorgen. Gehe schlafen."*

"What did she just say?" Beth asked her mother.

"Oh my." Ruth took Jenny's hand. "She just told me not to vorry. To go to sleep."

"Errinnerst du dich an mich?" Ruth asked. "Do you remember me?"

Jenny nodded. *"Du bist mein Baby von dem Kindertransport."*

"She remembers!" Ruth cried. "She said, 'You're my baby from the Kindertransport.'"

"It's a miracle!" Rhoda hugged Stan.

"What is, Nana?" Ricky asked.

"All of it, darling. All of it."

"Here is to family and friends." Stan raised his glass. "To life! *L'chayim!*"

"L'chayim!" they all shouted.

"L'chayim!" Aaron toasted Artie and drank the entire glass of wine.

"Hey slow down, son," Artie laughed. "We've got three more cups to go."

"I like being Jewish." He refilled his glass. "You guys really know how to party."

"That's right." Mindy hugged him. "Next to suffering, it's what we do best."

Twenty-seven

Six Weeks Later

Finally! Noah Blum, former-boyfriend-turned-hummus-selling psychic, got back to Mindy. "Fortunately it was just a social call," she scoffed. "Nothing very important going on in my life since I called you two months ago."

He apologized but said he never got her message. The reason he was calling was because he'd heard about the plane crash and was concerned. Also, he had great news to share. He was getting remarried and his fiancée was a girl who graduated from their high school a few years after them.

"How many years after?" Mindy asked. "Six, seven . . ."

"Ten," he coughed. "But a great girl. A dead ringer for Jennifer Anniston. You'll love her. She doesn't take my crap, ha-ha."

"I'm sure she's terrific, ha-ha. *Poor kid!* Send me pictures of the wedding."

"No, I want you to come to the wedding. We're getting married over Thanksgiving."

"And you call yourself a psychic? We have a bat mitzvah that weekend. And unless you tell me it's a horrible idea, we'll be living in Oregon by then. But wait. I need to know if it's okay to get on a plane again. I'm flying to Portland in a few days to go house hunting and I'm terrified. Speaking of houses, will we get close to our asking price? We got one offer but it was so low, I asked the guy if he was only bidding on the downstairs."

Say what you would about Noah, he could be a source of comfort. He assured Mindy that the move would work out great and that he saw the house selling to a nice couple who didn't care that it needed work, as the husband was a contractor and would be gutting it anyway.

As for future flights, he promised she had nothing to worry about. He did, however, caution her about their finances. "I see this big windfall. Did you make a killing in the stock market?"

"Yes! Oh my God."

"Well don't blow the money on the first thing you see . . . you've got a lot of extra expenses coming up. Are you guys planning on having another kid because I'm hearing about a boy, but it's more like an adoption. Name has an A sound."

She gasped, then said, "This is why people pay you the big bucks."

Then Noah confessed. A nervous Artie had called the day before, told him the whole story, then asked for his guidance.

"I'm in shock," Mindy laughed.

"Why? Because your husband claims he doesn't believe in psychics?"

"No, because he looked up your number without me. That's a first!"

Nadine was so jealous. Mindy and Beth had their houses all to themselves, as Stacie, Jamie, Jessica, and Emma were away at camp; little Ricky was in Florida with family friends; and God help them, Artie, Aaron, and Richard were living in Portland, having rented a three-bedroom condo near Nike.

"You're so lucky," Nadine called. "No laundry, no making dinner, no annoying kids."

"I know. It's like a Club Med vacation. I spend the entire day trying to throw out eight years' worth of crap, then I go over to Beth's to give her a hand."

"I'm still jealous. No laundry, no making dinner, no annoying kids."

True, and plenty of time to talk.

As Mindy helped Beth pack the fragile items she wouldn't be letting the movers touch (all of them), they pondered how their kids would handle this major upheaval, if any of them would survive without New York bagels, and if the women who moved in would become friends.

The one who had promised to bring her husband back for a second look at Mindy's house had twin boys, first graders who looked like middle linebackers. The one showing interest in Beth's house was a law professor whose ten-year-old daughter was a music prodigy. "The moms would totally hate each other," Mindy said as she taped a box.

"Forget that car pool!" Beth said, and handed her another Lladro.

"So have you guys decided anything about Jess's bat mitzvah?" Mindy sneezed.

"Please! Not on 'A Moment's Pause.' It's a limited edition. . . . Every time I bring it up, Richard says not to worry. Portland is a modern city with running water and DJs."

"He's not worried about losing all the deposits?"

"He said he'd rather lose his money than his family. Plus, I forgot to tell you. He spoke to that Andy Levinger guy and found out the temple they belong to has the Thanksgiving weekend available, so if we joined there, at least we could keep the same date."

"That's perfect for your out-of-towners."

"You mean the entire guest list?" Beth collapsed on the couch.

"Hey! We'll be local, hard as that is to believe."

"You can't believe?" Beth shifted to a more comfortable position. "At least you won't be taking a bath when you sell. Every night I wake up in a sweat."

"Duh . . . pregnancy and perimenopause equals the hormone hotel. Some are checkin' in, some are checkin' out!"

"I wish that's all it was. I'm still having nightmares about the crash, and still having anxiety attacks about the baby. I thought I'd feel different by now . . . not so depressed."

"Are you sure you're depressed? Maybe you're just over-whelmed. I mean who wouldn't be going crazy if they were moving across the country and planning a bat mitzvah and a bris for the same week?"

"I feel so much better now, thank you. . . . You really think I'm having a boy?"

"Yep."

"I think it's a boy, too. It just feels different than it did with the girls."

"Are you going to find out before?"

"I don't want to, but Richard is already hocking me. He's dying for a son!"

"That's what he told Artie. And the doctor is sure about the due date?"

"Positive. I almost fell off the table when he told me late November."

"Oh my God. What if you went into labor at Jessica's service?"

"And you wonder why I'm depressed?"

"Well, look at it this way," Mindy said. "You kept telling me how miserable you were, how you hated your life, your friends, and now look. Instant makeover! You're getting to start over in a brand-new city, in a brand-new house, with a brand-new baby—"

"And the same old husband."

"C'mon, think positive. He's working his ass off; he's seeing a shrink, he's been out house hunting with Artie; he's excited about the baby. You should be thrilled."

"Why do you always have to see the bright side and ruin everything?"

"It's the new me! I finally realized my bad attitude was making every situation worse."

"Okay, but let's be honest. The reason you're so calm now is you're not flat broke. It helps to have money."

"No, it helps to have faith. And perspective. Those things turned out to be free of charge. It's like my dad would say: 'Mindeleh, nothing is ever as bad as it seems or as good.'"

"Then why do I keep fantasizing about running away, which of course I can't do because I've got this ball and chain around me."

"Not a ball and chain." Mindy smiled. "An anchor. A reason to stay with your family and build this new life together. I swear this baby was so meant to be."

"Oh, please. Not the whole bashert thing. I don't buy it. Not everything is fate."

"Really? Then how do you explain that in Hebrew there is no literal translation for the word *coincidence*? The closest meaning is 'hand of God.' What does that tell you?"

"It tells me that you've been talking to my mother. It's God's will. It's in the cards. . . ."

"Got any better philosophies of life?"

"No, but speaking of cards, I have one for you."

"Why? It's not my birthday."

"Yeah, when is that?" Beth reached in a desk drawer. "January, right?"

"April, but you were close." Mindy stared at the envelope.

"Well, open it already!" Beth ordered.

"Stop being so bossy." She slid her finger across the top and smiled at the charming photo of two little girls locked arm in arm, one a strawberry blonde, the other a dark-haired child.

"This is how cards work." Beth stood over her. "There's an outside *and* an inside, often with a nice message."

Mindy rolled her eyes as she read the inscription: *To my dearest friend, Mindy, who taught me this and more.*

Success
by Ralph Waldo Emerson

*To laugh often and much, to win the respect of intelli-
    gent people
and the affection of children; to earn the appreciation
    of honest critics
and endure the betrayal of false friends,
to appreciate beauty,
to find the best in others,
to leave the world a bit better
whether by a healthy child,
a garden patch
or a redeemed social condition,
to know even one life
has breathed easier
because you have lived.
This is to have succeeded.*

"Oh my God." Mindy touched her heart. "I am so touched. It's the most perfect poem."

"I thought you'd like it. It's everything you've been trying to tell me . . . and everything I wanted to thank you for. I don't know what I would have done without you these past few months. You literally saved my life."

"Stop. I'm just glad we finally became friends. And what an adventure it's been!"

"Yes! We almost died together."

"Not that!" Mindy laughed. "I mean discovering our family ties, getting into a business venture, and now making this huge move. The only reason I'm not scared is because I think it's going to be a blast figuring everything out with you."

"Hope you're right."

"I mean even the contest thing worked out okay."

"What are you talking about? It was a disaster."

"Yes, but look at how much we learned. We found out we made a great team and that we had real potential in this business. Who knows? Maybe one day we'll start our own little greeting card company."

"I was actually thinking that," Beth said. "Of course I'd have to be president."

"No, no. You're razzle-dazzle, I'm management."

"Like hell! You don't even have a business suit."

"And when would I wear it? When I'm burping your baby and changing poopy diapers?"

"You'd do that? You'd come over and change poopy diapers?"

"Hell, yes! I've put up with your shit, why wouldn't I put up with your kid's?"

Richard was pumped! He'd found the house of Beth's dreams and even though it was farther north than he wanted to travel, he was willing to add time to his commute because the development was perfect and the owner had been transferred, so the house was empty.

"Did Artie look in the same development?" Beth asked.

"No. I told you. They want to look in a lower price range."

"Then so will we. I'm not making this move unless we stick together."

"Beth, that's ridiculous. We're not talking about buying matching pocketbooks. Don't you want to love the house?"

"How can I love a house when I don't know the neighbors? And don't you think the girls would feel better if they were close to Stacie and Jamie? They're all we've got."

"So you don't even want me to put a bid on it?"

"No. You need to find the house of my dreams that's right next to the house of theirs."

"They're not being all that picky. It's crazy, but the only thing Artie asks about is if the house has a shed."

"Well, whatever. This is not negotiable."

"You're impossible."

"Surprise!"

Richard laughed but agreed to keep looking. "Maybe it's best. Now that I think of it, there was one thing you wouldn't have liked."

"The master suite was small?"

"The couple next door was strange. Actually the husband seemed like a nice enough guy, but the wife was a piece of work. She made a face when I pulled up in the rental car, then she kept pumping me for information to make sure we were in their league. I thought she was going to ask me for a credit report and a tax return."

"Oh my God! Who would want to live next door to anyone that obnoxious?"

"I don't know. Let's ask Mindy."

Epilogue

On an unseasonably warm November morning, ten days before Jessica's bat mitzvah, Beth went into labor, endured six miserable hours of pushing, then gave birth by Cesarean section to a beautiful, eight-pound, three-ounce baby boy, who was promptly dubbed Mushy-Tushie by his adoring older sisters.

Richard thanked them for their suggestion but said that they had decided on a name that wouldn't get the kid beaten up on the first day of school: Alexander Daniel.

Quite by coincidence, down the hall, another mother was in labor, who though for the first time, did have one thing in common with Beth. She too had chosen Mindy Sherman as her birthing coach, never expecting that they would be needing her on the same day.

Her name was Rainbow Everhardt, and in the few months that she had gotten to know her good friend Aaron's stepmom, she felt a strong kinship to this wise and funny woman from New York who seemed to know everything about babies. And though Rainbow was being tended to by her mother and Aaron, who was suddenly too emotional to sing, it was Mindy's hand she squeezed in the middle of her contractions while screaming for drugs.

Later that night, Rainbow, also gave birth to a beautiful boy, though her mother asked her to hold off on naming him until they met with an elder from their tribal community, or a name was spiritually divined. But when it was time to fill out the birth certificate, Rainbow chose not to wait. Her son would be known as Takoda, friend to all, and though it was yet to be confirmed by DNA, the father would be listed as the deliriously happy eighteen-year-old Aaron Sherman.

Eight days later, in the midst of final preparations for Jess's bat mitzvah, the Diamonds braced themselves for the barrage of out-of-town guests expected to arrive early for Alex's bris.

Next door, in a house just as big and beautiful as the Diamonds, but with an extra upgrade, the shed of Artie's dreams, the Shermans were operating a central command post, organizing airport transportation and hotel accommodations. Within a four-hour span they would be picking up Beth's and Richard's families, Stan and Rhoda, Mindy's mom, Helene, and the indomitable Grandma Jenny.

Though the elderly woman had not traveled by plane in nearly a decade, this was an occasion she would not miss, for in the months since reuniting with the former Ruchel Freund, she had been regaling everyone with stories and songs of her youth. Caregivers at the nursing home marveled at her increased mental capacity and rosier disposition, attributing the positive changes to Ruth's daily visits.

And no question, Jenny Baumann understood that she was traveling a far distance in order to witness the next generation of Jewish children carrying out the ancient traditions of circumcision and being called to the Torah. "A slep in the face to Hitler," she repeated every step of the journey. "Thenk God I'm alife to see it."

But it wasn't just people that the Shermans were transporting, it was mounds of delicacies that had been shipped from Bagel Boss in New York, for no Jewish celebration was complete without bagels, lox, whitefish salad, an assortment of cream cheeses, and fifty pounds of rugulah.

It was the most festive bris the rabbi could recall, and certainly the only one where the celebrant was outfitted from head to toe in Nike apparel. "Between all the love in this room and these Nike sneakers, little Avraham Daniel here is certainly beginning life on the right foot."

But the rabbi's joy did not end there, for that Saturday morning, she officiated at the b'nai mitzvah of her two newest students, Jessica and Aaron. Seems that the young man's first order of business after reaching legal age was to both change his last name back to Sherman and to study Torah with the rabbi after school.

Artie was in complete shock, given Aaron's insistence that religion had no place in his life. But after having experienced a plane crash, Passover, and a huge payout from the insurance company all in the same week, he was suddenly willing to consider the possibility that there was a higher power that looked out for you.

What didn't come as a surprise to the Sherman family was that the father and grandfather of the bar mitzvah boy had to be asked several times to stop crying long enough for Aaron's voice to be heard as he recited the blessings.

At the reception in the social hall, Mindy pulled Beth aside for a quiet moment.

"If I told you a year ago that we would be next-door neighbors living in Portland, Oregon, that we would be celebrating Jess's bat mitzvah here, that you would be back with Richard and the proud parents of this adorable little boy, would you have believed me?"

"Absolutely." Beth kissed baby Alex's head. "About as much as you would have believed it if I told you that you would be a grandmother."

"Good point." Mindy laughed. "Although you know what's even more unbelievable than that? That we ended up as best friends."

"You're right. *That* I never would have believed!"

"And what about your being back with Richard and so happy? Could you have seen that coming?"

"Not in a million years." Beth swallowed. "I forgot we could be so good together. He's been wonderful to me. The move out here was the best thing that ever happened to us."

"Only one way to explain it," Mindy said as she nuzzled Alex. "It had to be bashert. Oh look! He's grabbing my finger. Such a smart boy you are."

"Of course he's smart," Beth beamed. "He's my son."

"And my godson." Mindy took him. "I think he wants us to dance."

"Be careful . . . he might spit up on you."

"It's fine." She twirled him. "I've always gone for guys who drool."

"Ladies and Gentlemen, may I please have your attention?" the DJ announced. Right now we're going to dedicate a song to a very special guest. And to make the introduction, please give a warm welcome to a good friend of the Diamond family, Aaron Sherman."

"What's going on?" Beth asked Mindy.

"How should I know? It's your party."

"Hey. How ya doin'?" Aaron adjusted the mike stand. "I'm Aaron. Just wanted to say mazel tov, Jessie. This is the most awesome bat mitzvah I've ever been to. Actually, it's the only one I've ever been to, but you did an amazing job today. Almost as good as me! Anyway, for those of you who don't know me, music has been like my whole life . . . really helped me get through some rough times . . . but you gotta have good people in your life, too, and there's this one great lady I couldn't have gotten by without. So I want to dedicate this next song to her for helping me see what I'm all about, what I can do with my life. Her name is Mindy, and believe it or not, she's my new mom. Mindy, you're the best! I'm never going to disappoint you. Hope you like this one from Boyz II Men. It's called, "Song for Mama."

"Oh my God." Mindy burst into tears and shook so that she frightened Alex, who wailed for his mother. "Oh no. Sorry sweetie . . . sorry. Here you go." She handed him to Beth. "See? He only wants his mommy. They can't live without us, not even for a second."

"Hey, little man." Beth swayed with him. "I'm here . . . you're okay."

Aaron surprised Mindy with a tap on her shoulder. "So do you like wanna dance?"

"Oh my God, yes!" She held out her hand. "You've made this such a great day for me. I'm so proud of you."

"I'm proud of me, too," he laughed. "I hate talkin' in front of lots of people."

"Well, you'd never know it. You were great. Artie! Over here! Get the photographer. Beth! Move closer. It's mother and son's first dance. I want to capture this moment forever!"

"She is so damn bossy," Beth said to Aaron.

"I know," he said, then shrugged, "but things didn't start getting good until I listened to her."

"Same with me." Beth kissed her son. "Same with me."

A+

**AUTHOR
INSIGHTS,
EXTRAS, &
MORE...**

FROM

**SARALEE
ROSENBERG**

AND

AVON A

With Apologies to the Trees in Oregon

Photo by Taryn Rosenberg

Two thousand pieces of paper later, a book is born

Creativity is mind over matter, and with my mind it doesn't matter.

You know how sometimes you get dragged into doing something in which you have zero interest, but you feel too guilty to say no, so you show up with a bad attitude? Then to your surprise, you realize you were glad you came?

When my previous novel FATE AND MS. FORTUNE was first published, I was invited to speak to a group of early-stage Alzheimer's patients about the book and the writing life. Exactly. Is this how Carrie Bradshaw got to launch her publicity tour? Didn't I deserve splashy cocktail parties and big window displays, too? Clearly, these nice people wouldn't remember a word I said after I left, let alone go out and buy my book.

But I was wrong. This group, including a former surgeon, judge, and dentist, responded to my talk, laughing at all the right times (unlike a certain snooty New York City book club). And how they perked up when I confided that what I loved best about the writing process was getting to inhabit a make-believe world where inner voices told me what to do.

Welcome to our world, they said. Just hope you don't ever end up wandering in the middle of a street unsure of how you got there, or more important, how you're getting home. To which I replied, welcome to *my* world! When I write, there are no maps or directions. I can wander aimlessly through chapters for weeks, trying to figure out how to get back to the point. (Note to self: writing is akin to losing your mind.)

Then you had to see their reaction when I asked if they wanted to do some brainstorming for a new novel I was toying with:

EARLY BIRD SPECIAL. Faster than you could say "Seinfeld" writers, they were throwing out ideas for characters and story lines. They may have been struggling with memory loss, but their creative sides were on full burn.

"Make one guy Joseph Flaherty, a retired badass cop from the Bronx. His wife still calls him Joey." "There has to be a woman, too. How about Dolly Rothman? A widow from Staten Island who used to be a Rockette." "My guy is Sidney Berkowitz, a proctologist from Great Neck. He's dumpy but a great dancer. Don't forget the pinky ring."

It was wonderful watching these once-thriving adults rediscover their creative sides, and it taught me a valuable lesson. No, two lessons. One, ditch the bad attitude. Every situation has some value and if you're lucky, even more than you expect. Second, oftentimes we lose our intuitive voice and talents for fear of being judged. But those who are battling Alzheimer's don't care about rejection or ridicule, as one of the side effects is losing your filter, your capacity to be aware of what is socially correct. How sad that it sometimes takes a debilitating disorder in order to remember the joy of taking creative risks.

Meanwhile, if I ever do write a book about a group of seniors from Pompano Beach who meet weekly for dinner, and then discover that each of them has a big secret, my inspiration will come from the brave soul in the room who shouted, "Hey! This nudnik over here doesn't know what the hell he's talking about. My idea is great!" Damn right!

As for working with this group, I jumped at the chance to return recently to lead a writer's workshop (and had a blast). Now there is even a possibility I'll be developing a special program that gives these early-stage patients a chance to write short stories based on their life experiences.

Hopefully they will be able to recall past events that shaped their journeys, and then commit words to paper so that they have something unique and personal to pass on.

There but for the grace of God go I.

Birth of DEAR NEIGHBOR, DROP DEAD took nine years of labor

Readers always ask about the genesis of my stories, though for whatever reason, they have already made up their minds that the crazy plots and characters have to be based on actual events and people. But guess what? My first three novels grew solely from my imagination and keggers of Dunkin' Donuts coffee (large hazelnut, light with half and half, no sugar, in case you're treating).

DEAR NEIGHBOR, however, did start as a seed of an idea after hearing stories about a friend's next-door neighbor. She lived next door to Mother Perfect, a beautiful blonde whose home was always immaculate, whose kids were little darlings, and who really did lay out creative art projects before school.

Meanwhile, my friend could barely get her kids out without needing an assist from the fire department or a plumber. And that was before engaging in battles with Mother Perfect over car pools, test scores, and birthday parties.

But follow the trail. I began working on my first novel in 1994, basing it on her next-door neighbor from hell. I called it ALL IN THE CARDS, and it was a caper about a greeting card contest that attracted the attention of two warring neighbors, Mindy and Beth.

It took three years to write and another year to find an agent. Then miracle of miracles, it had a close encounter of the third degree. Bette Midler and her All Girl Productions optioned the story with the idea of making it her follow-up film to *First Wives Club*.

You say you missed the movie? Never read the book? That's

because the deal fell apart, as they so often do. My only choice was to focus on my second novel, A LITTLE HELP FROM ABOVE. Fortunately, that story found a wonderful home with Lyssa Keusch at Avon.

Now fast-forward to 2006. I'd written three novels and was gearing up for the next when I decided to pitch the idea of reviving ALL IN THE CARDS. I thought the story of hostile neighbors still had a universal truth to it, and all I'd have to do is put cell phones in Mindy's and Beth's hands, update their clothes and cars, and maybe sprinkle in a few current events.

No such luck! About a month after I began the revision it hit me that I was no longer in love. I was older and wiser, a more confident writer, and the original plot, while still entertaining, no longer felt relevant. The world had changed dramatically after 9-11, Iraq, and Katrina, and even if suburban sparring was still a matter of interest, I wanted to dig deeper into the psyche of family life—marriage, stepchildren, pregnancy, infidelity, and death.

Ah, but what to call this new version?

Titling a book is no different than naming your baby. Everyone has an opinion and no one cares that you're the mother. "Seriously? You like Ophelia? Don't you want this kid to have friends?" In the end, however, you want/need a consensus. So, too, with a title.

Not sure if I broke any records, but I did submit dozens of ideas, none of which got a thumbs-up. And probably with good reason. Still, I thought you'd get a kick out seeing some of the ones that remain dear to my heart:

Hot, Hungry, and Hormonal; Ask Your Doctor if Stress Is Right for You; Where Have I Been All My Life?; I Exam; If You're Happy and You Know It; By the Book; Mother Bored; She Had It Coming; The Bitch Next Door; And You're Telling Me This Because . . . ; Bed, *Beth,* and Beyond; Fences and Defenses; If Lucy Hated Ethel; Dear Neighbor, Please Move; Neighbor for Sale; Is It Just Me?; You Try to Be Nice; Love the House, Hate the Neighbors.

But want to know my favorite? The one I really, really wanted but knew would never fly? Same Shit, Different Zip Code! (You laughed, right?) The reason I thought this was a perfect choice was because the manuscript then included several entries from a blogger mom in Georgia who carried on about annoying husbands, in-laws, kids, teachers, and, of course, bitchy, Botox-crazy neighbors. Point being that it didn't matter where you lived, it was the same crap everywhere.

For fun, here is one of my favorite blogs that got left on the cutting-room floor:

You Say You Want a Revelation

Anybody NOT doing Botox????

3-20-08

   Hey it's Becky from Georgia . . . SO I'M AT THE DENTIST
OFFICE *and ever since he started bribing me with laughing gas,
boom, the stress is gone. Plus, I get whiter than white teeth AND
a nice little twenty-minute buzz* . . . *Anyway, sure wish I'd had my
little high while I was waitin' in the waitin' room 'cause I picked
up one of those stupid ladies' magazines, Atlanta Gal* . . . *uch!
Pisses me off!!! Why don't they just call it* **You Suck Magazine**
or **Yo You're Ugly**? *Every page is another ad for some miracle
doctor who can't wait to inject me with cow poison or whatever
the hell is in Botox* . . . *Step right up for your free aesthetic evalu-
ation so we can point out the obvious. You ain't what you used
to be darlin'. Damn straight. I used to be the Crisco Kid 'cause I
had more rolls than a bakery and if it wasn't fried in lard, I gave
it to the cat. Now I eat so much salad and veggies I poop in green
* . . . *But is that good enough? No Ma'am! There is something
wrong if you don't want to get rid of the bags under your eyes,
the hair over your lip, and the cellulite on your ass. You can't seriously want to live another day with purple veins, flabby necks,
and breasts that do the limbo* . . . HOW LOW CAN YOU GO????
*Lucky you if you've got a couple of grand you don't need for the
mortgage or food. It's time for the supermarket sweep. Be sure
to check out the vanity aisle* . . . *Facelifts, liposuction, meso-
therapy, permanent lash extensions, threadlifts, veneers, and my
personal favorite, laser tattoo removal* . . . *And what about those*

headlines: *I LOVE THE WAY HE SMILES AT ME NOW! Really? Is that 'cause you've got a steak in one hand and a beer in the other? YOU KNOW YOU WANT TO. Yes I do. I want to bitch slap the girls who swear they've had nothing done after they've mysteriously disappeared for a week . . . and trust me, they're too old to be having babies out of wedlock . . . WOULD YOU LIKE TO KNOW HOW SHE DOES IT? Yes, do tell. How does my sister's friend juggle an affair with her personal trainer and still find the time to run the holiday gift wrap sale? ONE WEEK TO A NEW YOU! But I don't want a new me. I want a new couch for the den and maybe some new friends who won't forget my birthday even though I never forget theirs. . . . (hint: BLG you are so on my #$%^&& list). . . . Wait. I almost forgot the most hilarious part. Know what the cover of the magazine said: Need a Support Group? Help is On the Way. . . . Don't they get it? We wouldn't need support if they'd just leave us the hell alone. I say if you're good to yourself and the people in your life, you're a beauty! And as my sixty-eight-year-old grandma, the most gorgeous woman in the world, always says, "Rebecca darling, you can fool the mirror but never the stairs!"*

Who knows? Maybe this is the start of a whole new novel. Just have to come up with a title that won't get censored.

Love Thy Neighbor? Not!

Writing about awful neighbors was fun, but living next door to them is no laughing matter. Wouldn't it be great to be able to warn people in advance? Now there is a Web site that lets you tell it like it is or, even better, check an address so you are forewarned before the movers unload (www.rottenneighbor.com). But let the accuser beware. If the source of your aggravation retaliates and writes an equally disparaging memo about you, it could work against you when you try to sell the house.

Meanwhile, what to do if you live in a place inhabited by inconsiderate people who blast their sound systems, throw late parties, set off firecrackers, and have turned their backyard into Dirt Bike Village?

I asked Robert Borzatta, a leading expert on neighbor relations and the founder of www.neighborsfromhell.com to see if short of moving or committing a felony, there were effective ways to deal with a variety of neighbor abusers.

Q. Your NFH (neighbor from hell) is a SIC (selfish inconsiderate bitch). You could write a book about all the mean things she's done. Is retaliation ever okay?

A. Retaliation is usually the weapon of choice by the bad neighbor—a good neighbor might call police about a noisy party, then the bad neighbor retaliates by slashing the good one's tires. As long as it's within the law, some forms of retaliation may work. If my neighbor refuses to bring in her yappy dog by 11:00 p.m., I may set off my car alarm at 6:00 a.m.–unless it will disturb other neighbors. The idea is to send the message that there are consequences for being un-neighborly.

Q. Okay, but before the battle escalates, what's step one?

A. Step one is communication, but not by a note in the mail-box, or even an e-mail. You don't want the neighbor having written proof that they've been "harassed" by you. The best approach, though intimidating, is to meet face-to-face. Be po-lite, use a nice speaking voice, and don't show up with the rest of the block, putting the person on the defensive. Express your concerns and ask for their understanding. It might nip things in the bud, and if it doesn't, feel free to involve authori-ties (though that offers no guarantee, either).

Q. Meet face-to-face? But what if the person seems really, really scary?

A. Obviously don't endanger your life, but often when there are hostilities between neighbors, they've never met or don't know each other's names. The good neighbor may only know the bad neighbor by their offending behavior and judge them on race, religion, age, etc. By introducing yourself, you're showing you're not easily intimidated, and it becomes per-sonal. Why would they want to alienate a nice person like you? I know of an instance where the good neighbor gave the bad one a gift basket, mentioned the noise problem, and that was all it took.

Q. Okay, let's say the neighbor is nice but the ten-year-old son is a beast. He tramples rose-bushes, harasses dogs, and threatens little kids. The mom shrugs and says boys will be boys.

A. Oh. Her. Inside that giant-SUV-driving, overcaffeinated, mentally-absent Mom of the Year is a definite Neighbor from Hell. But at the same time, "live where you belong." The suburbs and other family-friendly neighborhoods are prone to misbehaving kids, barking dogs, roving teens, and disputes over snow shoveling. It goes with the territory, so in all fairness, be a little tolerant. Also consider that restoring civility in any dispute is a process, one that can take a lot out of the better neighbors. The key is not to let it make you ill. Be patient, be persistent, be proactive. Over time, the bad neighbor may either compromise or decide to annoy someone else.

Q. What is it about suburbia that fosters such competitiveness and resentment among neighbors?

A. Insecurity can bloom anywhere–but a suburban neighborhood can be a prime breeding ground because of the close proximity between houses, giving people an amazing view of how the neighbors live, what they drive, etc. Also, there are more opportunities to interact— driveways, yards, school-bus stops, etc., and it's hard to hide your new BMW (not that you're trying to). Just know that the better someone gets to know you, the more likely they will judge you fairly. Neighbor disputes escalate much more quickly when the parties are strangers.

Q. What is the key to achieving lasting peace when next-door neighbors are like hostile nations?

A. The only way to guarantee a resolution is if one neighbor moves away or dies, which is why I say it's better to try to manage the hostilities rather than expect to resolve them. Best way to quiet the tensions is to back off for a while. If you feed the fire, you get engulfed in the flames.

Q. What's worse? Neighbors who never got along, or ones who had a falling-out?

A. Neither feels good. Friends-turned-enemies make for ongoing battles because there is personal pain on both sides. But when we don't know our neighbors, we're less tolerant of their occasional disturbances. It helps to be friendly to everyone so that if a problem arises, the trigger finger isn't as quick to go off.

Q. Now that we can keep tabs on each other through the Internet, cell phones, nanny cams, have we become a nation of Peeping Cyber Toms?

A. Good people won't suddenly change because of the advent of technology. They will still abide by common decency. However, a word of caution. If you don't want your antics to be seen on YouTube, lower the shade. Also, good behavior caught on tape isn't news. No one is going to watch you bringing over a pie to the new neighbors.

Q. Finally, what is the best way to keep your cool when all you think about is revenge?

A. My doctor once told me that the intestine is the mirror of the mind. Do you really want to have to surgically repair your digestive tract because of a neighbor dispute? If you've tried to overcome the hostilities to no end, try relaxation techniques and stay on the high road. Sometimes we win by not losing our minds.

Robert Borzatta, a former investigative journalist for the Philadelphia Inquirer *and a frequent guest on ABCs* 20/20, *is the founder and online counselor at neighborsfromhell.com. His book and nationally syndicated radio talk show of the same name will debut in 2008.*

A Few Words About Those Great Fakes

Prada. Louis Vuitton. Fendi. Gucci . . . Love 'em, but why spend big bucks on a designer handbag when the copies look amazing and cost a fraction of the retail price? Just like in the story, where Mindy gets a fake Chanel after throwing a pocketbook party, I've bought them, worn them, and enjoyed them (until the handles broke or the glued-on labels fell off). Still, I'm a sucker for a bargain and what fun to watch someone eyeing my bag. Does she or doesn't she? Only the vendor on Canal Street knows for sure.

But now word comes from Dana Thomas in a story from the *New York Times* that money spent on faux designer watches, handbags, and fashions is linked to supporting international crime and terrorism (Op-Ed page, August 30, 2007).

She reported that most fakes are produced in China and that it's no myth that children are sold off to work in the factories that produce these counterfeit goods. In fact, when she toured the distant cities like Guangzhou, where many of the factories were located, she saw children as young as eight years old slaving over machines.

Bottom line? The rip-off racket is not a victimless crime. It is run almost exclusively by syndicates (including Hezbollah and the Shiites) dealing in narcotics, weapons, child prostitution, human trafficking, and terrorism. The only way to stop their illicit actions is by banding together and resisting the temptation to buy these fakes. The designers and retailers will be happy with the boycott, but more important, it's the right thing to do. There are enough crimes against humanity without contributing to the muck just so we can look fashionable and rich. I hope you'll spread the word.

Celebrating the Kindertransport

In early November 1938, days after Kristallnacht (the night of broken glass), a pogrom against Jews in Germany and Austria, a delegation of Jewish leaders in Britain appealed to the prime minister and the cabinet to organize a rescue mission that would allow Jewish children from Germany, Austria, and Czechoslovakia to enter the country unaccompanied, and then be placed with foster families until they could be reunited with their parents.

On December 1, the first group left from Berlin, and over the next two years, ten thousand more followed. The youngest were a few months old, the oldest, age seventeen.

The Kindertransport (*kinder* is German for "children") trains crossed into the Netherlands, and from there the children traveled by ferry to the British ports of Harwich or Southampton.

Thankfully, most of the children survived. However, only a very small percentage were ever reunited with family, as most had perished at the hands of the Nazis.

You may be wondering if I wrote about the Kindertransport because of a personal connection, but that was not the case. Over the years I had read many stories about this extraordinary rescue mission, as well as seen Deborah Oppenheimer's incredibly moving film *Into the Arms of Strangers,* which won the Academy Award for best documentary feature in 2001. So when I learned that 2008 marked the seventieth anniversary of this journey of hope, it was an easy decision to try to find a way to incorporate this little piece of history into the story.

I would like to thank Margaret and Kurt Goldberger for providing wonderful source material and for sharing their incredible journeys on the Kindertransport. Interestingly, they left Germany six months apart and did not meet until arriving in New York years later. But their common bond united them, and they have been happily married for fifty-eight years, residing in the same home in Long Island since 1952. They and their daughter's family feel truly blessed to have enjoyed a lifetime of good health and happiness together.

For more information about this miraculous mission, visit the official website: www.kindertransport.org

In Gratitude

This is a book of fiction, but all the more reason to try to get the facts straight. I am indebted to those who shared their expertise: Dr. Kenneth Margules, Dr. Ivan Jacobs, Dr. Heidi Rosenberg, Debbie Bergen, Patrick O'Hagan, Mira Temkin, Arlene Napshin, and Steve Johnson of the Portland International Airport.

And in testimony to the unbroken bonds that link the generations, I am honored to be a descendant of the real Gittle Soloweichyk, her daughter (my grandmother), Jenny Solomon Belinkoff and her daughter (my mother), Doris Belinkoff Hymen.

And in Conclusion . . .

I love that the editors at Avon have given their authors a unique forum in which to share anecdotes and behind-the-scenes stories with readers. It's a great way to bond, but more important, it's a very cool way to say in one big breath, the world has gone mad, but as long as we can support each other, laugh together, and marvel at all that is good, there is hope.

My wish for you and yours is that your blessings outweigh your burdens and that you continue to enrich your lives with your love of reading and anything else that is legal and gives you pleasure. Meanwhile, please keep in touch, as it totally makes my day when you write.

Best,
Saralee Rosenberg
www.saraleerosenberg.com
Saralee@saraleerosenberg.com
October 10, 2007

Photo by Glenmar

SARALEE ROSENBERG is also the author of *A Little Help From Above*, *Claire Voyant*, and *Fate and Ms. Fortune*. She promises you laughter, or your money back (no, just kidding about the refund). For a good time, visit her website at *www.saraleerosenberg.com*.

Saralee Rosenberg